SWEET TEMPTATION

"Sizzle, sex appeal, and sensuality! Maya Banks has it all . . . This book is on the inferno side of hot and it shows on every page . . . You will not want to miss out on this story."
—*Romance Junkies*

"An enjoyable tale of [a] second chance at life."
—*Genre Go Round Reviews*

SWEET SEDUCTION

"Maya Banks never fails to tell compelling tales that evoke an emotional reaction in readers . . . Kept me on the edge of my seat." —*Romance Junkies*

SWEET PERSUASION

"Surpassed all my expectations. Incredibly intense and complex characters, delicious conflict, and explosive sex scenes that fairly melt the print off the pages, *Sweet Persuasion* will have Maya Banks fans, new and existing alike, lasciviously begging for more."
—*Romantic Times* (4½ stars)

"Ignites the pages . . . Readers will relish Maya Banks's exciting erotic romance." —*The Best Reviews*

"Well written and evocative." —*Dear Author*

continued . . .

BE WITH ME

"I absolutely loved it! Simply wonderful writing. There's a new star on the rise and her name is Maya Banks."
—Sunny, national bestselling author of *Lucinda, Dangerously*

"Fascinating erotic romantic suspense."
—*Midwest Book Review*

SWEET SURRENDER

"This story ran my heart through the wringer more than once." —*CK²S Kwips and Kritiques*

"From page one, I was drawn into the story and literally could not stop reading until the last page."
—*The Romance Studio*

"Maya Banks's story lines are always full of situations that captivate readers, but it's the emotional pull you experience which brings the story to life." —*Romance Junkies*

FOR HER PLEASURE

"[It] is the ultimate in pleasurable reading. Enticing, enchanting and sinfully sensual, I couldn't have asked for a better anthology." —*Joyfully Reviewed*

"Full of emotional situations, lovable characters and kick-butt story lines that will leave you desperate for more . . . For readers who like spicy romances with a suspenseful element—it's definitely a must read!" —*Romance Junkies*

"Totally intoxicating, *For Her Pleasure* is one of those reads you won't be forgetting anytime soon."
—*The Road to Romance*

HIDDEN AWAY

MAYA BANKS

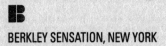

BERKLEY SENSATION, NEW YORK

THE BERKLEY PUBLISHING GROUP
Published by the Penguin Group
Penguin Group (USA) LLC
375 Hudson Street, New York, New York 10014

USA • Canada • UK • Ireland • Australia • New Zealand • India • South Africa • China

penguin.com

A Penguin Random House Company

HIDDEN AWAY

A Berkley Sensation Book / published by arrangement with the author

Berkley Sensation Books are published by The Berkley Publishing Group.
BERKLEY SENSATION® is a registered trademark of Penguin Group (USA) LLC.
The "B" design is a trademark of Penguin Group (USA) LLC.

For information, address: The Berkley Publishing Group
a division of Penguin Group (USA) LLC,
375 Hudson Street, New York, New York 10014.

ISBN: 978-0-425-24017-5

PUBLISHING HISTORY
Berkley Sensation mass-market edition / March 2011

PRINTED IN THE UNITED STATES OF AMERICA

10   9

Cover art by Craig White.
Cover design by Rita Frangie.
Interior text design by Laura K. Corless.

To Cindy Hwang, for her never-ending patience with this book and with me as I struggled to get it just right.

To Kim Whalen, who always goes to bat for me and tells me endlessly not to stress. I still stress, but you make it so much easier for me. Thank you.

To the MB Readers, Annmarie, Valerie, Fatin and Lillie. You guys are the best. I totally don't deserve you.

And finally, for T.J., who shares all the ups and downs, highs and lows, and always offers me encouragement and support when I need it the most. I truly couldn't do this without you. You're absolutely the most integral part of my life and my career. Love you always.

CHAPTER 1

THERE were any number of men who would do any job Marcus Lattimer wanted done. He'd amassed a fortune and countless connections during his lifetime, most of which were steeped in murky shades of gray. The men directly employed by Lattimer were absolute in their loyalty—he would tolerate no less—but he never allowed himself to fully trust anyone.

Some jobs . . . Some jobs demanded personal satisfaction. This one was a matter of honor. Others might argue that Marcus had none. By their definition, they'd be right. But he was bound by a fierce loyal code. *His* honor was what mattered.

Allen Cross was an arrogant, coattail-riding asshole. The world would be a better place without his kind of filth, and Marcus was determined that the task would be completed this day.

Marcus attached the silencer and tucked the gun into the waist of his slacks. Drawing the Armani suit coat closed, he left the confines of his car and instructed his driver to wait. He walked at an unhurried pace toward the entrance of the high-rise that housed Cross Enterprises. Around him the city lights twinkled in the darkening of dusk, and headlights from passing cars bounced along the alleyways.

The streets were mostly empty and the building barren of the weekday horde of employees who scurried in and out with regularity. He paused a short distance from the entrance and checked his watch. The security guard that manned the front entrance on the weekends was a family guy and, like most family guys, had a moderate amount of debt and stretched his budget from payday to payday.

After tonight, the guard wouldn't have the financial worries of others in his class. Marcus had seen to that. Right now, the guard would take a strategic break from his post, and at the same moment, the surveillance cameras would go down.

Money bought many things. Loyalty. Disloyalty. A blind eye. A moment's distraction. Fifteen minutes was all Marcus needed to rid the world of Allen Cross.

Cross was a creature of habit. He came into his offices every Saturday after seven and remained until nine P.M., when his car service collected him and drove him to the same restaurant ten blocks away. He liked the few hours of solitude to go over paperwork—but what he perhaps liked the most was the freedom to victimize a helpless woman with impunity.

Marcus's jaw tightened in fury. Predictability killed a man. As Cross was about to find out.

Marcus rode the elevator to the twenty-first floor and stepped onto the cheap, fake Italian marble flooring, his shoes issuing a faint echo as he walked through the empty reception area.

The door to Cross's office was ajar, and a faint light shone through the crack. Marcus pushed at the door and let it slide soundlessly open. Cross was behind his desk, kicked back in his chair, a glass of wine in one hand as he read a sheaf of papers with the other.

Marcus watched, content to wait for his prey to become aware he was hunted.

After a moment, Cross set his glass down and leaned forward. He halted in mid-motion, and his head snapped up, his gaze locked on Marcus. Cross's eyes widened in alarm and then he recovered, a sneer rolling over his lips.

"Who are you and what the hell are you doing in my office?"

Marcus strolled forward, his expression purposely bland as he loosened his coat. Cross rose, his hand inching toward the intercom on his desk.

"Get out or I'll summon security."

Marcus smiled. "I think you'll find him unavailable."

A flicker of unease skittered across Cross's face when Marcus continued to smile. Marcus pulled out the gun, enjoying the slide of the stock over his palm. He thumbed the safety, and leveled the barrel at Cross's chest.

"Would you prefer to die sitting or standing?"

Cross blanched, and he staggered, his hands slapping the polished mahogany of his executive desk. "What do you want?" he asked hoarsely. "Money? I have money. Just tell me how much. Anything. I'll give you anything."

A sneer twisted Marcus's lips. "You couldn't afford my shoes."

His finger tightened on the trigger, and he watched the awareness in Cross's eyes, the panicked realization that he was going to die.

Cross lunged sideways, and the sound of the bullet smacking into his chest resonated through the spacious office. Cross hit the floor, his arm outstretched in desperation. Blood seeped through the white silk shirt, growing as he gasped for breath.

As much as Marcus wanted to watch the life slowly fade from the bastard's eyes, he had to finish this now. He raised the gun and aimed between Cross's eyes. He saw the finality, the gray acceptance of death in his victim's gaze. He pulled the trigger and then turned away, satisfied that justice had been served.

THE cab pulled to an abrupt halt outside the building where Sarah Daniels had worked for a period of six months. She hadn't been back in a year. The mere thought of walking into Cross Enterprises made her physically ill.

She flung a twenty at the cabbie and ignored his offer to give her change. Clumsily opening the door, she bolted from the cab and entered the high-rise at a dead run.

The lobby was empty. Not even the security guard was at his post. Was she too late? What would she have even said to the man? That her brother was here to kill Stanley Cross?

She bolted toward the elevator and pounded on the up button, praying it would be here. She heaved a sigh of relief and threw herself through the doors as they slid open.

She jammed her thumb on the button for the twenty-first floor and then hit the close door button repeatedly.

Hurry. Hurry. Hurry.

She had to be on time. She wouldn't let Marcus go through with it.

Stupid. So stupid.

She should have known. She'd seen the rage in Marcus's eyes. He'd been way too quiet. Too collected as he'd calmly told her that he was taking her away. She hadn't argued. She'd allowed him to make all the plans. All the decisions. She hadn't even known where they were going, only that Marcus's private jet was fueled and waiting for them.

Finally the elevator doors slid open, and she rushed into the reception area and turned in the direction of Allen's office. She saw Allen's door wide open, saw Marcus's profile and then watched as Marcus tucked the gun back into his waistband.

Her horrified gaze tracked downward to see Allen Cross lying on the floor, blood staining his pristine white shirt.

Her hand flew to her mouth and she backed hastily away.

Oh God. Oh God. Oh God.

She was too late. She hadn't gotten here in time.

Allen was dead. Marcus had killed him.

Oh God.

Nausea welled in her throat. She nearly tripped on her feet as she steadily backpedaled. She had to get away. The police would be here soon. Wouldn't they? Surely someone couldn't just walk off the streets and kill someone in an office building.

She turned and ran back toward the elevator, praying it was still there. She knew that at least two were taken out of service on the weekends, but that left two working on this side of the building.

She jabbed at the down button with her thumb and held her breath, prepared to make a run for the stairs if she had to. The door slid open and she fell over herself getting in. She punched the button for the ground floor and turned just as the doors started to close, only to find herself staring at Marcus's frozen expression several feet away.

"Sarah—"

The doors closed, cutting him off. The elevator descended, sending Sarah's stomach into even more turmoil.

She simply couldn't process what she'd just witnessed. Marcus had killed Allen Cross. She couldn't even muster any regret. Only fear. Fear for Marcus. How could he think he could get away with something so bold?

The elevator came to a stop and she shoved at the doors, trying to make them open quicker. She pitched headlong into the lobby, stumbling to gain her footing. Just as she righted herself, a hand curled around her arm and yanked her upright.

"What the hell are you doing here?"

She gasped and stared into the eyes of evil.

Stanley Cross, Allen's brother, gripped her arm until she cried out in pain. His eyes sparked fury, but more than that, they warned her of just what kind of man he was. She knew all too well.

A sob welled in her throat as she faced down the man who was in her nightmares for the last year. She hadn't seen him since that night in Allen's office when he and Allen had forever changed the course of her life.

She hated them both more than she ever imagined being able to hate another human being.

Fear paralyzed her for what seemed an interminable amount of time. Her throat closed in and the ball in her stomach knotted painfully until it was all she could do not to vomit all over Stanley's shoes.

"I asked you a question," Stanley snapped. "What the hell are you doing here?"

Oh God, he'd find Allen's body and think she murdered him. Or worse, he'd see Marcus and then Marcus would go to jail. Stanley could place them both at the scene. Even if she wasn't herself accused of the crime, she could be forced to testify against Marcus.

Something snapped inside her. Rage mounted and swirled like a tornado. She thrust her knee into his groin, balled her fist and swung as hard as she could just as he howled in pain and doubled over.

Her fist met his jaw and he went sprawling.

As he started to scramble up, she ran for the entrance, burst into the night and bolted toward the street. She saw an off-duty cab rounding the corner and she ran in front of it, her arm held up to stop him. The cab screeched to a halt a mere inch from her knee. The driver threw his fist out the window, and obscenities blistered the air.

Ignoring his outrage, Sarah yanked open the back door and crawled in, slamming the door behind her. "Drive!"

The cabbie gave her a disgruntled look in the rearview mirror, then accelerated sharply, muttering about crazy women as he swerved through traffic. "Lady, I was not in service."

"I'll make it worth your while. Just drive!"

He heaved an exasperated sigh. "Where to?"

She slammed her eyes shut for a moment as she sought to regain her bearings. Where could she go?

Think. God. What did one do in a situation like this?

She stared down at the purse slung over her neck. She had some cash, her passport, a credit card, her driver's license. She couldn't go back to her apartment, could she?

Stanley would have found his brother's body by now. He'd probably already called the police.

Think, Sarah, think!

"Airport," she managed to get out.

Her cell phone rang, startling her. She rummaged in her purse and turned it over to check the LCD. Marcus.

Tears burned her eyelids. Her brother. The one person in the world who loved her. He was all she had and now he'd killed for her.

She opened the phone and put it to her ear.

"Sarah," Marcus barked before she could even get a greeting out.

"Marcus," she croaked out in a cracked and scratchy voice.

"Sarah, honey, where are you?"

"It doesn't matter. I can't . . . we can't . . . I have to stay away. I need to go away."

She was babbling, but she didn't care.

"Sarah, stop. Listen to me."

"No." She cut him off, her voice firmer now. "I have to go. Don't you see? They'll know. They'll know I saw you. They have surveillance in that building. All they have to do is play the security tape back and they'll know we were both there. You have to get out of here, Marcus. Go. I'm going too."

"Sarah, goddamn it, listen to me!"

She closed the phone and turned it off so he couldn't call back. She leaned her head back against the seat and closed her eyes.

She had no idea where she was going or what she'd do when she got there, but she couldn't stay here. She could never come back.

"I'm so sorry, Marcus. It should have been me who killed him," she whispered.

GARRETT Kelly came awake with a start, his muscles tense, sweat beading his brow. His breaths came in rapid, harsh huffs. For a moment he lay there, his unfocused gaze sliding across the window to the darkness beyond.

Explosions echoed in his ears. The staccato of gunfire made him flinch, and the smell of blood and burning flesh assaulted his nostrils, making them flare as his breaths tore from his lungs.

God.

He shook his head and raised his hand to scrub the sleep from his eyes. His shoulder protested, and he snarled with impatience at the ache, which still nagged. He rolled and sat up in bed, planting his feet on the floor. He stayed there, head hanging toward his knees, sucking in air like some pantywaist in basic training about to puke his guts up after a two-mile run.

It pissed him off when past memories ambushed him. He'd gone a long time without the images that interrupted his sleep. For some reason, after taking a bullet for his sister-in-law, he'd had a harder time sleeping. His consciousness seemed more vulnerable to things he'd shut out.

He cast a sideways glance at the clock. He wouldn't be going back to sleep and everyone would be up in an hour anyway. Maybe a run would clear his head and get his blood flowing again.

With a sigh, he hit the shower and turned it cold to shake the cobwebs and the lingering smell of blood. After he was dried off and dressed, he walked quietly down the hall and out the front door.

It was still dark when he started off down the winding road that paralleled the lake. He ran farther this morning, pushing himself beyond his normal routine. He could still hear the explosions and still hear his teammates. He closed his eyes and increased his pace until his lungs screamed and his side ached.

It was over. A lifetime ago. He needed to get over it. He *had* gotten over it. All this R and R was for the birds. It had only served to make him lazy and idle. Fuck it. He wanted back in. A mission. Something besides all this goddamn free time.

By the time he returned to the house, he was sucking serious wind. The sky had lightened to shades of lavender and a diamond-sized star hung stubbornly over the lake, blanketed in the soft hues of dawn. He stood on the dock staring over the water—smooth, not a single ripple disturbing the surface— and breathed the clean, unspoiled air.

He let the peace of home and the lake he loved envelop him until all the noises of the past dulled and receded.

CHAPTER 2

SWEAT beaded Garrett's brow as he completed his last pull-up. He held himself, chin hovering above the bar, until his muscles rolled and contorted and his shoulder burned. His lips thinned and nostrils flared. When his arms began shaking, he dropped to the floor and palmed the scar on his shoulder.

Impatient with the twinge of discomfort that still plagued him, he dropped down and began a series of push-ups. He forced everything from his mind but the goal of complete recovery—a process that had already taken too long for his liking.

After yesterday morning's run and a full day of PT, he'd slept marginally better last night than he had the night before. But he still couldn't rid himself of the lingering images of his dreams. Dreams that hadn't haunted him in some time but now seemed determined to shove themselves back to the forefront of his consciousness.

"Hey, man."

Garrett extended his arms to hold his position and turned to see his brother Donovan standing in the doorway to the basement.

"Why the hell are you interrupting my workout?"

"Resnick's paying us a visit. Should be here in the next few."

Garrett sighed and hopped to his feet. He rose and picked

up the towel he'd tossed on the couch and wiped the sweat from his face. "What the hell does he want?"

"He didn't say. But you know he wouldn't come out here unless he wanted something."

"Doesn't anyone use the goddamn phone anymore?"

Donovan chuckled. "I'll be over in the war room. A word of warning. Sophie's on a tear in the kitchen."

Garrett groaned. His very pregnant sister-in-law had been nesting furiously in the last week. She'd already cleaned the house top to bottom, and her next project was cooking enough food to outlast Armageddon.

Since marrying Sam, she'd bullied everyone into family time. They were her family now—as she liked to constantly remind them—and they would eat as a family, which meant everyone at the table, all accounted for, on time. The only excuse for missing a meal was hospitalization.

Garrett and his brothers indulged her because family was the one thing she'd always lacked. At first she'd been overwhelmed and cautious with the very large Kelly family, but then she embraced them all and took to her new life like a duck to water.

As he climbed the stairs from the basement, he rolled his shoulder, testing the wound. It had been months since he left the hospital, and it still wasn't healed to his satisfaction. He had residual soreness when he worked out, but if he went more than a day without pushing the exercises, it got stiff.

He was still rotating his arm when he got into the living room. Sophie looked up from the stove and frowned. "Is your shoulder still bothering you?"

Not waiting for his answer, she hurried around the corner— as fast as a woman in her condition could—and stood in front of him. Her belly protruded, nearly bumping into his hip. She looked about thirteen months' pregnant—not that he'd tell her that.

"I'm fine, Soph," he said good-naturedly.

"You've been working out again. Should you be pushing yourself so hard?"

He rolled his eyes and dropped a kiss on her cheek. "I'm fine. It's never going to get to one hundred percent unless I strengthen it."

Her blue eyes clouded and she briefly looked away. He sighed. She was the reason he'd taken the bullet, and she was also the only one determined not to forget that fact. He tugged at her hair just to annoy her, and when she looked back at him, he scowled.

Her sadness lasted all of two seconds. Her shoulders started shaking and her lips split into a wide smile. "Okay, okay," she said, putting her hands up as she backed away. "I'll stop the guilt and the mother hen act."

"Yeah, save it for the kiddo."

She walked back into the kitchen and he followed, sniffing the air.

"What are you cooking? It smells good."

"I think the question is, what am I *not* cooking." She gestured at the table, which had food scattered over the entire surface. It looked like a mad chef had butchered a cow and an entire garden. "I'm making lasagna to freeze, chicken and dumplings, a few casseroles and a gumbo. You hungry?"

He rubbed his stomach. "I could eat."

She checked her watch. "Lunch will be on the table in an hour."

"You're going to make me wait an hour?" he asked in horror.

She raised an eyebrow. "If I let you eat then Donovan and Sam would want to eat and then there'd be no one to have lunch with when it's time."

"You're a cruel, cruel woman," Garrett complained. "I don't know why Sam puts up with you."

Her look said she wasn't impressed with his whining.

"Speaking of Sam, where is he?"

Sophie peered over the pot and sniffed. "He went over to the office with Donovan. They had some calls to make. Sam said the contractors were supposed to break ground on the helipad at the compound today."

Garrett shook his head at her insistence on calling it the "office." "I'm headed over to the war room now. What are we having for lunch? Do I get to pick since I'm injured?"

"Oh now you want to be all pitiful," she muttered. "I suppose. What would you like?"

He grinned. "I'll take chicken and dumplings. Good comfort food for someone in my condition."

He turned to go but swiped a bite of the chicken she'd deboned and left in a flurry of threats to kick his ass.

Chuckling, he crossed the driveway to the building on the lot adjacent to the house. It had a stark look, completely in contrast to the homey log cabin that he and his brothers lived in, nestled on the banks of Kentucky Lake. It was square and imposing looking with grey cement–steel reinforced walls, no windows and a security system—thanks to Donovan's technical expertise—the CIA couldn't get into. Which was funny, considering the CIA would be arriving any moment now.

He punched in the access code and entered when the door slid open. Donovan was sitting in front of Hoss, the computer—the love of his life—and Sam was standing behind Donovan, reading off the screen.

He'd actually miss this place when construction was complete on the KGI compound he and his brothers had designed. They all liked to give Sam shit about his paranoia, but the truth was Garrett thought it was a damn good idea. He wanted his family protected. Especially after all that had happened in the months before, when his mom had been abducted.

If moving KGI to a secure, state-of-the-art facility would ensure that all the Kellys would be better protected, then Garrett was ready to make the move yesterday. The problem was, such a massive undertaking was going to take time. It would be months before everything would be complete.

"So what's up Resnick's ass?" he asked as he ambled over to his brothers.

Sam turned. "Dunno. He called, said he was about twenty minutes out. He sounded agitated."

"When doesn't he sound agitated? He's an uptight son of a bitch."

Donovan turned in his chair, looked at Sam and then both burst into laughter.

"What?" Garrett demanded.

Sam shook his head. "Hello, pot. Calling kettle uptight?"

Garrett flipped up his middle finger as he turned away and plopped onto the couch. Whatever Resnick wanted, it couldn't be good. The last time they'd seen him in person was when all the shit went down with Sophie. He'd been quiet since.

Just the way Garrett liked him. Trouble always followed in Resnick's wake.

Sam followed and slouched on the other end of the couch. "Mom is having a party for Rusty, and she's made it clear the entire family is to attend."

Garrett sighed. "What's the party for? Her staying out of trouble for a month?"

Donovan snorted and resumed typing on his keyboard.

"It's to celebrate the start of her senior year in school. And you have to hand it to the twerp, she's done well since Mom took her in hand and made her sit her ass in class."

Garrett grunted. Okay, yeah, the girl their mom had taken in—another of the strays Marlene Kelly was so famous for—had shaped up despite having a piss-poor attitude and a mouth to match. But Garrett wasn't into being all congratulatory for doing what she should be doing anyway, which was take responsibility and act like an adult.

"Jesus, they'll probably be buying her a car next," he muttered.

"Already did," Donovan called out.

At that Sam's eyebrows shot up. "They did? When did this happen?"

"I talked to Mom earlier and she said Dad was out car shopping. It's supposed to be a surprise for this party they're throwing," Donovan said.

Sam closed his eyes and Garrett shook his head. "Christ. That's just what we need. A crazy-ass teenager with her own car. I hope to hell they insure her out the yin yang. She'll get into a wreck and Mom and Dad will be sued and living on the streets in a month's time."

"We can always count on you to find the bright side in everything," Sam said dryly.

Silence fell and Garrett leaned his head back, closing his eyes. Between the haphazard sleep and two days of extended workouts, he was wiped.

"You sleeping okay?" Sam asked.

Garrett opened his eyes and turned his head to see his brother watching him with a thoughtful expression. "Yeah, I'm good."

"Sophie said you've been up a lot."

Garrett scowled. Definite drawback to living in a damn commune. "If she wasn't up going to the bathroom fourteen times a night, she wouldn't know I wasn't sleeping."

Sam chuckled but then he sobered. "Stuff bothering you, man?"

Garrett shoved impatiently at his hair, which needed a good clipping. Right now it stuck out on his head like some beach bum–surfer wannabe. "I'm good, okay?"

The last thing he wanted was to rehash the past. It was bad enough his brothers had to pick up the pieces and nurse his ass back to health when his mission had gone to shit six years ago. He didn't want to be babysat again just because he was having a few bad dreams.

"Sophie said the contractors were breaking ground on the helipad today."

Sam nodded. "I plan to go over after we meet with Resnick. Take a look around and see how the rest is coming along. I have Sophie studying house plans. She can't decide how many bedrooms we need because, as much as she wants more children, she swears this one may be an only child."

Garrett chuckled. "Ethan said Rachel's already decided on their house."

"Yeah, and what about you?"

Garrett frowned. A house? Hell, he hadn't given it much thought. He'd lived with his brothers for so long that the idea of having his own place hadn't really sunk it. But it would be nice. Yeah, he needed to start giving it some thought.

The beep of the intercom prevented his response.

Donovan rose from his chair at the computer. "Looks like Resnick is here."

"Don't get up," Sam said when Garrett remained on the couch. "I'll show him in."

Garrett grinned. "Thanks. I was comfortable."

Sam shot him a look and went to let their visitor in.

A few moments later, Sam returned with Resnick in tow. Typically, Resnick had one hand in his hair and the other piddling with the cigarette dangling from the corner of his mouth. He took quick, short steps and his gaze constantly moved from side to side. Yep, he was a nervous, high-strung son of a bitch.

Garrett raised an eyebrow in Resnick's direction. "Nice to see you, Adam. To what do we owe this unexpected pleasure?"

Resnick fixed Garrett with his stare and pulled the cigarette from his mouth, holding it between his thumb and forefinger. "Lattimer's finally fucked up."

For a moment Garrett stared at the other man, his mind completely blank. Gunfire echoed through his ears, and the acrid smell of blood filled his nostrils. He was taken back six years. To a place and time when his team had been set-up by the very man they'd been sent to save.

Rage seared through his veins despite his attempt to keep cool and not let the others know just how affected he was by the mere mention of Marcus Lattimer's name.

"Get to the point," Sam cut in. "Why are you here and what's Lattimer fucking up got to do with us?"

Resnick's gaze never left Garrett. He knew. It pissed Garrett off that Resnick knew just what buttons to push and how to exploit his weakness.

"We've got the best opportunity we're ever likely to get to take Lattimer down. I need you for the job," he said to Garrett.

Donovan rose from his seat and came to stand to the side of the couch where Garrett sat. "Garrett's out of commission right now. Find someone else."

Garrett held up his hand. Donovan meant well, and for that, Garrett couldn't get pissed. Sam was already frowning, fully prepared to get the corncob wedged farther up his ass.

"Talk," Garrett said shortly. "The abbreviated version, if you don't mind."

"There is no abbreviated version of Marcus Lattimer," Resnick said. "I don't need to tell you all the shit he's involved in. Or what he's done in the past."

"No, you damn well don't need to tell me. He's a goddamn traitor and the son of a bitch doesn't deserve to live."

"It's personal for me too," Resnick said softly. "But I'm not right for the job. You are."

Garrett's interest was solidly piqued. He had no doubt that over the years, Lattimer had pissed off a lot of people and betrayed just as many. It didn't surprise him that the CIA had a major hard-on for him, but for Garrett, nothing else

mattered but the faces of the men he'd lost on the day his team
went in to rescue Lattimer.

"Why am I right for the job? You still haven't told me how
Lattimer fucked up."

Resnick shoved the cigarette back into his mouth and ran
his hand repeatedly through his hair until it looked like he'd
stuck a finger in a light socket.

"Two weeks ago, he walked into a high-rise office building
in Boston. Fifteen minutes later he walked out and Allen Cross
was discovered shot to death in his office. Metro surveillance
captured Lattimer entering the building and fifteen minutes
later leaving the same way he came in. We don't have inside
surveillance because the system was conveniently down as
soon as Lattimer walked in. As an added convenience, the
security guard who was on duty that night has disappeared.
With his entire family."

"Yeah, pretty damn convenient," Garrett muttered.

"That's a pretty big fuckup for a man like Lattimer," Sam
said. "What made Allen Cross so special that Lattimer would
do the job himself?"

"That I don't know," Resnick admitted. "We're still trying
to connect the dots."

"So where do I come in?" Garrett asked.

Resnick fidgeted with his cigarette and Garrett was
tempted to tell him to just light the damn thing and get it over
with. It wasn't as if he didn't already smoke like a chimney.

"I'm getting to that. Sarah Daniels, who had a prior working relationship with Allen Cross, entered the building in an
agitated state not long after Lattimer went in. She ran out just
a few minutes later looking like Satan himself was after her.
To add to an already fucked up situation, Stanley Cross was
caught on surveillance entering the building not long before
Sarah ran out. He's the one who reported the murder after he
found his brother's body. But he denies seeing either Sarah or
Lattimer."

Garrett made a sound of disbelief. Marcus nodded. "Yeah.
I figure Lattimer got to him and he's scared shitless to say
anything."

"Think she witnessed Lattimer killing Cross?" Donovan
asked.

Resnick inhaled and blew out his breath around the cigarette. "I think that not only did she see it go down, but I think she knew it was going to happen."

"Whoa, you lost me there," Garrett said. "That's a hell of a stretch to make."

Resnick held up his hand. "Sarah Daniels is a dot we haven't been able to connect until now. Not only did she know the victim, but we believe that she has a relationship with Lattimer."

"What kind of relationship?" Sam prompted. "You're saying Sarah worked for Cross, was involved romantically with Lattimer and Lattimer shoots her boss?"

Resnick shook his head. "She's Lattimer's half sister."

Garrett sat forward on the couch. "He doesn't have any family. Hell, he killed his own father and then took over the old man's business. His mother died when he was a child and he didn't have any other siblings. I should know. I've looked for a way to get to that bastard for years. Even Van hasn't come up with anything and there's not much he can't find."

"We had someone undercover in Lattimer's organization," Resnick said. "We were this close to bringing Lattimer down when he got suspicious and my guy disappeared. I want Lattimer for this. I want him bad. Before he disappeared, my agent relayed information about Sarah. And here's the thing. Resnick cares about her. He's extremely protective of her. He's gone to great lengths to keep his relationship to her secret because he doesn't want his shit touching her. Remarkable, isn't it? I'd have laid odds the bastard didn't have a heart or a conscience.

"We were moving in on Sarah and setting up surveillance. I was in the process of getting wiretaps for her phone when this thing with Cross went down. We were in the same goddamn city as the bastard and he slipped through our fingers."

Garrett rubbed absently at his shoulder as he let Resnick's words sink in. Lattimer had a weakness. Weaknesses could be exploited.

"I want in."

"Wait just a fucking minute, Garrett," Sam said. "You don't know what the job is."

"It doesn't matter. Whatever it is, I want in."

Donovan frowned and shook his head "You're not ready to

go back into action yet, man. This isn't some pansy-ass cake job we're talking, not to mention this is way too personal for you."

Resnick cleared his throat. "It's actually perfect for him. It's why I came. It's true I know how much you hate the bastard, Garrett, and I'm certainly not above using that to my advantage. But your injury provides the perfect cover."

"Get to the point," Garrett snapped.

"Sarah disappeared after she ran from the building where Cross was killed. It took us a while to find her. She used her real name to hop a flight to Miami but it got a little murky after that. Took some digging, but we found a pilot who took her to Isle de Bijoux. She paid via a wire transfer and used a fake name. Marcus is obviously funding her. She's currently holed up in a cottage on a remote section of the beach."

Donovan crossed his arms over his chest and sat on the arm of the couch next to Garrett. "I can already tell I don't like where this is going."

"So why aren't you sending one of your men in?" Sam asked.

"Isle de Bijoux is small, not a lot of tourists. I need someone who'd blend. Someone with a reason for being there. Plus Garrett's motivated. He hates Lattimer's guts. And I wanted to give him the opportunity to take him down," he added in an even voice.

"Blend? You think *he'd* blend?" Donovan asked in amusement.

"He's perfect," Resnick said. "He already looks like shit. He needs a shave and a haircut. He's recovering from an injury. You'd take the beach cottage down from Sarah's. Do a little fishing. Hang out on the beach. Get some rest. It'd be a mini vacation and all you have to do is keep an eye on Sarah Daniels until Lattimer shows up."

Garrett stood and began to pace back and forth in front of the couch. His shoulder was aching, but he'd be damned if he gave in to the urge to rub it. Sam and Donovan would be on him about taking it easy, and the last thing he wanted to do right now was take it easy. He was damned tired of being laid up like some invalid. He was itching to get back in the game. Go to work. Even if it was some cake babysitting job. That wasn't what appealed. Beach and sun and sand did nothing for him. But the opportunity to nail Lattimer? He didn't give a shit if it meant him going to Bumfuck Africa.

He paused in mid-pace and turned his stare on Resick. "You're so sure he's going to show."

"Yeah. He'll show. Sarah's too important to him. She's the only damn thing he seems to care about in the world. If he doesn't show, he'll eventually get her to come to him. Either way, if you're on her tail, we nail him."

"So that's it. I go to this island and I keep an eye on her. Wait for Lattimer to show his hand and nail his ass to the wall."

Resnick blew out his breath. "Hell, I don't care if you sleep with her or play priest to her nun. I just need you close enough that you know when she so much as takes a piss. I want to know if Lattimer contacts her or she contacts him. And another thing, Garrett. I don't want you to lose your goddamn head over this. Do it right. Don't try to be a hero. If Lattimer shows, don't try anything stupid. We want him alive."

Sam's eyes narrowed. "What kind of backup will he have if things go to shit? I don't like the idea of sending one man in on any job, no matter how simple it sounds."

"The full power of my resources," Resnick said. "Whatever you need."

Garrett glanced first at Sam, who didn't look thrilled, and then to Donovan who simply looked worried. Then he looked back at Resnick. "Do you have a file on Sarah? Photos? Age? Habits?"

Resnick's eye twitched and he reached for his cigarette again. "Of course." He reached into his suit and pulled out a folder. He thrust it at Garrett who took it and flipped it open. Paper clipped to the first page was a photo.

Sarah was beautiful. Not classical and elegant like Rachel or cute and sweet looking like Sophie, but a quiet beauty that didn't jump off the page at you but rather settled in nice and comfortably.

She had long chestnut hair, a light dusting of freckles over her nose and deep green eyes. She wasn't smiling in the picture but he'd bet his last dollar that when she did smile, it lit up her entire face.

He thumbed through her information, glancing at her job. She was an administrative assistant. She'd taken the job as

Allen Cross's executive assistant eighteen months prior. That had only lasted six months. She hadn't taken a job since. He raised an eyebrow at that. Maybe her brother was footing her bills.

She lived in Boston but had been born and raised in Alabama. No siblings—officially. No parents. According to her records, she'd been raised in foster care for most of her childhood. He frowned. If she was Lattimer's half sister, then why the hell had she been raised in foster care when he'd grown up with a silver spoon?

She had an apartment in a modest area of Boston. Lived alone. She had acquaintances, but no apparent close friends. She seemed to have lost touch with people she'd formerly hung out with after she'd quit her job with Cross.

He traced the outline of her face on the picture. So she was a loner. Probably what she was used to. In another life, Garrett imagined he was a hermit, and if his overbearing family would allow it, he'd be a total cave dweller now.

Garrett rubbed his neck and then glanced back at Resnick. "You aren't holding out any other information from me, are you? This is it? I stick to Sarah Daniels and nail Lattimer when the time comes."

"In a nutshell, yeah. Think of it as paid vacation. With a pretty woman at that."

Garrett blew out his breath. "Okay, when do you want me down there?"

Resnick shot him a rueful glance. "Try yesterday."

CHAPTER 3

PARADISE had become hell. Despite the beauty of her surroundings, Sarah Daniels spent every minute of every day looking over her shoulder and waiting. Waiting to be discovered. After her arrival on the island, she'd spent the entire first week holed up in the tiny cottage she'd rented, barely able to sleep for fear of discovery.

Marcus had always been determined to take care of her. It frustrated him that she wouldn't accept his lavish gifts, his money or his offer to buy her a house complete with staff to see to her every need. What he had done was set up a bank account and deposited sums at intervals until a hefty balance had accumulated. As much as she'd been determined not to draw on those reserves, she was grateful now that he'd done it.

She'd use the money to protect him, just as he'd protected her.

Demons past and present haunted her dreams until she was exhausted and worn thin. On the eighth day of her self-imposed solitude, she'd risen at dawn and watched the first fingers of the sun spread over the deep blue water. Watched as the waves gently foamed onto the sand, reaching and then retreating.

Drawn to the peace it seemingly offered, she'd walked barefoot onto the sand and stood at the water's edge, face turned up into the sun. Here, her past didn't matter. It was a chance to be reborn. She just had to take it. She had to believe in it.

Though the sun warmed her skin, she was still cold on the inside. She was in survival mode. Everything was locked down. She didn't feel. She *couldn't* feel.

Gradually she ventured out to buy groceries, figuring she'd gain more suspicion by never leaving her cottage than if she mingled with the locals. The island was a fascinating mix of cultures, and people from all over the globe seemed to have traveled to this place for a new beginning.

Tourists hadn't yet found the island. It was inhabited largely by year-rounders, corporate people who'd left the rat race, artists seeking inspiration and loners like herself who sought refuge in a sparsely populated island where everyone pretty much kept to themselves.

Today she left her cottage wearing a tank top and casual trousers. Flip-flops and slides were the shoes of choice and she'd purchased a few pair days earlier in her attempt to blend in with the local scenery. Her destination was the coffee shop perched haphazardly on a beach overlook a mile from the cottage. It was a popular haunt. The coffee was good and they served a variety of sandwiches and croissants. It also had free Wi-Fi.

She tucked her laptop into her bag and then felt inside the pocket of her pants for the paper with the instructions on how to check the email account she communicated with Marcus from. Even though it had been her and Marcus's primary method of communication for a few years now, she hadn't yet committed the intricate steps to memory. Marcus had despaired of her, exasperated by the fact she made lists and notes for everything. He preached to her about paper trails, but she'd never considered his grumblings. Never considered that she'd be in a position to actually worry about such a thing.

She'd made a mistake already. She'd used her real name. Her passport. Like an idiot. She'd left Boston in such a rush that she hadn't really thought about the potential pitfalls of the very thing Marcus feared. A paper trail. Even her destination hadn't been planned. At the ticket counter in the airport, she'd plunked down her credit card and asked for the first available flight out of Boston. It just happened to be going to Miami. On the plane, she'd sat by an elderly couple whose final destination was Isle de Bijoux. It sounded perfect. By the time she landed in Miami, she'd had time to actually think about what she was doing, so from there, she chartered a private Cessna to the island, used a fake name and paid via wire transfer from the account Marcus has set up for her. The pilot probably thought she was a drug dealer, but he hadn't turned down the money she offered.

Then she'd booked another commercial flight to Los Angeles, though if anyone really looked hard, they'd know she never got on that flight. And it wasn't as if she'd made it difficult for anyone to track her to Miami. Still, she felt some sense of satisfaction that with as little experience as she had with subterfuge, she'd managed to get to the island and not stick out like a sore thumb. But the stress of not knowing if she was being hunted—by the authorities or Stanley Cross— had worn away at her already frayed mental state.

So one of the first things she'd done was to weigh her options and plan an escape route. It amused her that she was acting like a character in some ridiculous spy movie. She'd flown here, and flying back out in a hurry simply wasn't an option. If she ever had to bolt, her best avenue of escape would be by sea.

Instead of looking up the two larger charter services, she'd instead opted for a small, hole-in-the wall, one-boat operation that looked as though it was usually passed over for the two other services. She gave the owner a ridiculous story about how she was an author doing research and writing a crime novel and that she wanted to arrange for him to be on call to pick her up on the western tip of the island and take her to the neighboring island.

To his further amusement, she made him do a test run. He probably couldn't care less about why she was acting so ridiculous as long as she paid him, and she made sure it was worth his while, but she remained in character, even bringing a notebook where she pretended to take copious notes while they rode the two hours to the next island.

To her delight, there were a few charter services to choose from there, but she nearly did a victory dance when she found out that one of them made routine flights to Mexico to deliver goods to a retail store. After again spinning a yarn about researching a thriller, she convinced the pilot to allow her to hitch a ride when she got ready. She didn't bother to tell him that she preferred never to be ready, but at least she had a viable and somewhat secure escape route from her island should the need arise.

All the way back to the island aboard the small boat, she'd patted herself on the back and asserted that while she was a decided amateur at matters of deception, she wasn't a complete idiot. Then she'd spent an afternoon in the coffee shop researching her options in Mexico.

She'd come a long way from the spineless coward she'd been after Allen Cross raped her. So she'd changed one hiding place for another, but she was far more in control of her destiny here than she'd been in Boston. And she wasn't about to let go of the reins again.

After three weeks on the island, she settled into a routine, but she didn't dare let her guard down. Mistakes could get her killed. Only a fool became complacent. But she did allow herself a few simple pleasures. Such as coffee at the shop in town and occasional trips to the market to see what struck her fancy.

She barely remembered the walk to the coffee shop, so deep was her concentration on her circumstances. She stayed on the narrow beach path rather than take the winding, pothole-riddled main road that that ended just a few hundred yards beyond her cottage. When she reached the crumbling stone steps that led up to the ramshackle hut, she paused to look around. Satisfied that nothing seemed amiss, she hurried up the path to the rear entrance of the shop.

Once inside, the aroma of coffee surrounded her and filled her nostrils. She breathed in and then took a seat in the far corner, where her back was to the wall. Marie, the regular waitress with a soft French accent brought her a cup of the local brew, offered a smile and then faded away as quickly as she'd come.

Sarah liked that. Loved that everyone didn't want to be her friend, find out her life's story or pry into her circumstances. She opened her laptop after savoring the first sips of her coffee, then carefully pulled out the folded-up instructions.

She glanced up to make sure no one was nearby and then quickly went through the series of steps to access the secure server. She held her breath waiting for the page to load and then she saw that she had not one but several messages. Nearly a dozen. All from Marcus. Most saying the same thing with little variation.

Damn it, Sarah, where are you?

Sarah, contact me immediately. I'll come for you.

I'm worried. You shouldn't have gone off on your own. Tell me where you are.

And then the last.

Sarah, I'm sorry you had to see that. I didn't want you anywhere near. It had to be done. I don't regret it. I don't want you to be afraid of me. Never of me. People will be looking for you. Because of me. I need you to tell me where you are so I can make arrangements.

With shaking fingers she typed a response to the last email.

I'm okay. I'm safe. It's better if you don't know where I am. I don't want to be used against you. I'm not afraid of you. I'm afraid for you. You're the only one who's ever stood up for me. It's time I stood up for myself. I promise to contact you if I need you. Let me know when things are safe for you.

Then she hurriedly shut the laptop. She closed her eyes against the ache in her throat. There was so many "if only"s. They ran through her mind like an out-of-control merry-go-round. But it was time to put the "if only"s behind her. Move forward. New life. New resolve.

A sound jerked her from sleep. Sarah came fully awake, sitting up in bed, hands shaking and nausea welling in her stomach. For a moment she was paralyzed with fear, and then she realized the room was steeped in darkness. Her gaze swung frantically to the lamp she always left on. She rolled, reaching for it and nearly knocking it off the nightstand in her haste to turn it back on. She twisted the knob but nothing happened. Had the bulb burned out? It had to have gone off after she'd fallen asleep. Her shoulder brushed against the book she'd been reading, and she shoved it under her pillow.

She listened, straining for the sound. Had she imagined it?

She swung her legs over the side of the bed, her bare feet hitting the old wooden floor. It creaked in protest when she rose and she reached down for the only means of self-defense she had—an old pipe she'd found lying outside the cottage.

Her fingers curled around it and she pulled it up to her chest as she peered through her open doorway into the hall. Her vision blurred and her head swam before she realized she was holding her breath. She let it out slow but it stuttered across her lips and she clamped then shut so she didn't make any sound.

She crept down the hall, so terrified and yet determined not to be a powerless victim again. If only she could have that moment back. She'd replayed it so many times in her mind. She could have fought harder. She could have defended herself better. But no matter how many times she went back, the result was always the same. She'd failed.

She wouldn't fail again.

With renewed determination and courage, she gripped the pipe and increased her pace down the hall. At the end, she hesitated, surveying the small living room. The night-light plugged into the wall cast a glow over the area, and nothing looked out of place.

A faint rustle from the kitchen sent her pulse soaring. She leaned against the wall and pondered her options. She could run out the front door, but to where? The beach? She was a mile from town and at least two hundred yards from the closest cottage, which was currently vacant.

Still, outside was away from whatever was in her kitchen, and avoidance was always preferable to confrontation.

She swallowed, closed her eyes and then reopened them, her sights on the front door. There were two dead bolts, a chain and the regular lock to contend with. She'd need to be fast because as soon as she started fumbling with the door, the intruder would be alerted.

Before she could overthink it, she lunged for the front door, her fingers reaching for the first dead bolt. She had it undone, when she heard a very distinct *meow*.

She froze. A cat?

She whirled around to see a scruffy calico cat standing in the doorway to the kitchen. The cat looked at her, then

meowed again and proceeded to pad across the floor to rub
against Sarah's leg.

Her relief was so staggering that she sagged to the floor
still clutching the pipe. She leaned her head forward onto her
knees, eyes closed and laughed. She laughed until tears ran
down her cheeks and then she gave up and sobbed.

Warm fur rubbed against her arm and the low rumble of a
purr reached her ears. She raised her head to see the cat up on
its hind legs, paws on her thigh as she rubbed her head against
Sarah's skin.

"You scared me to death," Sarah said hoarsely. "How did
you get in here?"

The cat meowed and dipped her head, obviously wanting
Sarah to pet her. Sarah laid the pipe on the floor and reached to
scratch the cat's ears. The cat responded with an even louder
purr and a ripply sound of pleasure. She began kneading Sarah's arm and Sarah gently removed the claws from her skin.

Pitifully grateful for the affection of the cat, she gathered the animal closer, putting her against her chest. The cat
nudged at Sarah's chin and repeatedly bumped her head over
Sarah's jaw.

"Are you hungry? Is that what you were doing in the kitchen?"

Had she been so lost in her thoughts when she'd returned
from town that she hadn't seen the cat come in? Or had she
left the door ajar earlier? The thought worried her. She was
going to have to be more careful. She couldn't afford any
lapse in attention.

The cat responded with more purring and Sarah smiled as
she wiped the tears from her cheek. Gathering the cat under
one arm, she got to her feet and walked into the kitchen. She
flipped on the light and grimaced. The cat had knocked a
glass off the counter and it lay in pieces on the floor, the edges
gleaming in the light.

Sarah sighed and put the cat up on the counter so she
wouldn't cut her paws. "You were a very naughty cat," she
chided. "Stay there while I clean the mess up and I'll find you
something to eat."

The cat settled on its haunches and began licking her paw
and wiping it over her jowls. Sarah collected the dustpan
and the broom from the pantry and cleaned up the shards.

Afterward she perused the contents of the small refrigerator and decided that leftover chicken breast was the most suitable meal until she could buy dry food from the market.

The cat tried to stick her nose in the chicken multiple times as Sarah sliced it into bite-sized pieces. She pushed at the cat's head to ward it off but it only purred and rubbed against her palm. With a laugh, Sarah piled the chicken onto a saucer and set it in front of the cat.

She leaned tiredly against the counter, watching as the poor animal devoured the meal like it was her last. Unable to resist, she slid her hand over the cat's fur, petting as the cat continued to scarf down the bites.

Every once in a while the cat would pick her head up and give Sarah sweet eyes and Sarah smiled. "You don't look or act like you have a home, sweetie. Do you want to stay with me?" In truth, the idea of having a pet here appealed. It made the cottage less intimidating and the idea that she wasn't alone—even with just a cat for company—was a huge relief.

After the last bite was demolished, the cat licked the saucer and then looked up at Sarah and meowed. Sarah scooped her off the counter and headed for the bedroom. Tomorrow, in addition to food, she'd need litter and a pan. For tonight, she'd just have to hope the cat could hold it until morning, because she was closing her bedroom door and locking it.

Even though her fears had been unfounded, she was still jittery from the scare, and she wanted to feel as safe as possible. She dropped the cat onto the bed and then crawled on the mattress to get under the covers.

To her surprise, the cat padded up to her head, pawed at the covers until Sarah pulled them back and then snuggled down just under the sheet at Sarah's side. Sarah lay there, the cat vibrating against her side and smiled. It was a nice feeling. Very nice. She and the cat would get along just fine. Sarah would fill a need for the cat by offering food and shelter and the cat would provide some much-needed sanity for Sarah.

CHAPTER 4

GARRETT lugged his two bags through the door of the cottage and grimly surveyed the surroundings. When he'd imagined a beachfront house with great views and just steps from the water, he'd envisioned something a little more modern. Flat-screen TV, front porch with a hammock, fully stocked kitchen and maybe a hot tub that overlooked the beach.

What he'd got was a ramshackle cottage that looked like it didn't survive the last hurricane season, with a dilapidated front porch and sagging steps. The inside smelled like his grandmother's house. Musty and old. The furniture was threadbare and at least thirty years old. The kitchen had been designed in the sixties and had appliances to match. Worse, there wasn't a TV at all, and his hopes for a hot tub went down the toilet.

With a shrug, he dropped his bags and began opening windows to air the rooms out. He'd certainly had worse accommodations during his years in the Marines.

He peeked out his bedroom window down the beach to where Sarah's cottage stood in the distance. It wasn't optimal. He'd prefer closer proximity to the woman he was supposed to shadow, but the houses were sparse along this stretch of the shore.

The first order of business was a trip into town for food. He

planned to take the path down the beach that went directly in
front of her house. He didn't want to be too obvious right off
the bat and force a meeting, but if she happened to be out and
around when he passed, it was as good an opportunity as any
to meet his new neighbor.

As he went back out the front door and stood on the tilted
porch to look out over the ocean, he realized this wasn't going
to be as bad as he imagined. As much as he protested the need
for any recovery time, a few weeks on a beach to exercise,
eat good food and not trip over all the people who currently
inhabited his house sounded pretty damn good. If it put him
back to one hundred percent so he could go back to work, he'd
take the downtime.

He felt a little ridiculous in beach khaki shorts, muscle
shirt and flip-flops, but with the hint of scruff on his jaw and
the fact he hadn't cut his hair on his usual schedule, he passed
for a man only concerned with kicking back and relaxing.

The sun beat down on him and warmed his shoulders as he
set off down the worn path toward Sarah's cottage. He flexed
his arm and was happy to note that his shoulder was limber and
not stiff despite the long time he'd spent traveling and cooped
up in a way-too-small seat. Puddle jumpers weren't built for
men his size, and they were damn claustrophobic to boot.

Sand got between his toes and between the bottoms of
his feet and the flip-flops. Worthless shoes. He stopped periodically to shake the sand from them and then continued on
down the beach.

He was careful not to show any undue curiosity as he
neared Sarah's cottage, though he memorized every detail of
the place from his periphery. Like his accommodations, it had
seen its better days, although hers had underwent fresh paint
recently. Still, it would take nothing to get inside. A good kick
to the door—or hell, even the walls—and it would probably
knock right down.

He continued past, wondering if she was unconcerned as
she appeared. Simply using a fake name to rent a beach house
didn't guarantee anonymity. Her trail was sloppy all the way
from Boston. She'd done a better job of covering her tracks
once she reached Miami, but it still wasn't clean. Resnick had
been able to find her. Garrett supposed he couldn't fault her,

though. It wasn't like people got lessons in school on how to be a fugitive. Not that she was classified as a fugitive, but she may as well be. There were certainly enough people interested in her whereabouts.

The closer he got to town, the higher the dunes on his left stacked up. There were a few shoddily fashioned walkways up over the dune to turnouts on the road. Public access to the beach, but he hadn't come across a single beachgoer on his walk into town.

The sand ran smack into a rock outcropping, and cut into the stones were steps leading up to a coffee shack. He climbed but circled around the front to cross the cobblestone street to where the market was located. Outside the front were stands of fresh fruits and vegetables. He bypassed those for now and went inside to find the essentials. Red meat.

He soon learned that to the locals, "meat" meant fish or other seafood. He grumbled through the selection of ground meat and winced at only finding two steaks. He bought up all the pork chops and put a healthy dent in the chicken breasts. He wasn't a fish person. Oh, he'd put a hook in one, but eating them didn't appeal. Not enough substance.

Which reminded him, he really needed to check out the local bait shop, pick up a surf casting rod so he could spend some time fishing. It would give him a good excuse to be on the beach, where he could watch Sarah's cottage and get an idea of her routine.

At least the locals appreciated beer. There was a ton of variety, and well, when it came to beer, he wasn't picky. He picked up several six-packs, tossed them in the cart and headed down the aisles to see what else he needed to feed himself for the next while.

Eggs, stuff for his protein shakes. Then he frowned. What were the odds of his cottage having a blender? He was lucky to have a few pots and pans to cook in. Cheese, bread, mayo, mustard and ketchup. Definitely ketchup. What meal was complete without it?

He smiled at the memory of his mother grumbling about his need to pour ketchup on everything.

When he finally rolled the cart to the front of the store, he was treated to several curious stares. It was then he realized that most everyone else had a basket with maybe one day's worth of food. It took a while to check out since there was only one clerk, and the line piled up behind him as everyone waited for all his groceries to be tallied.

A young guy who looked to be in his teens approached Garrett as he finished paying.

"You want I deliver the groceries to where you stay? I can get my friends to help. We work cheap."

Garrett eyed the eager kid. "How cheap?"

"Twenty euros apiece."

"I wasn't born yesterday," Garrett said dryly. "I'll give you twenty American and you split it with your friends."

The kid beamed at him. "Deal."

Garrett pulled out his wallet. "I'm the last cottage down the beach from the coffee shack."

"Yes, I know it. I'll bring them down and leave them on your porch. Don't be long. You wouldn't want your meat to spoil."

No, he didn't want his food to spoil. Who knew how long it took the grocery to restock their non-fish meat items.

Since the kid was taking the groceries, Garrett ambled down to one of the shops that boasted fishing supplies. He walked in to see the shopkeeper sitting behind the register with his feet propped up on the counter. He had a floppy hat pulled low over his eyes, and it looked like he was taking a nap. Garrett was nearly by him when the guy tipped up the brim, gave him a cursory onceover and then nodded.

"Feel free to look around. If you need any help, just holler."

Garrett was surprised to hear an American drawl. Not just American, but clearly southern. "Got a recommendation for something to do a little surf fishing with?"

The shop owner slid his feet off the counter and they landed with a clunk on the floor. He pushed back the hat and sized up Garrett more fully. Then he grunted. "Military, though probably not for a few years. Injury to your shoulder. Recent. Looking for some R and R and don't much like other people. Am I right?"

Garrett raised an eyebrow, immediately suspicious.

"Relax. I read people. Nothing much else to do around here when what little tourist season we have is over." He stuck out his hand to Garrett. "Rob Garner. Retired army. Opened up shop here five years ago. Doesn't take much to live here and the scenery's good. I got in at a good time. In a few years, the rest of the world will catch on to what we have here and the property values will soar. Then I can sell and live high on the hog."

Garrett returned his hand shake. "Garrett Kelly. Marine Corps. And yeah, here for some R and R and no, I don't like people much."

Rob laughed and clapped his hands together. "I don't have much use for them myself. Now, if you want to do some surf fishing, I'd suggest a casting rod that you can get out there a ways with. Then you can slip it into the holder, kick back with a beer and wait for the fish to bite. All the casting and reeling those bass fishermen do is for idiots. Fishing's supposed to be relaxing."

Garrett cracked a smile. "Fuckin' A."

"Come on, I'll get you what you need. For bait you can use shad or shrimp. Cut bait is good too."

Garrett watched as Rob pulled down about a twelve-foot rod, handed it to Garrett and then went down another aisle to get hooks, surf weights and liters. A few moments later, he piled everything onto the counter. "You're all set. I'll ring you up and you can be fishing this afternoon if you want."

"Thanks. I might do that. Got the beer already. Maybe I'll grill some steak and have dinner on the beach."

Rob nodded. "Yep, that sounds like a pretty good damn day to me. Enjoy it. If there's anything else you need, don't hesitate to come back in."

Garrett broke down the rod to make it more manageable to carry, then collected the bag with all the other supplies. With a nod, he headed back outside.

Hopefully the kid had delivered the groceries while Garrett was in the bait shop. Breakfast had consisted of a dry bagel on the plane, and his stomach was doing some serious protesting. A steak and a little fishing sounded next to heaven.

He glanced over to the market to see a woman step out, bag clutched close to her chest. She glanced furtively left and right and then strode toward the coffee shack. His pulse picked up. If he wasn't mistaken, he'd just gotten his first real-life glimpse of Sarah Daniels.

On impulse, he crossed the street toward the coffee shack. He'd intended to take the main road back, but carrying the fishing pole and supplies, he had a ready excuse to take the beach path.

When he rounded the corner of the shack, he saw her head bob down the stone steps leading to the beach. He waited a moment to give her a bigger head start and then took out after her.

At first she didn't realize he was following her. Which further cemented his opinion that she was hopelessly naïve. When she did look over her shoulder, her eyes flared in alarm. Then she made a concerted effort to shield her reaction. She even offered a semblance of a smile as she took in the fishing gear he carried before turning around and increasing her pace.

Twice more she turned just enough that she could see him and each time she sped up. By the time she reached her cottage, he could tell she was alarmed by the fact he still trailed her. She hurried up her steps, and in her haste to open the door, she dropped one of the bags she carried.

She yanked the door open then turned so she could see him while she picked up her things. Her gaze never left him as she shoved the items back into her bag. Garrett found himself strangely transfixed and unable to look away. The pictures hadn't done her justice, nor had they captured the haunted, frightened eyes rimmed with shadows. She looked infinitely fragile, scared out of her mind, but he also saw something else. Maybe it was the way she *tried* not to look scared or maybe it was subtle stiffening of her shoulders and the rebellious twist to her lips. She was a fighter, not the timid mouse he'd imagined.

Awareness prickled over his skin and tightened the hairs at his nape. He rubbed the back of his neck in an attempt to dispel the momentary discomfort. His reaction irritated and intrigued him all at the same time.

He offered a friendly wave and continued on his way, though he found it hard to drag his gaze away from her. He didn't want her to feel threatened by him, because he planned to see a lot more of her.

CHAPTER 5

SARAH watched from between the slats of her wooden blinds as the man jogged down the beach. Every so often he'd stop, drop down and do a series of push-ups. Sweat gleamed in the sunlight and she could see the strain on his face as he pushed himself harder.

Ever since she'd freaked out two days ago when she'd realized he was following her, she paid careful attention to her new neighbor. Granted, her imagination had run wild, but she didn't get down on herself for being careful.

He was a big man. Beautiful. She chided herself for her fanciful thoughts, but the man *was* beautiful. He was solidly built, lean and muscled with no amount of spare flesh anywhere that she could see. His black hair was mussed on top, as if he'd outgrown a more severe military cut. Judging by the amount of time he spent working out and the way he'd roll his shoulder with a grimace, she figured he'd been injured. Maybe he was on leave or maybe he'd been discharged after his injury.

Or maybe she was just trying to convince herself that her new neighbor wasn't a threat to her.

She closed her eyes and let the slat fall. Not everyone was the enemy. The problem was figuring out who wasn't, and she didn't have the luxury of differentiating.

It relieved her that she felt the stirrings of interest—
feminine interest—in this man. That she could look and
appreciate and even wonder about him made her want to do a
fist pump in the air. *Up yours, Allen Cross. You haven't won.
You didn't destroy me.*

A plaintive meow broke her from her thoughts and she
turned to see the cat sitting on the countertop, eyeing her
expectantly. Sarah smiled and walked over to rub her hand
over the cat's head.

"I suppose I need to name you. I can't continue calling you
Cat, can I?"

The cat blinked and let out a purr, then walked over to the
cabinet where Sarah kept the cat food. She reared up on her
hind legs and pawed at the door. Sarah chuckled and went to
oblige the hungry animal.

Her new neighbor had already established a routine. She
felt like some stalker watching his every movement. Part of
it was her wariness, but the other part was curiosity. There
wasn't much else to do out here but watch the water. There
wasn't a lot of traffic down this way because of the smaller
number of houses, most of which were rentals. He was the
only other person she saw on her end of the beach with any
regularity, and she found herself fascinated by him.

He was up early in the mornings, jogging, sometimes running. Then he'd disappear into his cottage only to reappear
later with his fishing gear. He'd set up, wade out into the surf
to cast his line and then wade back and position his pole in the
holder. Then he'd kick back in a rickety-looking lawn chair,
ice chest on the ground next to him and wait.

She had to admire his patience. He'd sit for long periods of
time until the rod tip bent, when he'd leap up to set the hook
and begin reeling in. Most of the fish were smaller, but she'd
stood in her window watching for a solid half hour watching
him wrestle a huge catch to the shores.

He'd unhook it, admire it, hold it up in the sun and then wade
out to free it again. Then he'd begin the process all over again.

She envied his freedom. The complete lack of care. He
didn't look as though he had a worry in the world other than
enjoying his quiet day in the sun. She poured the cat food into

the bowl and set it on the floor, then stood back as the kitty began devouring it like it was a piece of prime steak.

"Patches," she decided. "Not terribly original. I'm sure there are thousands of other calicos out there with the same exact name, but I bet you're the only one on this island."

Patches didn't look up from her food.

Sarah went back to the window to see if she could catch another glimpse of her neighbor. To her surprise, he'd changed into a pair of swim trunks and was now standing at the water's edge. The waves foamed and covered his feet as he stared over the horizon.

He raised his arms and then began a series of motions that looked to her like a martial arts workout. Maybe Tai Chi? She watched, absorbed by the sensuality of his movements. She might have expected a man of his size to be clumsy, but he moved with a grace that surprised her.

Lyrical. He moved in harmony with the water, as though he blocked out everything but the beauty immediately surrounding him. She was, in that moment, insanely jealous of the peace that surrounded him like an aura.

She stared unabashedly as he went through the motions. At one point he turned, and she could swear he saw her watching him, but she shook off the notion. She was staring through an opening no bigger than an inch and he was at least fifty yards away. Maybe farther.

Still, it was enough to pull her away from the window. She needed something else to focus on. The isolation was driving her insane. Her gaze snagged on her laptop bag.

The waiting was making her crazy. Maybe she could check out the little bookstore in the town square. She'd even seen a section in the market where they rented DVDs. She hadn't even turned on the television to see if it or the DVD player worked but movies would be a welcome distraction.

And she totally needed to get out of this cottage before she lost her mind.

She grabbed her bag, made sure the cat was nowhere near the door and let herself out. As she descended the steps to the beach, she looked to her right to see her neighbor swimming at a fast stroke away from shore. She stood and watched for a

moment until he got so far away she could no longer see him
and then she headed down the beach in the opposite direction.

Her first stop was at the coffee shack, where she set up
in her usual corner, accepted a cup of the local brew from
Marie and then she went through the steps to check her email.
As suspected, she had no new messages. It was tempting to
search the local news in Boston but she was too paranoid. The
last thing she wanted was to tip off anyone as to her location.
And who knew what could be accomplished on the Internet?

Yes, she was paranoid, but she could live with that. It
might just save her life. It didn't help that she was a complete
idiot about technology.

Her instinct was to hurry through her coffee, go to the bookshop and rush back to her cottage. But she tempered that urge
and remained to sip at her coffee and watch the goings on in
the little café, such as they were. She hated the idea of going
back to the cottage, where she'd once again be alone. She hated
being alone. She was a people person. She liked being around
people even if she didn't interact with them much, loved the big
city with all the flashes of color and culture.

She glanced out the front window to watch the passersby
and speculate on their circumstances, where they came from,
where they were going. When the waitress came to offer her a
refill, she smiled and accepted, determined to stay and enjoy
her break from isolation.

After the second cup, she was jittery from the double jolt
of caffeine and anxious to be off. She slid out of her chair,
careful to tuck her laptop into her bag and then exited the
front of the shop to cross the street to the bookstore. It was
two doors down from the market with only a fishing supply
shop to separate them.

When she entered, she was instantly assailed by the smell
of old books. She sniffed appreciatively and went to the
shelves to browse the selection. An older lady with a warm
smile waved from her chair behind the register and Sarah
offered a brief acknowledgment before turning back to the
shelf in front of her.

It was easy to get lost in books. It was more than an hour
later when she realized how long she'd been there picking
over the titles. She looked ruefully at the dozen or so books

she'd stacked to the side and decided it was enough for now. It would give her a good excuse to return when she'd finished them.

She hauled her loot to the register and plunked them down in front of the woman.

"Hi there, you like to read, I see," the woman said cheerfully. "Most folks who come through here just pick up one or two. Beach reads they call them. If you ask me, any book is good for the beach."

Sarah smiled. "I do enjoy books. I don't think these will last me long, but they're all I can carry with me right now."

"I'm Martine," the woman said, extending her hand.

"I'm . . . Sarah."

"Well, Sarah, it's very nice to meet another book lover. When you're done with these, you can bring them back in. I'll give you credit toward more book purchases."

"Thank you, I will."

Martine rang up the books and Sarah paid her in cash. Then Martine placed the books in a plastic grocery store bag and handed it over to Sarah. Sarah juggled her laptop bag, hauling it farther over her shoulder, and took the sack from the shop owner. With a wave, she headed back outside.

Just the little bit of human interaction warmed Sarah on the inside. She needed this. Needed to connect to other people, even in a superficial way. Head down, she turned the corner of the bookshop into the small alley that separated the store from its neighbor. The DVD rental place was behind the market. She'd make a quick stop, pick up a few movies and then she'd be set for entertainment for the next several days. Between the times she spent watching her neighbor, that is.

She was so absorbed in her thoughts that she didn't see the person in front of her until she ran smack into the man. She bounced off as adrenaline spiked in her veins. *Stupid, stupid, stupid!*

Before she could react, the dull gleam of a knife flashed in her face and the strap from her bag carrying her laptop nearly wrenched her shoulder from its socket. She dropped the bag of books and grabbed the strap before her assailant could wrest it free.

She pulled and stumbled back, and came face to face with a grubby-looking man who looked to be in his early twenties. He was unwashed and unshaven and her nostrils flared at the overwhelming smell of body odor.

"Give me the bag," he ordered in clipped English.

He gripped her hair and yanked, pulling her closer to him—and to the knife he held barely an inch in front of her nose.

She couldn't lose her laptop. Her whole life was in that laptop. Panic and hysteria rose and slammed through her veins with the force of a cement truck.

"No!"

The exclamation rose in her throat and was forced out before she could think better of it.

The hand tightened in her hair and then she was slammed against the outside wall of the shop with enough force to knock the breath from her and make her eyes water. The man grabbed clumsily for her bag, and the knife wavered in her vision. Taking advantage of his lapse, she grabbed his wrist and knocked the knife from his hand.

And suddenly she was free. She stood against the wall, shaking violently, not comprehending what had just happened. She watched in disbelief as her neighbor, seemingly appearing out of nowhere, let out a snarl of rage as he smashed his fist into the face of her attacker.

The noise attracted onlookers. Several gathered at the end of the alley and a moment later, the constable ran down to intervene. It was over almost as soon as it began. Her attacker lay bleeding on the ground, begging pitifully for mercy. Her neighbor hauled him up and shoved him in the direction of the approaching constable. Then he turned to Sarah, concern etched on his brow.

"Hey, are you okay?"

He moved closer and gripped her shoulders. She flinched and tried to move away, but he held tight as he stared into her eyes.

"I-I'm fine."

"Did he hurt you?" he demanded.

She shook her head and to her consternation, her teeth started to clink together like ice tumbling into a glass.

He touched her cheek, then pushed back the hair that had fallen over her eyes. She glanced away to see the constable putting her attacker in handcuffs. "He had a knife." She pointed to the ground, where it had fallen.

Her neighbor bent and retrieved the knife, holding it up as he inspected it in the sunlight. Then he frowned and handed it over to the constable.

"You've gone too far this time, Didier," the constable snapped at her attacker.

Sarah frowned and pushed herself around her neighbor. "What do you mean? Do you know this man?"

The constable sighed. "He's a troublemaker. I've picked him up a few times, but he's never resorted to violence. He's a petty thief."

Heat suffused her cheeks. "He threatened me! I hope you'll keep him locked up this time so he doesn't terrorize others."

The constable's brows drew together as if he had no liking for her telling him how to perform his duties.

"He pulled a knife on the lady," her neighbor said in a dangerous voice. "If you won't deal with the matter, I'll report this matter to your superiors."

"Of course the matter will be dealt with," the constable huffed. "He's going to jail. He'll be summoned to appear before the judge." He looked to both Sarah and her neighbor. "I'll need the both of you to come with me and give a proper report."

The pulse at the base of her neck pounded viciously. Report the crime. What she hadn't, in her cowardice and shame, done before. She so indignantly informed the constable that she didn't want this man to be free to terrorize others, and yet she'd done just that when she'd refused to report the crime against her so many months ago.

She eyed her attacker bleakly, shame crowding her mind, pushing her fear and anger and everything else solidly aside. She was a hypocrite. And a coward. She didn't deserve justice because she'd never sought it for herself.

"You don't have to be afraid," her neighbor murmured. "I'll go with you."

Startled, she took a step back and found herself pinned against the wall again. She stared warily at the big man who'd come to her rescue, hating the inadvertent fear that raced up her spine.

He stood there waiting, not making a move toward her, almost as if he knew how badly he scared her. He watched calmly, waiting, his gaze drifting over her face, taking in every detail. It unnerved her and exposed her vulnerability.

"If you'll come to the station straightaway," the constable urged as he pushed Didier down the alleyway in cuffs. "I'll need to log a full report so the proper charges can be pressed."

Sarah swallowed the nausea that welled in her throat. Regret burned in her chest over past mistakes. But she wouldn't make that mistake again. She was through being a victim. She wanted control back, and she was tired of living in fear.

Her neighbor held out his hand, palm up, his expression devoid of any emotion. It was though he wanted to appear as nonthreatening as possible; and the thing of it was, she wanted to take his hand. She wanted to lean on someone else, just for a few minutes. She wanted it more than anything.

She wiped her hand over her mouth to disguise the tremble and then averted her gaze. "We should go," she said without taking his hand. She started after the constable, leaving her rescuer to follow.

He fell into step behind her, but he kept at least a foot between them. Still, he loomed over her, blocking the sun as they stepped onto the street. She quickened her pace, unsettled by him, and why, she wasn't sure.

When they reached the small station at the far end of the town square, her neighbor held the door open and ushered her inside. There was no air-conditioning and it was a good twenty degrees hotter inside the boxlike building. None of the windows were open to allow the sea breeze in, and she glanced nervously back toward the door. She couldn't remain in this airless place for more than a few minutes. She'd go nuts.

A younger officer sat at a desk idly flipping through paperwork. He looked up when she and her neighbor entered.

"Comment puis-je vous aider, madame?"

"English please," she said. *"Parlez-vous Anglais?"*

The officer nodded. "But of course."

"We're here to give the constable our statement," her neighbor said.

"Ah, very good. If you'll have a seat, he'll be with you momentarily."

Sarah nodded and sank onto one of the metal chairs, relieved to be off her feet. She stiffened when her neighbor sat next to her, their legs grazing as he shifted to get comfortable.

"My name is Garrett."

"I'm Sarah," she said quietly.

"Pretty name. Very classic. I like non-frou-frou names."

She glanced up and smiled. He smiled back and she found herself mesmerized by his deep blue eyes.

"Thank you."

He cocked his head. "You're welcome."

"We're neighbors," she blurted.

He smiled again. "I know."

"He tried to take my bag. I couldn't let him."

The words came pouring out and she winced at how defensive and silly she sounded. She hadn't done anything wrong.

"It's not worth your life," he pointed out.

She shook her head. "You wouldn't understand. Everything is in that bag. I can't . . . I can't lose it. Especially not to some bullying jackass."

Garrett chuckled. "I'm not convinced you even needed my help. You had him disarmed before I got to you."

She made a face. "I was scared out of my mind. I'm so grateful you were there." Then she frowned. "You were swimming when I left the cottage. How did you get into town so fast?"

He lifted a brow and amusement gleamed in his eyes. "Keeping tabs on me?"

She flushed and looked down. "I saw you exercising. When I left, you were in the water."

"I came into town after my swim. I'd only just arrived when I heard the commotion in the alley."

"You have excellent timing," she said ruefully.

The constable strode into the tiny waiting room and gestured for Sarah and Garrett to follow him back. Sarah rose and nervously ran her palms down her sides. It occurred to her that as angry as she was, and as much as she wanted the asshole to pay for his crime, it was stupid of her to draw attention to herself. Even dumber to go on record where her name and information would be a matter of public record.

The problem was, she hadn't thought. She'd reacted. She'd allowed emotion to overshadow common sense.

"I've changed my mind," she blurted. "I don't want to press charges."

Ignoring the constable's open mouth and Garrett's frown, she bolted from the station, cursing herself with every step. The door banged closed behind her as she hurried onto the street. Garrett caught up to her before she'd even made it a block. Though he didn't touch her, he stepped in front of her, effectively halting her in her tracks.

A scowl darkened his face. "Hey, what happened back there?"

She tried to step around him but he blocked her escape. "Nothing, okay? I changed my mind."

"You're going to just let him get away with that?" Garrett demanded.

She blew out her breath as rage curdled her veins. "Look, my preference would be to let the little bastard rot, but I can't afford to draw attention to myself."

She closed her eyes. Damn it, but she was a walking disaster today. Nothing was coming out right. She may as well have told him everything about her situation. She'd already slipped up and told him her first name. But that was okay. Sarah was a common enough name, and her neighbor didn't strike her as the type to get chatty with the locals.

"Okay, I get that."

Garrett's deep voice washed over her, soothing her fraught nerves. To her surprise, there was no reprimand in his voice. Just an intimate gentleness that made her shiver.

"Why don't I walk you home?" he offered. "Since I'm going the same way and all."

She hesitated for a moment, lips pursed in concentration. Then she realized how ridiculous she was being. They were going the same way. They'd end up walking together whether he was officially escorting her or not.

She relaxed and offered the most convincing smile she could muster. "I'd like that. Thanks."

CHAPTER 6

GARRETT kept pace with Sarah as they hit the center of town square. "Want to take the beach path back?"

She nodded and turned toward the coffee shack, leaving him to follow. He kept just a step behind her, taking the opportunity to study her up close. She'd been scared out of her mind when he'd pulled the asshole off her in the alley. She was still scared. She put on a brave front, but she was pale as death and her fingers shook uncontrollably.

He needed to get on the sat phone and talk to Resnick asap, but his first priority was making sure she was safe. More than that, he wanted to give her a chance to calm down and rid herself of the haunted look.

Something had happened to her beyond the day's events. He knew that look. He'd seen it in his sister-in-law's eyes more times than he cared to remember. Sarah had flinched when he'd touched her in the alley and she'd made it a point to keep her distance at every opportunity. Someone had hurt her.

All he knew was that she had barriers around her like most people wore clothes. She had a don't- touch-me air that enveloped her and reflected in her frightened gaze.

Even though Sarah hadn't pressed charges, and he understood why, he had no intention of allowing the little bastard to get away with what he'd done. He'd let Resnick deal with the asshole.

They walked in silence and he didn't attempt to break it. He wanted to come off as concerned but not intrusive. Gaining her trust was going to be more difficult than he'd thought, and he had to tread lightly or risk scaring her away.

When they reached her cottage, she took a step toward her porch but then stopped and turned around to face him. He sensed that it took a lot of courage to stand there in front of him. She looked as though she wanted nothing more than to run for her cottage and bar the door. But she stood there, bottom lip pinched between her teeth and she leveled her gaze directly at him, her light green eyes catching the light and warming.

"Thank you again," she said in a low voice. "I know you think I'm nuts, but thank you for everything you did and for walking me home. And . . . for not forcing the issue back there."

He offered a casual smile and shrugged as if it didn't matter to him one iota what she decided. "You're welcome. Glad I was in the right place at the right time."

Not wanting her to feel awkward, he broke away first and headed toward his own cottage. Right place right time. He nearly snorted at how easily that fabrication had fallen off his lips. He'd tagged her as soon as she left her cottage. It had only taken him twenty minutes to return to his place, change and head into town after her.

He let himself into the house and went immediately for the sat phone. He called Resnick first and relayed the events along with the name of the constable and Sarah's attacker. In half an hour, Resnick would know his dick size and the last time he took a shit. If there was anything Garrett needed to do, Resnick would tag him later.

His next call was to Sam, and he waited impatiently for his brother to answer.

"How goes the babysitting?" Sam asked.

"Just a hello works," Garrett said sourly.

"But not nearly as fun. What's up? Everything okay in paradise?"

Garrett rummaged in the fridge with one hand and pulled out a beer before diving back in for sandwich fixings. "It's not bad. Got some fishing in. Been working out, doing some swimming. Not a bad vacation."

Sam muttered something indecipherable, and Garrett grinned, knowing it would irritate Sam that Garrett was on a tropical island while Sam was stuck home on pins and needles waiting for his daughter to be born.

"Hey, is Van back from his gig?"

"Yeah, this morning," Sam replied. "He's sleeping."

"Get him up. I need him to do something for me."

"Can't it wait? He's on day four of no rest."

"No, it can't wait," Garrett said impatiently. "I wouldn't have called if it could wait."

"Impatient bastard," Sam grumbled. "If you get me into trouble with my wife for this, I'll kick your ass. She's ruthless right now."

Garrett chuckled. "Still hasn't dropped the kid, huh."

"Hell, no. If she doesn't pop soon, I'm seriously contemplating moving out."

Garrett rolled his eyes. "I don't know why you say that shit. You're full of crap and we both know it."

"Hang on, I'll wake Van up."

Garrett heard muffled voices and one distinct groan. He grinned. Donovan did love his sleep and he wouldn't appreciate being pulled out of bed. But Garrett didn't want to wait another twenty-four hours to find out what his brother needed while Donovan caught up on his beauty rest.

"What the fuck do you want?" Donovan's bleary voice bled over the line.

"Hello to you too. I need you to run something for me."

"This couldn't wait a few goddamn hours?"

Garrett's eyebrows went up. Cranky son of a bitch. He really must have missed some serious sleep to be this grouchy.

"No, it can't wait."

"Well hell," Donovan muttered. "Give me a sec to get to Hoss."

Garrett waited patiently, drumming his fingers on the counter by the can of beer. Deciding to utilize the time wisely, he propped the phone between his shoulder and ear and set about fixing a couple of sandwiches to go with the beer.

A few minutes later, Donovan's irritable grunt sounded.

"What the hell is so important that you couldn't wait for me to catch a few hours' sleep?"

"I need you to dig up some info on Sarah Daniels."

"What? I already gave you her file. I can't believe this."

Garrett stuffed a bite of the sandwich into his mouth and then mumbled around it. "No, no, I need you to dig deeper. I think I'm missing something here. I want you to check on any police reports that might have her name in it. Hospital records. Anything that suggests she was a victim."

There was a long pause. "Victim of what, Garrett?"

"That's what I need you to find out. That file Resnick gave us just gave info on her as it related to Lattimer and the guy he supposedly killed. I need to know more about Sarah herself and what makes her tick. She's skittish as hell, and she was attacked today."

"What the hell?" Donovan cut in. "Is everything okay there? Do you need us?"

Garrett chugged down a swallow of beer. "Nothing I can't handle. Some asshole tried to nab her bag. But she fell apart. I mean, not that it wouldn't be normal for her to be scared to death, but it was eerie. And then we get to the constable's office and suddenly she changes her mind, says she doesn't want to press charges and walks out. Part of it is I think she realized at the last minute that she would draw unwanted attention to herself, but I also think something else is going on here and I want to know what. I'm going to need all the ammo I can get, because she's going to be a hard nut to crack."

"Okay, I'll see what I can dig up. You want me to call you when I'm done or you want to call me back later?"

"I'll call you in an hour or so," Garrett replied.

Donovan snorted. "That confident I can find what you want by then?"

"You're the geek."

"That's Mr. Geek to you, and you can kiss my ass."

Garrett made a smooching noise through the phone and then hung up. He finished the half-eaten sandwich and chugged the last of his beer before ambling over to his window to peer down the beach at Sarah's cottage.

He frowned and leaned closer when he saw her sitting on her steps, head down. She looked utterly defeated, her shoulders slumped, the ends of her hair lifting and blowing this way and that in the steady ocean breeze. Had she ever gone into her cottage?

He wasn't sure what bothered him about her. It could be she was sitting out, enjoying the day, but after what had happened earlier, he couldn't quite believe that. He'd expected he wouldn't see her again for a while and that she'd hole up in her cottage.

She moved but it was only to bury her face in her hands and then her fingers slid over her forehead and into her hair. Hell. She was crying.

His stomach tightened and he turned away, unsettled by her obvious distress. This was a prime opportunity to go over and be sensitive or whatever it was women liked for men to be. But he'd rather go another round with the shithead Didier than face a woman's tears.

He sighed and blew out his breath. He was going to have to go over there. If she did hole up, he probably wouldn't see her for days. And he couldn't very keep an eye on her if she wasn't in sight.

Vacation or not, he'd prefer to be knee-deep in a jungle viewing the world through his scope. At least he knew what the hell to do in those kinds of situations. Shoot first, no questions later. That was easy. Figuring out how to gain the trust of a woman scared shitless? Yeah, he was fucked.

Chocolate. Weren't women supposed to be rabid predators of chocolate? He'd waved a chocolate bar in front of Sophie's nose more than once and been forgiven for all manner of transgressions.

He went into the bedroom and dug into his pack. There were plenty of protein bars but he always had a stash of the good stuff. Chocolate caramel bar. No, he wouldn't sacrifice that for the cause. He opted for the plain milk chocolate and tossed the pack back onto his bed.

Feeling like a genius, he headed out to the beach and glanced in Sarah's direction again. She hadn't moved so he set off at a brisk pace. He wanted to get as close as he could with his chocolate before she bolted inside.

He was just a few yards away when she looked up and saw him. She reached for the bag at her feet and wrapped her hands around the strap like she thought he was going to make a grab for it.

He was wrong. She hadn't been crying. She was, however, upset. Her face was raw and her eyes glittered with . . . grief? Slowly she released her grip on her bag. She rubbed her face and hastily shoved her hair back, then put her hands down on the steps like she was bracing herself for attack. Hell, he couldn't blame her after the morning she'd had.

"Hey," he said casually. "I saw you were still out. I brought you a present. My sisters-in-law inform me that a woman can refuse no man bearing chocolate."

Her brow wrinkled in confusion as he held out the chocolate bar. She glanced up at him then back at the candy, clearly baffled. Then her face crumbled and she dropped her head again.

"I can't go in," she said in a low voice.

Taking the chance that she wouldn't kill herself backing away from him, he eased onto the step beside her. "Your cottage?"

She nodded, her hair falling forward again to partially obscure her face. His fingers were up to brush it away before he got ahold of himself. He dropped his hand back to his lap and stared over the water.

Casually he extended the candy bar sideways so it crossed her vision. After a hesitation, she took it and held it, her finger stroking over the aluminum wrapping. He felt like a man trying to tame a wild animal with a food offering.

"Yeah, my cottage," she finally said. "Oh God, I feel so stupid. I stood there in front of the door and couldn't go in."

"Why?"

Her head dipped lower, and she gripped the candy bar with enough force that coupled with the hot sun, she was going to have a handful of chocolate syrup.

"Fear," she said in an aching voice. "God, I hate it. I feel so . . . powerless." She turned her head, her eyes blazing as she sought his gaze. "Do you have any idea what that feels like?" Then she gave a derisive laugh and looked away again. "Probably not. You don't look like you've ever been scared of anything."

"Crying women scare me," he admitted.

She laughed. "Lucky for you I used up all my tears months ago."

"Plenty of things scare me. Pregnant women scare me."

She turned to face him again, her lips twitching. Some of the wildness had faced from her eyes. "I'm getting the impression that women, in any form, scare you."

He shrugged. "They're the more violent species. And unpredictable. I'd rather take on a wild boar. You can't shoot women."

This time her laugh came from deep within. It was full and throaty and so fucking beautiful that he simply stared at her, gutshot over his reaction.

"Okay, be serious. Aren't you ever afraid of anything?"

"Plenty of times," he said softly.

"Even when what you're afraid of defies all logic?"

"Especially then. It's been my experience that fear doesn't have a set of parameters. We can't turn it off just by realizing we shouldn't be afraid."

She nodded, a rueful twist to her lips.

"Tell you what. Why don't you let me go into your cottage first. I'll check it out. You stay on the porch. I'll kick the shit out of any bogeymen and then you can come in."

Her head swung up again and the relief in her eyes staggered him. Shit, she'd really been scared. Her fingers were curled into tight fists in her lap, so tight that her knuckles were white. He took in the dampness on her forehead and at her hairline. No, not just scared. Terrified.

Unable to resist, he reached with a tentative hand to touch her shoulder. Though she didn't outright flinch away as she had before, she tensed and trembled underneath his fingers. Not wanting to cause her more stress, he pulled quickly away. He rose and then reached a hand down to help her up. He stood there, waiting for her to accept the gesture, allowing her to touch him on her own terms.

Finally she reached up and slid her damp palm over his. She wrapped her other hand in the strap of her bag and hauled it to her shoulder. He curled his fingers around hers and pulled as she got up from the steps.

"You don't mind?" she asked nervously.

He smiled. "Not at all."

Her shoulders lifted and then sagged as she breathed out. "Thank you. I know this is stupid. Irrational even. I—"

"Shhh," he said, cutting her off in mid babble. "It's not stupid and it's not irrational. You had a hell of a scare earlier. Now, wait here while I go in."

He started for the door when suddenly she bounded up the step after him.

"I forgot to tell you about the cat," she rushed out. "Don't let her out, I mean watch out for her. Her name is Patches." She broke off then took a step back and sighed. "I'm babbling again."

He smiled to reassure her. "I'll look out for Patches and make sure the bogeyman didn't get her either."

"Oh, the key. You'll need the key." She hastily dug into her bag, her face drawn into a frustrated frown. Finally she pulled out a key ring that sported three keys and thrust it in his direction. "You'll need them all. I mean, there are two dead bolts and the regular lock."

He raised an eyebrow but didn't say anything as he turned to the door. She was careful. He'd give her that.

After a few moments of figuring out which key went where, he pushed open the door and stepped inside. Patches meowed from her position on the couch and then laid her ears flat when she figured out Garrett was a stranger.

Garrett glanced around, noting the bareness of the room. It wasn't much more updated than his own, though he did note she'd gotten the better draw. And she had a TV. Silence blanketed the house. Only the sounds of his footsteps echoed as he made his way down the hallway to the bedroom. He peeked in the bathroom, surprised that it wasn't littered with girly paraphernalia. Then he entered the bedroom, taking note of the pristinely made bed and the fact that wasn't so much as a shoe on the floor.

Neat freak. God save him.

Nothing out of place. In fact, nothing was *in* place. He glanced at the still-packed suitcase to the side of her bed. She was living out of her suitcase. Not even her toiletries were unpacked and in the bathroom.

She was prepared to run at a moment's notice.

If he thought she wasn't fully aware of the situation she

was in, he was wrong. Resnick was wrong. This was a woman who knew full well that her time could be limited. She lived and breathed fear, waiting each minute for her world to upend.

Christ, that was no way to live.

Anger boiled up in his throat until the taste of acid was strong on his tongue. And frustration. He was intensely frustrated by not knowing everything. Resnick hadn't done his job worth shit, because Garrett was faced with a woman with secrets. And he needed to know every damn piece of her past if he was going to figure out the best way to handle Sarah.

If she'd witnessed a murder, it wasn't all that had happened. Someone had hurt her or scared the hell out of her, and it enraged him. Yeah, she was a job and he took each and every job seriously. He took his duty damn seriously. But the surge of protectiveness he felt whenever he looked at this scared, fragile woman went beyond that of a job. And he was at a loss to explain it.

He turned and finished his sweep of the house. Though he noted the two dead bolts on the front door, the windows in the house were completely unsecure. It would be a cakewalk to get through any of them, although he did notice that she'd moved the dresser directly in front of the window in the bedroom. It blocked any and all view, but then she wasn't here for the scenery.

He walked back outside, where Sarah stood clutching her bag like a lifeline. "All clear."

Her shoulders drooped and relief washed over her face. "Thank you."

He waited for the inevitable dismissal. For her to walk past him, go inside and close the door behind her. But she just stood there, staring at the entrance like she was trying to gather the courage to take that first step.

"Hey," he said gently, "I have an idea."

Her gaze swung to him and she blinked, almost as if she'd forgotten his presence.

"I stocked up on groceries after I got here. I think I wiped out most of the meat from the market. Why don't I head over, get all the fixings then come back and grill us a steak. You like beer? I have a good stock of that."

She was surprised by his offer and equally unsure of what

to say. She frowned and then pressed her lips together. She glanced down the beach at his house then back to him as she battled her indecision.

"Thought it might be good to have company until you've settled down from your fright. It'll make your cottage less scary."

"Yes," she murmured. She took a deep breath. "Okay. Thank you. A steak sounds nice."

He smiled, and careful not to crowd into her space, he descended the steps and started for his cottage. When he reached the beach, he turned to find her watching him.

"Give me just a few minutes and I'll be back. You can wait out here for me if you prefer not to go in alone."

A smile crept over her mouth, lifting the corners until he saw the flash of her teeth. "Thank you."

CHAPTER 7

SARAH eased her bag onto the steps and then rubbed her hands up and down her arms to ward off the chill. The sun beat down on her but she still felt cold on the inside. She watched as Garrett sauntered down the beach, his pace unhurried.

He was a puzzle to her. He seemed so big and intense yet he was laid-back and . . . casual. *Easygoing*. It didn't compute. He should terrify her, and in some ways he did. And yet the idea of him being in her cottage even for a little while sent waves of relief down her spine.

"He saved you, dumbass," she muttered. "It's the rescue syndrome. You feel safe because he saved your ass."

And now she'd invited him in. To her house. To a place she should feel safe. *Idiot*.

Her hands shook and nausea rose, sharp and overwhelming. She looked at the door to her cottage and then back down the beach where Garrett had disappeared. Then making a decision, she hurried up the steps, ducked into the cottage and closed the door behind her. She leaned heavily on it, her heart slamming against her chest like a fist.

She pried open one eye to see Patches on the couch watching her as she bathed a paw. Sarah walked over to the couch and collapsed beside the cat. Her bag hit the floor with a thump and she sat there, head turned up so she stared at the ceiling.

"I'm a mess, kitty. One big ball of mess. I can't live like this."

Tears pricked her eyelids and she blinked, refusing to let even one fall. The time for crying was over. It didn't do anything other than bring back the feeling of abject helplessness.

The knock on the door startled her. She shook her head at her idiocy. It was just Garrett. Garrett, who she was supposed to have waited for on the porch. Garrett, who she'd agreed to have dinner with.

She sat there for a minute, indecision wracking her mind.

"Sarah, it's me, Garrett. Can you come grab one of these bags?"

The request acted like a slap in the face. She lurched to her feet and hurried over to open the door, forgetting that she planned to hide in the house and ignore him when he came over. Yeah, that was mature.

She swung the door open to see him looming in the doorway, his arms full. She reached for the bag on top, which leaned precariously, and pulled it away. She stepped back but he didn't make a move to enter. He just looked at her while she fidgeted like a moron.

"Come in," she invited, stepping back again.

He smiled and walked past her. "Mind if I put these on your table?"

She hurried around him to put her own bag down. "No, go right ahead. Whatever you need. The fridge is over there." She pointed at the obvious and then felt ridiculous. "Of course it's there. Hard to miss."

Garrett plopped the stuff down on the table and then turned to her. His expression was serious but he didn't make a move toward her. "Relax, Sarah. You don't have to be nervous. If you aren't comfortable with me being here, I can go. No problem."

Was this guy for real? He was so calm and . . . unthreatening. Which, God, she needed. She couldn't do threatening right now. She needed something sturdy. Something to believe in even if just for the space of a dinner.

"I'm losing my mind," she said in a cracked voice. "I want you to stay. That is, if you still want to."

"What I want is for you not to be afraid. I want you to feel safe." He took one step toward her but hesitated as if testing her willingness to let him close. Then he touched her jaw—just a fingertip. But she felt it all the way to her soul. "You're safe with me, Sarah. I'm not going to let anyone hurt you."

Coming from anyone else, the statement would be melodramatic and corny. But he didn't so much as blink when he made the declaration. He was dead serious, and the thing was, she totally believed him. She *wanted* to believe him.

She stood there, not flinching away from his touch. It was . . . nice. Comforting on a deeper level she didn't quite understand. It had been a long time since she'd taken so much pleasure in a man's touch. Just the simple gesture, the brush of his fingers. It touched something inside her that had been paralyzed with fear for so long.

"Who are you?" she blurted. "Are you real? Or did I conjure you up?"

He looked startled by her question. He cocked his head to the side and then emitted a soft chuckle. "I don't know about me, but the food's real."

She peered curiously at the bags on the counter. "What did you bring?"

He turned and open up one of the sacks and pulled out a package of steaks. "I thought we'd start with a little meat, progress to more meat and finish with—"

"Let me guess. More meat?"

He grinned. "I'm a growing boy. Need my protein."

She rolled her eyes and then frowned when her gaze lighted on his shoulder. "How did you hurt yourself?"

He lifted one brow and leaned his hip against the counter.

She flushed. "I watched you from the window. It seems to bother you when you're exercising."

He flashed a wry smile. "Yeah, I might have met with the wrong end of a bullet."

She blinked. "Is either end of a bullet good?"

For a moment he stared at her and then he threw his head back and laughed. "Okay, you totally got me there."

"So what happened?"

"Let's just say some bad people were trying to hurt someone I love."

"And shot you in the process? You look military. Were you in the army?"

He visibly shuddered. "Army? Hell no."

She studied him through narrow eyes. "Marine? You used to be a Marine?"

"I *am* a Marine," he corrected.

"Oh, you're still enlisted then? Are you on leave?"

"You sure do ask a lot of questions. I feel like I'm playing volleyball."

She flushed. "Sorry. I get carried away."

"S'okay. And no, I'm not enlisted anymore. But we don't exactly call ourselves former Marines."

"Oh, yeah. Once a Marine . . ."

He nodded.

She pursed her lips, ready to ask another question then thought better of it. He smiled. "You can ask. I was only kidding about you asking so many questions. Well, not kidding, but I don't mind."

"You're awfully laid-back," she said.

He looked at her in astonishment and then laughed again.

"What's so funny?"

"Oh man, I gotta tell my brothers you said that. They'd kill themselves laughing. They think I'm the most uptight son of a bitch who ever lived."

Shock widened her eyes. "Really? But you seem so easy-going. So . . . calm."

He rubbed a hand through his mussed hair and grinned ruefully. "Maybe it's the downtime. I haven't exactly taken any in . . . well, forever. Kind of hard to be uptight when all you can see for miles is beach, water and blue skies."

She rubbed her hands up her arms, drawn to the image he painted. Peace. That was the word that seemed to personify him. Longing welled like a giant wave, falling over her until it was all she could process. What would she do for peace? True peace. The kind that settled into your bones and invaded your veins until contentment ached bittersweet.

She'd sell her soul to own even a little part of the peace that seemed to surround him.

"What are you thinking?"

"I'm thinking I envy you," she said honestly.

Their gazes connected and his blue eyes flickered, just a hint of reaction in their depths. He didn't respond. Didn't offer some hokey sentiment. He just watched and studied her as if no words were needed because he understood. She shook her head to rid herself of the ridiculous thoughts dancing around in her head. How could he understand anything when he was a complete stranger?

She turned away, no longer able to look into his eyes, into so much warmth. He made her stupid. Completely and utterly stupid. He'd get no free passes just because he saved her. Her gratitude? Yes. She was extremely grateful, and not just for rescuing her, but for going beyond that to make her feel safe.

Mentally, she put about six feet of distance between them. When she turned back around, her lips were set into a firm line. "Do you want me to make a salad?"

"Nah. Would ruin the whole effect. You can season the meat though, while I go out and fire up the grill."

Relieved to have something to do and that he was leaving the room for a bit, she nodded and went to retrieve spices from the small pantry. By the time she returned to the table, Garrett had disappeared out the front door. She heaved a sigh of relief and sagged against the counter.

Never before had she had such a confusing reaction to a man. Garrett terrified her and yet he made her feel as though nothing could hurt her as long as he was near. She feared allowing him too close, and yet she didn't want him to leave.

She smiled when she saw that in addition to the steaks, he'd brought over chicken breasts and pork chops. He hadn't been kidding when he'd suggested a three-course meat dinner. As much as he worked out and as muscled as he was, he probably had to consume a gazillion calories in a day. And lots and lots of protein.

She liberally seasoned the meat and then washed her hands in the sink. As she gazed out the window overlooking the porch, she saw the fire blazing in the small grill. Garrett stood watching the flames and when they finally died down, he closed the lid and started back toward the front door.

"Want to sit out on the porch while the meat cooks?" he asked when he returned to the kitchen.

The idea was instantly appealing. She'd spent most of her

time watching the ocean from the safety of her cottage. But sitting outside, smelling the air, feeling the ocean breeze on her face sounded wonderful. She wouldn't be vulnerable and alone. She had Garrett.

"That sounds wonderful." She even managed to smile as she said it.

Suddenly eager to be outside and enjoy an afternoon of freedom, she rummaged in the sack for the still-cold beer. She held up three bottles, all different, and raised a questioning eyebrow in his direction.

He grinned. "Pick one. I'm not particular."

She shrugged and put one down on the counter. The rest she shoved into her fridge for later. Garrett picked up the beer and returned her questioning look.

"Not having one?"

She wrinkled her nose. "I'm not much of a beer person, I'm afraid."

"Ah."

There was a lot in that one little word and her gaze sharpened. "What?"

"Just ah. You look more like a wine person."

"What's that supposed to mean?"

He cocked his head to the side and studied her. "You have this refined, elegant look about you. I bet you enjoy classical music, going to the opera, fine wine and fancy food."

She flushed. "You think I'm a snob?"

His eyes widened in surprise. "Not at all. I don't know you. Just a guess. Am I right?"

"Hmm, yes and no. I do love classical music, but can honestly say I've never been to an opera nor do I particularly desire to go. I do enjoy wine. White only. But as for food, I'm afraid I'm a burger-and-fry kind of girl."

Garrett clutched his chest with his free hand and staggered back. "Be still my beating heart. You're speaking my language. I make a mean hamburger."

"So you think I'm elegant and refined? Is that a veiled insult?" she asked with a smile.

"No. I like elegant and refined. You look . . . classic."

"Well thank you. I think."

"It was totally a compliment. You're a beautiful woman."

Her cheeks heated under his scrutiny and she looked away, suddenly self-conscious. She'd all but fished for the compliment and now she was embarrassed by how obvious she'd been.

Garrett reached around her for the platter of meat. "Can you get the door? I wouldn't want to drop my beer."

Sarah chuckled. "Oh the horror."

She moved ahead of him to open the door and they both walked out onto the sun-warmed porch. It was an incredibly beautiful day. One she hadn't had the chance to fully appreciate once her trip into town ended in disaster. She perched on the steps while Garrett put the meat on to cook.

A few seconds later, he sat next to her, stretching his long, tanned legs down the steps. He took a long swallow of his beer and sighed.

"It doesn't get much better than this."

She wanted to agree but couldn't really. In other circumstances, yeah, this was truly paradise. She made a sound that could be construed as agreement and he glanced sideways at her as he lowered his beer.

"So what were you in town for this morning? Did you need something? I can always run back in for you."

Surprised by his thoughtfulness, she shook her head. "I went by the bookstore to pick up a few books. I dropped them when the idiot attacked me."

"Sorry, I didn't even see them. I was too focused on you."

"It's all right. Maybe I'll go get some more in a few days. If I ever get the courage to leave my cottage again."

He reached over to where her hand rested on top of the step and covered it lightly. "You'll be fine."

When he left his hand there, she edged it sideways until her hand came free. She brought it up to her lap and laced her fingers into a tight ball. She tried to imagine how she might have responded to Garrett a year ago. Would she have encouraged him? Would she have flirted and flashed him playful smiles?

It was hard to remember acting so freely with a man. For the past year, she'd been consumed with self-preservation, and for her that meant avoidance. But avoidance hadn't done anything to stop the shame, the frequent anxiety attacks or the sleepless nights. There were days she couldn't remember what her life had been like before . . .

You can say it, Sarah. You were raped. You were violated.
You were attacked by someone you trusted.

Her lips wouldn't form the syllables but it screamed
through her head until she shook it from side to side to rid
herself of the word, which was as brutal as the act.

And here she sat, next to a stranger. Someone she didn't
know from Adam. Someone she didn't trust and knew nothing
more than that he was here recovering from a bullet wound. If
someone she had trusted could do something so horrible, how
could she possibly believe that a complete stranger wouldn't
do the same?

CHAPTER 8

SENSING her tension, Garrett got up and needlessly went to turn the meat. He piddled at the grill longer than necessary and took the time to watch Sarah. He'd made a mistake touching her, but found that he was unable to resist the urge to offer comfort. Comforting women was something entirely alien to him. That was something his brothers were far more adept at. He was lovey with Rachel—okay, and now with Sophie. Maybe he wasn't a complete failure when it came to women, but it didn't mean he understood them either.

What he did know of Sarah in turns pissed him off and made him hurt. There just wasn't an excuse for hurting a woman. Ever. It was the one thing designed to infuriate him above all else. And Sarah had been hurt. He knew it. He felt it. Saw it in her eyes every time she looked at him.

A normal guy would ask her questions. And he was supposed to be a normal guy. Most men would be curious about a woman like Sarah. They might even try to cozy up for a vacation fling. He blew out his breath, remembering that Resnick had all but suggested it. The problem was, he wasn't a normal guy. He was here on a job and he couldn't feign casual interest.

But he wasn't supposed to know anything about Sarah, and

a normal guy would be a little freaked out by her seemingly bizarre behavior. Garrett? He understood it. Only too well.

Still it might seem strange if he didn't try to pry a little.

He grunted under his breath. He hated this kind of shit. He didn't do undercover crap. That was more Sam's forte. He'd much rather go in, blow the shit out of the bad guys then go home and have a beer.

Well, at least he had the beer covered.

"I'm going to grab another beer. You want anything?"

She turned to look at him with those big eyes and his stomach tightened. Damn. He had to chill on this bizarre . . . attraction. No matter what Resnick suggested, he wasn't going to try to get into a woman's pants just to get on her good side.

"No, I'm good," she said.

He went inside and was greeted by Patches, who jumped onto the counter to watch as he pulled another beer from the fridge.

"You want some?" he asked the cat.

She eyed him balefully then turned with a swish of her tail and proceeded to ignore him.

He shrugged. Typical female.

He walked back onto the porch and sat back down by Sarah. She didn't move away, which gave him an absurd thrill. He took a swig of his beer and stared out at the incoming waves.

"So what brings you here? Vacation?"

She gave him a startled look. Great. He'd caught her off guard even though it was the most innocuous inquiry he could summon. Maybe she hadn't considered fielding such a question, but wasn't it something anyone would ask her? She wasn't going to blend in if she freaked every time someone got friendly with her.

"Yeah. Vacation. Needed some time away."

He nodded. "I hear that. Where you from?"

She was growing more uncomfortable with each passing second, but she managed to smile though it was so fake she could be one of those beauty pageant queens whom Donovan liked to watch on television.

"All over, actually. I moved a lot as a kid."

"Really? I lived in pretty much the same place my entire life. Except when I was in the military."

"Oh? Where's home?"

He didn't miss the obvious way in which she turned the tables on him or her evident relief that she'd avoided his original question. But he went with it. He could play the dumb tourist as well as anyone.

"Tennessee. Little town on Kentucky Lake. My entire family lives there."

She sighed. "It sounds nice. You have a big family?"

"You could say that. There's my mom and dad. I have five brothers. I'm second oldest. I also have two sisters-in-law, one of whom is ready to pop out a kid any day now. Then there are my mom's adopted chicks. Her most recent find is a surly-ass teenage girl who she's determined to keep on the straight and narrow. My brothers and I have given up and wished Ma luck."

Sarah chuckled. "Aren't all teenage girls surly?"

"Hell, I don't know. They're all deranged, if you ask me." He glanced sideways at her. "What about you?"

A slight grin flirted with the edges of her mouth. "I'm pretty sure I was deranged at sixteen."

"Smart-ass. I meant what about your family?"

Her expression became more pensive. "I grew up in foster homes."

He shifted uncomfortably. He already knew that but he wasn't supposed to and now he had to sit here and play dumb. He was dying to ask her about Lattimer, and why, if she was his sister and he was so protective of her, had she grown up without all the benefits he had? Instead he offered a lame reply that said he didn't really know what to say at all.

"Ouch. That had to be hard."

"It wasn't so bad. But it did involve a lot of moving. Most placements were temporary until something more permanent came along. The problem was that the permanent situations never were . . . permanent."

His lips twisted in sympathy. "That sucks."

She shrugged. "It's not like I was abused. I had food and clothes. A place to live. There were a lot of children far less fortunate than I was. I don't spend my adult life lamenting my childhood. I had some good times."

He wasn't sure what to say to that. He liked her attitude.

Shit happens and you deal. Only second to the Kelly motto, in his mind. No one fucks with the Kellys.

"So how long are you here for?"

She frowned. "I don't know. I haven't decided yet."

"Ah. Extended vacation then. Must have really needed this one. Stressful job?"

Tension snaked across her face. "I'm sort of taking a breather right now. I'm thinking of a career change. Maybe something a little less . . . stressful, as you put it."

"Any ideas yet?"

She smiled ruefully. "No. Not really. Maybe teaching. Something with kids. I'm kind of tired of adults."

"Oh hell, and you think teaching's less stressful? My mom and my sister-in-law used to teach. I never figured out how they survived that with their sanity intact."

"Let me guess. You're scared of children too?"

He scowled. "Not scared. Cautious. Maybe a little apprehensive. Okay, terrified. I mean, they're terrorists disguised as cute little people."

She laughed that full throaty laugh that sent a shiver up his spine. Damn but she was beautiful when she laughed. She lit up like a Christmas tree and her eyes sparkled. Too bad he wasn't a humorous guy. He'd give anything to make her laugh again.

"They aren't that bad. They just need attention. And love. Just like everyone else."

"Everyone else doesn't puke on you. Or rub their snot on your shirt."

She grinned. "That's what antibacterial wipes are for."

"Try full-body armor," Garrett muttered.

She rolled her eyes. "A big muscled out guy like you, terrified of women and children. What a wimp."

"Hey." He pressed the cold bottle against the bare skin of her leg and she yelped as she slid away. "No need to get personal."

She laughed again and God if he didn't get all gooey inside. She was right. He was a first-class pansy. He scowled and gave thanks his brothers weren't here to give him shit.

"Better check the steaks. It's a sin to burn good meat."

He hoisted himself to his feet and made it a point to

"accidentally" get her with the cold bottle again. She giggled and pushed herself up as well. She followed him toward the grill and sniffed appreciatively when he propped open the lid.

"Smells great."

"Yeah, just needs another minute or two. Want to grab plates and eat out here?"

She glanced over to the small patio table with the umbrella that tilted precariously to one side. "Yeah, that sounds great. I'll get the stuff and set the table."

They ate in companionable silence as dusk settled over the water. The skies faded from the brilliant blue of earlier, and shades of pink and gold spread like gossamer wings over the horizon. There was something to be said for this whole R and R thing. Not that he'd ever admit it to his brothers. But damn if he wasn't enjoying himself. And the company.

When they pushed aside their plates, neither made a move to get up, and he was content to follow her lead. He settled back in his chair as the water turned dark with impending nightfall. The moon was barely visible as it crept over the horizon. It was nearly full and in two nights it would be, but it was still bright as it splashed across the surface of the ocean.

"I've kept you far too long," Sarah said, breaking the silence. There was a note of discomfort in her voice, not that she'd spent the time with him, but a hesitancy that signaled her regret for what she considered an inconvenience.

"I had a good time. You're great company."

"So are you," she said after a pause. "I had a good time too."

The tone of her voice suggested that fact surprised her. And it probably did. Kind of tough to relax for a few hours when you're looking over your shoulder at every turn.

He rose and began collecting the plates, but she reached over and put her hand on his wrist. Cool soft fingers and yet they burned his skin like coals.

"I'll do it," she said huskily. "You already did so much."

"You sure you're going to be okay?"

She nodded and released his wrist. He wanted to take her hand back so she kept touching him. He liked her hands. Small and so dainty and feminine. She had slender fingers with tapered nails. And the pads of her fingertips were smooth and infinitely soft.

"I'll be fine, and again, thank you for doing so much to make me feel better. I really appreciate it."

He wondered what she'd do if he told her he wanted to kiss her. Not that he would. Tell her, that is. If he was going to kiss her, he'd want her to have no warning. No time to think. But he didn't want to scare the hell out of her either. So he stood there, watching her mouth and wondering what she'd taste like.

"If you need anything, don't hesitate, okay? I'm just down the beach. And I mean anything. If you get scared, I'll come over. It's not a problem."

For a long moment she simply stared at him, her heart in her eyes. They gleamed shiny in the soft moonlight and her lips were drawn almost as if she were in pain.

"I stopped believing they made men like you," she said in a voice that made him ache. "Thank you for proving me wrong."

He almost went back and kissed her anyway. It was the hardest thing he'd ever done, but he turned and walked down the beach to his cottage. He stopped midway to look back and she was still standing there, moon splashing silver on her skin.

He lifted his hand in a wave and then traveled the rest of the way in the dark.

When he entered his cottage, he groaned as he caught sight of the sat phone where he'd left it on the kitchen counter. Donovan was going to kill him. Better to get it over with sooner rather than later, and he was eager to hear what his brother had dug up on Sarah Daniels.

He dialed the number and waited as it rang. A moment later, a decidedly feminine voice bled over the line.

"Hello?"

"Sophie? What the hell are you doing answering this line?" Garrett asked. "Everything okay there?"

"Hi, Garrett."

"Still pregnant, sweetheart?"

She made a sound that came out as a grunt. Maybe he should have just kept his mouth shut.

"Where's Van?"

"He's asleep at the computer," his sister-in-law said. "Ethan and Rachel came over after you called earlier so he never went back to bed."

"How is Rachel doing?"

"She seems to be doing well. She and Ethan went swimming. Sam wouldn't let me go. He said if I started to drown there wasn't a life preserver that would fit around me."

Garrett snorted. "What an asshole. Want me to kick his ass for you?"

She laughed and Garrett smiled. "Rachel kicked him for me. I couldn't lift my leg that high without falling over."

"You take good care of yourself and my niece. I'll expect a phone call the minute you go into labor."

"I think the entire world will know when the day finally comes," she said tiredly. "I mean, I don't think even elephants are pregnant this long."

"Poor sweetie. Make Sam give you a foot rub."

"Donovan is stirring and I need to wipe up the drool off the desk. Do you want to speak to him?" Sophie asked.

"Yeah, thanks. Take care, okay?"

Muffled sounds came through the phone and then Donovan's irritated growl and Sophie's laughter.

"For someone who was in such a goddamn hurry, you took your sweet time calling back."

Garrett winced. "Sorry, Van. Something came up. You got anything for me?"

Donovan sighed. "Actually, no. I've been on it all afternoon. If something happened to her, it's not on record anywhere. I have a contact in Boston who is doing some more digging for me. He'll poke around her neighbors, acquaintances and coworkers to see what he can come up with but we have to be careful because she has a lot of damn people looking for her."

Garrett sighed. No record. Meaning whatever had happened to her went unreported. He wanted to put his fist through the wall. Had she been in an abusive relationship? Was she a victim of random violence?

"Do me a favor, Van. Look up any past relationships. Boyfriends, casual dates, whatever. I need some blanks filled. Resnick either didn't tell us the whole story or he doesn't know it himself, which is hard to believe since he's such a meticulous bastard."

"What are you really looking for, Garrett? Help me out here. I need to know what I'm searching for."

Garrett rubbed a hand over his face. "I think she was attacked. Maybe raped. I feel pretty sure it was by someone she trusted. So I don't know if she was abused, if some guy she was with beat the hell out of her or sexually assaulted her. There's something going on here beyond her witnessing someone being murdered."

"Christ," Donovan muttered.

"Yeah, tell me about it."

All of the Kellys had a strong protective urge when it came to women and children, but Donovan especially had a soft spot a mile wide for women and children. A lot of times it was to his detriment because he simply couldn't turn down a job if a child or a woman was in jeopardy. He was putty in a woman's hands. He adored women and they adored him. Garrett teased him that it was the geek that appealed to the "fairer sex." But the truth of the matter was, Donovan was extremely intelligent and he was good to his toes. Women sensed that and they flocked to him like flies.

He was quieter than his brothers. He wasn't as big and broad shouldered as the rest. Often he was most comfortable taking a backseat to everyone else. He stood on the fringes and watched. As a result, Donovan had more dirt on people than Garrett could imagine.

And there wasn't anyone else Garrett would rather have at his back.

"Garrett, that bullshit Resnick spouted . . . You can't go in like that if some son of a bitch hurt her."

Garrett controlled his irritation because he knew Donovan was doing what Donovan did best. Looking out for the woman. "I know that, Van. Sarah . . . She's vulnerable right now. She needs a friend. I intend to be that friend."

"Let me know if you need me, okay? I can be over there in a day. In the meantime, I'll do some more digging and let you know what I find out."

"Thanks, Van. Now go get some sleep. You sound like hell."

"Fuck you."

Garrett grinned and cut the connection. He rubbed the

back of his neck, fingers digging into the base of his skull. He was tired and right now a hot shower sounded better than sex. He needed to get to bed and get some rest because he had an early morning errand to run the next day. Preferably before Sarah had a chance to get up and around.

CHAPTER 9

SARAH opened her eyes to sunlight streaming through her window. She blinked the grogginess away and turned to look at the clock. Sure she hadn't seen the numbers correctly, she shoved to her elbow and squinted to get a better look. Ten A.M.? Holy cow.

Patches jumped onto the bed and eyed her suspiciously. Usually Sarah was the first out of bed and the cat always protested being moved from her warm spot.

Sarah flopped back onto her pillow and stared up at the ceiling. The cat rubbed against her side and purred loudly. Sarah put her hand down to rub the animal's ears and received a delicate meow in thanks.

It was the most she'd slept since arriving. Most nights she was lucky to get in a few hours. Her dreams haunted her, and at times she refused to close her eyes because she'd do anything to keep the demons at bay.

Somehow she'd managed not only an entire night's sleep, but she'd slept well past daybreak into midmorning. She stretched and then cuddled deeper into her covers. It was then she realized that some of her sense of panic was gone. Anxiety had been ever present for months, so much so that she couldn't remember what her life had felt like without it. This morning she felt remarkably . . . light.

She lay there for another half hour, simply enjoying the peace. The growl of her stomach finally forced her into the bathroom to take a quick shower. When she was done, she wrapped a towel around her head and headed into the kitchen.

She put on a pot of coffee to brew and stared out the window as it bubbled and hissed. The water was so blue it almost hurt her eyes to look at it. The sun bounced off the surface and reflected like a million tiny diamonds. There wasn't a single cloud in sight although the talk in town the day before had been a storm system expected through by the evening.

As the coffeemaker hissed its last, she removed the pot and poured a cupful of the savory brew. It was too perfect a morning to waste indoors. Sitting on her porch with a cup of coffee sounded heavenly, and maybe she'd see Garrett.

Heat tingled her cheeks and she shook her head. She was acting like a giddy teenager crushing on her first boy. Still, she smiled as she opened her front door. Her gaze was drawn to the water and she nearly tripped over something in the doorway. She stumbled and her coffee sloshed over the rim. She righted herself, put down her coffee on the window ledge and then looked down to see a basket sitting on her porch.

Astonished, she knelt to find two bottles of white wine and the books that she'd dropped in the alley when she'd been attacked. She lovingly stroked the spines of the paperbacks and pulled them away so she could see each of the titles. There were even a few additions to the ones she'd purchased. Next to the wine, were several chocolate bars and a folded note with her name on it.

Her chest was so tight and she was smiling so big her cheeks ached. With shaking fingers, she opened the note.

I'm told no woman can resist wine, books and chocolate. Enjoy your day.

                                                    —G

She hugged the note to her and stared down at her goodies. He'd gone and gotten her books! She was ridiculously

touched by the notion of him making a special trip to retrieve
her books and to buy her wine and chocolate.

Her eyes were suspiciously watery as she rose and hoisted
the basket into her arms. Her coffee forgotten, she set the basket on the patio table and began going through the assortment
of paperbacks. After settling on the one she wanted to read
first, she hurried back inside to set the wine to chilling in the
fridge. She added the chocolate so it wouldn't melt and then
returned outside to her book.

After an hour, she went back inside to prepare lunch.
The wine was cold and she poured a glass to have with her
meal. She took her time, actually enjoying the food as the sun
soaked into her skin. Today . . . she was in no hurry today.
The events of the previous day melted away and she savored
the freedom to just . . . enjoy.

She dozed off with a book propped on her chest, her feet
resting in the chair opposite her. A fat raindrop hit her square
in the forehead, startling her from her slumber. Her eyes flew
open to find the sky vastly changed. Instead of the sheer blue
canvas, angry thunderheads had rolled in, billowing in the
sky like giant mushroom caps.

It was dark and shadows fell over the beach, turning the
serene paradise into something sinister. The water rolled and
frothy wave caps blew over the surface, rolling onto the beach
and spreading over the sand.

She put her feet down and stretched her aching muscles.
After collecting her wineglass and book, she retreated indoors.
Disappointment nagged at her. She hadn't seen Garrett even
once.

Garrett stood at his window and watched as Sarah went
indoors. He'd been on the verge of going over there himself to
wake her before the storm kicked up too bad. She'd been sleeping the entire afternoon, and he'd watched over her from afar.

He's purposely stayed away today to give her time to process the evening they spent together. He wanted her trust and
found that he was willing for things to progress as slowly as
necessary to achieve that goal.

Lightning stabbed through the sky, flashing and illuminat-
ing the rolling sea. Thunder echoed in the distance. The storm
was moving fast and getting closer with each passing second.

He turned away and let the curtain fall. He loved a good thunderstorm. It was a perfect evening to kick back with a beer and listen to the rain.

Soon the rain picked up and fell with steady rhythm. It beat against the tin roof of the cottage with a muted roar. Just the sound made him yawn; lethargy stole over him, turning his muscles to jelly.

He slouched on the sofa and kicked his legs up. Of course as soon as he got comfortable, the sat phone beeped. He raised his head and glared across the room to where it lay on the on the chair by the window.

Grumbling the entire way, he pushed himself up and went over to snag the phone.

"This better be good," he said as he sank back onto the couch.

"This coming from the asshole who woke me up twice?"

Garrett chuckled. "I was comfortable, man. Just laid down on the couch."

Donovan made a derisive noise before continuing. "Do you want what I got or what?"

Garrett sat up, suddenly very serious. His stomach knotted and he sucked in a deep breath. Yeah, he wanted to know but then again he wasn't sure he did. He sighed. "Yeah, hit me with it."

"Sarah Daniels leads a very ordinary life, lives in a very ordinary apartment. No one has a single bad word to say about her. As far as I can tell there are no recent boyfriends. No medical records other than a few routine check-ups. I'm trying to get the actual reports now but it'll take some time. She's been jobless for months. She has conservative spending habits but her bank account isn't hefty so she's getting support from somewhere. My bet is Lattimer. But in short, she's normal. She's disgustingly perfect."

No. Not perfect. Broken. And infinitely fragile.

Garrett blew out his breath. "Then what the fuck?"

"Maybe you're misinterpreting things, Garrett. She witnessed a murder. She's either scared of her brother. Or she's trying to protect him. That's a lot of shit to deal with. Of course she's jumpy."

Bullshit. Yeah, she was scared, and she was cautious, but

there was more to it. Garrett wasn't wrong about this. He'd touched her. He'd felt her tension. Saw the grief and the pain in her eyes.

"I'm not wrong about this, Van."

Donovan sighed. "The thing is, if she was attacked but never reported it, she probably didn't tell anyone. Not even those closest to her. Unfortunately a lot of crimes against women go unreported."

Garrett cursed, knowing that Donovan was right. If Sarah had been hurt, there was a distinct possibility that the only person who knew anything of it . . . was her. And the son of a bitch who attacked her.

"Damn it," Garrett muttered. "This is complicated."

"I'll keep digging. If I come up with anything, I'll call you."

"Thanks, man. How is Sophie doing? And have you talked to Rachel?"

Donovan chuckled. "Trust you to want to know about the women."

Garrett scowled. "I didn't get to go by and see Rachel before I left. I just want to make sure she's doing okay. I worry about her. And Sophie. She looked about fourteen months' pregnant when I left."

"Dude, you're on speakerphone," Donovan said.

Garrett winced. "Oh fuck. She didn't hear that, did she?"

"She might have just started crying, and Sam is threatening to kick your ass."

"Crying?" Hell. He'd need to send chocolate. Lots and lots of chocolate. Pregnant women were demented.

"I'm joking," Donovan said with a chuckle.

"Asshole."

"Rachel is doing fine. She's called at least once a day to ask if we've heard from you."

Garrett went soft on the inside. He loved Rachel to pieces. Always had. The idea that she worried about him made him feel a little mushy.

"And Sophie has slowed down, much to mine and Sam's relief. Today she spent on the couch with her feet propped up while Sam fussed over her. She's tired and I think if she doesn't deliver soon, Sam's going to have a kitten. He's already threatened to kick the doctor's ass if he doesn't induce her."

As much as he dearly loved his sisters-in-law and his family, right now he was grateful to be away from Sam. The man was a bit touchy when it came to his wife and until she delivered safely, Sam was going to be a complete basket case.

"How is Dad? Is he taking it easy?"

Donovan laughed. "Mom and Rusty are driving him insane. He's called over here at least twice a day, begging for one of us to go rescue him. They won't let him eat what he wants to eat. They won't let him work for more than a few hours at the hardware store."

Garrett grinned at the image of his burly father being bullied by the women in the family. That was the way it usually went. Marlene Kelly was ruthless when she put her mind to something. She kept her husband and all six of her sons on a straight line and it was pointless to resist.

Ever since his dad's heart attack months before, she'd kept him on a tight leash and ruled with an iron fist.

"What about Beavis and Butthead? They still off on some supersecret mission for Uncle Sam?"

"Uh, about them."

A prickle of alarm shot up Garrett's spine. His youngest brothers were still active military, and he worried about them constantly. "Uh-oh. What's up?"

"Nothing bad," Donovan hurried to say. "Joe called Sam yesterday. Said he and Nathan weren't re-upping and wanted to know if they could work for KGI."

"Well, duh," Garrett said with a snort. Relief lessened the pressure in his chest. Not that KGI was a cakewalk. They handled their fair share of dangerous assignments, but he'd much prefer to have all his brothers right in front of him where he could watch their backs.

"Yeah, that's what Sam said. They're bugging out again in a week. Joe didn't say where, which bothers me. He usually at least has a location for me. Tells me it isn't good. But when this tour's up, they both want to come home."

"Ma will be beside herself," Garrett said dryly.

Donovan chuckled. "All her chicks in one spot for more than a week or so? That hasn't happened since Sam was a senior in high school. She'll drive us all insane."

"It'll be nice."

"Yeah," Donovan agreed. "It will be."

"Okay enough chitchat. I gotta go. I have a date with the couch," Garrett said. "Kiss the sisters-in-law for me."

"I'm flipping you the bird right now," Donovan grumbled.

Garrett grinned and tossed the sat phone onto the coffee table. The rain still beat the roof and flashes of lightning went off outside the windows like strobe lights. The rumble of thunder acted like a sedative, luring him into the promise of a nice long sleep.

He yawned. He should probably go to bed. But that would require moving.

CHAPTER 10

THE next morning, Sarah stood on her porch and stared over the debris-ridden beach and watched frothy waves foam onto the shore. Palm leaves, tree branches and an assortment of driftwood sprawled across the sand, remnants of last night's storm.

The skies were clear this morning and a light breeze lifted her hair and blew over her face as she stood gazing over the water. She was trying to work up the nerve to go back into town. Alone. Without asking for Garrett's help.

During the night as she lay listening to the wind and rain, she'd decided she wanted to do something to repay his kindness and understanding. He'd cooked her dinner and he'd retrieved her books, not to mention gave her chocolate and wine. That deserved something in her mind, and she was through being a ninny around him.

If she was going to spend all this time laying low, she was at least going to enjoy herself.

Now she just had to conquer her fear of returning to town alone and she'd be set. She took a deep breath and stepped onto the sand. Meat and beer were obviously the way to Garrett's heart, but she was going to throw in something sweet as well.

She lugged her laptop bag over her shoulder and started at a fast clip down the beach before she changed her mind.

While she was in town, she'd check her email and send Marcus reassurance so he didn't get edgy and come after her. Surely he realized the necessity for them to stay as far away from one another as possible.

As long as she kept quiet and away from Boston, everything would be fine. She'd never risk running into Stanley Cross again. Allen was gone—a fact she couldn't bring herself to feel any regret over. Just that Marcus had been the one to do the deed. She should have left Boston a long time ago, but she'd stayed locked in her apartment, terrified to go out. Terrified to live.

Well, that was over. It was time to regain control of her life. Even if it was here on this island. It wasn't as if she wasn't used to being uprooted and having to adjust all over again. She'd spent her life moving and adjusting.

She hit the café first. Enjoyed a cup of coffee while she checked her email. Her heart sped up when she saw a new one from Marcus.

Let me know you're okay.

She typed a quick response assuring him she was fine. She even made her response a little wordier than she had in previous emails. She made it sound like she was taking an extended vacation. And maybe she was. Who was to say she wasn't?

After packing up her laptop, she drained the rest of her coffee and headed toward the market. Remembering Garrett's tastes, she chose a small brisket, large baking potatoes and all the fixings. She preferred salad with meat courses but Garrett obviously didn't waste stomach space on lighter fare like lettuce and tomatoes.

She studied the array of beer, frowning because she couldn't remember what kind Garrett had when he'd come over. Deciding it didn't really matter, she chose three different brands and hauled them into her basket.

The small section that served as the bakery didn't have anything she thought Garrett would go for. It was all too frou-frou and fruity, whereas she pictured him as more of a pure sugar guy.

Cake would have to do. She didn't have time to go all-out on something exotic and complicated. Not if she was going to invite him to dinner tonight.

She picked a mix and bought ready-made frosting even though she quivered at the sin of it all. Then she made her way to the check-out and paid for delivery of the heavy groceries to her cottage.

On her way home, she found herself humming. She actually stopped in the sand and grinned as she realized she had this ridiculous giddy thrill at the idea of seeing Garrett again. She hugged her arms and squeezed, so happy and grateful that the idea of having a man in her personal space didn't freak her out anymore.

It wasn't as if she considered herself miraculously cured. Obviously it couldn't be just any man. Garrett was different. He made her feel safe. And for the first time since her attack, she felt a stirring of interest in the opposite sex. For that alone, she'd always be grateful.

She started back down the beach, a ridiculous smile plastered on her face. It was a good day. And it would only get better.

Two hours later, she stood on Garrett's porch and second-guessed her chirpy assertion that the day was so wonderful. Her hands were clammy, her mouth was dry and her heart was about to beat out of her chest.

Why was this so hard? She wasn't afraid of Garrett. She wasn't! It was though her psyche refused to cooperate and had hit the panic button in her brain. It was completely irrational, but then she'd already acknowledged that fear was anything but rational.

More than a little pissed that panic was putting a serious damper on her good mood, she set her jaw and knocked briskly on the door. A moment later, Garrett opened the door and his eyes widened in surprise. That might have put her off but then he smiled broadly and she could see pleasure in his expression. Her heart jolted and did a funny flip.

He was only wearing swim trunks and she was afforded a prime, up-close view of his chest. The same chest she'd drooled over from afar. He wasn't one of those polished, hairless, pretty boys with an even tan and skin as soft as hers. No, he was rugged, paler on his belly and chest than he was on his arms and face. And he was hairy. Not in a gross, man-wolf way. There was a smattering over his upper chest, enough to give him a rougher edge, and it tapered downward to a dark line to his navel and low enough to fire her imagination about what was beneath the band of those swim trunks.

Her face lit on fire and her cheeks were so tight, she thought she might explode. Whether from embarrassment or awareness, she wasn't sure.

Her gaze jerked up to the fresh scar on his shoulder. There were other scars. Much older. Some more faded than others. The one at his shoulder was still angry and puckered looking. He followed her stare and slid his palm over the scar.

She flushed guiltily. "I'm sorry. I didn't mean to stare. Well, I guess I did. I was curious. Sorry, though. Does it still hurt?" And God, was she babbling. Like an idiot.

He shrugged. "Some days more than others. Hey, I was about to go for a swim. Want to come?"

She blinked in surprise and took a step back. "Swimming?"

His eyes glittered with amusement. "Yeah. You know, that thing you do in the ocean? In bathing suits usually, although I wouldn't be opposed to skinny-dipping."

"Oh. Well. I mean, I came over to invite you to dinner."

"Really? I'd be happy to. But no reason we couldn't go for a swim first. Unless you're cooking a pig or something and have to start on it now."

He was totally ribbing her and she grinned as some of the panic melted away under the warmth of this smile. "No pig, but I did buy a fair piece of a cow."

He rubbed his belly and sighed. "You do know how to tempt a man. So, how about that swim? I'll help cook after we're done."

"Oh no you don't," she said with a shake of her head. "You did all the cooking last time. This time, you're going to sit on the deck with the beer I bought for you while I do all the cooking. I already baked a cake."

"Damn. You're spoiling me, woman."

Her cheeks tightened again and the warmth spread into her chest. "And yes, I think I would like to swim. I'll just go change and meet you back here."

"Great. I'll wait for you on the beach."

Sarah flew back to her cottage and rummaged through her things for the swimsuit she'd purchased just a few days after arriving on the island. She hadn't used it yet. Not even once. But suddenly she was eager to feel the ocean.

It was a modest one-piece, and by modest, it covered everything. High-necked, broad shoulder straps and a skirt that fell midway to her knees. She felt like a granny, although she doubted many grandmothers wore suits this ugly.

Knowing she was about as attractive as a toad should have dimmed some of her enthusiasm, but she found she just didn't care. Garrett didn't seem to mind her odd behavior and her eccentricities. She was going to enjoy today if it killed her.

She mentally flipped Allen and Stanley Cross the bird as she trekked down the steps of her deck and onto the sun-warmed sand. Allen was already in hell, and Stanley could kiss her ass. If there was any justice in the world, he'd join his brother there eventually.

As promised, Garrett waited in front of his cottage, a towel slung over his shoulder. She slowed as she approached and realized she'd forgotten to bring one.

"I'm an idiot," she said.

Garrett raised a brow.

"I forgot a towel. I need to go back and get one."

He grinned. "No need. You can use one of mine. Let's hit the water."

She turned her gaze to the ocean and the gorgeous canvas of blue that sparkled like a cascade of diamonds. "Is it cold?"

He gaped in exaggerated fashion. "You mean you don't know? You haven't been in yet?"

She shook her head and grimaced.

"It's warm. Feels pretty damn good. No crap on the bottom. Sand is smooth. No seaweed."

Laughter bubbled up. "Well, thank goodness there's no crap on the bottom. That would suck."

He winked at her. "When you've waded through as much shit as I have, you tend to appreciate nice, clean water."

"Last one in is a rotten egg," she yelled, just as she took off for the water.

"Why, you little!" Garrett yelled. "Cheater!"

She hit the water with a resounding splash. Garrett barged in behind her and promptly tipped her into the surf. She came up sputtering, hair in her face but grinning like an idiot.

"I won," she said triumphantly.

"You cheated."

She sniffed and shoved at her bedraggled hair. "According to my rules, I won."

Garrett laughed. "I know better by now than to argue with a woman when it comes to rules."

She flopped back, rocking over the gentle swells as she stared up at the sky. "You were right. The water's great and no crap on the bottom."

He turned over onto his back and spread out his arms as he floated lazily beside her. "It's good. I didn't think it would be. I was thoroughly prepared to hate it here."

Her brow scrunched up and she tried to glance over at him, but got a face full of water. "Why on earth did you come here then?"

He went silent for a minute. "Let's just say my family was leaning on me pretty heavily to take a vacation. They put me on a plane and here I am. I hate to admit it, but they were right. I needed the downtime. I feel almost a hundred percent again."

"Almost?"

"Yeah, I'm getting there."

"Me too," she murmured.

His fingers brushed hers as he stroked in the water. He snagged her finger, just one, but he held on, keeping that connection between them as they bobbed along with the waves. Here in a vast body of water, no one around for miles, she should have felt incredibly isolated and alone. She didn't. For the first time in a year, she felt a connection to another person. A man. It helped heal a little part of her soul. The part that wondered if she was doomed to forever lock herself away from other people.

After a while, Garrett tugged at her hand and pulled her closer. He flipped and treaded water beside her while she continued to float on her back. "Having fun?"

She put her feet down and realized she couldn't touch bottom. She grabbed a hold of his arm and righted herself until she was keeping above the water along with him. "Yeah. Thanks. I am. It's . . . peaceful out here."

"We're pretty far from the shore now. Think you'll be able to make it back?"

She glanced up and gasped as she realized how far they'd drifted from the beach. She swam decently enough, but that was a long way back.

He nudged her cheek with a wet knuckle. "Hey, don't worry about it. I didn't mention it to make you frown. All you have to do is hang on to my shoulder and float. I'll do all the work."

Just like he'd been doing all along. Always helping her. Always shouldering the effort.

"Come on," he said. "Grab hold. I'm hungry."

She laughed. "We can't have that. Clearly you're in danger of starving to death with that body."

"You like my body?"

The devilish glint in his eyes was nearly her undoing. The man was incorrigible. And his family thought he was an "uptight bastard?" It didn't compute. Maybe his family didn't understand him, or maybe they were the uptight ones. She'd never met a man as easygoing and understanding as Garrett.

She rolled her eyes at his fishing. "You know you have a great body."

"You've been checking me out," he said smugly.

"Duh," she muttered under her breath.

He took her hand and slid it over a solid wall of muscle until her fingers were hooked over his shoulder. Damn but the man felt good.

"Hang on. Here we go."

With a kick he was off. She attempted to help for a while until she realized her flailing about was actually hindering him, not helping. So she concentrated on staying afloat and was content to go along for the ride.

When he had them close enough to the shore that he could stand, he stopped swimming and began wading forward while she still grasped his shoulder. He tentatively slid his fingers over the top of her hand and then reached back in a gesture for her to give him her other hand.

She kicked until she was behind him and no longer beside him and gave him her other hand. He pulled until her arms were looped around his neck and she was hugged up against his back. Then he continued forward, pulling them both effortlessly through the water.

The shallower the water got, the higher he rose from the

water and the higher she had to reach. He stopped when he was a little over waist deep, patted her hands to show her she should still hold on and then he reached back to grasp her behind the knees. He hoisted her up and wrapped her legs around his waist and continued to forge ahead.

Okay, so she could totally stand right now, but she was enjoying the piggyback ride way too much to point out that she could make it on her own. She was wrapped around his hard body, and his big hands burned her thighs where he had hold above her knees.

He trudged out of the water and onto the sand, and still, he made no effort to put her down. He started down the beach toward her cottage. She rested her chin atop his head and sighed in contentment. She almost wished he'd slow down just to make the ride last longer. But all too soon he reached her deck and he turned so he could deposit her on the bottom step.

"Thanks," she said lightly.

"Not a problem. Now you don't have sand all over you."

She glanced down at the sand caked on his feet and legs. "Wait right here. I'll get some water to rinse you off."

She hurried inside and filled a pitcher of water and then went back out where he was now sitting in one of the lawn chairs. He dutifully raised each foot for her to rinse and then plopped them back down onto the deck.

"After all that discussion about towels, I left mine back on the beach," he said.

She blinked. A towel had been the last thing on her mind. "That's okay. I'll run in and get us one. If you can wait just a few minutes, I'll go ahead and change before I come back out."

"I'm not going anywhere," he said lazily as he stretched his arms over his head like he was seeking the sun. He tucked his hands behind his head and closed his eyes, and for a long moment she was riveted to just how beautiful the man was. She was utterly fascinated by him. The idea that man with such hard edges and scarred body—clearly the body of a warrior—could also be so gentle and understanding simply astounded her.

Forcing herself away, she let herself into the house and hurried for her bedroom, where she stripped out of her suit.

With a grimace, she glanced down to see that sand had accumulated in some interesting places.

She ducked into the bathroom, turned on the shower and stepped underneath the chilly spray. Shivering the whole time, she quickly rinsed the sand off and decided while she was at it, she'd wash her hair.

Fifteen minutes later and feeling guilty for leaving Garrett for so long, she walked back onto the deck, towel in hand, to see him exactly as she'd left him. Kicked back in the chair, head back, eyes closed and looking completely relaxed.

"Sorry I took so long," she said. "I had sand everywhere so I showered."

He cracked one eye open and stared at her. "Yeah, sand in the sensitive parts is a bitch. It can cause some chafing issues."

"Do you . . . do you want to use my shower? You probably have sand issues too."

He chuckled. "Yeah, I could use a quick rinse if you don't mind me staying in my swim trunks. Otherwise I can just run back over to my place and shower and change."

It made the most sense for him to just go home. It wasn't as if he were a long distance. But she hated the idea of him leaving. Even for just a few minutes.

"I don't mind. You're welcome to my shower and towels. I only have girly soap. Sorry."

"I'll just rinse if you can bear the smell," he drawled.

It was on the tip of her tongue to tell him he smelled so damn good that it would be a sin to use soap at all.

"I'm going to start dinner while you clean up."

He plopped his legs down and ambled into the cottage ahead of her. He disappeared into her bedroom and she went into the kitchen, so many butterflies scurrying around her belly she felt dizzy.

There was a man in her bedroom. In her bathroom. Taking a shower in her shower. Naked. Right now. She grinned. And she wasn't even running the other way, hyperventilating or otherwise freaking out. It was a start.

This might even constitute a date. An actual evening with a gorgeous specimen of a man.

She seasoned the brisket, washed the potatoes and put everything into the oven. Then she pulled out the three kinds of beer and her own bottle of wine and went out to the deck to wait for Garrett.

Just a few minutes later, he came out, barefooted and in his swim trunks and looking so delicious she wanted to lick him. He rubbed at his damp hair and then spotted the beer as he closed the glass door behind him.

"Oh hell, you didn't lie about the beer. I feel so honored that you bought it just for me."

She gestured toward the bottles. "Take your pick. I had no idea what to get so I grabbed what I could."

"It looks good to me. It's wet and cold. That's all that matters."

They sat enjoying the afternoon, her with her wine and him with his beer. The sun was settling over the western horizon, plunging the sky into vibrant shades of gold, pink and purple. The huge orange orb reflected and shimmered on the water, sending fingers of fire racing across the still ocean.

"This is my favorite time of day," she murmured. "The sunsets are so beautiful here. They take my breath away."

"They remind me of home," Garrett said. "My brothers and I used to sit out on our back deck, drink a few beers after a long day and watch the sun go down over the lake. We haven't done that in a while. I'm thinking when I get back home, we need to do it more often."

Sarah smiled. Then she remembered dinner. "Oh crap! I need to check the brisket!"

She hurried into the house and was immediately surrounded by the scent of cooking meat. It smelled homey and delicious. More importantly, it didn't smell burnt. She took the casserole dish out of the oven and set it on the stovetop and then she reached in with an oven mitt and retrieved the two potatoes.

The brisket looked perfect. It needed to rest a few minutes so she put the potatoes on a platter along with butter, cheese and sour cream and carried it outside so Garrett could dress his potato while it was still hot.

Then she returned inside to prepare a small salad for herself, get more beer for Garrett and sliced the brisket and arranged it artfully on a chipped platter. Bumping the door open with her hip, she carried the food and drink outside and set everything on the table so they could eat.

"It smells wonderful," he said with an appreciative sniff.

"We need to eat quick or it'll cool too fast with all this breeze."

He chuckled. "I don't ever dally when it comes to food."

She sat and they both dug in. Garrett put away a shocking amount of food, but then she'd seen his exercise regime and it was clear he needed a lot of calories. By the time they'd finished dinner, the sun was barely hanging in the distance and in the east, stars had begun popping in the darkening sky.

"I have dessert," she said.

He visibly perked up at that.

"Chocolate cake. Chocolate frosting. I'll apologize in advance for the fact the frosting is store-bought."

"I'm not picky when it comes to sugar."

She smiled and then hesitated. "Would you . . . Would you like to come inside and eat? The bugs will be bad if I turn on the outside light."

"I'd like that," he said softly.

She stood and began collecting the dishes. Garrett piled several up and followed her inside to the kitchen.

"Have a seat," she directed. "I'll clean the mess later."

He settled his large frame on the other side of the bar and watched while she uncovered the cake and took out saucers. She cut a huge hunk for Garrett and a much smaller piece for herself and then slid his across the counter to him.

She opted to stand so they faced each other. In truth, she liked watching him.

"Thank you for today," she said.

He glanced up, his expression curious.

"Swimming. I had fun. It was nice to just relax. The water is fantastic. Everything here is fantastic."

She tried hard to keep her tone light, speaking as anyone might on vacation, but she couldn't quite keep the wistful note from her voice. It was hard not to feel guilt or to allow herself to drop her guard even for a moment when the truth lingered so close to the surface. A man was dead and she was involved—responsible—even if she hadn't pulled the trigger herself.

Even now, there were probably any number of people looking for her. Marcus included, though she couldn't imagine him not being able to find her if he was set on it. She thought it likely he already knew of her whereabouts, but he was no fool. He had to know that it wasn't smart for her to be anywhere near him while Allen's murder was being investigated. His emails had gone from where the hell are you to asking her if she was okay. Yeah, he probably knew exactly where she was.

Stanley Cross was another matter. A shiver stole down her neck. He wasn't the type to sit idle and allow just the authorities to investigate his brother's death. He too would be looking for her and she was well aware of how ruthless he could be.

"You don't look like you're thinking fantastic thoughts," Garrett broke in.

Startled, she settled her gaze back on him to see him watching her thoughtfully. "Sorry. Wandered off for a minute there."

"Wherever it was, I'd say it wasn't a pleasant trip."

"It wasn't."

"Want to talk about it?"

She wasn't sure what surprised her more. His blunt question or the fact that for a moment she had an overwhelming urge to unburden herself. She could just see the direction of that conversation. Garrett struck her as a black-and-white kind of guy. No shades of gray. And her entire situation was so murky that it would make swamp water look like the crystal Caribbean waters.

"Wouldn't want to ruin what's been a perfect day," she said lightly.

He stared intently into her eyes. "Everyone needs somebody to talk to, Sarah. If you ever change your mind, I don't mind being that person."

She smiled, warmed to her toes by the sincerity in his tone. "Thank you, Garrett. You've been so wonderful."

"No, thank you," he countered. "Dinner was wonderful. Dessert was delicious. But the company was superb."

He rose as he said the last, and panic hit her. She nearly laughed. She wasn't panicking because he was here in her personal space. She was panicking because he was about to leave.

"It was the least I could do. You've done so much for me, Garrett. I really can't thank you enough."

He smiled. "Ain't no thang. Maybe I'll see you tomorrow."

It came out more as a question, and she realized he was leaving it up to her.

"I'd like that. Maybe we could swim again."

He reached across the bar and cupped his hand over hers. Warm and slightly rough. The feel of his fingers over her skin was electric. Heat pooled in her belly and she was shocked by the instant reaction, that she was capable of responding. She wanted to run around the bar and hug him. She wanted to do a lot more than that, but she stood there, stock still, not wanting the moment to end.

"I'll be around."

His hand slid away from hers and she curled her fingers, determined to keep the sensation alive for as long as possible. With a grin and a jaunty wave, he let himself out the door, leaving her in the kitchen to stare after him long after he'd gone.

CHAPTER 11

THE next day another storm rolled in and by early afternoon, the skies were black and threatening and the wind blew in a ceaseless line from the water to shore. Sarah was vexed. She'd woken up feeling alive and ready to roll. She'd planned a trip into town for picnic supplies and then she was going to march over to Garrett's cottage and invite him to go swimming and have a late lunch.

Now she was stuck indoors watching it rain when she wanted to be outside. With Garrett.

Instead, she curled up with one of the books Garrett had bought her and she cracked open the last chocolate bar. Still, there was a niggling of hope that Garrett would pop over. At what point she'd come to rely on his company, she wasn't sure, but he'd crept in, slipped through her defenses and she found she quite liked it—a lot. It was nice to have a friend. Someone she could let her guard down around even just for a little while.

She ate some of the leftover brisket. Even cut a piece of the chocolate cake. Then she went back to her book, but unease had settled over her as the sky grew blacker and the wind blew harder. Eventually she gave up on trying to read when she figured out she'd read the same page no less than a dozen times.

She walked back and forth between the front window, which overlooked the beach, and the side window, which afforded her a view of Garrett's cottage. Waves crashed on the beach with angry slaps and the water, which the day before had been aquamarine was now gray and ominous.

She was being fanciful and letting her anxiety have far too much control.

Then her lights flickered and her pulse ratcheted up about twenty beats per minute. She held her breath as the flickering stopped and let out a sigh of relief.

Her head pounded from all the stress. What she needed was some Tylenol and then she was going to bed and hoping for a better tomorrow. No reason she couldn't have that swim and picnic then.

She chased the medication down with a glass of water and then changed into her pajamas. Patches was waiting on the bed, having given up her perch beside Sarah on the couch at the first boom of thunder.

"Coward," Sarah muttered as she crawled under the covers.

Patches gave her a bored look and began licking her paw.

"The least you could have done was keep me company."

Patches settled her chin flat on the mattress and closed her eyes to show Sarah how really impressed she was with her disdain. With a sigh, Sarah flipped off the lamp and snuggled under the sheets.

Sleep was a long time coming and when it did, it was fractured with images from the past blending with present circumstances. In her dream she was running and Stanley pursued her with a bloody knife. Even as she fought the dream, knowing it wasn't rational, she couldn't shake the veil of sleep so that the images would stop.

He called her name. It sounded like a crackly whisper. She frowned. He had a foreign accent. Stanley didn't have an accent.

She heard it again and this time her eyes flew open just as another boom of thunder exploded across the sky. She lay there, so still her chest barely rose and fell with her breaths. A creak sounded down the hall toward the kitchen.

She bolted from the covers, sending Patches scrambling from the bed. Oh God, oh God. How was she supposed to get

out if someone was in her kitchen? Her gaze latched on to the
rickety dresser she'd shoved in front of the window. Not such
a good idea in hindsight. Still, if she was quiet, she could push
it aside enough that she could crawl out the window and run
down to Garrett's cottage.

Who could possibly be after her? If it was the authorities,
surely they wouldn't skulk around in her kitchen. They'd bust
in, arrest her and haul her away. But what if Stanley had sent
someone after her?

The idea sent a chill snaking down her spine that nearly
paralyzed her. She had to force herself to move, to overcome
the panic spreading through her like a wildfire.

She inched the dresser away from the window, holding her
breath and praying she wouldn't alert her intruder to the fact
she was escaping.

The window slid upward with a groan. Sarah didn't wait
to find out if her intruder had heard. She threw herself out the
window and hit the ground below with a painful thud. She
slipped in the mud as she struggled to her feet, put her hands
down to catch herself and then threw herself forward again.

She hit the beach at a dead run, her feet bogging in the
saturated sand. Rain beat down on her, slicking her hair and
pajamas to her like a second skin. Her only thought was to get
to Garrett.

A prickle of alarm went up Garrett's nape and tightened every
hair on his head. His eyes flew open just seconds before his
front door reverberated with fierce pounding. He came awake
instantly, reached for the gun underneath the cushion and
leapt to his feet.

He was halfway across the room when he heard Sarah's
voice. "Garrett!"

He yanked open the door to see Sarah standing on his
porch, soaked to the skin, her hair plastered to her face as
water dripped from the ends. Before he could say or ask anything she launched herself at him.

She hit him square in the chest and he wrapped his arms
around her to keep them both from going down. She shook
violently against him and burrowed deeper as if seeking a

way to bury herself completely in his protection. Her heart pounded against his chest, way too fast. As much as he wanted to stand there holding her, he had to find out what the hell had scared her so bad.

He maneuvered them inside and kicked the door shut behind her. Then he laid his gun down on the small table by the window and gently pried her away from his chest.

"Sarah." He took her shoulders in his hands and forced her to look up at him. He couldn't tell if the wet was from the rain or her tears, but her eyes were huge and the pupils dilated. He touched her cheek and found her skin icy cold. She shivered underneath his touch and tried to push her way into his arms again. "Sarah," he said again. With more force this time. "What happened? What's wrong?"

The blankness in her expression concerned him. The shaking hadn't stop and had in fact gotten worse as reaction seemed to settle in. She shook so hard that her knees buckled, and she would have gone down if he hadn't tightened his grip on her arms to keep her standing upright.

With a curse, he hauled her toward the couch and sat her down. He left her long enough to grab a blanket and then he wrapped it gently around her, gathering the ends under her chin so she would be warm.

Her lips quivered and she closed her eyes, her face crumpling. She lowered her head, and her shoulders hunched inward as if she was closing herself off from the world.

He sat beside her and pulled her into his arms, holding her against him so his warmth would bleed into her too-cold skin. Ignoring the fact that she was soaked, he tucked her head underneath his chin and smoothed a hand over her tangled, wet hair.

"Hey, it's okay now. I've got you. I won't let anything hurt you. You're safe."

She snuggled farther into his embrace, her arms leaving the confines of the blanket to clutch desperately at his waist. Finally he gave up on trying to keep her in one place and hauled her into his lap. He leaned back and reached with one arm to gather the blanket around the both of them.

Realizing he wasn't going to get a word out of her until some of the shock had receded, he concentrated instead on getting her warm and soothing some of the horrible fear in her eyes.

"It's all right," he crooned as he stroked down her arm. "You're safe now. Take some deep breaths."

She shuddered against him and he tightened his hold until they were wound so tight around each other that his clothing soaked up all the wetness from hers.

Gradually her heartbeat slowed and he could no longer feel the erratic thump of her pulse. She raised her head, bumping his chin as she stared across the room at the table where his gun rested.

"You have a gun," she whispered.

He winced. Trust her to notice that detail. She was probably one of those women who fainted at the sight of a weapon.

"Yeah."

She raised herself off his chest to look into his eyes. "Can I have it?"

As what-the-fuck moments went, this one was one of the bigger ones. The thing was, she was dead serious. There was an earnestness to her gaze that said she really wanted him to give her his gun. Shit.

He touched her cheek and let his fingers trail down her jaw. He tugged at a wet strand that stubbornly clung to her skin and tucked it up over her ear. "Sarah, honey, tell me what happened."

She took a deep breath and exhaled again. It came out as a staccato stuttering over her lips. "Someone was in my cottage. I heard him."

Garrett sat up, nearly upending her from his lap. He caught her arms and pulled her back against him, but he sat up straight, processing what she'd just said.

"How the hell did you get out? Did he hurt you? Tell me what happened. Everything."

"I crawled out my window. I know I sound like the world's biggest coward, but all I could do was lie there, terrified. I had to make myself get up."

He brushed his lips across her hair in an unconscious gesture of comfort. "Don't be so hard on yourself, sweetheart. Fear can render even the most powerful person immobile. Now tell me the rest."

"I pushed the dresser away from the window and crawled out."

"Where did you hear the noise?"

She frowned. "In the kitchen. There was a creaking sound. Like maybe a cabinet opening. It was what woke me up. I thought I was dreaming it at first."

"Do you think maybe you *were* dreaming?"

Her head popped back up and fire blazed in her eyes. "I'm not crazy, Garrett. He was there. I *heard* him."

"Shhh. I believe you, Sarah."

"I can't stay there." It came out as a sob. "Oh God, I can't do this." She beat her fist against his chest and then her head fell forward onto his shoulder.

Garrett gathered her in his arms and rocked back and forth, murmuring soothing nonsense in her ear. She reminded him so much of Rachel, so broken and afraid. Sarah was teetering on the edge and he wondered if this would be the final straw in the tight grip she kept on her composure. Sooner or later she would break. No one could hold up under the strain for so long. Not with everything that had happened to her.

"You don't have to stay there," he murmured. "You can stay here with me."

She went still against him and then she pushed herself away. It was then he knew she realized that she was close to him. Touching him. Allowing him to comfort her. Her initial terror had faded enough that the barriers had gone back up and she had returned to self-preservation mode.

Her eyes became troubled and she edged backward, but for the first time, he forced the issue and kept a tight hold on her. He watched her closely for signs of true distress but what he saw was uncertainty. Not fear.

"Listen to me, Sarah. I want you to stay here while I go check out things at your cottage."

She shook her head but he put a finger to her lips to staunch the denial.

"What I want you to do is to take a hot shower while I'm at your cottage. I'll bring back your things. You're freezing."

She clutched at his hand, her cold fingers curling around his. "Garrett, you can't! What if he's still there?"

"I hope to hell he is."

He lifted her and set her over to the side and then he pulled the blanket up over her knees and tucked the ends around her neck.

"Please be careful," she begged.

"I'll have my gun. I tend to shoot first and ask questions later. While I'm gone I want you into a hot shower before you make yourself sick." He nudged her chin up with his fingers. "Okay?"

She nodded and he got up. She had more color in her cheeks now, and she seemed more cognizant of her surroundings. She'd be fine while he checked things out. But he wasn't taking any chances.

"When you go into the bathroom, I want you to lock the door. Don't come out until I get back and tell you it's okay."

She nodded again and he picked up his Glock as he headed toward the door. He turned as he stood in the open doorway and instilled enough force into his words that she'd pay heed. "Get on into the bathroom. Do it now."

CHAPTER 12

SARAH pushed her face under the spray of the shower. Instead of going for hot and steaming, she'd turned the cold on, determined to rid herself of the horrific fear that still crowded the edges of her mind. When she was no longer able to bear the icy water sluicing over her skin, she turned it to scalding hot.

She stood there, thawing out as steam rose in the tiny bathroom. She closed her eyes and let the spray cascade over her icy-cold skin, warming the blood that slugged through her veins. Was she going crazy? Had tonight been one big hallucination?

No, there had been someone in her kitchen. In her house. She hadn't imagined it. She was too in tune with every sound her cottage made. She knew which boards creaked. Knew how the walls groaned when the wind blew too hard. The sounds she'd heard had been an intruder and she'd come awake instantly with the unshakable knowledge that she wasn't alone.

She stayed in the shower until she was completely waterlogged and sweat beaded her brow from the overwhelming heat. She was completely limber, and warmth had seeped deep to where the cold had captured her in its relentless grip.

She reached up to turn off the water and stood sucking in deep breaths for several seconds before she shoved the curtain aside and stepped onto a ratty mat. She grabbed one of the towels neatly folded on the shelf over the toilet and wrapped it around her. She took another and wound it tightly around her hair before unwrapping herself again to finish drying.

Remembering Garrett's instructions, she closed the lid to the commode and sank down and clutched the towel tightly around her. What was Garrett doing?

She couldn't bear it if something happened to him. What if she'd sent him into a trap? What if whoever had been in her cottage was still there, waiting for her to return? If Garrett surprised him, Garrett could be hurt or killed. And she was stuck here. Alone.

She never should have let Garrett leave. They could have waited until morning when it was light and the storm had passed. Then she could go collect her things and get the hell out.

The time went by agonizingly slow. Unable to bear sitting, she stood and paced the impossibly small area. Two steps to the door. Two steps back to the toilet. Where was he?

She yanked the towel from her hair and ran her fingers through the damp strands, arranging it around her face. She still looked like a drowned, scared rat, but some of the wildness from her eyes had receded. Her pupils were normal size and color suffused her cheeks, probably thanks to the enormous heat from the shower.

How long had it been? It seemed like an hour but maybe it had only been a few minutes. Still, she stayed where she'd been told and kept the door locked. As much as not knowing frightened her, the idea of being vulnerable made her more so.

Her hair was nearly dry before she heard the footsteps down the hall. She held her breath and went completely still, her ears straining.

"Sarah, it's me, Garrett. I'm back. You can open the door."

She deflated like a pricked balloon. For a moment she simply sat there, her relief so staggering she couldn't summon the energy to get up. Finally she stumbled to her feet and took the two steps to fumble with the lock on the bathroom door.

It swung open and Garrett stood there holding Patches. The cat was clearly not happy and was wet from the tip of her tail to her bedraggled ears. Garrett didn't look much better.

She whirled around and grabbed one of the dry towels

and then took the cat from Garrett and held her close to her chest. Garrett extended his other hand, which held her bag. "I packed your clothes. Get dressed and come into the kitchen. After I change, I'll get us something to eat and drink."

He dropped the bag at her feet and it was then she remembered she was only wearing a towel. And a very wet cat.

"Want me to take Patches so you can dress?"

Wordlessly, she thrust the cat back at him, towel and all and held both arms over her chest so the other towel didn't slip. He backed out without a word and pulled the door shut behind him.

She hurriedly dressed, not paying attention to whether anything matched. She was anxious to hear what Garrett had found at her cottage. He hadn't seemed too ruffled so maybe her visitor was long gone.

She shoved everything back into her bag and hung the towels on the rack to dry. Not bothering with any of the toiletries Garrett had brought, she hurried out of the bathroom and back toward the living room.

Patches sat on the couch grooming herself, and Garrett was clanking around in the kitchen. She went in his direction, pausing in the doorway as she watched him pour two glasses of tea. "What did you find?"

He turned, tea in hand and extended it to her. She took the cold glass and cupped it between her hands as she sipped at the sweet brew.

"Nothing," he answered.

"Nothing? He was gone? I guess that's good. I worried about you going over there and surprising him," she babbled.

Garrett eyed her, a gleam of sympathy in his eyes. She didn't like that look. It was a precursor to something she didn't want to hear.

She set her tea down on the counter and squared her shoulders. "What?"

Garrett grimaced and put a hand on her shoulder to guide her back into the living room. "Honey, I didn't find any sign of an intruder."

She whirled around in agitation. "What are you saying? Do you think I imagined it? You think I'm crazy, don't you?"

He frowned. "Sit down and calm down."

Blinking at the force of his command, she unconsciously obeyed, sinking onto the couch beside Patches.

"I don't think you're crazy, okay? All I'm saying is that I couldn't find any sign that someone was in your cottage. But it's raining like a son of a bitch outside. Evidence could have washed away. I couldn't see very well, but I didn't find any sign that anyone had been inside your cottage. I'll be able to take a better look tomorrow. All I can tell you is that if there was someone there, he's gone now."

Another crack of lightning flashed through the living room and the floor vibrated under Sarah's feet.

"I didn't imagine it. I couldn't have. Could I?" Her voice cracked and the last word came out in a high, hysterical note.

Garrett sighed. He nudged her chin and stared into her eyes, the deep blue of his burning her with their intensity. "Listen to me, Sarah. I didn't say I didn't believe you. I'm telling you what I found. Or didn't find."

"I'm sorry," she said in a low voice. "I'm sorry. It's not your fault. God, I came over here like a lunatic. Woke you up. Made you go out in the rain to find some nonexistent intruder." She stood, knocking Garrett's hand from her face. "I should go. Really. I've put you through too much trouble."

She started to shove by him, but he caught her arm, his fingers curling gently into her flesh. He pulled her to him until she was shockingly close to his mouth.

"You're not going anywhere. You're going to stay here with me."

She started to open her mouth, but to her shock, Garrett sealed his lips over hers.

It was electric, a jolt to her system that fried her entire nerve system. He curved his hand around her nape and dug his fingers into her hair as he held her in place. His mouth moved sensuously over hers, gentle, but so demanding that her knees shook under the power of his touch.

Never had she been kissed like this. It wasn't a touching of lips or a casual gesture of affection. It was carnal. Heated and possessive. He was placing a silent claim and it should have terrified her. She should be screaming the roof down but instead she stared dumbly at him as he drew away, his eyes gleaming in the soft light.

"You'll stay," he said, his tone brooking no argument.

And she found herself nodding.

"Good. Now that we have that out of the way, I'll go put some clean sheets on the bed for you."

She caught his arm, still so rattled she could barely process what she wanted to say. "No. I'll sleep here on the couch."

He shook his head. "You can have the bed."

"Garrett, no. Okay? I'm fine. I swear it. There is no way you can fit onto this couch and you damn sure aren't sleeping on the floor. I can take the sofa."

He gave her an impatient look and then sighed. "Tell you what. We'll share the bed."

She found herself shaking her head before he could even get the words out. Panic raced up her spine. Chill bumps rose and fanned out, prickling over her skin like tiny razors.

He touched the side of her face. "Listen to me, Sarah. I'm not going to hurt you. Okay? The bed is plenty big. We can put pillows between us. I'll stay on my side and you stay on yours. I don't want you in this front room alone, so we either both sleep in the bed, or if you insist on taking the couch, I'll have to camp out on the floor next to you."

She was being stupid. She knew it but couldn't fight the overwhelming fear that gripped her. It was irrational. It was blind. But when was fear ever sensible? She wanted to trust this man. That didn't make any sense either, but there it was. The problem was, it wasn't a matter of her deciding she trusted him or wanted to trust him and she could go on like a normal human being.

Her head didn't care what her heart said. Her head was telling her to stop being a twit and to wise up.

Garrett stared at her a long moment and then reached behind his back and pulled out the gun. He gripped the barrel and extended the stock toward her.

She stared at the gun and then raised her gaze to his, her brow furrowed with confusion.

"You can sleep with this under your pillow. That way you'll be safe from me. I won't move the entire night. Not only am I used to sleeping in one position, but I damn sure don't want to risk scaring you and getting my balls blown off."

She tried to smile but could only think how pitiful her

life had gotten. The only way she could allow a man to sleep in the same bed with her was if he offered her a gun for self-protection?

She closed her eyes. Jesus. It made her angry. So damn angry.

Finally she shook her head.

Garrett's gaze softened as he tucked the gun back into his waistband. "I swear to you that you have nothing to fear from me, Sarah."

She nodded her acceptance of his vow and lowered herself back onto the couch. Patches quit grooming herself and came over to rub against Sarah's hand. She petted the cat, allowing the simple gesture to calm her fried nerves. And she tried not to think about the fact that she'd be sleeping mere inches away from Garrett.

CHAPTER 13

PALE shades of dawn painted the room in gradually lightening shadows. Garrett lay on his side, his head propped in his hand as he stared over the barrier of pillows to where Sarah slept. She hadn't moved the entire night. He knew because he'd slept lightly and he woke up regularly to check on her.

She was huddled on her side facing him, and she'd inched as far to the edge of the bed as she could without falling off. Patches lay against her chest, curled into a ball of fur. At the moment, the cat was awake and batting lazily at the strands of Sarah's hair that fell over her shoulder.

Though Sarah was asleep, there was no peace to her expression. Her brow was wrinkled and her lips drawn into a tight line as if her jaw was clenched tight. Dark smudges lay underneath her eyes as though she hadn't rested in many nights. She probably hadn't. He was glad that she'd slept soundly here. Maybe she felt safe with him. Or as safe as she could feel with a strange man.

He reached over and touched her cheekbone with one finger and then softly traced a line downward to her jaw and then to her lips. Lips he'd tasted the night before. She uttered a breathy sigh and her features relaxed, the tension easing from her face.

He was a dumbass to get all mushy about a woman who obviously had a great deal of baggage. There were so many reasons why he needed to treat this just like any other job. He had to be the world's biggest pussy for being so soft-hearted when it came to her. It was, unfortunately an affliction he seemed to have around women. Rachel. Then Sophie. And now Sarah. He hadn't even liked Sophie in the beginning, but that hadn't stopped him from taking a bullet for her. And now he'd do damn near anything for his two sisters-in-law.

The difference here was that he hadn't ever wanted to kiss his sisters-in-law. Oh he was hugely protective of them. No doubt there. But with Sarah, it was different. And he didn't like it. Not even a little bit. But neither could he help the reaction to her.

It was as if he went on auto pilot around her. No matter what he thought, it all went out the window the moment he looked into her eyes.

"This bullshit has to stop," he muttered. He was fast losing objectivity and worse, he was forgetting the task at hand. All he was supposed to do was keep her safe and wait for Lattimer to make his move.

The sun hadn't yet to creep over the horizon. Sarah would likely sleep awhile. It would give him a chance to go back over to her cottage and check things out. The copious downpour from the night before made it difficult to find outside evidence, but he was going to give the cottage a thorough checking-over now that it was getting light.

SARAH opened her eyes as soon as she heard the front door close. She scrambled out of bed and peeked out the window to see Garrett jog down the beach toward her cottage. She would have to move fast if she was going to get out before he came back.

She might very well be going crazy. Maybe there hadn't been anyone in her cottage, but she wasn't about to stick around on the off chance she was losing her marbles. She had an escape plan—a darn good one for as little resources as she had. And it was time to ask Marcus for help, as much as the thought scared her.

She went to her bag and hauled out a change of clothing but dug deeper until her fingers glanced over the bulge in the inside pocket. She pulled out the pay-as-you-go cell phone she'd only used once so far and punched in the number she'd committed to memory.

"Allo?"

"Frederick, it's Sarah. It's time."

"D'accord."

She ignored the sound of amusement in his voice and hung up. Her heart beat so fast and hard that she couldn't squeeze in a breath. She closed her eyes to shake the light-headedness, and when she reopened them, the room spun at a dizzying speed.

"Get it together," she bit out.

Her gaze snagged on the note that Garrett had left her. She paused and then went back to the bed where Patches lay purring. She picked up the piece of paper and scanned the uneven scrawl.

Be back soon. Don't worry.

She blew out a long breath. There was a part of her that hated leaving. Maybe the entire night had been her imagination, but it had shaken her confidence enough that she knew she couldn't stay here. She was terrified to go back to her cottage, and she couldn't stay with Garrett forever. She didn't even know how long he was here for.

And if she hadn't imagined her intruder, she'd only bring trouble, and with him recovering from a bullet wound, trouble was the last thing Garrett needed.

She picked up the pen on the nightstand and turned the paper over. She sighed. How to tell him everything she wanted to? That the days spent here on the island with him had saved her life. Well, if she survived her current problems, he'd saved it. Okay, she was being way too melodramatic. A simple thanks would have to suffice. She scribbled a quick note and laid it back on the bed next to the cat. She rubbed Patches on the head and whispered good-bye before hurrying out the front door.

Once on the beach, she turned in the opposite direction of town. The path narrowed to nothing and the sand gave way to a rocky coastline the farther west she went. There were no houses on the westernmost point of the island. The beach was rugged and gave no opportunity for lounging.

By the time she reached the rendezvous point, she was winded and stood holding her side as she sucked in breaths. She scanned the water, looking for a boat, but all she saw were the waves crashing against the rock outcroppings.

Then a distant sound, like the wine of an engine, drifted to her on the breeze. It grew louder and louder until she saw what looked like an inflatable boat with an engine 'round the bend and zip between two outcroppings. It sped toward the beach and the pilot cut the engine just as the nose slid onto the sand.

She hurried forward, clutching her bag and the carryall with her laptop in it.

Frederick waved to her and smiled. The man thought she was an idiot—but an idiot who paid well nonetheless.

He held out his hand to help her into the boat. She climbed over, making sure she didn't drop her bags, and the pilot gestured for her to take a seat in the middle.

He backed away from the beach and executed a sharp turn just as a wave rolled in. He gunned it over the swell and sped away.

Sarah huddled in her seat, holding on to her bags as the craft bounced and swayed over the water. She looked back as the island got smaller and smaller in the distance. Her throat knotted and she rubbed to assuage the ache. It was silly to have regret over what she'd left behind. There was nothing. She had no ties to the island. She'd only been there a short time. But still, she couldn't shake the sense of sadness over leaving Garrett—a man who had helped her when he didn't have to. A man who seemed to understand the demons she fought.

GARRETT left the constable's office in town and started to jog down the road back to his cottage. After closely scrutinizing the area around Sarah's cottage, he'd discovered a few footprints that hadn't been washed out by the rain. He also found a window with muddy fingerprints.

He hadn't spent a lot of time the night before because it was as dark as sin and he'd been anxious to get back to Sarah, but there had been someone at her cottage and whoever it was hadn't been the least bit careful. Which to him meant it was likely someone local looking to score a little cash or whatever he could come across. But on the other hand, it could be someone else completely. Garrett couldn't afford to assume anything.

Sarah would just stay with him from now on. It'd make Garrett's job a hell of a lot easier. Not to mention a good deal more pleasurable.

Several minutes later, he jogged up to his porch and opened the door. It was quiet inside, which meant Sarah probably hadn't rolled out of bed yet. It was still early and she needed her sleep. Still, he found himself quietly approaching the bedroom. He just wanted to check in on her. That was all. It wasn't like he wanted to watch her sleep. Never mind the fact he'd spent a good portion of the early predawn hours doing just that.

When he pushed open the cracked door, he frowned when he saw the bed empty save for the cat, who was still curled into a ball next to the pillows. He pushed in farther. "Sarah?"

Lying on the bed was the note he'd left her, only it was folded out so that what he'd written was on the outside. He picked it up and saw that on the inside she'd written him a note.

Thank you for everything, Garrett. I have to go. Please take care of Patches for me.

His gaze flew to the spot on the floor where her bag had lain. Only now it was empty.

"Son of a bitch!"

He tossed the note aside and took off at a dead run. He checked the other rooms in the house just in case she hadn't left yet, but came up empty. He hit the porch and leaped off the steps, his gaze scanning the beach. She hadn't come into town on the main road. He would have seen her. And there were no footprints leading down the beach path.

But to the west . . .

Small imprints in the still damp sand led away from the cottage toward the more remote edge of the island.

"Son of a bitch, son of a bitch," he cursed over and over as he took off.

Where the hell was she going? And how the hell could he protect her when she wasn't where he could see her at all times? Damn it. He'd only just convinced her to stay in his cottage, a point he planned to press. He was going to make damn sure she stayed under his watchful eye. Yeah, that had worked just great. He'd fucked up and left her alone, thinking she wouldn't—couldn't—run in the short time he'd left her.

He'd learned the hard way with Sophie that it never paid to underestimate a woman and fuck it all, he'd done exactly that with Sarah. Again. Christ but he was the world's biggest idiot. Here he was, Mr. Bad-Ass Special Ops dude and he couldn't keep track of one defenseless female. When would he learn that women never stayed where you put them?

He followed the erratic footprints, losing them once or twice when the path became rockier. Several times he had to backtrack, and he overshot the last time. It wasn't until he climbed down to the beach over the outcroppings that he saw where her footprints picked back up. Only this time they didn't parallel the shore. They led directly into the surf, disappearing as the water rolled onto the beach.

He stood staring left and right but they ended here at the water's edge. Holy fuck. Someone had picked her up in a boat. It was the only explanation unless she'd lost her ever-loving mind and walked into the water.

She may be a lot of things, but no fucking way had she committed suicide.

He glanced around again, but there was nothing to be seen. No houses. No people. She'd picked the most remote spot possible to make her escape and that hadn't been dumb luck. She'd planned her escape route, and the time in which she'd pulled it off wasn't left to panic and last minute. She'd planned for this eventuality.

Yeah, he'd totally underestimated her and that pissed him off more than her flight. He felt like a first-class fool, and he hated feeling like a dumbass.

Christ, he'd been handed this cake job, and he couldn't even manage to keep a defenseless, scared-out-of-her-mind woman in his sights. Yeah, nice. This was why he'd gone into the military. None of the missions he'd ever gone on had involved chasing a damn woman all over the world.

He turned and stalked back down the path he'd come. She couldn't have gotten far, and hell, what was out there anyway? The only thing that made sense was that she'd hopped to the next island. If he had any hope of catching her, he had to get there quick.

When he reached his cottage, he threw his crap into his bag and started to walk out. A plaintive meow halted him in his tracks.

Goddamn cat.

He stared at it for a long time and then shook his head. He reached down, picked up the limp ball of fur and stuffed her into his bag. She yowled once but he zipped it up, leaving a small opening for her to breathe and set off for town.

By the time he reached the row of shops, Patches was making her displeasure widely known. Garrett glanced at the bookstore. Weren't little old ladies who ran bookstores supposed to love cats?

He entered, throwing the door open so hard that the bell gave a disgruntled clank instead of the light tinkle. The shop owner gave him a wary glance from behind the register as he approached.

He plopped the bag onto the counter and the woman took a step back, looking at the bag like she expected the antichrist to pop out.

"I have a cat," Garrett began. "Well, it belonged to Sarah. She was in here a day or so ago?"

The woman nodded but she still looked at Garrett like he was an axe murderer.

"Sarah had to leave unexpectedly and, well, so do I. I was hoping you could take the cat?"

He smiled, hoping to soften her obvious wariness but it felt more like a grimace. He couldn't believe he was standing here with a goddamn cat. He should have just left her at the cottage. Cats could fend for themselves, right? While he was standing here fucking around with the animal, Sarah was getting farther away.

He unzipped the pack and put a hand down to make sure Patches didn't bolt at the first sign of freedom. But the cat just licked him and began purring loud enough for the store owner to hear.

The woman peered over the edge of the bag and her eyes lit up. "Oh, she's adorable!"

"So you'll take her?" Garrett asked hopefully.

The woman looked startled and very much like she would refuse.

"I'd hate for her to starve. She's a sweet cat. Probably a good mouser."

He hated the cajoling, whiny way his words came out. If his brothers could see him now, he'd never hear the end of their torment.

The woman looked at the cat and then back up at Garrett. She set her lips together as her eyes narrowed and then finally she said, "Okay, I'll take her. It's obvious she isn't going to do okay in your bag."

Garrett didn't even flinch over the disapproval in her voice. He'd saved the animal from starvation, hadn't he? He peeled Patches from the bag and unhooked her claws from his shirt then thrust her toward the woman.

"Thanks, I appreciate this."

He turned and left before the woman could say anything further. He'd done as Sarah had asked and made sure the cat had a decent home. At least it wouldn't starve to death now.

His next stop was at the dock where there were three charter services. He asked benign questions like whether it was possible to hire a boat to take him to the neighboring island. The first two were more than happy to accommodate his request and could arrange it immediately. The third, however, the woman informed him that her husband was already on a trip to the next island and wouldn't return for some time. When he pressed her, she clammed up and all but shoved him out the door.

Oookay. So it seemed that Sarah had arranged for a charter to make her escape and that she'd likely done it well in advance of her actual departure. He needed to get there a hell of a lot faster than the couple hours it would take by boat.

He hopped one of the two taxis on the island and got dropped off at the airfield on the east end. The guy at the counter eyed him with a speculative gleam when Garrett told him he wanted to charter a helicopter to the next island. Immediately. It was a look that told Garrett this was going to cost him a fuckload of money.

"Sure, I can take you over. I had a client supposed to come in for an aerial tour of the island chain, but I can cancel if the price is right."

Yeah like Garrett didn't know that was coming. "You take plastic?"

The guy grinned broadly at Garrett. "Of course."

Garrett pulled out his wallet and ripped out his credit card. On KGI's dime, of course. Sam would have a kitten, but oh well. He could always bill Resnick.

"How soon can we leave?"

The guy picked up Garrett's credit card and smiled. "Just as soon as I run your card."

CHAPTER 14

PEOPLE just don't goddamn disappear. Did they? Garrett was tired. He was hungry. And he was one pissed-off motherfucker. He'd been over every inch of this island and there was no sign of Sarah. No one in the harbor had seen her—or so they said. There wasn't a flight with her on it—as near as he could tell.

The woman had simply vanished into thin air.

He wanted nothing more than to say fuck it all, go home and let Resnick deal with Sarah Daniels. It was what he should do. His sister-in-law was about to deliver. Sam's hands were tied if they got another job because Garrett was off fucking around in paradise. And quite frankly, he'd have a hell of a lot better time blowing some shit up over playing junior detective. Hell, that was Donovan's job.

He should just go home and call it good.

But he'd kissed her.

It was a pansy-ass excuse. But if he hadn't kissed her. If he hadn't gotten close to her. Hadn't seen her fear. Hadn't felt her tremble beneath his fingers. If she hadn't tasted so damn good. If he hadn't kissed her, he could go home and forget she ever existed. He could leave her to Resnick and company.

But he couldn't. Somehow in the course of a few days she'd become his. His responsibility. His to protect.

It was a fucked-up scenario no matter how he looked at it. He couldn't make it go away no matter how hard he wanted it to. All he knew was that somehow, some way, he and Sarah Daniels were connected.

No, he didn't like it. But there it was. All laid out, sort of like he felt right now. Balls flapping in the wind.

No man should ever get so damn tied up in a woman. Especially one he barely knew.

Yeah, go home. It's precisely what he should do.

Then he could better prepare himself for the job of protecting her. While Donovan ran her to ground, he could haul out his arsenal and start planning for the eventualities. Hell, he never went anywhere without at least four rifles and a few handguns. And yet here he was with only a Glock and his winning personality to get himself out of a scrape on this shit hole of an island. And he'd have to leave the Glock behind.

He stalked into the tiny-ass terminal that served as ticketing desk, luggage check and security all in one and tossed his bag onto the stuttering conveyor belt.

"I want to get the hell out of here," he announced to the startled agent. "What's your next flight out?"

"Miami," she said nervously.

"Done. When does it leave?"

"Half hour, sir. They'll be boarding in the next few minutes."

Garrett scanned the waiting room to see four other people all watching him like he was the shoe bomber. He smiled through gritted teeth. "Bad breakup. Girlfriend dragged me down here for a vacation and dumped me for the first dude she saw in a Speedo."

The two men grimaced in sympathy while the two women looked like they thought it was no wonder.

He tossed his credit card onto the counter and hoped to hell Sam hadn't already discovered the last charge and frozen the account. The agent hastily shoved a printed boarding pass over the counter and then went to secure the routing ticket onto Garrett's bag.

"You say I have thirty minutes? When is last boarding call?" he asked.

The agent checked her watch. "You have twenty minutes before final boarding. The plane takes off in thirty."

He nodded and walked back outside, where he pulled out the sat phone. This time Donovan actually answered the phone.

"We have a problem," Garrett began.

"We?" Donovan echoed. "I don't see a 'we' in this equation."

"Fuck you," Garrett growled. "I need your help."

Donovan sighed. "What else is new? What, did you forget your bathing suit? Oh wait, no, the sunblock right? Give me a minute. I'm actually mustering real sympathy for you here. I might even manage to squeeze out a tear or two."

"Are you done yet?" Garrett asked impatiently. "Sarah took off."

There was dead silence.

"She gave you the slip?"

Garrett closed his eyes and braced for what was to come.

Donovan laughed in his ear. "Let me get this straight. All you had to do was stay close to a beautiful woman. Watch over her. Even cozy up to her, if that's what it took. And she gave you the slip?"

Garrett could hear the fool wheezing through the phone. He pinched the bridge of his nose between his thumb and forefinger and closed his eyes. "I'm going to beat your ass when I get home."

"Ah man, I wish I could be there to see this one," Donovan said. "So what are you going to do now?"

"It's not what *I'm* going to do. It's what *you're* going to do. I'm hopping a flight home. I need you to find out where the hell Sarah has gone. She took a boat off the island but her trail was cold when I got here. I need to know if she flew, swam, took a boat or what. I'm counting on you to find out, Van."

"Well hell," Donovan grumbled. "I like how you take an assignment and I do all the work."

"Oh and by the way. You can't use Resnick or his resources. I don't want him to know about any of this."

Again there was a long silence. "You want to explain to me why you're holding out on the man you took the assignment from?"

Garrett checked his watch. "Look, I don't have a lot of time. I'll explain when I get there. In the meantime, if Resnick knocks, you play dumb. And find out where the hell Sarah is."

He cut the connection and turned to go back into the terminal. What he needed was about twelve hours' sleep. He wouldn't sleep a wink on the plane. He hated commercial flights.

GARRETT pulled into the driveway of his house and frowned when he didn't see Sam's or Donovan's truck parked. Sophie's SUV was under the carport and he pulled in behind it. Where the fuck was everyone? He was tired from the flights, pissed over the entire deal, and he'd called Donovan as soon as he'd landed in Nashville to tell him he was on his way home.

He needed to get in, get whatever info Donovan had and get the hell back on the road. Hopefully this time, one of the Kelly jets would be available, because damn, this going-through-security-hoops at airports was for the birds.

He opened the front door and stepped inside. "Hello? Anyone home?" Where the hell was everyone?

Frustration frayed his already worn patience. He didn't have time for this.

"Garrett?"

He turned in the direction of the kitchen to see Sophie standing in the doorway, her face pale, her hand palming her enormous belly. He strode across the room, concerned by her pallor.

"Hey, you okay, sweetheart?"

She clutched at his shirt when he got close and swayed unsteadily on her feet. "No. I mean, yes. I'm in labor. I need you to take me to the hospital."

Oh hell. "Where is Sam?"

She frowned. "I don't know. He's not answering his cell. He went over to Ethan and Rachel's but when I called over there no one answered. I was just about to call Marlene when I heard you come in."

Seeing the anxiety etched in her expression, he put his arm around her and squeezed reassuringly. "It's okay. I don't want you to worry. Have you got your bag packed?"

"By the door," she said.

Suddenly she went still and gripped his hand with enough force to cut off his circulation. Damn, but for a little woman she packed a mean grip. She closed her eyes and took in several light breaths through her nose. Shouldn't she be taking deeper breaths or something?

Panic hit him in the stomach like a baseball bat. Give him a fucking war, but a pregnant woman in labor? He was clammy just thinking about it.

When the contraction passed, she started for the door and he hurried beside her. He bent down to retrieve her bag and reached for his cell phone at the same time. This was a hell of a time for Sam to go MIA. What the fuck was he thinking? Sophie could have been completely alone. She *had* been alone until Garrett showed up.

He ushered Sophie to his truck and instead of helping her to climb up, he lifted her and eased her down onto the seat. Then he gave her an awkward pat on the leg and hurried around to the driver's side.

He called Sam first but when he got no answer, he called his mom next.

"Mom, is Sam over there?" he demanded as soon as his mom answered.

"Garrett? You're home?"

"Yeah, Ma, look I don't mean to be rude, but I need Sam. Where the hell is he?"

There was a pause. "He's helping your father and brothers look for Rusty. She didn't come home after school today."

Fuck. Just what he needed was Rusty's irresponsible ass to cause trouble when everything else was going to shit.

"Sophie's in labor. I'm on the way to the hospital with her. Sam isn't answering his phone. He needs to get his ass to the hospital to be with his wife."

Rusty could rot. He didn't say it but his mom wasn't an idiot. It was there in his voice to hear.

"Oh my goodness," Marlene breathed out. "I'll get him. I'll call your father. Tell Sophie I'm on my way over right now. Tell her not to worry."

Yeah, he was going to tell a pregnant woman not to worry about pushing a bowling ball out of her uterus.

"I gotta go, Ma. Find Sam for me. I'm going to take care of Sophie."

He tossed down the phone and glanced over at Sophie, who had a tight grip on the door handle.

"It's going to be all right." He hoped he wasn't lying. What the hell did he know about women in labor? "Ma is going to run down Sam. He'll be there. No way would he miss this."

To her credit, Sophie looked less worried than Garrett felt.

"What's going on?" she asked.

"Goddamn Rusty," he bit out. "She didn't show up after school. Apparently they're all out looking for her."

Sophie frowned. "Oh, I hope she's all right."

Garrett shook his head. "She better damn well have a good reason for this and I'm thinking unless *she's* in the hospital, there isn't one."

Sophie laid her hand on his arm. "I'm fine, Garrett. Really. I'm having contractions, but I'm pretty sure she isn't coming anytime soon."

"Shouldn't I be the one comforting you?"

She smiled. "Well, yeah, I wouldn't turn down sympathy or a little petting. I am a little nervous about all of this. I think I've been in a state of denial over the actual labor process. This stuff hurts!"

Garrett grimaced and then took her hand, squeezing to reassure her. "Sorry, sweetheart. I'm an insensitive jerk, but then I think you already knew that. Is there anything I can do to make it better?"

"You could have the baby for me."

"Oh hell no," he muttered.

She laughed. "What a baby. You took a bullet without whining."

"Yeah, well that's different."

"How about just getting me there as quickly as possible. Maybe I'm far enough along to have an epidural right away."

"I can do that."

He drove as fast as possible without wrapping them around a tree. It was about a thirty-minute drive to the hospital. He made it there in twenty.

"Don't make a big deal," she pleaded as he roared into the parking lot. "No big entrance at the E.R. Just park and we'll walk into the hospital's front entrance."

"Isn't this an emergency?" he demanded.

She gripped his arm and was silent for a moment. Then she took a deep breath and exhaled. "No, it isn't an emergency. I don't want to look like a moron. Just park and help me inside. They'll take me up to the right floor."

Garrett frowned but he did what she asked, although he did make a new parking place right up close to the front entrance. They could kiss his ass or tow his truck. He wasn't making her walk all the way across the lot no matter what she said.

He jumped out of his truck and walked around to open the door for Sophie. She put both her hands out to brace on his arms, but again, he just plucked her from the seat and eased her down onto the pavement.

"Good?" he asked.

She nodded and took a step forward toward the entrance. The doors slid open and she stopped and held on to his arm for a long moment.

"Okay, granted I'm no expert on having babies, but are you sure this baby isn't coming soon? Those contractions seem to be awfully close together."

She blew out and started forward again. "They're irregular. Some are close. Others are spaced ten to fifteen minutes apart."

"And you're relying on the kid to realize they're supposed to be regular?"

Her sides shook with laughter as an elderly woman in a volunteer uniform hurried over.

"Are you in labor, dear?"

Sophie grimaced and nodded.

"Stay right here with your husband. I'll call for a wheelchair."

"Yeah," Sophie said as the volunteer hustled away. "Be a good husband and stand here without losing your mind."

"I'm so going to kill Sam for this. I took a bullet for you. He should at least have to be here for the delivery."

Again Sophie laughed. "Trust you to prefer the bullet." But she squeezed his arm and this time it wasn't because of a contraction. "Thank you. Really. I was scared back at the house."

He gathered her in a hug and kissed the top of her head. "That's what family is for."

"So you keep reminding me."

A few minutes later, an orderly entered the lobby pushing a wheelchair. Garrett got Sophie settled in, fussed over her a few seconds and then followed alongside them as the orderly pushed her toward the elevator.

Once upstairs, they were greeted by a smiling nurse who took over the wheelchair and wheeled Sophie into a small room with a rather uncomfortable-looking exam table. Weren't they supposed to have beds? Like comfortable beds? Geez, childbirth clearly wasn't for sissies.

"Is there where you're putting her?" Garrett blurted.

The nurse smiled and set a hospital gown on the "bed." "No, this is only temporary. We need to see how far along she is. Sometimes we send the mothers back home for a while. False alarm and all that. But if she's progressed enough, we'll move her to a delivery suite."

Garrett scowled. "Send her home? She's in labor. You can't send her home. Can't you see she's in pain? Can't you give her an epidural now?"

Sophie laughed. "Calm down, Garrett. We've got it handled. I promise."

The nurse patted the gown. "I'm going to leave you to change. I'll be right back to do an exam and hook you up to a monitor." She glanced at Garrett with barely veiled amusement as she walked back out.

Sophie picked up the gown and Garrett froze. "Uh, you don't need help or anything, right? I mean, you'll be okay if I just go over . . ." He glanced around. There wasn't anywhere else to go in the tiny room except out. "Uhm, I'll just step out unless you need . . . help." Oh God, don't let her need help.

"You can leave or you can turn your back," Sophie said calmly. "It's not going to take but a second to slip into the gown."

He whipped around to face the door and raised his eyes heavenward. Where the fuck was Sam?

He heard the rustle of clothing and even though he was facing away, he closed his eyes and listened for any sign that she was having trouble. Or a thump.

"Okay, all done," she said. "I could use your help getting onto the bed if you don't mind."

Garrett turned back around and kept his gaze averted just long enough to make sure he wasn't going to see anything he shouldn't. Slowly he let his gaze travel upward, relieved to see that the gown covered all the necessary parts.

She was trying to climb up but with her belly and her holding the gap closed on the gown, it looked awkward as hell.

"You hold the gown, I'll lift you up," he said gruffly.

Her lips twitched suspiciously as she gathered the material in her hands. He lifted her onto the bed and hastily arranged the sheet so she was modestly covered. A few seconds later, a knock sounded and the nurse returned.

"I need to see how much you're dilated," she said.

That didn't sound good. Garrett kept his eye from twitching. Barely.

"I'll just wait outside," he said.

Sophie waved him off and he stepped outside the room. He leaned against the wall in relief. Christ but he hated hospitals. He didn't even want to know what the nurse was doing in there. His imagination was in overdrive and it was frying his brain.

He waited. And waited. He started to pick up his cell phone and realized he'd left it in the truck. Just great. If Sam had tried to call, he was probably losing his mind by now.

Several long minutes later, the nurse stepped into the hallway and motioned for Garrett to step inside again.

"She's already dilated to five," she said in way-too-cheerful a voice. "We'll be moving her to a delivery room and the good news is she can get her epidural just as soon as the anesthesiologist can be paged."

Garrett looked over to where Sophie lay but she was watching the monitor at her bedside.

"Uh, so how long does she have? I mean until the baby gets here."

The nurse patted him on the arm. "No way of knowing really. It could be soon or it could be hours yet. We'll monitor her progress. No need to worry, Dad!"

"I'm not her husband. I mean, I'm not the father. I'm her brother-in-law. The father should be here any time." Where the fuck was he?

"Oh, well, then just relax and help keep Sophie calm and comfortable. There's nothing to worry about. The baby is doing just fine."

A commotion outside the door had Garrett turning. He breathed a huge sigh of relief just as Sam barreled inside, a crazed look in his eyes.

"Sophie? Baby, are you all right?" Sam demanded as he rushed to her bedside.

Sophie raised her head and smiled. Her entire face lit up and Garrett could see the tension ease in her expression. "I'm good. Really. Garrett took good care of me."

Sam took her hand and then leaned over to kiss her. "I'm so sorry I wasn't there. My damn phone went down and we were out looking for Rusty. I never should have left you. I didn't think I'd be gone but a few minutes to Ethan and Rachel's and then Ma called."

Sophie put a finger over his lips and then followed with a soft brush of her mouth. "Shhh. I'm fine, Sam. Garrett was great."

Sam turned to look at Garrett for the first time. "Thanks, man. I'm glad you got home when you did." He studied him for a long moment. "Everything okay with you?"

Garrett nodded. "Yeah, now that you're here."

Sophie laughed. "He was afraid he'd have to coach me through delivery. He was pretty green there for a while."

Sam settled into the chair beside Sophie's bed and laced his fingers through hers. "No chance I'd miss this." He smoothed a hand over her swollen belly. "I can't wait to meet our little girl."

"I hate to interrupt, but we need to move Mrs. Kelly to another room now," the nurse said from the door.

The nurse moved forward to unhook the monitor. Sam helped Sophie from the bed and she walked awkwardly toward the door after the nurse. Not knowing what else to do, Garrett followed the group down the hallway to a larger, much more comfortable-looking room. The bed was certainly bigger and it didn't look like a slab at the morgue.

As the nurse settled Sophie into the bed, Sam stepped back to stand beside Garrett. Garrett turned to his brother. "I should probably leave now."

"You aren't going to stick around for the birth of your niece?"

Garrett swallowed. "You want me to watch?" He tried to keep the horror from his voice but knew he failed miserably.

Sam laughed and slapped him on the back. "You can stick around until the messy part comes and then move into the hall.

Hell, before it's over with, I imagine the entire family will wind up here."

Garrett ran a hand through his hair. He needed to get with Donovan and figure shit out about Sarah. And he needed to get on the road, but how could he leave when his niece was about to arrive? Donovan would want to be here, not stuck in the war room on his computer looking for Sarah.

Sam's eyes narrowed. "What's going on with Sarah Daniels? Besides the fact she gave you the slip."

"Someone broke into her cottage and scared the shit out of her. So she bolted."

"And what is this about keeping Resnick in the dark?"

"How about you worry about Sophie and let me deal with Resnick and Sarah Daniels."

Sam frowned but the nurses were moving away from Sophie and Sophie looked over to find Sam. Sam left Garrett and returned to Sophie's bedside. He took her hand and kissed each finger, his smile warm and contented.

Garrett leaned back against the wall and wondered how the hell he'd gotten himself in the middle of childbirth.

CHAPTER 15

SEAN Cameron turned his patrol car onto another county road that led away from the lake and scanned the tree line and farther down the dirt road. It really pissed him off that Rusty had pulled this crap after all the Kellys had done for her. He'd questioned some of the students at her school and had been told she drove off with Matt Winfree after school ended.

When he got his hands on both of them, he was going to wring their necks. Especially Rusty's. Marlene and Frank were sick with worry and now Sophie was in the hospital about to deliver. Something that should be a joyous occasion for all the Kellys. They should all be at the hospital, not scouring the countryside looking for an ungrateful twit.

When he rounded the bin, he fishtailed to a quick stop, coming only inches from running over a person in the road. He looked up to see Rusty staring at him through the windshield. Her hair was a mess. She had blood trickling from the corner of her mouth, and her eyes were wide and frightened.

As soon as she recognized him, her expression grew hard and cold. Her lips twisted belligerently and she limped past him and continued down the road. He shot out of the car and charged after her. He grabbed her arm and spun her around.

"What the hell happened?" he demanded. "Where's your car?"

Her nostrils flared. "Get your hands off me, copper."

"It's either my hand or the cuffs. Take your pick," he snarled back.

He pulled her back toward his car and pushed her against the side. She trembled underneath his fingers and he let go, standing in front of her, arms across his chest in an intimidating manner.

"Start talking, Rusty."

She refused to meet his stare. "It's about a mile up."

"Did you wreck it? Where is Matt Winfree?"

Her head popped up and anger burned through her eyes. "What do you know about Matt?"

"I know you left school with him when you should have been going home. And that you took off without telling anyone where you were. Damn it, Rusty, the Kellys are worried sick about you. Sophie's in labor and the family should be with her but they're all out looking for your irresponsible ass."

Her face fell and for the first time he saw beyond the belligerent front to the pain that lurked deep in her eyes. He frowned as he took in not only the trickle of blood but the redness of her face. His gaze swept downward to take in her torn shirt and the welts around her neck.

"Son of a bitch," he bit out.

Rusty flinched away and would have taken off but he put his hand on the car to block her.

"Talk to me, Rusty. What the hell happened? Did that little bastard hurt you?"

She shook her head mutinously and Sean blew out his breath in frustration. "Get in. Show me where your car is."

He walked around to put her in the passenger side and she looked briefly up as she slid in. "Not going to make me ride in back like the other prisoners?"

"I haven't arrested you. Yet."

He slammed the door and went back around. He needed to call Marlene to put her mind at ease but he wanted to find out what the hell had happened first. Rusty was holding out—not that it was any shock.

They drove up the road and about a mile up, he saw the car nosefirst in a deep ravine.

"Goddamn," he muttered. "Is Matt still inside?"

Anger flashed on her face again and she shook her head.

"Mind telling me where he is?"

"He took off."

Sean pulled up beside the wrecked car and rested his hand over the steering wheel as he looked over at Rusty. "Any reason why?"

"Because I threatened to call you," she blurted.

His eyes narrowed. "Call me?"

"Yeah, okay? It was a bluff. Pretty stupid. You wouldn't piss on me if I was on fire."

Sean reached over and touched the blood drying at the corner of her mouth. Then he lowered his hand and pulled the collar of her shirt back just an inch to reveal the already discolored places on her neck.

Rusty stared back at him, her gaze challenging.

Sean picked up his phone and punched in Frank's number.

"Frank. I've found Rusty. I'll bring her home after I've straightened things out. No, don't come. I'll take care of it. You and Marlene just worry about Sophie."

He hung up before Frank could press further and then he stared back at Rusty.

"We can do this one of two ways. You can tell me exactly what happened, or I can take you back to the station and you can tell me there. Your choice. But you are going to give me an exact accounting or I'm going to find Matt Winfree and get his side."

Rusty closed her eyes. "It doesn't matter. You won't believe me. Nobody will believe me."

"Try me."

She turned her face toward the window and stared out. More bruises shadowed the slim column of her neck up to her ear. He was getting more pissed off by the minute. Then she looked down and her shoulders shook as if she was valiantly trying to hold on to her control.

"I didn't mean to make them worry," she said in a cracked voice. "It wasn't supposed to be anything more than a ride home. Matt Winfree is cute and popular and I thought he was interested in me. He asked if I'd give him a ride home. So I said yeah. I mean, what girl wouldn't? After we left the school, he asked if he could drive. He thought the car was cool and wanted to get behind the wheel. I know I should have said no, but I wanted him to like me."

The pained vulnerability in her voice gripped Sean by the throat. Christ, she was just a kid. It was hard to remember that sometimes, but she was still just a seventeen-year-old kid who'd had a hell of a hard life.

"So I pulled over and told him he could drive to his house and that was all. I knew Marlene would worry if I wasn't home, but I figured she wouldn't mind five minutes."

She went silent and locked her gaze on some distant object out her window.

"Go on," Sean urged.

She dragged her hand through her hair and he saw two nails, broken to the quick, tiny lines of blood at the tips. He had a very bad feeling about this.

"He drove past his house. I asked him what the hell and he laughed and said he wanted to show me something. I was pissed because I'd already told him just to drive to his house. He came out here, with me yelling at him the entire way. He tried . . ."

She leaned her forehead on the glass and hunched her shoulders inward as if to hide herself completely from Sean.

"What did he try?" Sean asked quietly.

Rusty whirled around, tears swimming in her eyes, but they blazed with fury. "He wanted sex, okay? He wanted me to put out. Apparently it's the hot gossip at school that any boy can get into my pants, and so he wanted his turn."

Sean's jaw clenched so tight his teeth ached. "Did he rape you?"

She gave a dry laugh. "He tried. He tried, okay? I told him I'd tell you, and he laughed. Said you'd never believe me over him, that everyone knew what kind of girl I am. I fought him off and he drove my car into the ditch. Then he took off. Probably called a friend on his cell phone to come get him. I don't know. I don't care."

"He's wrong."

She lifted pain-filled eyes to his. "What?"

"I believe you."

Relief was crushing in her eyes. Tears slipped down her cheeks and then she raised her hands to her face as sobs billowed out. He reached over to lay his hand against her hair.

"He won't get away with this, Rusty."

She jerked her head up again. "No. You can't tell anyone. No one will believe me. No one. Do you understand? My life will be ruined. I won't be able to go back to school."

The sad thing was she was right about a lot of people not believing her. But that didn't mean that Sean and the rest of the Kellys couldn't make the little bastard's life miserable.

"I won't press charges," she said vehemently. "I won't. I'll say nothing ever happened. You can't make me."

Sean slid his hand underneath her chin and nudged it upward. "Trust me, Rusty. I know you and I don't see eye to eye. I know you hate me. But trust me. I'll take care of this."

The hope in her eyes damn near undid him. It was gone in a flash, and her expression went dim again.

"Now tell me where you're hurt. Do you need to go to the hospital?"

She flushed and shook her head. "He hit me a few times. Tore my clothes."

He touched the side of her neck where the bruises had already formed. "What happened here?"

She twisted away and pulled her torn shirt up to cover it. "It's nothing. He held me by my neck while he ripped my shirt."

Sean itched to get his hands around *Matt's* neck.

"Tell me what you want to do then. I'll take you to the hospital if you want to go."

"I just want Marlene," she said in a small voice.

"Then I'll take you home. Okay? I'll call ahead to make sure she's there."

"Won't she be at the hospital with Sophie?"

"I think right now you need her more," Sean said gently.

Rusty breathed a sigh of relief and then she looked at him. "Thanks. You're not so bad, you know? For a cop."

Sean shook his head. "We're not the bad guys, Rusty." He glanced over at her car. "Do you need anything out of there before we go?"

"My purse. And my school stuff."

"Okay, sit tight while I go get it. I'll need to call a wrecker to come get the car."

"Frank and Marlene are going to be so upset," she said. "They just got me that car and I promised to take care of it."

Sean paused and then leaned back into the car to look over at Rusty. "They'll be happy you're okay. They don't give a damn about that car."

As he walked toward the wrecked car, he pulled out his cell phone. "Marlene? This is Sean. Yeah, Rusty's okay. Look I know you're probably on your way to the hospital but . . . Rusty really needs you right now. I'm going to take her home if you can meet me there."

CHAPTER 16

SEAN parked his patrol car outside Matt Winfree's home and sat for a moment trying to get his anger under control. Dealing with teenage punks of Matt's ilk wasn't anything new, but this time really set him off. It was no secret there was no love lost between him and Rusty. She'd been obstinate, obnoxious and rebellious from the first moment she'd learned that Sean was a cop. Half the time he wanted to shake her senseless. The other half, he preferred to just avoid her. But she didn't deserve this shit with Matt. For all her faults, he knew beyond her tough-girl exterior lay a very frightened, insecure girl who just wanted what other teenagers took for granted. Someone to love her and give a damn.

He got out and walked toward the front door. Matt's father, Tom, opened it when he was halfway up the walk.

"Sean," he greeted. "What can I do for you?"

Sean stopped a foot in front of the bottom step. "I need to talk to Matt, Tom."

Tom frowned and his brow drew together. "Is there a problem? He just got in from school. He's up doing his homework."

"You need to get him. I need to have a private word with him."

"I'll get him, but I'll hear whatever it is you have to say."

Sean shrugged. "If you insist."

He stood outside, hands shoved into his pockets while he waited. A few minutes later, Tom returned with Matt and they stepped outside onto the porch. Matt glanced nervously between Sean and his father and then his lips curled and he went on the offensive.

"No matter what that little bitch said, I didn't do anything."

"Watch your mouth," Tom barked. "You'll show some respect."

Sean leveled a stare at Matt and enjoyed watching him squirm. "Well now, I hadn't said anything at all. Interesting that you get on the defensive right away now, isn't it?"

Tom's eyes narrowed and he fell silent as he stared at his son. Then he turned to Sean. "What's going on here, Sean? Just spit it out. What is it you think Matt has done?"

"I don't think anything," Sean said softly. He looked past Tom to Matt and then took a step forward. "You're damn lucky I don't haul you down to lockup."

Matt smirked, though his eyes betrayed his panic.

"Rusty isn't pressing charges, though I tried to talk her into it. Nothing would give me more pleasure than to stuff you into a cell. But let me tell you this. If you so much as breathe her name—even once—I'll make your life miserable. You got me? You don't talk about her. You don't brag to your buddies that you got next to her. If I hear a single word that you've done anything to make her miserable at school, I'll come down on you so hard you won't be able to take a piss without me breathing down your neck and then you can kiss your football scholarship to UT good-bye."

Matt paled and Tom's perplexed expression turned angry. "Matt, what the hell is he talking about? What did you do?"

"I didn't do anything," Matt spat out. "The little bitch is a prick tease."

"I saw the bruises on her neck. I saw the tears in her shirt. You wrecked her new car—which, by the way, you are going to make restitution for. You're getting off scot-free, which pisses me the hell off. But it ends right here and now. If you don't think I'm serious, you just try me. I can ruin your life, and moreover, I'd take great pleasure in doing so if you do anything to give Rusty a hard time."

Tom closed his eyes and shook his head. All the color had drained from his cheeks, and Sean felt sorry for him. Tom was a good man. He was a longtime school board member and a huge supporter of the high school. He didn't think for a minute that Tom would condone his son's behavior.

"He'll do whatever it takes to make amends," Tom said hoarsely. "You have my word on it."

Matt's face reddened and swelled up with anger, but his father's look prevented him from speaking his mind.

"I want him to stay away from Rusty and keep his mouth shut."

Tom nodded. "He will."

Sean turned and started toward his car when Matt's outburst reached him.

"She's nothing! Just some little tramp. Why do you give a shit about her?"

Sean stopped and then slowly turned back around. He pinned Matt with the full force of his glare until he saw fear glimmer back in Matt's eyes.

"That's where you're wrong, you little prick. Take my advice. Forget you ever heard Rusty's name. She's very much a part of the Kelly family now, and if you know anything about them, then you know they don't suffer any insult to their family. She now has six older brothers who'd love nothing more than to kick your little arrogant ass all over Stewart County."

"Matt, for God's sake, shut up," Tom snarled. "You're in enough trouble as it is."

Sean tipped his hat in Tom's direction and then continued to his car.

Satisfied that he'd given Matt Winfree plenty of incentive to keep his mouth shut and to leave Rusty alone, he drove toward the Kelly house.

A few minutes later, he pulled to a stop beside Marlene's car and sighed. This sucked all the way around. Especially for Rusty. But he could at least allay her fears of the incident making the rounds at school.

He knocked and waited. Marlene opened the door, her eyes fiery. Oh, he'd seen that look plenty of times. She was such an easygoing, loving woman, but God help the fool who messed with one of her chicks.

"How is she?" he asked quietly.

Marlene sighed. "Upset but trying not to let me know how much. She's playing it off, of course, but it scared her to death. Tell me you beat the shit out of that little asshole."

Sean's shoulders shook with laughter. "I might have threatened to."

Marlene made a disgruntled sound.

"Can I see her?" he asked.

Marlene opened the door wider. "Of course. Come on in. She's in the kitchen. I made her put an ice pack on those bruises."

Sean scowled at the mention of those bruises. It made him want to go back over and bruise Matt Winfree's face.

He followed Marlene into the kitchen and braced himself for Rusty's belligerence. But when she looked up, he saw no sign of anger or hostility. She looked . . . young and extremely vulnerable.

"How are you doing?" he asked.

She leaned against the kitchen sink and let the hand holding the ice pack fall away. "I'm okay. Thanks to you."

She sounded subdued. He almost preferred her mouthy and obnoxious. He didn't know how to take the quiet and beaten-down Rusty.

"I just came by to tell you that you don't have to worry about Matt Winfree causing you any more trouble. And school won't be a problem. He won't be running his mouth."

Her eyes widened in surprise and to his extreme discomfort tears shimmered on the surface.

"What did you do?" she asked hoarsely.

He shook his head. "What I did isn't important. What is, is that he won't be a problem for you. And Rusty? If you ever need me, you call, okay? You seem to think that no one is on your side and that you can't depend on anyone. By now you should know that isn't true. The Kellys stand by you, and so do I."

Her eyes held the faint glaze of shock as she stared wordlessly at him. Marlene's phone rang, breaking the growing silence that followed his announcement. She picked it up and he listened as she said hello and then broke into a wide smile.

"Sophie's had her baby!" she said over the mouth of the phone.

Sean smiled. "That's great. Tell Sam I said congratulations."

Marlene spoke on the phone a few more seconds and then hung up, beaming from ear to ear.

"Why don't I drive you two up to the hospital to see Sophie and the new baby?" he offered. He glanced at Rusty as he spoke. "Seems to me this is a good time to be surrounded by your family."

A smile hovered over her mouth, the corners lifting as her eyes lightened.

Marlene looked over at Rusty and then reached out her hand to squeeze Rusty's. "What do you say? Want to go up and see the newest addition to the Kelly clan?"

"I'd like that," Rusty said in a soft voice.

"Well come on then. I'll give you code-three treatment," he said with a grin.

CHAPTER 17

"**MEXICO?** What the hell is she doing in Mexico?" Garrett demanded.

Donovan rubbed his hand over his hair and yawned as he stared with bleary eyes at his computer. "Yeah. A cargo pilot gave her a ride. She paid him a bundle."

Garrett's eyes narrowed. "Apparently not enough to buy his silence. How'd you dig this up so quickly?"

Donovan lifted one eyebrow. "Like I'm going to tell you. You and Sam just think you run this operation. Neither of you could manage without me."

"Feeling unappreciated, Van?"

"Fuck you."

Garrett chuckled. "I think Sam and I are both well aware of who's the brain in this camp. It definitely ain't me. So give me everything. Jesus, but I had no desire to go back to Mexico anytime soon."

"Want me to go?" Donovan offered. "I've had time to rest up. You can stay here and watch over KGI while Sam makes goo-goo eyes at his new daughter."

"Hell, no."

Donovan raised an eyebrow. "Why not? Besides, how's it going to look for the beach bum who saved her ass on Isle de

Bijoux to show up in Mexico? There ain't no amount of explaining that'll make her believe in that big of a coincidence."

"I'm going to have to lie."

"Yeah, that's going to go over real well."

Donovan wasn't telling Garrett anything he didn't already know. He'd wrestled with his conscience ever since Sarah bolted. He knew he'd gained her trust, or at least some degree of it while they were on the island. He was going to have a damn good explanation for showing up again. One that didn't get the door slammed in his face and didn't have her bolting again at the first opportunity.

Garrett pushed out his breath in an angry huff. "I'm going to tell her Lattimer sent me. That he wanted me there all along. It'll shock her enough that she'll buy it because no one's supposed to know. I was with her a lot on the island. I don't think she's in constant contact with Lattimer so I think it'll buy me some time. And if she talks to Lattimer, and her asking about me draws him out, all the better."

"It's a good plan," Donovan said. He stared thoughtfully at Garrett. "So why does it have you so pissed off?"

"Because I hate lying to her, goddamn it," Garrett exploded. He dragged a hand over his head to the back of his neck and shook his head. "She's already been fucked over once. I *hate* the idea of lying to her, of using her, even if the end justifies the means."

Donovan nodded slowly. "Yeah, I get it, man. My offer still stands. I can go. She doesn't know me. I can stash her someplace and we can lay a trap for Lattimer sans Resnick. You get the girl. Uncle Sam gets Lattimer. Everyone's happy."

"No. I go. You find me a place I can safely stash Sarah. I'd feel better if we pulled in a few team members and send them ahead to the safe house. I may have to lie to Sarah, but that doesn't mean I won't protect her with everything I have."

"I'm going to say this and it's probably going to piss you off, but I think you should stay the hell away from this one, Garrett. It's personal with Lattimer and now it sounds personal with Sarah. I can do this with a clear head. You can't."

"You aren't going near Sarah."

Surprise flashed in Donovan's eyes. Garrett cleared his throat in disgust and refused to say anything else on the matter. Donovan wasn't stupid. He knew Garrett was ass-deep in some uncomfortable shit. But that didn't mean his brother was going to get all chatty about it.

"It'll take me an hour or so to make the arrangements and get the jet ready," Donovan said.

"I never unpacked so I'm ready to hit the road as soon as you give me the green light. While you do all that, I'm going to run by the hospital to say good-bye to Sophie and see our niece. I'm also going to drop by Ethan and Rachel's on my way back over so Rachel won't worry."

Donovan offered a snappy two-finger salute to which Garrett responded with his middle finger. He was almost to the door when Donovan's voice stopped him.

"Be careful, Garrett. This obviously goes deeper than we know. Get down there and do whatever you have to do to get her to trust you. Then you need to grab her and get the hell out of there."

Garrett turned, his hand gripping the doorframe. "Yeah, I hear you. And thanks, Van. I appreciate this."

MARCUS Lattimer stared coldly at the man standing in front of him. Two of Marcus's men flanked the dirty, bloodied traitor, their guns pointed at his sides. Marcus's lip curled in distaste. He had no use for disloyalty. This man had infiltrated Marcus's organization, gained his trust, and the entire time he'd been working for the CIA.

He let Douglas Culpepper stew for a moment before Marcus addressed him directly.

"Welcome back, Douglas. I've been looking for you."

The flicker in Douglas's eyes betrayed him as Marcus called the man by his name. He remained silent as he stared dully at Marcus, the knowledge of his fate reflected on his face.

"You sold me out, Douglas, but tell me, did you sell out my sister too?"

It was one of the few mistakes Marcus could remember making. He'd made a life of being careful. But Douglas had been good. Marcus had let his guard down, a fact that still made him furious. He'd told Douglas things. Things he hadn't ever divulged to anyone else in his organization. He'd told him about Sarah.

Marcus's jaw twitched as Douglas remained silent.

"I might have let you go except for that," Marcus continued. "Are they hunting her?"

Douglas's lips tightened and his nostrils flared.

Marcus shot to his feet, his palms slapping the top of his desk as he leaned toward Douglas. "You'll talk, you son of a bitch. I guarantee you before this day's over, you'll talk. You're going to tell me everything you reported back to your superiors."

"Fuck you."

"No," Marcus said. "Fuck you, Douglas."

He made a motion with his hand and Douglas was dragged from the room by three of Marcus's men. Marcus sank into his seat and leaned back as he turned to stare out the window. Douglas would talk. Not that it really mattered. Marcus had to operate under the assumption that Sarah was no longer a secret. Which meant she was in danger. The CIA and countless other operations would have no qualms about using her to get to him. A fact Sarah herself knew, since she'd naively fled to protect Marcus.

He smiled at the idea that his little sister would protect him. He was one of the most feared men in the world and yet a woman with a soft heart and little to no knowledge of just how bad the world was had it set in her mind that he needed her protection.

No, it didn't matter if Douglas talked but he sure as hell was going to regret betraying Marcus's trust. Marcus didn't want a quick end to Douglas's suffering. His men had been instructed to keep him alive for as long as possible. Eventually he'd die in the worst sort of agony. Until then he'd pray for death with every breath.

Marcus opened his laptop and checked the email account where Sarah sent him messages. There was a new one from her. Grim satisfaction gripped him as he scanned the contents. She was finally asking him for help. He rapidly typed in a detailed response, giving her curt instructions on where to go and what to do when she got there.

Once he was done, he closed his computer and hoped she had the sense to listen to him.

He leaned back again in his chair and studied the patterns in the painting that adorned his wall. Then slowly pulled open the drawer where he kept a photo of Sarah locked away in a small lockbox.

He couldn't allow anything to happen to her. She'd already suffered far too much. If their father had done his duty, Sarah would have been raised with the protection and privilege she deserved.

He hoped the bastard was rotting in hell. Right alongside Allen Cross.

"Soon, Sarah," he murmured. "I'll make sure you never want for another thing. I just need a little more time."

CHAPTER 18

THERE was no ocean view. No sound of incoming waves and no cool breeze from the water. It was hot. The humid, cloying type of heat that made Sarah's edgier than she already was.

She'd arrived the day before after hiding in a ridiculously small, run-down hotel room in a town she couldn't even remember the name of. When she'd received Marcus's email with explicit instructions, she'd been both fearful and relieved. As much as she didn't want to involve her brother in her mess, she needed help and he'd provided wonderfully.

Fiona, the caretaker of the house Marcus owned, had stocked groceries and all the necessities, and as soon as Sarah arrived, she'd discreetly disappeared leaving only a telephone number where she could be reached if Sarah needed anything.

The area was remote but not without its escape routes. She'd spent every moment of her first hours here meticulously planning for any eventuality. She'd been a little—okay a lot—naïve when she'd arrived on the island weeks earlier. Not that she hadn't been exceedingly cautious, but even so, she'd been caught unawares and without a way to protect herself. Escape route, yes. She'd made sure of that from the moment she'd arrived on Isle de Bijoux. But she hadn't considered her own protection. Ridiculous, considering her circumstances.

It was no longer an issue. Thanks to Marcus, she now owned a gun and while she wasn't exactly able to test-fire it, she'd been over every inch of the weapon, loading and unloading, testing the stiffness of the safety, the weight of the gun and how the stock rested in the cradle of her palm. It was big and a little awkward for her, but in a pinch, it would work.

She'd raised it, pointing at an imaginary enemy and tested her resolve to kill another human being. When all else failed, she pictured Allen Cross and imagined facing him down and putting a bullet through his heart.

She could look out for herself. It was *time* to look out for herself and stop being the scared, defenseless twit she'd turned into over the past year.

In a former life, she would have been able to stay on the island and perhaps enjoy a vacation romance with Garrett. He'd certainly seemed interested enough. He'd kissed her. She'd seen the way he looked at her. She wasn't immune to the man despite the faint sense of alarm he raised whenever he was near.

No, it wasn't fear of him as someone who posed a potential risk to her safety. It was the fear a woman had when she sensed a man who could overpower her senses and reduce her instincts to those of a primal being.

It was a heady sensation. It filled her mind and soul with a vibrancy that awakened a deep longing. To possess and be possessed.

Mocking laughter bubbled up in her throat as she stared at the lush terrain surrounding the house. She stood in the window and rubbed her hands up and down her arms. She was running for her life and was standing here contemplating the what-ifs involving a fling with a hot guy.

But she was encouraged by the flare of attraction, the ability to think of a handsome man without fear and mistrust overwhelming her. It was . . . a step in the right direction. Progress. Healing. Sweet, sweet healing.

Amidst such turmoil and the knowledge that her life was irrevocably changed, hope burned. That maybe, just maybe, her future wasn't the bleak horizon it had been months ago. It was . . . liberating.

Hunger drove her toward the kitchen. Reluctantly, she left her perch high above the surrounding acreage. Here she felt more secure. She could see an approaching threat.

The kitchen, while small, was well stocked and surprisingly had updated appliances. It was more modern than her apartment back in Boston. After checking the fridge and pantry, she decided to go for simple and made herself a sandwich. She'd cook later when she wasn't feeling so antsy, as if someone would pop out of the woods at any moment and storm the house.

She poured herself a glass of wine and started to put the bottle up but then decided an entire bottle wasn't a bad idea. It would definitely help take the edge off the previous days of all-consuming stress.

She tucked the bottle under her arm, picked up the saucer with her sandwich and then collected her wineglass with the other. She went back to the living room with all the windows and positioned herself so she had the best view. By the time she was halfway through her sandwich, she'd already refilled her glass twice.

Mellowed by the wine, exhaustion crept like a slow-moving fog, seeping through her veins until her limbs went slack and her eyelids were so heavy that she struggled to keep them open.

She kicked off her shoes and leaned forward to put her plate on the coffee table next to the almost-empty wine bottle. After staring a moment at her glass, she drained the contents and then slumped back on the couch, her head bouncing gently against the plump cushion.

Probably not the best idea to get soused when she was supposed to be on her guard, but she hadn't slept in three straight days, and she was fried. She had to sleep or she was going to go crazy.

There was one other thing she had to do before she succumbed to exhaustion. She dragged her laptop over to her from the end of the couch and opened it. It took a moment for her computer to find the wireless network, and she held her breath, hoping the Internet connection was reliable enough for her to check her email.

The screen blurred and she reached up to rub her eyes and

massage her forehead as she tapped at the keys with her other hand and completed the series of steps to access her account. Her connection was slow and it seemed to take forever for the page to load. When finally, the screen bearing the message that she had new emails popped up, she tapped impatiently at the keypad to access the content.

The first was merely one line.

Let me know you made it safely.

The second contained all the impatience and worry she knew Marcus was capable of.

Damn it, Sarah, what's going on? Check in the minute you get this. I'm worried.

She opened a blank email and typed a short response.

I made it. Thank you. Please don't worry. I'm waiting like you told me to.

She shut the laptop and pushed it toward the end of the couch. Her eyelids drooped more precariously than before. Sleep. Finally, fatigue was fast overtaking her. She glanced over to the end table to her right and reached out her hand to grasp the gun. After checking to make sure the safety was engaged, she placed it in front of her on the table by her discarded sandwich, making sure the weapon was within easy reach of her position on the couch.

She yawned broadly and welcomed the approaching oblivion of sleep. Aided by the wine and three days of adrenaline-induced wakefulness, she slipped under. But even so, her sleep was fractured and she dreamed of dark shadows and of something else entirely. She dreamed of Garrett.

GARRETT didn't immediately intrude on Sarah's newfound sanctuary. He spent the first day scouting the area, keeping his ear to the ground and making damn certain that he wasn't walking into a trap—and furthermore that when he did make his presence known, they'd have a clear escape path.

Donovan was positive that the house Sarah was holed up in belonged to Lattimer, which meant Sarah had been in contact with him since leaving the island. He was going to have to talk fast and make damn sure Sarah didn't contact him again after Garrett made his presence known or his cover would be blown to high heaven.

Whatever had prevented her from accepting help from her brother before evidently had gone out the window as soon as she'd run scared. Or maybe this had been the plan all along. Who knew how Lattimer thought. It pissed Garrett off that Sarah's brother had left her vulnerable for so long while she was on the island. If she was so damn important to him, then Lattimer should have hauled her away to one of his many holdings whether she liked it or not.

As a result of Sarah's flit, Garrett had no idea what he was getting into. For all he knew, Lattimer could be here with her, although it would make him the dumbest son of a bitch on the planet, and Lattimer hadn't stayed alive as long as he had by being stupid. Still, stranger things had happened, and one thing Garrett had learned in his years in the military and the missions that KGI had taken over the years, was that crazy shit happened all the time and rule number one was to be prepared for anything.

He shifted his backpack, and switched his rifle to his other hand as he climbed another hill in the wooded area surrounding Sarah's house. He was nearing an end to his recon after having made a complete 360 of the terrain. What he'd seen so far pleased him. There was no sign of recent activity, no indication that anyone had found her before he had. But still he paid careful attention to the smallest indicator that anyone but him had been watching the house.

He rested on his stomach and moved his field glasses to his eyes. He trained them on the many glass windows of the house. The openness made him twitchy, although it being one of Lattimer's holdings, it was likely all state-of-the-art bulletproofed.

Garrett scowled even harder when he found her, standing

at one of the windows looking out with a worried frown. It didn't matter if the glass was bulletproof or not. Her parading around in the opening was an invitation to anyone hunting her.

He was going to have a long talk with her about safety measures just as soon as he explained to her the magnitude of the danger she was in. Hell, everyone in the world wanted a piece of her. Resnick was probably having a kitten right this moment and would be breathing hard down Sarah's neck. If Donovan had found Sarah, so could Resnick.

He didn't even want to think of who else was looking for her. The break-in on the island still weighed heavily on his mind.

When he was through with his surveillance, and satisfied that an immediate threat didn't exist, he stashed his gear between two rocks and began the slow journey toward the house. He'd get his equipment after his come-to-Jesus moment with Sarah. If he barged in fully armed, he'd only scare the shit out of her, and she was already going to have a big enough what-the-fuck moment over his arrival. And he didn't have chocolate to wave under her nose this time.

Since he didn't want her to have any advance warning of his coming—she'd probably take off again—he was careful to keep his approach disguised and circled to the back edge of the property so he could access the back entrance.

Subtlety had never been his strong point, but now he warred between whether to knock like he was some casual guest—yeah, right—or just break in the back and corner her before she got any crazy notions. He was confident in his ability to talk fast once he was in.

He'd rather go in, explain later. Much more his style.

When he reached the solid wood door from the back terrace, he gave the knob an experimental tug. At least she'd locked it. He moved to the window a few feet from the door and peered in. He felt like a damn creepy stalker, and if she saw him, she wouldn't have reason to believe otherwise.

"Get in first. Explain later," he muttered.

She was a mission, and he shouldn't feel like he had to apologize for making sure she was safe.

"Keep telling yourself that, buddy. Maybe you'll believe it."

Christ. Now he was having pussy conversations with himself. Maybe he should have let Donovan take the job after all. It was apparent he was losing his damn mind.

After peering in, he didn't see her, and it was likely she was still standing by the damn windows in the front. He tested the window and found it locked as well. Not just locked, but there were sticks between the top of the sill and the middle to reinforce the security. No one would get in unless they broke the panes.

So it was back to the door.

He took out the small pouch that held his "tools." Hell, it had been a damn long time since he'd resorted to a breaking-and-entering that didn't involve explosives. It took him longer than he'd like, but he finally jimmied the lock and carefully opened the door.

Only to find two chains that prevented it opening more than two inches.

"Son of a bitch," he muttered.

There was no quiet way to do this. He didn't exactly carry around bolt cutters.

So he'd make an entrance anyway, despite his resolve not to scare the daylights out of her.

He pulled back and then rammed his shoulder into the heavy wood. It took two attempts before the chains gave way and he sprawled into the house. He hit the floor and rolled. Only to stop in front of a pair of female feet.

If he expected her to scream, panic or have an otherwise girly reaction, he was dead wrong. When he glanced upward, he was staring down the barrel of a fucking cannon. Jesus, she was holding a goddamn Desert Eagle .50 cal. When he looked higher, he met with one pissed-off woman. He dropped his gaze again to the gun to see that she had a haphazard grip around the stock, and worse, the safety was off, and her finger was curled way too tight around the trigger.

"Sarah," he said in a low voice.

"You bastard," she hissed. "It was you all along, wasn't it? You weren't there on some vacation. Someone sent you after me."

"In a manner of speaking," he said mildly, still keeping a very close eye on her trigger finger. "But if I'd been sent to kill you, you would already be dead."

Confusion flickered across her face. Clearly that hadn't been what she'd expected to hear. "Did Marcus send you?"

Interesting that she seemed to think someone else would have sent him. He'd get to that later. Right now he had to be damn convincing. "Yes. He sent me."

Her brow furrowed and she took a step back although she kept the damn gun pointed at him, and the problem was where she had it pointed—though he wasn't going to take the chance of pissing her off by asking her to target a different portion of his anatomy. There was a humiliating medical report he had no desire to file. Having his nuts shot off by a pissed-off woman.

Her eyes narrowed in suspicion as she stared down at him. "Who is Marcus? And you better know all the answers or I'm going to shoot."

There was a firm set to her chin. Her lips were pressed tight and her eyes glittered, and it wasn't with fear. No, she seemed more than capable of shooting him just because she was pissed off.

"Can I get up?" he asked calmly.

"No. Stay down. Start talking."

He sighed. He took a shot that Resnick knew what the hell he was talking about and hoped he wasn't wrong. "Your brother sent me. He doesn't want you unprotected."

Surprise made her suddenly unsteady, and he tensed, hoping she didn't shoot him by accident. Then her eyes narrowed again. "Why wouldn't he say anything?"

"When exactly would you have had this heart-to-heart?" He took another stab and hoped he was right about Sarah not being in constant contact with Lattimer. He suspected she corresponded solely by email, judging by how fanatical she was about that damn laptop. "Your brother isn't the type to spell things out through an email. Nothing's one hundred percent secure, you know. Plus, he didn't want to worry you. My job was to stay close and make sure you stayed safe."

She frowned. "So why all the elaborate charade? You didn't have to date me to watch out for me."

He met her gaze and remembered kissing her. Remembered touching her and stroking his hands over the curves of her body. And what he was about to tell her, while a lie, would be the absolute truth if her brother really had hired him to protect her.

"I wanted to spend the time with you. You intrigued me."

"So all that bullshit on the island was just you making sure our paths intersected repeatedly so you could do a job?"

The note of incredulity in her voice was hard to miss. As was the sarcasm. But there was also a hint of hurt in her voice that twisted the knife a little further in his gut.

"Hell no, and I think you know that."

She closed her eyes and shook her head for a moment. The hand holding the gun wavered precariously, and he seized the opportunity before she accidentally pulled the trigger and made a woman out of him.

He rolled and grasped her wrist, pointing the gun toward the wall. Then he squeezed until she yelped in pain and the gun dropped with a clatter to the floor. He immediately eased off her wrist but held on while he reached for the gun with his other hand.

Still holding on to her hand, he hoisted himself up and then turned her arm over and rubbed his thumb over the mark he'd made on the inside of her wrist. "I'm sorry. I didn't mean to hurt you."

She yanked her arm back and clutched her arm to her chest, her eyes troubled as she stared nervously at him.

"Who are you?"

He popped the clip out of her gun and pocketed it before laying the pistol on a nearby end table. "My name is Garrett. I didn't lie about that."

"That tells me precisely nothing."

"I work for different people," he said. "I protect people. It's what I do."

She arched a delicate brow. "You're a mercenary?"

"If you're asking if I take money in return for my services, then yes. I don't work for free."

Her eyes narrowed. "And how much are you being paid to protect me?"

"Does it matter? What's important is that I keep you safe. I'd think you'd take a keen interest in that part."

"And you expect me to trust you. Just like that."

He had to control the wince. Yes, he wanted her to trust him even as he fed her a huge lie. He went on the offensive instead.

"If I wanted you dead, you'd be dead," he said bluntly. "I damn sure wouldn't have gone through an elaborate charade to get close to you, and I damn sure wouldn't have kissed you."

Her eyes widened and he kicked himself for bringing it up. He wasn't trying to be manipulative and make it about emotions though it would certainly look that way in the end.

"Why did you then?"

"Because I wanted to." That much was the truth.

She didn't look like she knew what to say to that. Confusion flickered in her eyes and then she turned away, her hands going to rub at her temples. When he walked around enough that he could see her face again, her utter fatigue flashed like a neon sign.

"When was the last time you slept?" he demanded.

She looked even more startled by the question. Her hands came away from her head and she stared at him like he was a puzzle she couldn't quite figure out.

"I don't get you, Garrett. I don't get any of this. Why are you here? I don't need you."

"The hell you don't."

She raised her hand again and pressed her open palm to her forehead. "Let me rephrase then. I don't want you here. Go home. I've changed my mind. I don't want Marcus involved. Just leave me alone."

He snorted, growing more irritated by the minute. "You really think you can go it alone? Sarah, you're a victim waiting to happen. Hell, you've been standing in front of the windows, gawking around like an idiot."

Her head snapped up and she glared at him, her eyes flashing. "You've been watching me?"

"Hell yeah, I have. I've been here for two days scouting and making damn sure you weren't followed. You haven't exactly made it hard for anyone to find you. You may as well hang up a neon sign that says 'Sarah Daniels Is Here' and paint a big red X on your forehead."

She covered her face with her hand and closed her eyes. "God, I was careful. I *thought* I was careful. Am I deluding myself? I don't know anything about hiding. I've never had to hide."

She looked dangerously close to collapsing. Her shoulders slumped in a gesture of defeat, and she looked so damn small and vulnerable. He stepped forward, fully intending to pull her into his arms, but he hesitated. On the island he wouldn't have thought twice about it, but it was different now. He'd misled her. She probably thought everything that happened on the island was merely an effort to gain her trust. And while that had been his initial intention, it sure as hell wasn't why he kissed her or why he was dying to do the same right here and right now. Only now he'd upped the stakes. He'd never outright lied to her before now.

"Sarah," he said in a low voice.

She looked up, her eyes raw, exhaustion practically screaming back at him.

"I don't expect you to fully trust me yet, but right now you don't have a hell of a lot of choices. Until I know what the threat to you is and eliminate it, you're stuck with me. That has nothing to do with your brother or anyone else. It has to do with you being safe, and I'll do whatever I have to in order to make that happen."

"*Why*? Why would you care?"

He stared back at her for a long time. "I care. Let's just leave it at that."

CHAPTER 19

SARAH gawked back at Garrett, still trying to process the fact that he was standing in her house. In Mexico. She wanted to be furious—she *was* furious—but she was too damn tired and befuddled to do anything but stare like an idiot as she tried to take it all in.

Then she shook her head. Why the hell were they standing there talking about kissing?

He reached out and cupped his hand over her cheek. The touch was a jolt to her system and sent a flicker of awareness down her spine. He rubbed his thumb over her cheekbone, the pad rasping over her skin until a shiver crept up her nape.

"You need to sleep, Sarah. I'll watch over you. No one will hurt you. I need you at your best and then we need to get the hell out of here."

She swayed, hypnotized by the deep timbre of his voice. How easy he made it to fall under his spell.

"What's in this for you?" Then as if she remembered, "Besides the money," she said with a hint of bitterness.

His hand stilled on her face, and a slight current of tension raced through his fingertips. He seemed to struggle with the question, and she wondered if he'd bother answering. Then he dropped his thumb until it rubbed over her lips. "You. You're what's in it for me."

She took a step back, disconcerted by the utter seriousness she heard in his voice. He followed. She retreated until her back bumped against the wall and then he bumped into her, his body pressing against hers until his heat invaded her limbs.

She raised her hands, fully intent on shoving him back, but they stilled when they came into contact with his chest.

"I'm going to kiss you again, Sarah."

"No, you're not."

"The hell I'm not," he growled just as his lips melted over hers.

This was stupid. They were kissing. She'd just threatened him with a gun. He'd just called her an idiot who was trying to get herself killed. He'd purposely positioned himself on the island to get close to her. Their meeting hadn't been happenstance. He'd lied.

But he hadn't. Not really. She'd been an idiot for not being more careful. He hadn't had to lie to her because she'd never pressed him for information. He'd been there, a strong, steady presence and she'd latched on like some pathetic moron. Much like she was doing now.

She stood still, determined not to respond. Determined that she could show indifference. That she was still angry over his deception. But he was patient. Oh, the man was patient. And lethal. He wooed her with his mouth, tasting, kissing each part of her lips before he gently teased her mouth open so his tongue gained entrance.

He savored her like she was something decadent and delicious, his tongue dancing lightly over hers and then stroking, warm and soft. She closed her eyes and swayed into him, her fingers digging into the hardness of his chest. She froze when her belly pressed into his groin and she felt the evidence of his arousal, hard and hot against her softness.

He cursed softly and pulled his mouth away, leaving only an inch between them. "Ignore that," he said. "I didn't mean to scare you."

She laughed. She couldn't help it. Her shoulders shook and she looked down and laughed all over again.

"What the hell is so funny?" he demanded. "Definitely not good for a man's ego when a woman looks at his dick and laughs."

This time her laughter came out in breathless wheezes. She laughed so hard, tears gathered in the corners of her eyes and then streamed down her cheeks. He glared at her, his scowl growing more ferocious with every burst of laughter.

"On the contrary," she managed to get out. "You tell me to forget something that obvious?"

"I was trying not to be an asshole," he grumbled.

For some reason she found that even funnier. "You break into my house. You take my gun away from me. Informed me you lied about pretty much everything when we were on the island. Then tell me I'm an idiot who's trying to get herself killed. And you're worried about being an asshole?"

He opened his mouth then promptly shut it. Then he backed away and picked up her gun from the table he'd laid it on. He turned it over in his hand then looked back up at her. "Not a bad choice, but it's too big for you. You weren't holding it tight enough for it not to kick back and probably knock you on your ass. You need something smaller that fits your hand better. A .38 would be a good choice."

She frowned. "I was holding it tight enough to shoot you."

"You were aiming at my balls," he said in a disgruntled voice.

"Oh."

"And if you start laughing again, I'm going to kick your little ass."

She clapped a hand over her mouth to stifle the giggle that threatened to pop out.

"You need to get some rest. While you sleep, I'll figure out where we're going."

"I haven't said I would go anywhere with you," she said in a low voice.

"And we'll talk more about that after you've gotten some sleep."

It was really hard to maintain any semblance of anger or argue with him for that matter, when all she wanted was to lie down and do exactly as he suggested. And if he was telling the truth and really was here to protect her, then she could sleep without worry of who or what was out there.

"Yes, we'll talk," she said by way of agreement. "I want to know everything."

He nodded. "As do I, Sarah. There's a hell of a lot I need to know if I'm going to keep us both alive."

She was careful not to show any outward reaction, but panic curled in her stomach. She merely returned his nod, not trusting herself to speak. He wanted to know all, and she needed time to determine just how much of the truth she could tell him without telling him everything.

"Show me around the inside of the house. I want to make sure you're going to sleep in a secure area where there isn't a threat from the outside."

Her stomach still churning, she guided him toward the large open living area that served as dining room and living room all rolled into one. He alternated between shaking his head and cursing under his breath.

"You don't go into this room. Period. And stay the hell away from the windows."

"But this is where I stay most of the time. I can see everything from here. I'd know if someone was approaching."

"Like you knew I was here?" he asked balefully.

She flushed. "You aren't most people. You were probably skulking around in the bushes wearing camouflage paint and wearing shrubs on your head."

He stopped and held up his hand, and she braced herself for the lecture she knew he was about to deliver.

"First of all, if you can see out, they can damn well see in. And at night, you can't see a damn thing out there, but with the lights on, they can see you bright as day. Second, anyone who comes after you is damn well not going to walk up and knock on your front door. He'd position himself out there in the bushes and he'd put a bullet through your head the minute you stuck your head out of the house."

The blood drained from her face and she closed her eyes. "You're right. You're right, okay? I didn't think . . . I mean I don't know how to think like a . . . a killer."

"That's why you have me," he said. "Now let's get the hell out from in front of these windows. From now until we leave, this room is off limits."

She nodded and followed him toward the hall where the

two bedrooms were located. He poked his head in the first and promptly backed out, shaking his head. "Not this one. Too vulnerable."

She sighed.

He opened the door at the end of the hall and stood in the entryway for a few moments before motioning her in. It was the smaller of the two bedrooms with only a twin bed, but at the moment, she didn't care. There was only one window, a small square situated at the top of the wall just under the ceiling. Just right to let sunlight pour into the room but not large enough for a human to get in or out of.

He turned and nearly bumped into her. He grasped her shoulders to steady her and then guided her toward the bed.

"I want you to sleep. I'll wake you in a few hours and we'll get on the road. I'd rather not stay in Mexico a minute longer than I have to."

"We'll talk first," she said softly. "And then I'll decide whether or not I'm leaving with you. Marcus said I'd be safe here. I only just got here. Why would I leave?"

He gave her a look that suggested she wasn't going to get a choice in the matter. She glared back and curled her lip to show him her irritation. He merely winked at her and her mouth fell open in shock. He'd winked at her? Such a playful action was in direct contradiction to every opinion she'd formed about him. Then she scowled because she realized he was just messing with her.

"All yours," he said, gesturing grandly toward the bed. "I'll mosey on out—unless, of course, you need my help undressing."

"Don't push your luck," she muttered as she shoved by him to sit on the bed. "I'm too tired to get undressed anyway."

She flopped back onto the mattress and closed her eyes. The bed dipped, and alarmed, she opened her eyes only to find herself staring up at Garrett as he loomed over her.

He had both hands planted on either side of her shoulders and his knees were straddling her. He leaned down and brushed his lips across hers. This time he didn't linger. Didn't wade into a long, hot exchange as he had before. He touched his finger to the spot he'd kissed and then murmured, "Sweet dreams, Sarah. You're safe now."

Then he backed off the bed and left the room without a

backward glance. She lay there, stunned by her reaction to him. More stunned by the yearning that kicked through her soul with enough force to make her heart ache.

She needed to email Marcus and ask him about Garrett, but her laptop was in the living room shoved under one of the cushions of the couch. As soon as she got up, she'd take care of contacting Marcus. Maybe by then she'd be able to think. Perhaps Garrett was the solution. She could accept Marcus's protection—through Garrett—without having to be in close proximity to Marcus. They'd both be safe.

CHAPTER 20

GARRETT let himself back into the house with his bag and rifle. He did a quick run-through and secured most of his equipment to his belt. He slipped two knives into loops on either side of his pants and made damn sure his grenade was secure. He still hadn't lived down Sophie lifting a grenade from him when all the shit had gone down with her father.

He made the rounds again, securing the broken back door in the process. He rigged a nice little surprise for anyone who decided to make an unexpected entrance. He prowled down the hall and nudged Sarah's door open so he could peek inside. Not that she had an escape route. And not that he even expected to find her awake. She'd been dead on her feet, and the deep shadows under her eyes had lent a bruised, defeated look that hadn't improved his mood one iota.

No, he liked watching her sleep. There was something infinitely fragile—and angelic—about her. Delicate eyelashes rested on her cheeks and the soft, even rise of her chest signaled that she was deep under. He watched her for a long moment, still perplexed by the hold she seemed to have on him.

When he should have been motivated to grab her ass and beat a path out of the country as fast as he could, instead he'd kissed her and acted like an asshole on the make.

But she hadn't been pissed. She'd laughed—and lord but she had a beautiful laugh, even when she was laughing at his damn hard-on. He'd grumbled, but the truth was, he'd have stood there all day, dick flapping in the wind to bring such merriment to her eyes.

He backed out of her room and went into the kitchen to set up the sat phone and the small laptop he carried with him. Then he began a meticulous search of the house. He needed to find that laptop. There weren't many computers Donovan couldn't woo like a lover.

It didn't take too long to find, wedged underneath one of the cushions on the sofa. He needed to work fast because he wasn't sure how long Sarah would sleep even though she was completely dead on her feet.

He opened her laptop next to his equipment on the kitchen table and placed the call to Donovan. Donovan answered on the third ring. He sounded distracted though, and there were odd noises in the background that sounded like a cat in distress.

"What the hell is going on there?" Garrett demanded.

"Give me a minute. Charlotte isn't happy."

"You're holding the baby?"

"Well, yeah, Sophie needed a nap and Sam has been up all night. I think Charlotte needs a diaper change."

"By all means, don't let me interrupt all that domestic bliss," Garrett said dryly. "Never mind I'm on a tight schedule over here and need this done like yesterday."

"You ever try changing a baby's diaper while trying to save the world? It ain't easy. These things need to come with instruction manuals."

Garrett listened and cringed when he heard what sounded suspiciously like baby goo-goo nonsense coming from Donovan.

"You have lost your damn mind," Garrett muttered.

Several moments later, the noise died down and Donovan spoke back into the phone. "Miss Charlotte is all happy. Now, what can I do for you?"

"I've got my hands on Sarah's laptop. I was hoping to get you dialed in so you could poke around and eavesdrop on her conversations with Lattimer."

Donovan immediately went into a series of directions that

made Garrett's eyes roll back in his head. Garrett followed them to a T and listened to Donovan's satisfied exclamations as he "got in."

As Donovan continued to talk to himself and to the computer in question, Garrett glanced over to see a folded piece of paper that had fallen out of the laptop when he opened it. Idly, he picked it up and opened it up to see a bunch of stuff that didn't make a lot of sense to him. But he guaranteed it would mean something to Donovan.

"Hey Van, this might be something." He started reading off the list of what looked to be instructions and Donovan broke in excitedly.

"Wait, go back. From the beginning. Let me get all this down."

Garrett repeated everything on the piece of paper and periodically cocked his head in the direction of Sarah's bedroom, but all remained quiet.

"Give me a sec to get back to my desk. I think you just gave me access to her email account. I also have some other info for you."

Garrett sighed and waited for his brother to get his act together. Although he couldn't say much because of all the Kellys, Donovan was the most organized. It bordered on some obsessive-compulsive disorder that the rest of them damn sure didn't suffer from. Sam was probably the closest to being an anal bastard as Donovan.

"Okay, while I'm getting into this account, I'll tell what else I've found. I've been doing some digging. I've called in some huge favors—the kind that could get people in some deep shit, if you know what I mean."

Garrett perked up at that. "What kind of favors?"

"I wanted to know if Resnick has been feeding us a line of bullshit. I also wanted to see if I could figure out Lattimer's last known location. And what his connection to Allen Cross was."

"Resnick's already started squawking. He doesn't buy for a minute that you bailed on the mission. He's pissed and raising hell. Threatening Sam and KGI and making all sorts of threats against humanity."

Garrett rolled his eyes. "I'm sure that breaks Sam's heart."

"Anyway, no luck on running Lattimer down. Resnick

doesn't have a clue, which isn't making him happy, especially now that you've gone off the radar with Sarah. He's seeing his chance to nail Lattimer sliding down the toilet, and he wants Lattimer at any cost."

"That makes two of us," Garrett muttered. Although he wasn't as willing to throw Sarah to the wolves as Resnick was. Garrett wasn't a half-measure kind of guy. He figured there was no good reason why he couldn't nail Lattimer and also keep Sarah safe in the process.

"We've got an unknown in the equation here, Van. Lattimer wouldn't have someone break into her cottage and scare the shit out of her. Neither would Resnick. Resnick's going to sit back and bait the trap. Sarah was spooked enough that she hauled ass off the island. She had an escape route planned from the time she set foot there."

"There's two actually. Unless your guy on the island is the same lead I have."

Garrett shook his head. Of course there was. Donovan did love to tell a good story. Garrett was more of a get-to-the-point sort of guy. Donovan liked to drag shit out for maximum effect.

"Who now?" he asked wearily.

"Stanley Cross. Allen's brother. In my digging, I found out Resnick uncovered the fact that Cross has hired a private recovery firm to bring Sarah in. Interesting that Resnick didn't see fit to share that little tidbit with us. Stanley is throwing a lot of money around. He seems pretty desperate."

"Oh Jesus, that's all I need. Some mercenary wannabe wading in to throw Sarah over his shoulder and haul her home like a Neanderthal. He'd probably get her killed inside of an hour."

"And you're not planning to go all Neanderthal on her?" Donovan asked mildly.

"I won't get her killed."

Donovan chuckled and then his laughter trailed off. "Resnick doesn't know I know. And don't ask how I found out. Let's just say if I'm ever asked to donate a kidney, I won't have a choice but to say yes. He's holding out on us, which is why I haven't busted your chops for holding out on him. I figure you're in the situation, you know it better than anyone, so the call is yours."

"Thanks for that," Garrett said dryly. "I want to get the

hell out of here with Sarah. What do you have for me? I don't want to lure Lattimer on his own turf. I want him where we have the advantage."

"I've got a place. I didn't want to use any of the KGI usual haunts. Resnick would look there first. It'll be a little tricky getting there, but you've got to ditch her current digs quick."

"I hate when you use words like that. It's usually a gross understatement. Just how bad am I going to hate this?"

"Afognak Island, off the coast of Alaska. Logging camp and an out-of-commission lodge are all that's there and no one's on the island right now. They shut down operations last year. I have a contact with the tribe that owns the island and the lodge. The best part is that it will be virtually impossible for Lattimer to get on that island without our team knowing."

"Alaska? Could you have picked anywhere farther?"

"Yeah well, just wait until I tell you the roundabout way you're getting there."

"Fuck me. You're enjoying this way too much."

"No. I'm worried, Garrett. This is a complete clusterfuck. I have Steele and part of his team en route. They're going to completely secure the island before you and Sarah get there."

"Okay."

"Okay? You're not going to argue and tell me to fuck off and give me a line about how you're going out on your own?"

"Oh fuck you, Van."

"I feel the love. You're such a sensitive soul. I bet you read poetry to Sarah."

Garrett scowled. He may not have read poetry but leaving a basket of wine, books and chocolate on her porch came damn close.

"Can we get back to the matter at hand? What arrangements have you made?"

"You'll travel to Belize City. Guy at Pedro Air, a private charter service, fly-by-night operation, will take you to Jamaica. From there you'll hook up with Rio, who has a friend with a jet who'll fly you to Kodiak Island. From there you'll take a sea plane to Afognak Island."

"My eyes are crossing thinking about it. And what's Rio doing in Jamaica?"

"I've called in everyone I can on this, Garrett. This seemingly innocuous mission is a hell of a lot more complicated than we thought. I have a bad feeling about this one. At no point are we going to let our guard down."

"Thanks. I appreciate the backup."

"I'm sending you GPS coordinates so you know exactly where you're going, and I'm sending you all the contacts and their information. The charters are cargo based and there'll be no passenger manifest, so that you and Sarah can't easily be traced. Plus these guys aren't exactly known for their up-and-up business practices."

"I'll be on the lookout. Sarah's sleeping but as soon as I get everything, we're heading out. Hey, what about Lattimer's connection to Cross? Figured out that angle yet?"

Donovan sighed. "No, but more and more I think it has everything to do with Sarah."

Garrett had the exact same feeling. It settled deep into his belly like after eating bad Chinese food.

"Okay, I'm in. I was right. This is a secure email account. I'll have to be damn careful to wipe my fingerprints."

"What do they say? Is she emailing Lattimer? I just got through telling her he sent me. I need to know how long I've got before that busts wide open."

"I might be able to help you out there," Donovan murmured. "If you give me an hour or so, I can make it so her emails are rerouted to me. Then I can answer as if I were Lattimer and cover your ass in the process."

"She won't be emailing anyone for the next hour," Garrett said. "She's practically in a coma. What's been said so far and how many emails have they exchanged? I need all the information I can get if I'm pretending an association with the asshole."

"Not much. At first he was frantic wanting to know where she was. Then the tone changed once he seemed to know her location. She emailed him after she ditched you. Told him she was headed to Mexico and asked him for help. He told her where to go. His emails have been short and to the point. He's a careful bastard. He only gives her what is absolutely necessary. She isn't much better. She emailed him once she got there and told him she was fine and not to worry. Interestingly enough, all her emails have been about protecting him."

"What the fuck? What can she possibly do to protect him?" It was on the tip of his tongue to ask *why* she'd want to protect Lattimer, but he already had his answer to that. No matter what, Sarah was loyal and goodhearted to the bone, and Lattimer was her brother. Hell, for all he knew, she didn't know exactly what a bastard her brother was. He damn sure hadn't done anything to alleviate the loneliness of her childhood.

"Think about it, Garrett. If she saw him murder Cross and everything points to that being fact, she could be used to bring him down. It's certainly what the Cross family is thinking. To a lot of people Sarah represents a surefire way to get to Lattimer, Resnick included."

And himself. Garrett had to include himself in the number of people willing to exploit Sarah to get to her brother. He swallowed and refused to dwell on how much of a bastard it made him feel. He just had to keep reminding himself that the end justified the means.

"Sarah has to know that. If she can't be found, she can't be made to testify against her brother."

Garrett blew out his breath. Yeah, he'd buy that. Sarah would be intensely loyal, but he was also disappointed that she'd be so blind in her loyalty to her brother that she'd ignore the cold-blooded killing of another human being. Maybe his sense of justice was more black-and-white than Sarah's, but it bugged him that she'd walk way.

"That makes sense," Garrett said in a grim voice. "In a sick, twisted way, it makes sense. Thanks for covering my ass with the emails. It'll buy me some more time. If her emails are redirected and Lattimer is no longer getting them, it could work in my favor because she'll no longer be telling him she's okay. He'll worry. He'll no longer be content with a casual search while she's there reassuring him that all is well. He'll want to find her, and I'll be waiting."

"I don't envy you, brother. Sarah isn't going to be happy when the shit hits the fan."

No, she wouldn't. But Garrett couldn't dwell on that right now no matter how much it bothered him. He had a job to do. He had justice to see even if Sarah refused to do so. He had a longtime promise to his fallen teammates to fulfill. His honor wouldn't allow for anything else, even if he lost some of it in the process.

The greater good. It was all about the greater good. But somehow shitting on a woman like Sarah for that greater good didn't leave him with any satisfaction.

CHAPTER 21

SARAH came awake to a gentle hand on her shoulder. It became more persistent and her head wobbled as her eyelids fluttered open.

"Come on, Sarah. Time to wake up. We've got a lot to talk about."

"Garrett," she whispered.

"Yeah, it's me."

She rose up on one elbow and shoved her hair out of her face. She stared at him through bleary eyes as she tried to blink away the veil of sleep.

"So I didn't dream you."

"Not unless you had a very nice dream about a really good-looking guy."

Though he delivered his teasing with a perfectly straight face, his blue eyes held a devilish glint. She shook her head to rid herself of the cobwebs. Talk. He wanted to talk, which meant he also wanted answers she wasn't prepared to give. She definitely needed a clear head so she didn't screw this up.

"Do I have time for a shower before we have this talk?"

He made a show of checking his watch. "I'll give you five minutes and then we meet back here in this room. It's the safest place to be."

She scowled. "Five minutes? It's obvious you're not married and have probably never lived with a woman. You don't give a woman five minutes to take a shower."

He didn't look impressed by her response. "Five minutes or I come in after you. They start now."

Good God, he was serious. And he'd actually do it too. She didn't doubt that for a moment.

"You now have four minutes and forty-five seconds."

She dove for the end of the bed and ran for the bathroom, his chuckle following as she nearly killed herself getting out of the door.

"Five minutes," she grumbled as she turned on the shower. He was probably used to hosing off in three minutes in the military. Well, she wasn't in the military and furthermore, it took longer than five minutes just to wash her hair.

Still, his threat rang in her ears, and she wasn't entirely certain that he wouldn't come in after her so while she stuck her head under the spray to rinse the shampoo, she scrubbed the other parts of her body.

She momentarily got caught up in the absolute bliss of the hot water raining down over her. Instead of energizing her, as she'd hoped a shower would do, it made her want to crawl back into bed and sleep for about a year.

In disgust, she reached for the knob and turned the hot water completely off. The result was an icy blast that made her yelp as it pricked her body like little ice pellets. At least she wasn't mooning over how good the bed would feel again.

As she stepped from the shower, shivering, Garrett pounded on the door.

"Sarah? Is everything okay in there?"

"Yes, fine!" she called. The last thing she wanted was for him to make good on his threat. "I'll be out in just a minute, promise."

She hurriedly dried and then pulled on her underwear and jeans over her still-damp skin. She struggled with her bra, and in her haste, she managed to put the damn thing on inside out. God, but she was a mess. With a laugh, she righted her bra and then yanked on her shirt. She wasn't even going to bother with her hair. If he was so determined that she make it out in five minutes, then he'd just have to deal with her looking like a drowned rat. More like a horde of rats had taken up residence in her tangled tresses.

She gave one last wipe to her hair so it wasn't actually dripping and then gave up and opened the door. Garrett was leaning against the opposite wall and he raised an eyebrow.

She frowned. "What? You gave me five minutes. This is what happens when you give a woman only five minutes in the bathroom."

"Whoa, I didn't say a word."

"You didn't have to. It was that look you gave me like you were staring at Medusa."

He chuckled and kicked off the wall. "I wasn't looking at your hair."

"Then what the hell were you looking at?"

"I'm a man. Shouldn't be too hard to figure out."

She glanced downward and saw that her shirt was clinging very damply to her bra, which was also . . . damp, which in turn gave him a pretty darn good glimpse of her breasts and the outline of her nipples.

"Oh hell." She turned and charged back into the bathroom to get another towel. "This is all your fault."

"What were you hollering about?" he asked from the doorway.

She turned around, armed with a towel that she held strategically over her chest. "I turned the cold water on so I could wake up. You said you wanted to talk. I can't talk if all I want to do is go back to sleep."

He stepped back into the hallway and gestured for her to precede him back into the bedroom. She plopped onto the bed and switched the towel for a pillow and held it to her chest as she made herself comfortable.

Garrett loomed—there was no other word for it—over the end of the bed. He was a big man, and in such a small bedroom, he seemed to take up every available inch. He made her nervous.

"For God's sake, sit down or something. I can't think with you hovering like that."

He made a sound of amusement but accommodated her by settling on the end of the bed. But that only brought him closer and made the entire setting feel decidedly intimate.

"What do you want to talk about?"

He studied her for a moment, his gaze moving over her face in a way that made her think he was peeling her skin back. "Why are you so nervous?"

That was a stupid question. Something an oblivious man would totally ask. So she ignored him and stared pointedly, waiting for him to begin.

"I've put my cards on the table. It's time for you to deal yours."

Her eyes widened and then she narrowed them in irritation. "You haven't done anything of the sort. I know your name and that my brother supposedly sent you—which, by the way, I plan to confirm."

Garrett shook his head and sighed. "You have no sense of self-preservation, Sarah. You and I have to work on that."

"What's that supposed to mean?"

"If I was the bad guy feeding you a line about your brother sending me, you just tipped your hand and put me on notice. If I was threatened by that, it would be awfully damn easy to make you sure you weren't capable of checking in with Lattimer."

"Why are you telling me this then?"

"Because I'm the good guy, and I want to teach you not to make mistakes that could get you killed."

He looked indulgent, like he was having to display a large degree of patience with her naïveté. Okay, she got it. She was a complete moron. But in her defense, there weren't any classes where one learned the art of deception and cloak-and-dagger crap that was the hallmark of overwrought spy thriller movies.

Much was said about common sense, but common sense was for the generalities of life. No one she knew had experience with murder and hiding from the law.

"Cut me some slack," she muttered. "I know I'm an idiot. I get it. I do." She rubbed her hand over her forehead and a wave of hopelessness hit her like a tsunami. Who was she kidding? She was never going to survive on her own.

"You're not an idiot," Garrett said in a low voice. "You've had your very normal life upended. You've made some bad choices, and you haven't been as careful as you should, but that's where I come in. I'm going to do my damndest to make sure nothing happens to you."

"If you only knew," she murmured. Then she let out a dry laugh. "Bad decisions. If I could only go back."

"You can't think that way. You play with the cards your dealt and you move on."

"You strike me as someone who lives with no regrets," she said, intensely jealous of how grounded and confident he always appeared.

He seemed surprised by her observation and he laughed, but the sound wasn't one of amusement.

"My attitude is born of necessity. I've made mistakes. I've made decisions I regretted. I know what it's like to live with regret. I live with it every day. But if I let it take over, I'd never get out of bed in the morning."

The frank, raw note in his voice shook her. For a moment she got a glimpse of the man beyond the self-assured, steady exterior. For some reason it reassured her and put them on more of an equal footing.

He stared back at her, neither of them speaking. She was unwilling to break the brief moment of connection—true connection—and she savored that he'd shared something beyond casual conversation. He hadn't said much but it had been what he said. She wasn't the only person to make mistakes—though hers seemed so much larger and the consequences so much more far-reaching, but how was she to know the true depth of his mistakes?

"What happened in Boston, Sarah?"

Garrett watched as the blood drained from Sarah's face. She went as pale as the sheets rumpled around her. Her arms tightened around the pillow she held so close to her chest and she dug her chin into it until only her eyes shone over the top. Damn. He didn't want to scare the hell out of her, but he had to pry the information out.

"I need to know what you saw, Sarah," he said gently. "I need to know what kind of danger you're in."

If possible, she went even whiter. For a moment she closed her eyes and when she reopened them he saw a vulnerability so deep that he wanted to reach out and hold her.

"It was best that I left," she finally said. "I can't go back. I've resigned myself to that."

"So you'll spend the rest of your life running? That's no

way to live, Sarah. It doesn't have to be that way. I need . . ." He ran his hand through his hair back and forth in agitation. He hated the hypocrisy in what he was about to say to her. He hated that would ask her to give him something he had no right to given his deception. "I need for you to trust me."

She looked up, her eyes dull. "I don't trust anyone."

So starkly said, the words hit him hard. There was a wealth of emotion even when her expression was so dim and lifeless.

"Sarah."

She refocused on him, blinking as their gazes met.

"You can trust me."

And she could. With her life. Her well-being. He'd do whatever necessary to keep her safe. He wasn't being honest with her, and that was something he'd have to live with. But she could damn well trust that he'd never let anyone hurt her.

Somehow he would separate what he had to do in order to bring down her brother and shield her in the process. She would see it as a betrayal. She was too loyal, too loving and giving to accept what he had to do. But it was the right thing to do and somehow, someway, even if it took forever, he'd make her understand that. He didn't have a choice.

Her struggle was vivid, played across her face and awash in her eyes. He saw an intense desire to be able to trust him. She was so wary but she longed for someone to lean on. And damn it, he wanted to be that person.

"Sarah."

She locked gazes with him again.

"You *can* trust me."

The lie that wasn't a lie. Was anything ever straightforward? Life was a study in shades of gray. As black and white as he tended to view the world, here and now he understood the pull between right and wrong. Between what he had to do and what he wanted. He didn't like it. Not at all.

"Now tell me what happened the day you walked into the building where Allen Cross was murdered."

He watched her battle the tears, but she blinked them back and swallowed, her jaw tightening. "I saw Allen Cross die. I wasn't in time. I wasn't in time," she repeated helplessly.

Garrett's frowned and leaned forward. "Wasn't in time for what?"

"I could have prevented it. Oh God, I could have stopped it."

A spasm of grief crossed her face. It was uncomfortable to witness, and for a moment he wanted to pull her into his arms and drop the entire subject. It was a stupid, emotional reaction—one he couldn't afford to consider. Too much was at stake here.

"How could you have prevented it, Sarah? Did your brother threaten Cross?"

"Marcus doesn't make threats. He doesn't posture. He acts."

It was hard to tell by the inflection of her voice whether her statement was a criticism or a bleak statement of fact. There was no pride in the words.

"Then how could you have prevented it?" Garrett asked again.

He might not be that intuitive when it came to women, but his gut was starting to scream. Some of the puzzle pieces were coming together. He didn't know why it hadn't clicked for him before. But now the facts were there, laid out in front of him and he had a very bad feeling he knew exactly what had prompted Marcus Lattimer to go to Allen Cross's office and shoot him in cold blood.

He met her gaze, saw so much more than he had even five minutes ago. "Who hurt you, Sarah?"

Her face lost all color again and her eyes went blank, like a deep freeze or a white-out.

"I don't know what you're talking about."

The words stuttered out, utterly unconvincing.

He reached over to take her hand. She tried to retreat, but he held firm and gently rubbed his thumb up and down her fingers. "You're as skittish as an abused animal. Someone hurt you. I think I finally understand what happened and why."

"Then why ask if you already know everything? You have it all figured out. You don't need me to spill my insides."

He wasn't put off by the bitterness is her voice. He may have lied about Lattimer, but there was one thing he planned to be blindingly honest with her about.

"I need to know," he said simply. "And I need to know because I can't live every minute wanting to kiss you and touch you, all the while knowing that someone made you afraid. Not just of me but all men."

Her eyes widened and her lips parted in a gasp of surprise.

"I don't want you to be afraid of me, Sarah. More than anything, I want you to trust me. I want you to be able to feel my touch and know that I'm never going to hurt you. I want you to touch me."

He hadn't realized how much he wanted her to touch him until he'd said the words. He wanted to feel those soft hands on his skin. His groin ached and throbbed. He wanted her fingers wrapped around his dick, stroking with her feather-light caress and then firmer. He wanted her on every inch of his body. He wanted to see the contrast of her paleness against his darker skin.

He wanted to taste her and for her to taste him. Sweat beaded his forehead and his breaths had shallowed until it embarrassed him. He was panting after her like a moron, but she flipped every one of his switches, and some he hadn't even known he had.

He wanted to make love to her. He wanted her to trust him enough to take that step. He wanted to show her that he'd never hurt her.

Her surprise turned to hurt, her gaze growing dim. He hated the sadness that was deep seated there. It was like watching day turn to night as some of the light went out and shadows stretched like storm clouds through her eyes. She pulled her hand away and he let her this time.

"You were right, Garrett," she said in a brave voice that trembled with the effort it took her to make the admission. "Someone did hurt me. More than that, he took something away that I'm not sure I'll ever get back."

It was hard to control the rage that mounted with every breath he took. He willed himself to remain still and not to outwardly react. She seemed so hesitant—and vulnerable—almost as if she expected him to back away as though she had the plague.

But he knew. Goddamn it, he knew that Cross had been the one who raped her. Everything clicked together at light speed. Her quitting her job with Cross and not taking one since.

It even made sense why Lattimer had killed the son of a bitch, and as much as Garrett loathed Lattimer, he understood why. There was plenty to condemn Lattimer for, but not this.

Sarah turned her haunted gaze to Garrett, and he saw her visibly withdraw. The walls went up, almost as if bracing herself for his rejection.

Instead, he eased forward, moving inch by inch until he slid his hand over hers again, cupping it protectively in his palm. "You'll get it back."

"He raped me," she blurted. "I trusted him and he raped me."

He wished he was one of these guys who always knew the right thing to say at the right time, but he wasn't. He wasn't subtle. He didn't know how to be sensitive and he sucked at words. He acted. That was who he was.

He reached out and tenderly nudged her chin with his free hand until their gazes met again. Tears shimmered in her beautiful eyes and he remembered all the times before when she'd been so stalwart, on the verge of tears but never letting them fall. Had she ever cried for herself? Had she ever given herself permission to grieve?

"Honey, you gave him your trust. He shit on that. That's on him. Not you. Never you. I'd like to find the bastard and cut his nuts off, but I know that doesn't help you now."

She gave a shaky laugh and a single tear slipped down her cheek. He caught it with his thumb and whisked it away but continued to stroke her cheek.

"He's dead," she whispered. "Marcus killed him."

"I know," he said gently. "But it was a nice image, wasn't it?"

This time her laughter was stronger and some of the light flooded back into her eyes. And damn if he didn't want to pull her into his arms and tell her it would be okay. But he had no way of knowing that. It was just words, and she didn't need platitudes.

And just as quickly, her face crumpled and she took her hand from his and wiped at her eyes. "Oh God, I'm laughing and a man died because of me. Because I didn't stand up for myself."

"He deserved to die," Garrett said fiercely. "Any man who preys on a woman deserves a long, painful death. He doesn't deserve your regret or your guilt."

"It's not just him. My brother killed him for me. When he found out what Cross had done, he was so furious. I shouldn't have told him. But he knew. He knew something horrible had happened."

She was babbling now, talking fast, the words tumbling over each other, but he remained silent and let her get it out.

"I was so devastated. I couldn't even go out of my apartment. Isn't that ridiculous? I was afraid to go out because it would mean unlocking my door. I didn't want to chance seeing him even though the odds of our paths crossing when I no longer worked for him were nil. I didn't go to the police because I heard Allen telling me over and over that no one would ever believe me. It's so stupid. Why did I believe him? Why did I allow him control even after it was over?"

"Not stupid," he said.

Her eyes were glassy, and she was lost in another time and place. Locked in her past. Reliving it with each breath. He'd asked for her trust, but he hadn't realized what it would cost her. And he hadn't realized how painful it would be for him to hear. Even though he'd strongly suspected what had happened to her.

"Marcus doesn't visit. I mean, not often. I'm sure you know he . . ." She shook her head. "He doesn't spend much time in the States. But we email often. He always looks out for me. Wants to know if there's anything I need.

"He'd been trying to get in touch with me and was worried when he couldn't reach me so he came to my apartment. It had been months. *Months.* And for me, it was like it had just happened the week before. At first I refused to tell Marcus, but he wouldn't relent. He was so worried. He wanted to take me to a doctor. He thought I was ill. When I finally told him, he went crazy. I thought it was all talk. People say things in the heat of the moment all the time but they don't mean it."

"He meant it."

"He meant it," she repeated bleakly. "He spent so much time with me that it slid away, his threats, the words he said when he was so angry. He took me places. Bullied me to eat. Made me laugh again. I don't know what I would have done without him. He saved my life. I know that sounds so dramatic, and I know you think I'm probably still a mess and I'm this scared little mouse, but it was so much worse then. It felt like something broke inside me and I didn't know how to fix it. I've always been naïve. I know that about myself. I've been called a Goody Two-shoes. Miss See the Best in Everyone.

He took that from me. I never imagined in a million years that he would have done something like that.

"I've always considered myself a good person. I've never done anything to purposely hurt anyone. I was in shock that this happened to me, and because it did, I turned into this vengeful person. I've never truly hated anyone, but I was *glad* when I saw him lying there on the floor."

Garrett could stand it no longer. The ache in her voice, the absolute devastation was tangible. He pulled her into his arms and pressed her cheek to his chest. She didn't resist as he stroked his hand through her hair. He closed his eyes and pressed his lips to the top of her head.

When she spoke again, her voice was muffled by his shirt. He shifted and pulled her more firmly against him, but turning so that he could hear.

"Marcus began making plans. He talked of taking me away. I let him take charge. I thought at the time he was still worried and wanted to take me someplace he could keep an eye on me and so that I would get away from where it all happened. I didn't realize what he'd planned until the day we were supposed to leave. I was packed. Marcus had made all the arrangements. His jet was waiting for us. And then Marcus said he had a last-minute appointment. He asked me to wait and that he'd send his driver for me as soon as he was finished and he'd meet me at the airport.

"If I hadn't been in such a fog, I would have realized much sooner that Marcus would never have let it go. He was too furious after I told him. But that's just it. I didn't think. I never imagined . . ."

Garrett squeezed her lightly and rubbed his hand up and down her arm to offer her the comfort she needed.

"I think I know the rest," he said softly. "You went to try to stop Marcus. Allen was already dead. I think I know why you bolted instead of going ahead with the plan to go away with your brother."

She shifted and turned her face upward, which sent her body snuggling even closer to his chest. He caught her, wanting to keep her there as her gaze found his. "If I stayed—if someone saw me or placed me at the crime scene—I'd either be a suspect or I'd be forced to testify against Marcus. No one knows of our relationship. No one would have reason to connect us. It was better if I was as far away from him as possible."

Garrett was torn. Well and truly torn. If he didn't hate Lattimer so much, he'd shake his hand for taking care of the scumbag who'd hurt Sarah. Somehow the idea of taking him down didn't hold quite the appeal it did before. Sarah had been bitterly betrayed by a man she trusted, and now she'd be betrayed again. By a man who'd asked her to trust him, even knowing how much it cost her.

She was quiet for a moment before she laid her head back down against his shoulder and tentatively trailed her hand up his arm until she tucked her fingers around the ball of his other shoulder.

"I owe so much to Marcus. I can't—won't be used against him. He should never have done what he did. But he did it for me. Because he loves me. I know he isn't perfect. I suspect he's done some not-so-nice things, but thinking and knowing are two different things. No matter what he's done, I won't have him imprisoned because of me."

Garrett had to bite his tongue to keep from telling Sarah just what a bastard Marcus was. She'd already been dealt a shock, on top of a traumatic attack. He couldn't—and wouldn't—further destroy her illusions. Not until he had to.

CHAPTER 22

DESPITE her conversation with Garrett, Sarah pulled out her laptop from where she'd hidden it underneath the sofa cushion and carried it into the bedroom so she could check her email while she packed. Or that was her excuse. She hadn't *un*packed. All she had to do was put on her shoes and she was ready to leave. Again. This time not alone. With Garrett.

The relief she felt over that detail was telling. It was staggering even. She was weary to her toes and tired of the fear that seemed to overwhelm her more with each passing day.

There wasn't a new email from Marcus, so she opened a blank one and typed the longest message she'd sent to date. She allowed some of the emotion she'd kept under wraps to bleed into her words. She was still careful not to state specifics—she couldn't be absolutely certain her emails weren't intercepted. But she hoped she allayed Marcus's fears by telling him she'd agreed to accompany the man he'd sent to protect her.

She looked up when she saw Garrett step to her doorway and knock lightly on the frame.

"We need to make tracks. One thing you should be aware of is that Allen Cross's family has hired a private recovery firm to find you. His brother is footing the bill and apparently money is no object. It wasn't hard to find you here, and I expect it would be just as easy for anyone else, given the right motivation."

The blood drained from her cheeks, and she swayed from her perch on the edge of the bed. She put her hand down on the mattress to steady herself and gripped her laptop with the other.

"You won't let them take me back," she said in a low voice. She hadn't intended it to come out as a question, but it was so hesitantly said, that it conveyed her uncertainty in neon glow.

"Over my dead body."

Bolstered by the absolute confidence in his voice, she allowed some of the panic to recede. She hadn't dared tell Marcus all of it—of Stanley's involvement. Not after he'd killed Allen. There would be no more blood on her brother's—or her—hands, if she could help it.

She was reaching for her bag when she realized she had no idea where they were going. Garrett intercepted the large bag that held her clothes and tossed it over his shoulder. She stood and stuffed her laptop into its case and glanced around to make sure she hadn't missed anything.

"Where are we going?" she asked.

There was a slight quirk to the corner of his mouth, almost as if he was amused. "Alaska."

Her eyes widened and then narrowed. "Alaska? I'd prefer to stay out of the U.S. I don't want to risk going back there."

"There's nothing more risky than where you are right now. You've been found out at the two places you've chosen, so it's my turn. That trust thing we talked about? Now's the time for you to decide. I'm not going to do anything that puts you at risk, Sarah. Members of my team are already en route. They're going to secure the location and remain at the ready while we're there."

She glanced down at the T-shirt and pair of shorts she wore and grimaced. "Isn't it cold there?"

Garrett chuckled. "I'll keep you warm."

Just the words sent a blast of heat up her spine to her neck and over her cheeks. She couldn't even meet his gaze, because he'd see the effect he had on her. He was teasing her, but the images of her wrapped in his arms—warm and safe—was such a powerful enticement that she longed to make the fantasy a reality.

He held out his hand to her. "Are you ready? We need to hit the road."

The simple question was several inquiries all rolled into one. Did she trust him? Would she go with him? Was she agreeing to his protection?

She slid her palm over his and allowed him to twine his fingers with hers. He squeezed once and then leaned forward to brush his lips against her forehead. Then he tugged her toward the door and they walked down the hall. He veered toward the back door and tucked her securely behind him.

"I have the truck pulled up almost to the door. I'm going out and I want you to stick like glue to my back at all times. Don't stick any body part out that you don't want to part with. Okay?"

"You think someone's out there?" she asked anxiously.

He shrugged. "I always assume there is. We can't afford to take any chances."

She swallowed and nodded her agreement. He gave a brisk nod in return and then opened the back door. He reached behind him and wrapped one arm around her waist, pulling her flush against his back. He pulled out his gun with the other hand and stepped into the night.

"SO who pissed Van off?" Cole asked as he boarded the seaplane on Kodiak Island with his teammate P.J. Rutherford and team leader Steele. "And why did Dolphin and Baker get the get-out-of-jail-free card on this gig?"

"What are you whining about now, Coletraine?" P.J. asked as she slid in beside him. She tossed her duffel bag onto the floor between her legs and then stretched out in the seat. Not that her legs took up much room.

Steele, ever silent, crawled into the cockpit with the pilot and turned to glance at Cole and P.J. "Everyone set?"

At their nods, he motioned to the pilot they were ready and he revved up the engines in preparation for takeoff. The plane set off over the water, gathering speed as they left a foamy trail in the emerald-green sea.

"Alaska," Cole grumbled. "It's fucking cold here even in

summer, and it stays light too goddamn long. How are we supposed to sleep?"

P.J. chuckled. "I think the point is that we're not supposed to sleep."

"Easy for you to say. You're a damn robot. You're not human. No one can go as long as you without sleep."

She shrugged. "If I fall asleep, someone could die."

Cole shook his head. P.J. . . . P.J. was something of an enigma. She'd been part of his team for a few years now, and he'd yet to figure her out. He knew next to nothing about her past, only that she'd come from S.W.A.T. and that she was a damn good shot. Better than him—not that he ever admitted that in front of her.

They were competitive, and he liked to give her shit. He didn't always understand her, but then it had been his experience that all women were creatures from an alternate universe anyway. But she was steady. He could always count on her. The entire team could.

The plane sailed over the water and in the distance, the island was visible.

"What are we looking at here, Steele?" Cole asked. They hadn't had time for a full briefing. Steele had taken the call from Donovan and pulled him and P.J. They'd left on a minute's notice, not that it was anything new.

"Garrett is bringing Sarah Daniels here. Our job is to be invisible and make damn sure no one gets on this island," Steele replied.

"Well, that's nice, but who is Sarah Daniels?" P.J. piped in.

Steele's expression didn't change. "Does it matter? Our job is to keep her safe. Watch Garrett's back. Do the assignment, just as we do all the others."

"Don't you ever get curious?" P.J. grumbled.

Steele raised an eyebrow and turned back around in his seat. Cole shot her an amused look and she scowled and flipped him off.

"Steele, curious?" he mouthed.

P.J. rolled her eyes and said in a low enough voice that Steele wouldn't hear, "And you said I wasn't human. He's a machine."

The plane dipped and P.J. turned to look out the window as they nosed down toward the water.

"There's a bald eagle," she said in an excited voice as she pointed.

Cole ducked his head and leaned forward to look. "I had no idea you were such a wildlife buff."

"You're unpatriotic if you don't get a thrill at seeing a bald eagle," she said, shoving at his arm. "Aren't you army guys supposed to be more gung-ho about national symbols?"

He winced and then growled through his teeth, "I was not in the goddamn army and you damn well know it. Navy, P.J. I was a SEAL, for God's sake. Have some respect."

"I get you all confused," she said defensively. "Who the hell can keep up with all the branches of the military you people wimped out of."

Cole gave her a look of disgust. She was so full of shit. She had a memory like a steel trap. She didn't forget anything. She could probably name branch, serial number and rank for every single one of the KGI members.

"Yeah, well, what's your story, Rutherford? You talk shit about us, but all that I know is that you wimped out of S.W.A.T. after being the first female in your unit. Couldn't take the heat, or what?"

Though he was teasing, pain swamped her brown eyes followed quickly by ice so prevalent it shriveled his nipples. Her lips tightened into a line but he saw the betraying tremble. It was the first time he'd ever seen true emotion from her. She could joke and give hell with the best of the guys, but for the most part, she kept to herself, and when she wasn't teasing, she kept her mouth shut and followed orders.

He would apologize, but that would only piss her off, so he pretended he hadn't seen her reaction and dropped the subject. But it intrigued him. The first crack in her give-a-shit attitude. Somehow it made her more human. And it made him want to know more about the mystery that was P.J. Rutherford.

The plane skimmed the surface of the water before slowing and turning into a cove. They coasted to a stop alongside an aged, wooden dock and the pilot hopped out to secure the plane. Cole stepped out and reached back for his bag. He didn't offer to help P.J. He'd made that mistake before. She carried her own weight and never asked for help. It made her a damn good team member, but it bugged the shit out of Cole. He couldn't even put his finger on why.

After their bags were on the dock, the pilot gave them a wave and climbed back in. A few minutes later, he took off toward Kodiak Island. Cole stood with Steele and P.J. as they surveyed the immediate area.

"We've got a lot of ground to cover," Steele said grimly. "I expect Garrett in two days, maybe sooner. We need to be ready. We'll start with the lodge they'll be staying in and then we'll expand our perimeter to encompass as much of the island as we can cover in two days' time. We'll set up in a triangle around the lodge. Stay low and out of sight and keep your guard up at all times."

"Who, exactly, are we expecting to show up?" P.J. asked.

"Don't know," Steele said shortly.

Cole frowned. "Do we know anything?"

"Van has a bad feeling. His instincts are usually damn good and I trust them. Garrett took a job to find and protect a woman who witnessed a murder in Boston. A murder committed by Marcus Lattimer."

"Oh fuck," Cole muttered. "What the hell was Sam thinking letting G take that gig? One of us would have done it."

P.J.'s brows drew together in confusion. "What am I missing here?"

"Nothing important," Steele said. "What is important is that Garrett feels that there's a wild card and that someone other than Lattimer is after Sarah Daniels. The problem is they don't know who. Yet. Garrett is stashing her here until they know what they're dealing with. It's our job to make sure she stays safe."

Cole nodded. "Ain't no thang. Another day at the office."

P.J. pulled her pack over her shoulders as Cole did the same. As they turned to head up the incline toward the lodge, Steele called out, "One more thing."

Both Cole and P.J. turned and Cole was surprised by the amused glint in Steele's usually stoic expression.

"Watch out for the bears."

P.J.'s eyes widened. "Bears?"

Steele struggled to maintain a straight face. "Yeah, they

have Kodiaks here. Big-ass fucking bears. Make grizzlies look kind of friendly."

"Well, shit," P.J. swore. "Nothing like being trapped on an island with BAFBs."

Cole shot her an inquisitive look.

"Big-Ass Fucking Bears," she said patiently, echoing Steele's description. She cast him a sideways look and mischief danced in her eyes. "We can always use Cole for bear bait."

"You're all heart, Rutherford. All heart," Cole said.

"VAN, when was the last time you heard from Garrett?" Sam asked as he strode into the war room.

Donovan rotated in his chair and stared back at his brother. "He checked in a few hours ago. Said Sarah was sleeping and as soon as she woke up, he was getting them the hell out of there."

"Bring me up to speed. I hate feeling left in the dark."

Donovan grinned. "A new baby will do that to you."

Sam rubbed a hand over his unshaven jaw and barely managed to stifle a yawn. He was deeply and madly in love with his new daughter, but she was a whole new experience. Sophie was tired and trying to do it all in her quest not to interfere with the goings-on at KGI since Garrett was off on a mission, but Sam had nipped that in the bud quick.

She had exhausted herself by trying to do too much too soon and he'd put her to bed and taken over baby duty. Only Charlotte hadn't expressed a whole lot of interest in sleeping. She'd alternated fussing with wide-eyed staring at her father. She seemed perfectly content to be held. As soon as Sam tried to put her down, she put up a fuss that had him scrambling to soothe her before she woke Sophie up.

"Nothing in my years in the army prepared me for having a baby," Sam said wearily. "It's not for pussies, that's for sure."

Donovan chuckled. "Think how Sophie feels."

"Yeah, I know. I don't know how she does it. I had to make her take some downtime. She was running herself ragged trying to do everything."

"I thought Rachel coming over was nice," Donovan said.

"I have to admit, I was a little worried about how she'd take Sophie having a baby. She was so devastated when she remembered having the miscarriage."

Sam ran his hand over his face, wiping some of the sleep from his eyes. His younger brother's wife had spent a year a prisoner in South America, leaving Ethan and the rest of the family to think she was dead. When they discovered she was alive, KGI had gone in with the full force of their resources and rescued her, but she'd come home missing memories of her life—and of her difficulties in her marriage to Ethan.

"I was worried too. I wouldn't have her hurt for the world," Sam said. "Sophie was concerned too. She was reluctant to take the baby over to Mom's because she was worried about hurting Rachel."

"Sophie's a doll," Donovan said. "You're lucky to have her."

Sam smiled at that. "Yeah. Damn lucky."

"And Rachel has handled it well. She and Ethan have been doing so much better. She seems . . . stronger lately. I'm seeing more and more of the Rachel we knew before she disappeared."

The security doors opened and Sam swiveled to see Ethan walk into the war room. "Hey man," Sam greeted. "What are you doing here?"

"I was under the impression I was on your payroll now, even if I do still draw the pussy missions," Ethan said dryly.

"We were just talking about Rachel," Donovan said by way of subtly reminding Ethan why he was still drawing the light-duty tasks.

"Yeah? Any reason in particular?"

"No, just remarking on how much better she seems to be doing," Sam said. "I'll be honest. We were worried how she'd take the new baby. I worried it would upset her. Bring back bad memories."

Ethan shoved his hands into his pocket and rocked back on his heels. His expression was bland, but Sam could see the unease in his brother's stance. Rachel's miscarriage had been a catalyst for a chain of events that had led to the complete unraveling of Ethan and Rachel's marriage. Ethan still struggled with the guilt for what his wife had gone through and what she continued to battle on a daily basis.

"I think she'd like to try to get pregnant again."

Both Sam and Donovan exchanged surprised looks and then Sam went back to Ethan to check his reaction. He didn't look thrilled.

"How do you feel about that?" Sam asked.

"Christ but I hate these conversations," Ethan muttered. "She hasn't said anything. It's just a feeling I get. Or maybe I still just feel like a shithead and I'm projecting. Don't you love all the new words you learn in therapy?"

Donovan chuckled. "Okay, but you didn't answer the question. Are you guys ready for that kind of step?"

"No," Ethan said bluntly. "She's not ready. Damn it, she's still so fragile. If . . . if she got pregnant and miscarried again, I don't even want to imagine how she'd react. I don't think we can deal with that right now when she's getting better. It's like . . . God, there are times when it's just like old times. Before I fucked everything up. I feel like I have her back, the way she was before she forgot so much. I don't want to do anything to mess that up. I don't want her hurt again. I just want to protect her and make her happy."

"That's understandable," Sam said. "I get it, man. I really do. I'd do a hell of lot to make Sophie happy."

Ethan cupped his nape and glanced over at Donovan. "I didn't come over for couples therapy. I wanted to check in on Garrett and see what the hell is going on. No one's said jack to me beyond the fact Garrett was taking a job that Resnick asked him to take."

Donovan provided the details while Sam stood to the side and listened in. Damn but he was tired. And if he was tired, he couldn't imagine how wasted Sophie had to be. Her labor, despite its quick beginning, had actually gone longer than expected. And then there had been complications afterward. Not serious, but it had taken a lot out of her.

She and Charlotte were his world. And for the next few days, he was going to become even more intimately acquainted with his daughter, because her mother was going to do nothing but rest, if he had to all but tie her to the bed.

It took him a moment to realize that Ethan had asked him a question. He blinked and tuned back into the conversation. "What did you say about Rusty?"

"I talked to Sean yesterday. I wondered if he'd told you about what happened," Ethan said, a scowl darkening his face.

"About the Winfree punk roughing Rusty up and wrecking her car? Yeah, he told us. He also told us he threatened the little prick and scared him shitless," Sam said.

Donovan's eyes hardened. "I want to go over there myself. I may not see eye to eye with Rusty. Hell, half the time I wonder if Mom's lost her damn mind for taking on that project. But no little teenage bastard is going to get away with fucking with one of the family, Kelly-born or not. Any guy who goes around manhandling a teenage girl ought to have his balls removed and shoved down his throat."

"Part of this is our fault," Sam said evenly. "We haven't exactly been accepting of Rusty. Most of the time, we ignore her existence. That's created two problems. One, she doesn't feel like she can come to us with a problem like that. Hell, if Sean hadn't come up on her right after it happened, she probably never would have told anyone. And the little bastard probably would have went after her again and succeeded. Two, because we haven't been accepting of her, others pick up on our disinterest. We've done her a disservice. Whether we approve of her or not, she's a part of this family. She deserves our protection and she damn sure needs to feel like she can come to one of us if she's getting grief from some asshole at school."

Ethan sighed. "You're right. We've made her an outsider despite the fact that Mom has declared her a member of the family. No matter what our feelings, everyone else needs to know that she's one of us and no one fucks with the Kellys."

"That deserves a hooyah," Donovan said with a grin.

Ethan looked at him in mock horror. "Garrett would kick your ass over that. A Marine allowing a navy salute past his lips?"

"Garrett's too busy corralling his lady to worry about me," Donovan said with a smug grin.

Sam and Ethan looked at each other and then back at Donovan. "Okay, what's the deal? And you better spill," Sam threatened.

The look of unholy glee in Donovan's eyes made Sam feel instantly sorry for Garrett before even hearing the situation.

Whatever it was, he was probably already taking some heavy-duty shit from Donovan.

"Come on, give it up, Van," Ethan said.

"Sarah Daniels has Garrett chasing his tail and not in a fun way. He's been acting awfully strange about her. When I volunteered to take over the mission when he was home a few days ago, he damn near took my head off. He's got that possessive caveman thing going." Donovan looked at Ethan and smirked and then yanked his thumb in Sam's direction. "You know, like lover boy over here got when Sophie landed in our backyard."

Sam scowled. "Fuck you, Van."

"I'm hearing that a lot lately," Donovan said with exaggerated hurt.

Ethan rubbed his jaw in a thoughtful manner. "It's not unusual for Garrett to get all growly over a woman. He's extremely protective of Rachel. He'd take off someone's head if they posed any sort of threat to her."

"He didn't like Sophie at first," Sam pointed out.

"This is different," Donovan insisted. "I'm telling you. There is something going on with Garrett this time. He gets awfully tense over Sarah Daniels. They're heading to Alaska as we speak. I sent Steele and part of his team ahead. I don't have a good feeling about this."

Sam frowned. "Think we should go then?"

"I think the both of you are fine right where you are for the time being," Donovan said. "Your wives need you. I still have Rio and his team on tap, and I'm free if he needs more. Steele, Cole and P.J. are there and are providing protection. I have every confidence that they'll more than be able to handle anything that comes up."

CHAPTER 23

SARAH melted into the front seat of the black SUV and waited anxiously for Garrett to walk around to the driver's side after he closed her door. Thanks to his caution, she was now fully convinced people were poised to jump out of the trees at every turn.

Garrett tossed her bag and his into the backseat and then slid into the front. He quietly shut his door then cranked the engine. As he put it in gear, he glanced over at her.

"You okay?"

She gave a nervous nod.

"We've got a drive ahead of us, so get comfortable, but don't let your guard down. If I tell you to do something, do it. No questions."

Again she nodded and he started forward, navigating around the heavy tree cover where he'd parked the SUV.

They rocked and bumped over the broken-paved road toward the small village several miles away. But he turned off about a mile out of town and took an even smaller, one-lane dirt road to the north.

As if sensing her question, he said, "I want to stay off the main roads as much as possible and out of towns if I can help it. If I found you, so can others."

She grimaced. "I made it that easy to find me?"

"Sorry, sweetheart, but it wasn't that difficult. There isn't much my brother can't find out about someone. He probably knows your bra size."

She glared over at him. "I see. And did he share this information with you too?"

Garrett grinned. "No need. I plan to find out that one myself."

Her eyes widened and then she laughed at the blatant flirting. Just when she thought she had him figured out, he always did something to unbalance her. He might appear to be the uptight, grumpy person he swore his brothers labeled him, but he was also fun and a huge flirt. He was also extremely sensitive though if she told him that, he'd probably shoot himself. Or her.

"I've been so careful. Or I've tried to be. I still don't understand how anyone found me on Isle de Bijoux."

He gave her a look that suggested it was a stupid question and didn't require an answer.

"Clearly I'm not cut out for a life on the run."

"Why Isle de Bijoux anyway? It was a good choice. An obscure location. You just didn't cover your tracks well enough."

"You'll think it's stupid."

"Try me."

"After I took a cab to the airport in Boston, I picked the first flight out that I could book, which happened to be a nonstop to Miami. On the flight there, I sat next to a couple who were continuing on to Isle de Bijoux. I thought it sounded like a good plan since it wasn't an island I'd heard of. Since I'd made it easy to track me to Miami, when I arrived there, I hired a private Cessna and paid for it via a wire transfer from a bank account Marcus had set up for me years earlier." She grimaced. "It was the first time I've ever used his money. The idea always made me uncomfortable before, but I was desperate and knew I didn't have a choice."

"It wasn't a bad plan on the fly," Garrett conceded. "Unpredictability is always an advantage. If you can keep the people looking for you off balance, you can stay ahead of them with better success."

She swallowed and began her next question hesitantly.

"Could you arrange a fake passport, birth certificate, driver's license? All that stuff?"

He yanked his head around to look at her. "It's a little late to be thinking of all that now."

She growled in frustration. "Yes, I understand. Believe me I get it by now. I'm a fuckup. I suck at subterfuge. I can't lie worth a damn and I don't have a clue how to take care of myself. Well damn it, give me some credit for trying. It's not like I *want* to be some helpless twit."

His lips twitched suspiciously and he stared ahead at the road. "I was only going to say that it's not necessary now. I'll make sure you have everything you need, Sarah. I'm not about to give you the tools to ditch me again."

"It's not like it was personal," she muttered. "I didn't want you to get hurt. I didn't want me to get hurt. At the time I thought you were some poor ex-military guy who'd been injured and needed a vacation. The last thing I wanted was for you to get caught up in my mess."

"Hey I was a poor ex-military guy recovering from a wound," he protested. "I didn't lie about taking a bullet for my sister-in-law. It was a bonding experience for both of us."

She rolled her eyes and shook her head. "Are you sure it wasn't your sister-in-law who shot you? I have a feeling you're an infuriating person to be around on a constant basis."

He flashed her a grin that did suspicious things to her insides. "Well, now, I guess you're going to find out, aren't you?"

God help her but she was, and the fact that her insides lit up just a little at the thought made her smile. Then she frowned. "Oh my God. Patches! I didn't even ask you about the cat. Is she okay? Did you take care of her?"

He looked startled by the abrupt change in topic. "Yeah, I gave her to the lady who owns the bookstore. I'm sure Patches is very happy."

She sighed in relief. As ridiculous as it seemed to worry over a cat when she had so many other problems, the idea of the cat being alone and hungry bugged her endlessly.

"Thanks. That was a nice thing for you to do."

He scowled as if the last thing he wanted to be considered was nice.

"Do you know where you're going?" she asked as she stared dubiously into the night. There wasn't much recognizable, just landscape blanketed in black. There weren't even any stars out.

Fog hovered low to the ground and swirled around their headlights, making long-distance visibility impossible. It was spooky and only fired her already overactive imagination.

"I don't, but the trusty GPS does."

He tapped on the GPS mounted in the dashboard as he spoke and once again she felt like an idiot.

"I'll just shut up now," she sighed.

"Try to relax. I'd like to get out of Mexico as soon as possible. I hope you peed before you left."

She chuckled and leaned back in the leather seat.

They drove for an hour, but they couldn't have traveled very far because the road was impossible and visibility was so poor that he couldn't drive much more than twenty-five miles per hour for the majority of the time.

She'd just closed her eyes when she heard him swear under his breath. The truck ground to a halt and she popped open her eyes to see the road blocked by what looked to be the local police, or whatever it was they called Mexican law enforcement.

Garrett reached hastily into his pocket, pulled out a small electronic device and then reached under his seat. His hand came back up empty. He glanced once her way but then focused his attention to the roadblock before them.

"Listen to me, Sarah. I want you to sit tight, and don't say a word," Garrett said in a low voice. "I'm outnumbered and I don't want to do anything that puts you at risk. Which means I'm going to have to cooperate with these assholes."

Dread filled her stomach and rose into her throat, tightening until it was hard to breathe. Cooperate? Outnumbered? This sounded bad. Really, really bad. Three police cars were parked at angles and at least seven men were standing in the road. They began approaching the SUV with automatic rifles held high. One man shouted in Spanish.

Garrett kept his hands on the steering wheel and Sarah flinched when one of the men jerked open her door. At the same time, Garrett's door flew open and the officers motioned for them both to get out.

Sarah looked at Garrett, her heart damn near pounding out of her chest. He gave a short nod and then ducked out of the truck, careful to keep his hands up.

"No habla Español," Garrett said when one of the men barked at him in rapid-succession Spanish.

To Sarah's horror, the man drew his baton and rammed it into Garrett's stomach. Another officer cracked his baton over Garrett's head, dropping him to the ground. She screamed and tried to run for Garrett, to cover him, to somehow protect him from the unexpected attack.

She was quickly intercepted, a strong arm wrapping around her waist. The policeman who grabbed her uttered a guttural command she didn't understand when she kicked and fought like a woman possessed. It didn't take a rocket scientist to figure out he was telling her to cease and desist, but she wasn't about to let them beat Garrett to death.

She twisted in his arms and jabbed her fingers in his eyes. He howled in pain and dropped her like a stone. She flew to Garrett and threw herself over his body just as one of the policemen was about to deliver another blow. She tensed, expecting the pain, but it never came.

"Goddamn it, Sarah, what the hell are you doing?" Garrett hissed.

"Saving your ass."

"Get up," one of the men said in strongly accented English. "Do it slowly, señor. You wouldn't want the lady to get hurt."

"Do as he says," Garrett ordered. "And for God's sake, don't do anything to piss them off."

Strong fingers curled around Sarah's arm and hauled her off Garrett. She stumbled and nearly fell as she was shoved against the hood of the SUV. Garrett picked himself up off the ground and no less than three guns were pointed at him as he stood to his full height.

Two of the policemen went to the SUV and pulled out the bags from the back seat. They emptied the contents onto the ground, the first being Sarah's clothing. Humiliation burned in her throat as the men laughed when her underwear fluttered to the ground.

Next they pulled out Garrett's arsenal, frowning and talking to each other. They gestured at Garrett and rattled off more

Spanish as they picked through all his weapons. Guns still drawn on Garrett, the police officers converged and motioned for Garrett to turn around and face the vehicle.

They began patting him down and even she was amazed by the number of weapons they pulled from his belt, pockets and pants. Panic scuttled around her stomach until she was ready to puke. This couldn't be good.

Two of the men seized Garrett by the arms and directed him toward the backseat of the SUV. Before they stuffed him inside, they cuffed his hands behind his back and then slammed the door behind him. And suddenly their entire focus was on her and she'd never been so terrified in her life.

One wrapped his hand in her hair and yanked her sideways toward the other passenger door. She stumbled after him on tiptoe, drawn up by his grip on her hair. He opened the door and shoved her inside but didn't cuff her as they'd done Garrett. She landed with a thud against Garrett and stayed there, preferring the comfort of his body over the alternative.

Two men got into the front while the others returned to their vehicles. The SUV fell into line between two of the police cars and they raced down the narrow road too fast for the condition of the road or the weather.

"Where are they taking us?" she asked fearfully. "They didn't even ask us for identification or anything. They didn't say why they were detaining us."

"They won't," Garrett said grimly.

His voice was barely a whisper against her ear and she stayed in her position so they wouldn't be overheard.

"They aren't police," he continued. "They're not very discreet with their conversation."

"But I thought you didn't speak Spanish?"

"That's what I told them," he murmured.

Try as she might, she couldn't keep her voice from shaking. "What do they want?"

"Ransom. It isn't an uncommon practice. But listen to me, Sarah. No matter what happens, you do nothing to draw attention to yourself, do you understand me? No matter what they do to me, you aren't to put yourself in the way."

His voice was fierce and brooked no argument.

"Promise me," he demanded.

She nodded, knowing it was a lie.

One of the men turned around, baton in hand and swung in Sarah's direction. "Do not talk!" he said.

Garrett shoved her over and turned so that the blow landed on his shoulder. "Stay down and out of his way," he ordered.

Not wanting Garrett to suffer anymore, she huddled in the seat and remained silent as they bounced recklessly down the road. It was at least another hour before they came to a stop. The headlights slashed over a hacienda-style house with an iron gate. After a moment, the gate swung open and the vehicles drove the short distance to a circular drive in front of the house.

Again, the back doors opened and Sarah found herself hauled out. Garrett fared no better, and the men took it upon themselves to land a few more blows as they herded Garrett toward the front door.

She was sick with fear and fury. He couldn't defend himself with his hands cuffed behind his back and the bastards were taking full advantage.

"Stop it!" she screamed when at the steps, one of the men slammed his baton viciously into Garrett's back.

Garrett's knees buckled and he went down on one knee. He staggered back up and pinned her with his ferocious stare. "Damn it, Sarah, you promised me."

She bit her lip to keep the sob from welling out.

She was dragged through the front room and unceremoniously shoved into a room in the back that had bars over the window and a cement floor. It was, for all practical purposes, a jail cell. A ratty mattress lined one wall and in the center was what looked to be an old bloodstain.

Oh God, what hell had they stumbled into?

A single lightbulb hung from the ceiling and the man reached up and smashed it with his baton, plunging the room into darkness. She went cold. Ice invaded her veins as he trailed his fingers up her arm.

Fear. Panic. Horrible, unending shame. Memories crowded her mind until she wanted to scream them away.

She would die before she let another man take from her what she wasn't willing to give.

To her surprise, the man stepped away, leaving her standing in the middle of the room. Then he simply left and closed the door behind him.

She waited a few moments and flew to the door, testing the knob. It didn't budge, not that expected it to. She stared around, her eyes adjusting somewhat to the dark. Only a narrow beam shone from underneath the door, and it wasn't enough to make out much.

A light from outside cast just enough illumination through the window that she could make out her surroundings. Barely.

She began to pace back and forth, her mind short-circuiting with all that had happened. She didn't understand any of it. And she was scared out of her mind for Garrett.

Where had they taken him? What were they doing? What did they want?

She heard raised voices in Spanish and then in broken English. She strained to hear. Something. Anything. She listened for Garrett but never heard him utter a word. She jumped when she heard a crash. It sounded like a chair being knocked over to the floor.

Several long minutes elapsed. Silence. No voices.

Then the low murmur of voices again. She pressed her cheek to the filthy door listening and straining.

A sound filtered through from the next room and she froze. She didn't even breathe as a sick knot grew in her stomach. It sounded like . . . Oh God, there it was again.

It was the unmistakable sound of an object hitting flesh.

It was slow and methodical. Rhythmic almost. Garrett never made a sound and the beating only got louder and more forceful. She covered her ears, trying to shut out the horrible reality. Numb to her toes, she shuffled to the far side of the room, wanting nothing to do with the bloodstained mattress.

Her eyes stung and watered as the sound echoed again, and she slid down the wall, her knees hunched to her chest. She hadn't cried for herself. She couldn't. But when she heard Garrett's muffled sound of pain—the first noise he'd made at all—she bowed her head as the sobs welled in her throat. And she cried.

CHAPTER 24

WHEN the door opened, the flash of light blinded Sarah. She had no idea the passage of time, only that each minute that had passed had seemed an eternity. Her face was ravaged and raw, her eyes swollen. She scrambled to her feet as Garrett was shoved into the room.

The door slammed shut behind him, plunging the room into temporary darkness once more.

She rushed forward just as Garrett went to his knees. He put one hand down to brace himself and clutched his abdomen with his other.

"Oh my God," she whispered, her voice hoarse from crying. "Garrett, are you okay?"

She dropped down and wrapped her arms around him, holding on to him so he didn't fall completely down. His breaths came in low pain-filled rasps and he knelt there, leaning into her for a long moment.

"What did they do? Why did they do this?"

She could barely get the words out around her sobs.

"I'm okay," he said in a low voice. "Give me a minute."

She could feel his battle as he struggled for control. Then slowly he wrapped an arm around her waist, pulling her closer into him. He rested his forehead on her shoulder and sucked in long, steadying breaths.

She ran her hands over his back and up his sides, and then she pulled away to slide her fingers over his face and down his chest, feeling for blood or swelling. When she reached his mouth, her fingers came away slick with blood and her heart leapt.

"You're bleeding. Where else are you hurt? What did they do to you?"

"It's not too bad. Help me over to the mattress."

When she tried to rise supporting him, her knees buckled but she jammed one foot back to brace herself and willed herself not to stagger under his weight. By sheer determination, she managed to maneuver him over to where the bloodstained mattress lay, and her spirits plummeted even more as she realized that this wasn't the first time someone had been beaten and left in this room.

He went down onto the thin mattress, which did little to shield him from the hardness of the floor. She tried to help him lie down, but he put a hand down to block her effort.

"Don't. Let me do it. Only hurts when I try to move too fast."

She backed hastily away, not wanting to add to his discomfort. When he was settled on his side, she pushed forward again and knelt over him, unsure of what to do or even what she could do. She'd never felt so helpless in her life.

"What did they do?" she whispered again.

"Beat the hell out of me," he gritted out. "Mostly ribs. Hurts like hell to breathe. Everything else is okay though. Nothing broken."

Tears gathered in her eyes again and she leaned down, gently wrapping her arms around him. She didn't know what else to do—she wanted to offer comfort if nothing else.

He raised his hand and brushed it over her cheek, wiping at the wetness there. "Ah, Sarah, don't cry for me, honey. I've been in worse situations. This is nothing. Believe me."

She didn't want to know about those other situations. She hadn't lived through those with him. She'd lived through the sounds of his beating and knew there was nothing she could do to stop it. Rage built in her veins until her blood simmered and boiled like a volcano about to erupt.

"Those bastards," she spat. "Those goddamn bastards. Why did they do this? What do they want?"

His hand absently stroked through her hair, offering her comfort, and that only shamed her all the more. She hadn't been the one subjected to such brutality. She caught his hand and held it to her cheek, rubbing against his palm.

"Information," he said. "They aren't police. Not in an official capacity, although they probably have a pretty damn tight stranglehold on this part of the region. They want money. Want to know who I am and what potential threat I pose to them. They want ransom. These roadblocks are routine in some of the less-developed areas where the law is a nebulous being and left up to the ones doing the enforcing."

"What do we do?" she whispered.

"We wait," he said simply. "And in the meantime, you do nothing, and I mean *nothing* to draw their ire. You become invisible and if they question you, you cooperate. You do whatever it is you have to do to survive. I'll get us out of this, I swear."

She could feel his gaze burning into her even though the darkness prevented her from seeing much more than the outline of his face. He caressed her cheek, rubbing his thumb over her skin as she continued to rub against his palm. She knew what he was telling her. Don't fight. Even if it came to the worst. And he knew what he was asking because he already knew what she'd endured.

It was telling that even now when he was so beaten that his strength held them both up. It bled into her soul and firmed her resolve. If he could endure so much, then so could she.

"You survive, Sarah. Let me take the heat. It's nothing I haven't endured before and likely will again. My job takes me into bad situations all the time. It's knowledge I live with on a daily basis. Have faith that I can endure and don't react to anything they do to me."

Hot tears slipped over his fingers. "But this time . . . this time you're here because of me."

"This isn't your fault."

He slipped his hand around her nape and tugged her down until his lips touched hers. It was just a gentle brush and he was careful to keep the side of his mouth that was bleeding from her lips.

"Come here," he urged as he pulled her down farther.

"I don't want to hurt you," she protested.

"You won't. Lie next to me. Let me hold you."

"No," she said. "I'll hold you."

She could hear the smile in his voice when he spoke. "I won't argue one bit. Come hold me then."

Carefully she stretched out beside him, mindful of the injuries to his ribs. Only when he coaxed her closer, did she put herself flush against his body. Then she curled her arm over his waist and nuzzled her cheek against his chest.

"I'm sorry," she said, not knowing what else to offer. Her heart ached and she was so damn angry that she wanted to rage against the bastards who'd done this. She'd doubted that she would have the wherewithal to shoot a person when she'd procured the pistol, but now she knew without a doubt that she could. Without hesitation.

Hate was an emotion that she'd done without for most of her life. She hated Allen Cross and his bastard brother as much as she imagined ever hating anyone, but here and now, her anger was a terrible, ugly thing. It consumed her and with it came a hatred she didn't think she was capable of.

"Shhh," he said against her hair. "You have nothing to be sorry for."

"What now?" she asked, infusing strength into her voice. She didn't want to come across as a whiny twit. She wanted to sound positive and as confident as he did. The least she could do was offer whatever support she could.

"They'll probably leave us here. No food or water. Try to wear me down. Then they'll probably take another shot at me. If that doesn't work, they'll use you."

Despite her resolve not to show weakness, she couldn't control the shiver that racked her body.

"They're not going to get that far. My team will come for us, Sarah. I just have to buy us enough time for them to get here. That's why I want you to keep your head down. They will come for us. You can help me by doing as I ask you."

"Okay," she whispered.

He squeezed her a little and then tensed in pain. She raised her head and found his lips there in the dark. She didn't care about the blood. All she cared about was finding him, showing him her love. And maybe give him something of herself when he'd already given so much to her.

Love.

It was nothing like the movies or books. No big lightning bolt from the sky where she instantaneously discovered she'd fallen in love. As if it were something random, like winning the lottery or a momentary high caused by hormones.

Maybe she'd started falling the day he saved her on the island. Or when he left her books with wine and chocolate on her porch. Or maybe it was his unwavering devotion to keeping her safe.

What she knew was that he was a good man, the kind she'd always dreamed of having. Loyal and protective. Willing to sacrifice for her. But love also meant sacrificing for him, and no matter her promise, she could not and would not go down without a fight. She wouldn't allow him to suffer endlessly while they waited for rescue.

And what she knew was that she had fallen and was still falling for the badass with the big heart and gentle soul.

She whispered the words in her mind, savoring them as she rested in his arms. Now wasn't the time for emotional outbursts, but when they were safe—and they would be because she believed him without reservation—then she'd tell him what she thought about the man he was. The man she wanted.

And if he walked away, she'd never have any regrets. Love was a gift, but it was up to the recipient to accept and cherish or to reject the offering. All she could do was give unreservedly. And for the first time since her assault, she realized that she could give something she'd never thought to give again. Her trust and her love.

CHAPTER 25

"SON of a bitch. Son of a bitch!" Donovan exclaimed.

He got up from the desk and hit the floor at a dead run. He left the war room and sprinted over to the house. He burst into the living room, where Sophie was feeding Charlotte. Sam was sprawled on the couch beside her and looked up in alarm when he saw Donovan.

Donovan didn't waste time trying to preserve Sophie's modesty. Nor did he bother trying to hold back so as not to frighten her. "We've got a situation."

Sam was on his feet in an instant. Sophie's eyes widened in alarm and the baby let out a mewl of protest.

"Garrett?" she asked fearfully.

"His locater was activated several hours ago," Donovan said to Sam.

"Why the hell didn't we know until now?" Sam demanded.

"Fuck if I know," Donovan bit out. "Signal may have been interrupted. Maybe it was the damn satellite. But the time stamp was during the night."

"What does that mean?" Sophie asked. "Is he in trouble?"

Sam gave a short nod. Then his expression softened as he looked at his wife and child. "He wouldn't have activated unless he was in trouble and needed help. It's our SOS system. It means he's down or in deep shit."

"Go," she said. "He needs you. I'll be fine. I have Marlene and Rachel."

Sam only hesitated a brief moment before leaning down to kiss Sophie and then Charlotte.

"Bring him home, Sam," she said in an urgent voice.

"I will, baby. I promise."

Donovan had already turned and ran back toward the war room with Sam on his heels.

"Rio will be closest. I'll reroute Steele and his team from Alaska, but we'll get there first after Rio," Donovan said. "I don't know what we're dealing with but I'm going to assume the worst and pull every available man to get the hell down there."

While Donovan hailed Steele and gave him the order to pull out, Sam picked up the phone and punched in a number. A few moments later, he said, "Ethan, Garrett's in trouble. We need you."

Donovan was already opening the gun locker. He pulled out an array of weapons and tossed two rifles in Sam's direction. When they had their gear packed, they hustled out to the truck.

"I'll drive. We'll swing by to get Ethan and then head to the jet. You raise Rio and give him the coordinates," Sam said.

The drive was silent, but Donovan knew Sam was as worried as he was. And Donovan blamed himself. He should have put a team with Garrett from day one. When he smelled a rat, he put Rio and Steele in place but it was too little, too late. He should have hog-tied Garrett to a chair if necessary to make sure he didn't go to Mexico alone.

It was always the cake jobs that went all to shit.

GARRETT lay with Sarah in his arms listening to the quiet rhythm of her sleep. He'd shamelessly lied to her about the condition he was in. Not that he was ready for a pine box, but his ribs hurt like a bitch, and he hadn't been able to sleep for the discomfort.

But he hadn't wanted to scare her any more than she already was. He was damn proud of her for not losing it completely. She was scared witless, but she was also one pissed-off woman. It was the pissed-off part that worried him.

Pissed-off women were unpredictable.

He'd lost sense of time but he figured it ought to be daylight soon. Sarah had slipped into an uneasy sleep during the night and when she stirred, he'd soothed and quieted her as much for her peace of mind as to prevent her from moving too much against his ribs.

He hoped to hell he'd told her the truth about what their captors would do. Again there was that whole predictability factor at work. And while it made sense that they'd leave them to worry and wonder over their fate, wear them down, they'd already proved what stupid sons of bitches they were. He didn't have a whole lot of faith in their intelligence.

He hadn't fought them, which rankled. He'd meekly gone along, like some lamb to a slaughter, because he hadn't wanted to risk anything happening to Sarah. If it had been him alone, he would have kicked some serious ass and enjoyed every minute of it. But Sarah was with him, and he'd die before allowing any harm to come to her.

His growing discomfort signaled a need to shift positions, but he didn't want to wake Sarah. She'd finally settled into a more peaceful rhythm and he liked the sensation of her warm breath on his neck.

She'd kissed him the night before. The first time she'd initiated any intimacy between them. It was soft and so damn sweet he'd been able to forget the pain for that barest moment when her mouth had met his.

When he could stand the position no longer, he tried to edge to the side so he could turn more fully onto his back. She came awake instantly, her head shooting off his shoulder. She leaned over him, her hair falling onto his chest as she stared down at him, concern blazing in her eyes.

"Are you okay? Are you hurting?"

"I didn't mean to wake you. I just need to turn onto my back for a while."

Her hands ran lightly over his chest as she helped him roll the quarter turn onto his back. He felt an instant relief as some of the pressure on his ribs subsided. His breaths came easier and he took in several deep ones.

"Better?"

"Better," he said. "Now come back here. I like you close to me."

She settled into the crook of his arm and laid her head on his shoulder. Her hand ventured lightly over his chest and down toward his ribs. It was cool against the heat of his pain. A soothing balm; he closed his eyes at the sheer pleasure of her touch.

"Am I hurting you?" she asked.

"No, don't stop. It feels damn good. I like you touching me."

He felt her smile against his shoulder.

Carefully she skimmed over his shirt, her touch so light it was almost not there. She rubbed a path to his belly and then back up again, taking care around his rib cage. Then she settled her palm against his chest, right over his heart as if reassuring herself that he was there and alive with her.

After a moment, she retraced her path downward again. He could stand it no longer. The damn shirt was in the way and he wanted to feel her hands on his bare skin like he wanted nothing else.

"Push up my shirt," he said. "Touch me, not my shirt."

He waited to see if she'd balk, but she lifted the end and slowly pushed upward until his shirt was bunched under his arms. Then she put her palm on his bare chest and he almost groaned from the sheer pleasure of it.

Such gentleness in the face of such violence and pain. So warm and sweet. He drank it up greedily, wanting to be soothed by her fingers.

When she ventured lower, down to the band of his pants, his body reacted. His dick surged to life and swelled, begging to be included in her tender ministrations.

Hell, the last thing he wanted was to frighten her or put her off.

"Watch your hand," he said hoarsely. "I seem to have this problem around you."

She chuckled softly and raised her head up again. "I wouldn't have imagined, I mean not now. You have to be hurting so much."

"I'm not dead," he muttered. "And my dick isn't particularly concerned with what the rest of my body's feeling."

To his further surprise, she leaned down and pressed her lips to his chest. She kissed him softly and then moved down an inch and kissed him again. All the while her palm smoothed over the skin of his belly awfully damn close to his waistband. The discomfort in his groin was fast overtaking the pain in his ribs.

"I don't want to hurt you," she whispered. "Tell me to stop if I do."

Like that was ever going to happen. He could be missing a leg and he'd be damned if he called a halt to her sweet seduction. An angel in hell. That's the only descriptor he could come up with. His sweet angel.

"I can guarantee that I'm not going to tell you to stop," he groaned. "I only wish to hell I could make love to you. I want to touch you, damn it."

Again her husky laughter washed over him like a healing wind.

She lovingly kissed and caressed every part of him that hurt. Every bruise. Every cut. Her soft mouth moved over his flesh as if she were absorbing the pain. She placed one hand on the other side of him and pushed herself up and over him until her hair fell down around his face. Then she lowered her lips tentatively to his.

The first brush tasted like ambrosia. Sweet. So damn sweet. Fire raced through his veins when the tip of her tongue rubbed shyly over his mouth. Her hand left the mattress and cupped his cheek. Her fingers stroked gently over his jaw, feathering up to his temple as she kissed around the cut at the corner of his mouth.

He'd give anything to be able to turn her over, hold her tight and slide between her legs. It certainly gave him incentive to get the fuck out of this hellhole, because when they did, he was going to do everything to her that he was currently fantasizing about.

She continued her gentle ministrations, touching, petting lightly and following her caresses with her lips. No part of his battered face and abdomen was left out of her sweet lovemaking. She soothed his aches and pushed away his pain, replacing it with warm pleasure.

Finally she lay her head on his chest and slid her hand over his belly in a light, comforting pattern. He raised his hand and thrust his fingers into her hair, enjoying something so simple as touching her.

He couldn't think. He could only feel. Mellow and content, his woman lying on his chest snuggled into his body. He covered her hand with his other one and squeezed, unable to voice all that he felt. She squeezed back as if understanding his silence.

They rested there, their fingers laced together, and forgotten for the barest moment, was the hell that waited.

CHAPTER 26

MARLENE pulled into Sam's drive and hurried toward the front door. She didn't bother to knock but simply pushed in and called Sophie's name.

Sophie rounded the corner, Charlotte bundled in her arms, and Marlene saw the worry reflected in her daughter-in-law's eyes. She held out her arms and went to pull both mother and child into her embrace.

"How are you doing?" she asked Sophie.

Sophie posted a brave smile. "The question is, how are you? I can't imagine how you do this so often with all your sons gone and not knowing if they're safe." A quick shudder rolled over her shoulders and Marlene reached to take Charlotte from her.

"Oh, I'm okay. Worried, of course, but you get used to it." She smiled down at her granddaughter. Love, so strong, rushed like a flood through her heart. "She's so beautiful, Sophie."

Sophie smiled, but it was a tired smile laced with the strain Marlene knew she felt. Marlene squared her shoulders and eyed her daughter-in-law. "I want you to pack what you need for several days. Then you and I are going to go get Rachel, and we're going to hole up at the Kelly headquarters, as I like to call it. Oh, I know Sam has his war room here but honestly, my house has and always will be Kelly central. At a time like this, family has to stick together."

Relief shone bright in Sophie's eyes and her shoulders sagged just a bit. "That sounds wonderful, Marlene. Being alone right now . . . well, it sucks."

Marlene laughed. "Well, of course it does. You have a new baby. You're tired. And your husband is gone to rescue that fool son of mine who doesn't think he needs anyone. Get your things. It'll be one big sleepover. We'll drive Frank out of his mind. He'll likely flee the premises before it's over with."

Sophie smiled, lighting up her entire face. "Give me just a few minutes to get what I need for Charlotte."

While Sophie went off to pack, Marlene settled on the couch and gazed down at her sleeping granddaughter. She was more concerned about Rachel, truth be told, which is why she had no intention of letting either of her daughters-in-law weather the next few days alone. Ethan still stuck close to Rachel most days, and when he did go off on assignment, Marlene made sure she wasn't alone. The entire family checked in on her, Garrett especially.

Rachel and Garrett shared a special bond, and with Garrett MIA and Ethan going into an unknown situation, Marlene didn't like to think about how upset Rachel would be.

And what she didn't want either Rachel or Sophie to know was how worried she was. Oh, she gave Sophie that song and dance about being used to it, but did a mother ever get used to saying good-bye to her sons and not knowing if they'd come back? It was a worry she lived with every day.

Garrett was the loner and self-sufficient. He was the steadfast one. He could always be counted on when the chips were down. But now he was the one in need, and Marlene couldn't get rid of the sick feeling in her stomach.

Sophie returned carrying a huge baby bag slung over her shoulder and an additional bag with her things in her other hand. "I'm ready."

Marlene rose. "We'll take my van. I had Frank install a car seat for Charlotte so she's all set."

The women hustled from the house and Marlene settled Charlotte into her seat in the back. They tossed Sophie's bags in the rear compartment and Marlene started for the driver's side. To her surprise, Sophie stopped her and pulled her into a huge hug.

"Thank you," Sophie whispered. "I told Sam to go. I wanted him to go. But after he left, all I could think was that I didn't want to stay in that house alone, worried out of my mind that something horrible has happened."

Marlene squeezed her back. "You're welcome, honey. That's what family is for."

When she pulled away, tears shimmered in Sophie's eyes. Then she smiled. "You know, I'm getting used to it. I never had a real family. It feels . . . nice."

"Well come on then. Let's stop with all the emotional girly stuff and go get Rachel."

Fifteen minutes later, Marlene pulled into the driveway of Ethan and Rachel's house. Before she could get out, Rachel came out onto the front porch, her face pale and her eyes troubled.

"You stay here with Charlotte," Marlene said to Sophie. "I'll leave the van running. We won't be but a minute."

She hurried out and Rachel met her at the bottom of the steps.

"Have you heard anything? What's wrong?"

Marlene took both of her hands in hers and wished like anything she could get rid of the shadows that still lurked in Rachel's eyes. "Nothing's wrong, baby. Nothing at all. I just decided that at times like these, family should stick together. I've come to collect my daughters and we're going to drive Frank out of house and home for the next few days. Now go pack a bag. You're coming with me. None of us should be alone right now."

The relief was staggering in Rachel's eyes. It was as if she was prepared to hear the very worst.

"I'm so worried about Garrett. And now Ethan. God, Marlene, what could have happened? I hate not knowing."

Marlene pulled Rachel's hands together and squeezed a little harder. "They're coming home to us, Rachel. Just like you did. My boys are fighters. They fought for you. They fight for others. They damn well will fight for each other. Now go get your things. Sophie and the baby are waiting for us in the van."

Without another word, Rachel turned and hurried up the

steps. Marlene sighed, pulled herself together and turned back to the van to wait. A few minutes later, Rachel came running out and climbed into the middle seat beside Charlotte's carrier.

Marlene glanced over at Sophie and then over her shoulder to Rachel. "Okay, girls. Let's go home."

Both women smiled and Marlene drove out of the driveway and turned toward home.

When they pulled up to Marlene's house, to her surprise, Rusty was sitting on the front steps. She rose when the van came to a stop but remained where she was as she watched the women get out and get their bags.

"I could use some help with Charlotte," Marlene called to Rusty.

Rusty moved forward, looking a little hesitantly at the baby in Marlene's arms. "You want me to take her?" She glanced over at Sophie and then back at Marlene.

Marlene arranged the baby in Rusty's arms, gave her the necessary instructions about supporting the head and then shooed her toward the house. Rusty had a mixture of terror and wonder in her eyes as she slowly turned away and went up the steps into the house.

Marlene shook her head as she went to the back to help Rachel and Sophie with their things. "I swear, you give a teenage girl a baby to hold and it's like an exorcism."

Sophie and Rachel both burst into laughter.

"There now, that's better," Marlene said, offering a squeeze to both their arms. "We look like we're heading to a wake."

As they started to the house, Frank appeared on the porch. He simply held out his arms to Rachel and Sophie and pulled them both to his chest in a tight hug. "How are my girls?"

"Better," Rachel said softly.

Frank kissed her cheek. "Well, good. I'm going to fire up the grill later. Thought we'd have steaks for supper."

"That sounds wonderful," Sophie said.

"And you," Frank said to Sophie. "You're going to get some rest, young lady. You look tired. That granddaughter of mine is cute as a button, but she's got her days and nights mixed up from the look of you."

Sophie gave him a wry smile. "I'm afraid you're right."

"Leave your bags on the porch. I'll get them in a minute," he said. And with that, he turned, still holding both of the women to his side and pulled them into the house.

Marlene stood for a moment simply watching her family do what they did best. Then she turned her eyes heavenward. "Take care of my boys," she whispered. "Bring them home to us. This family isn't whole without them."

CHAPTER 27

SARAH sat on the floor beside the mattress, knees drawn to her chest as Garrett dozed beside her. She didn't want to be scared, but the truth was she was terrified. She didn't want to not believe that she and Garrett would be rescued, but despite her efforts, doubt crept insidiously into her mind.

He'd been right so far, though. Throughout the long day, their captors had left them alone in the dark and silence. No sounds could be heard through the door. No food. No water. The food didn't bother her yet, but she was thirsty.

Thoroughly humiliated by the fact that there was no place to relieve herself, she'd waited until Garrett had nodded off before crouching in the corner. She'd die if he'd been awake to witness her mortification.

She put her head down on her knees and rocked back and forth, trying to keep her focus, trying not to let panic overwhelm her. Garrett needed her strong, not helpless.

Not knowing the extent of his injuries worried the hell out of her. Every so often, she leaned over him to hear the reassuring sounds of his breathing. And then she resumed her vigil, sitting and waiting. Watching over Garrett as he'd watched over her.

Garrett stirred and she picked up her head to see him

raising his head to look around. His gaze found hers, and he reached for her hand as if to reassure himself she was there and safe. She took it and squeezed.

"How are you?" she whispered.

"I'm good. Don't worry. Just sore. I don't think it's as bad as it felt like at the time."

The cheer he forced into his voice melted her heart. He was doing everything he could to keep her spirits up and keep her optimistic.

"So you're ready to go kick some ass then," she teased. "What are you waiting for? I'm sure between us we can break the door down."

"Maybe not that chipper yet," he said dryly. "Can you help me sit up? I want to test the ribs out."

She got to her knees and looped his arm around her shoulders. "Ready?"

"Ready."

He grunted once as he pushed to a sitting position.

"Are you okay?" she asked anxiously.

He sat there for a moment catching his breath and then rubbed his hand over his midsection. "I'm good. Just bruised, I think. They seemed pretty careful to rough me up without breaking anything. Nothing feels broken anyway. Just stiff and sore."

She kept his arm over her shoulders and leaned into his side. She wrapped her arms around his waist and laid her head against him.

"I know you're scared, Sarah. But we'll get through this. I promise. My team will come."

She pressed her lips together for a short moment and then asked the question plaguing her since the night before when he'd told her the same thing. "How will they know? I mean, how will they know where to find us?"

He turned his face into her head and pressed his lips to her temple. "Tracking device. Our SOS system, so to speak. I activated it when we hit the roadblock and tossed it under the front seat of the SUV."

"So you knew," she murmured.

"That we were in bad shape? Yeah. And if it had turned into a false alarm, I could have always checked in, but nothing about that situation looked anything but fucked-up."

She laughed softly. "Anybody ever tell you that you have a way with words?"

"All the time," he drawled.

He reached under her chin and nudged upward. "Come here," he said as he lowered his mouth.

She went willingly, fusing her lips to his. Before she'd been achingly gentle with him, not wanting to hurt him. She'd wanted to offer comfort—and her love. Now, she kissed him desperately, wanting and needing his warmth and comfort.

He let his hand slid up to cup her face, and he held her there as he fed from her mouth. He was every bit as impatient as she felt, hungry and a little wild. He took her breath—returned it—then took it again, the exchange of hot, moist air elevating the itchy desire that grew with every moment she spent with him.

He drew away and stared down at her, stroking her cheek. "I hope to hell this isn't one of those situations where you go a little crazy because we're in a bad situation and you don't think we're going to get out so you do stuff you'd never dream of otherwise. Because baby, when we get out of here, I'm going to spend two days doing nothing but make love to you. And it won't have a damn thing to do with anything but the fact that I want to be inside of you more than I want to breathe."

Her breath hiccupped and stuttered. Her chest grew tight and she swallowed under the intensity of his gaze. Then she reached up to touch his face, allowing her fingertips to trace the strong lines of his jaw.

"I kissed you because I wanted to. That won't change tomorrow."

"It's a good damn thing," he growled.

He leaned in to kiss her again when a noise outside the door made him go rigid.

"Get behind me," he ordered. "Do it now. Don't make a goddamn sound. Don't talk. Don't react. You pretend you're invisible. You got it?"

Every single part of her wanted to argue like hell, but she did what he asked and scrambled behind him and made herself as small as she could against the wall.

The door burst open bringing with it a blinding flood of light. Garrett bolted to his feet, and she didn't know how he'd done it so fast and with such ease. It had to have been excruciating.

He stood, in an almost a casual pose, but his hands were fisted at his sides. A stream of Spanish erupted from the doorway and two of the men came into the room and took Garrett by the arms.

Fight, she silently willed him. Don't take it. But oh God, he went willingly and she knew why. She closed her eyes as the door shut and rage billowed inside her. He didn't want to do anything that would draw their attention to her. He didn't defy them, because he feared they'd retaliate by hurting her.

She rammed her fist into her mouth to stifle the sob that swelled like a malignant growth. She wouldn't cry. She wouldn't give in to the despair. Garrett would need her. Strong and steady. Like him. She wouldn't fail him. Not when he was sacrificing so much for her.

Bolting to her feet, she ran to the door and pressed her ear against it, straining to hear. She had to know. She didn't want to, but she owed that much to Garrett, to know what was being done to him.

The murmur of voices continued forever. They were questioning him in broken English and his answers were clipped, noncommittal, the subtle version of go fuck yourself. After each negative response he gave, she tensed, expecting to hear the sound of them beating him.

But the questioning continued. She sagged against the door for what seemed like hours. Her legs were numb, her knees shaky and her entire body was bathed in perspiration.

And then it started. She flinched when the first sound of violence reached her. She held her breath until she was light-headed. More questions. Another strike. They were slower and seemingly more measured this time.

Through it all Garrett remained silent, and she didn't know how. How could a person's will be so strong that they could suffer such pain and not give in to the urge to scream? When finally she heard the scrape of chairs and the sound of footsteps approaching the door, she flew back to the far wall, there next to the pallet. And she waited.

The door flew open, but this time, there was only one man and no sign of Garrett. He stared at her for a long moment and then crossed the room. He spit out a stream of Spanish and she never looked up, refusing to meet his gaze or to let him see how terrified she was.

He reached down and grabbed her hair with one hand and circled her arm with the other. He hauled her to her feet and shoved her toward the door, his grip never easing. The light blinded her and she closed her eyes and then blinked rapidly, trying to adjust as he forced her into the room.

She stumbled forward and gasped when she got her first good look of Garrett. He was tied to a chair, arms behind his back, completely vulnerable. Blood streamed from his nose and mouth. He looked tired and haggard, but the moment he looked up and saw her, something deadly entered his eyes.

They sharpened and where before he looked half unconscious, he was now fully alert, tense, his gaze taking in every detail.

The man standing to the side of Garrett put down the piece of wood in his hand and approached Sarah, his face expressionless. She looked past him, meeting Garrett's gaze, trying to infuse every ounce of her strength to him. She allowed no fear to show and it was the hardest thing she'd ever done. And she pleaded with him silently not to do anything crazy. Not to draw their wrath. He couldn't take much more.

The man circled her like a cat stalking his prey. He glanced up and down her body in a clear, suggestive manner and then he moved in close, his hand touching her cheek. She didn't flinch away, but neither did she look at him.

He turned then to Garrett all the while keeping his hand on her face, stroking up and down her cheekbone.

"My men are very eager to have your woman," the man said. "You've given me no reason to deny them."

This one spoke nearly perfect English, his accent light. It was clear he was the authority figure here. It was also clear that he was the one who'd inflicted the most damage to Garrett. It was all she could do not to ram her knee into his nuts.

But she stood there, stoic and unmoving, all the while staring at Garrett, telling him she was okay.

"Tell me what I want to know or I leave her to them."

Garrett's nostrils flared. His gaze was so deadly that she shivered under the impact.

"I'll tell you," he finally said. "Leave her alone. You'll never get what you want from her. It's me who can provide the ransom."

The man smiled, his eyes gleaming with triumph. "I had a feeling you'd see it my way." He turned and snapped his fingers at one of his men, who immediately came forward. The other man grabbed Sarah's arm and dragged her back toward the room. She turned her head, her gaze finding Garrett's one last time. To her astonishment, he winked at her. She almost missed the gesture, it was done so quickly. And just as fast, Garrett's focus was back on his captor.

Sarah found herself shoved once more into the dark room and the door shut behind her. She stumbled back over to the wall and this time, she lay on the mattress and curled into a tight ball. Something inside her had broken at the sight of Garrett. Nausea rose in her stomach and she scrambled to the corner as she heaved and gagged. There was nothing to come up, but her stomach still revolted. Dry heaves racked her body and she took in deep breaths, but the cloying smell of urine and sweat only made her sicker.

When she was finally able to gain control and stop the horrible twisting in her gut, she crawled back to the pallet and collapsed, weak and shaky—ashamed.

She had to get it together before they returned with Garrett—*if* they returned. These weren't men of honor. How was she to know they wouldn't kill him after he gave them what they wanted?

No, she wouldn't think of that. She couldn't. Garrett had promised her, and she believed him.

She lay there, eyes closed, sucking deep breaths and trying to ignore the horrible knot in her stomach. This time she didn't hear their approach. The sudden opening of the door startled her and she rose up on one elbow, shielding her eyes with the other. Garrett stumbled forward as he was shoved into the room, but this time he didn't go down. He stood defiantly until the door shut behind him and then he scanned the room. Looking for her.

He walked slowly toward her and then sank to his knees in front of the pallet where she lay. She opened her arms and swallowed back the sob. He gathered her close and, with a groan, lowered them both back to the pallet.

"I'm sorry," he murmured over and over. "I'd hoped they

wouldn't touch you, that you wouldn't be scared. I know you must have been terrified, but I'm so damn proud of you."

She pulled away and ran her hands over his face, wiping at the blood, uncaring that it stained her hands and clothes.

"It wasn't bad," he said quickly. "They figured out they weren't going to get anywhere with force. That's why they pulled you in. I should have done a better acting job. I could have pretended to be beaten down more. They would have left you alone then. Maybe."

The words tumbled out and she put a finger over his lips to silence him. He was apologizing. God. She replaced her finger with her lips and kissed him tenderly, peppering tiny little kisses over his bruised and battered mouth.

For a long while they lay in silence, tangled together, exchanging the occasional kiss.

"What now, that you've told them what they wanted to know?" she asked softly.

"I didn't tell them shit. I was just trying to buy us some time before. Time for my team to get here. I gave in now because by the time they figure out it was a bunch of nonsense, we should be out of here."

He sounded so sure that it elevated her flagging confidence.

"You need rest," she said. "For when your team gets here so you can help kick butt."

He chuckled. "Bet your ass."

"Garrett?"

"Yes, baby."

"Are you really okay? I mean, you don't need to tell me you are just to make it seem not so bad. I want to know."

He made a disgruntled sound. "I've been better. But I've been worse. I'll be fine."

"Tough guy," she chided.

"Bet your ass," he said again.

"Know what I want when we get out of here?"

"Me? Naked?"

She blushed and buried her head in his shoulder. "Besides that."

He laughed. "Okay, I give up."

"One of your three-course meat dinners. I'm thinking chicken, pork and steak will do nicely."

"Hell yeah," he breathed. "With ketchup."

"French fries," she said dreamily.

"And chocolate cake."

"Something caramel."

"You like caramel?" he asked.

"Oh yeah. My favorite. Anything caramel."

"Oh boy," he muttered. "I have a confession to make."

She lifted her head in curiosity.

"That time on the island when I brought you a chocolate bar?"

"Yeah."

"Well, I sort of had a chocolate and caramel bar in my stash too but I offered you the chocolate because caramel is *my* favorite."

"I should be pissed over that. Caramel hoarding is a sin."

"Yes, you should be," he agreed. "I'll make it up to you though. I make some of the best caramel num nums ever. It's the only thing besides meat that I can cook."

"Num nums?"

"Yeah, well, I don't know what the real name of it is. It's graham cracker crumbs with caramel poured over with a thin layer of chocolate on top. They're so damn good all you can say when eating them is num num num."

Her shoulders shook as she laughed and she squeezed him. He winced and she backed off, an apology on her lips. He put his finger over her mouth. "No, don't say it. I like you touching me. I'm okay. Really."

"I want those caramel num nums," she whispered.

He leaned in to kiss her again. "You'll get them."

CHAPTER 28

SARAH came awake to the sounds of footsteps—heavy, hurried footsteps—outside the door. But what alarmed her more than the potential threat was the fact that Garrett didn't rouse from sleep. He was extremely alert and quick to pick up on any noises, but he lay still. She put her hand down to rouse him and wondered if he was unconscious and then she yanked her hand back just as the door burst open.

Enough was enough. The bastards weren't going another round with him. She lunged to her feet and flew across the room to plant herself between the man and Garrett.

"Enough, you bastard," she hissed. "Take me. You've done enough to him already. What use is he to you if you kill him? If you want your jollies then take me and do your worst. I've already been there and survived, and I'm not going to let an asshole like you break me either."

She yanked at her shirt, determined to distract him from his goal. She had it up and her bra pushed aside, prepared to take it all off it that's what it took, when the man reached out and grabbed her wrist, preventing her from baring any more flesh.

"Take me," she said desperately. "I'm willing. I'll do whatever you want. I won't fight you. Just leave him alone."

Tears gathered in her eyes but she squeezed them back as she defiantly faced down the man who'd come for Garrett.

"Sarah, honey, it's okay. He's one of mine," Garrett said from behind her.

She whipped around to see Garrett leaned up on one elbow as he tried to get up. Then she turned back to the man who still held her wrist.

"Sarah," the man said gently. "It's okay now. My name is Rio. I've come for you and Garrett. Everything is going to be fine."

As he spoke, he carefully pulled her clothing back into place as she stood shocked and appalled by what she'd just done. Behind Rio, another man barreled into the doorway and she took a quick step back. Her knees buckled as realization set in. They'd come. Just like Garrett had promised.

Rio caught her before she fell but she batted away his arms. "No, no, I'm fine. You need to see to Garrett. He's hurt. Don't worry about me. Please just help him."

"No one touches her, Rio." Garrett's softly issued warning floated through the room. "Make sure your men know."

A look of understanding passed between the two men and Rio motioned for the man behind him to come through. Sarah backed away, hugging herself as she watched the flurry of activity begin.

The second man stopped by her side and stood with his gun up, clearly protecting her. When she glanced up, he nodded respectfully. "I'm Terrence, ma'am. We're here to take you home."

Still numb, she turned to see Rio help Garrett to his feet. He leaned heavily on Rio as they stood a moment to allow Garrett to get his bearings.

"How bad is it?" Rio asked grimly. "I have to tell you, you look like shit, man."

Garrett cracked a grin. "I'd worry more if you told me how pretty I looked."

Terrence snorted. "I've seen prettier jackasses."

"It's not too bad. They were fucking amateurs," Garrett said. "I guess for that I can be grateful. They worked me over pretty good but it's mostly bruises."

Sarah shook her head, trying to take it all in. They were

standing around like this was some big joke. "We should go," she blurted. "He's not safe here. He needs a hospital."

"Come here," Garrett said, holding out his free arm to her.

She went instantly, anchoring herself to his side, holding on to him for dear life. Dear God, she was trying to keep it together but she could feel the hysteria rising like a tidal wave. She didn't know whether to laugh or cry.

He squeezed her to him and kissed the top of her head. "We're safe now. My team is here. They're not going to let anything happen to us."

Garrett felt the betraying tremble of her body and knew she was hanging on by a thread. He tried to step forward, still holding her next to him, but his body was stove up from the beatings and every muscle screamed in protest. He'd been still for too long and the simple act of moving was damn near impossible.

"I'm going to need help," he said to Rio.

Rio frowned, and Garrett knew he was thinking it had to be bad for Garrett to admit he couldn't walk out under his own steam.

"Take Sarah out first," he said to Terrence. "Rio and I will be right behind you." Then he looked down at Sarah. "Go with him, honey. I won't be far."

She glanced a little nervously at Terrence but stepped away from Garrett and then followed the big man out of the room.

"What the hell happened?" Rio asked bluntly.

"I got the shit kicked out of me. Stupid bastards nabbed us at a roadblock. Wasn't much I could do facing down seven armed men, and I had Sarah with me to protect. I activated the SOS and then tried to buy us as much time as possible."

"Did they hurt her?" Rio asked, a deep scowl working over his face.

"No, they left her alone. Dragged her out to make me cooperate when they figured out their methods of making me talk weren't working. Scared her, but she's been fierce."

"Yeah I got that. I think she would have taken me on when I came in the door."

"I've never seen anything like it," Garrett said softly. "For her to do that. You don't even realize the courage it took."

"I think I do. She's been hurt before."

Garrett nodded. "That she was willing to . . . for me. Damn but I'm furious and awed all at the same time. She's . . ."

"Yeah," Rio agreed. "Fierce."

Rio started forward but Garrett held back. "I don't know if Van briefed you or what all you know, but Marcus Lattimer hired us. That's the story. Sarah is his sister and she doesn't know. I don't want her to find out until I have a chance to tell her."

Rio nodded. "Van gave me the rundown. My men have been briefed. We're cool. We're not going to blow your cover. Now let's get the fuck out of here. If I had to guess, we don't have a lot of time before your brothers come in and start a fucking war with Mexico."

Garrett grinned. "Family motto. No one fucks with the Kellys."

With Rio's help, Garrett walked out of the room and then out to the front of the house, where the rest of the team was assembled. They passed the bodies of the men who'd held him and Sarah captive and he frowned at what Sarah had seen on her way out.

Rio shook his head. "Terrence wouldn't have let her see all that crap. I know my man better than that. He's real protective when it comes to women."

Garrett shook off Rio's hold as they exited the house and he breathed in the fresh air. He automatically looked for Sarah and saw her standing off to the side, her arms wrapped around herself. She looked pale and completely lost. Terrence hovered over her and was speaking to her in low tones, but Garrett wasn't even sure she heard. The three other members of Rio's team were spread out and on careful watch duty.

As soon as she looked up and saw him, she broke away and ran to him. He braced himself for impact and opened his arms, but she stopped in front of him and then carefully went into his embrace.

She buried her face in his chest and wrapped her arms around his waist. She shook like a leaf.

"We need to make tracks," he whispered softly.

She shuddered and tilted her head to look up at him. "I don't want to stay here a minute longer than necessary."

Garrett caught Rio's gaze over Sarah's head and tilted his

head in the direction of the SUVs. Rio nodded and then took a step toward Sarah.

"Sarah, we need to get you inside the vehicle where it's safe. Will you come with me?"

Rio kept a foot of distance between himself and Sarah and was careful to keep his voice measured. She wouldn't even meet Rio's gaze. A flush swept over her cheeks, and Garrett's heart clenched at the humiliation in her eyes. For her to feel shame for what she'd done for him—that she was willing to sacrifice for him—made him sick. He was damn sure going to have a heart-to-heart with her at the first opportunity, because no way in hell was he going to allow her to be embarrassed over trying to protect him.

"What about you?" she asked Garrett. "You're coming, right?"

There was fear in her voice despite the fact that her words came out steady. Her hand trembled in his and he squeezed reassuringly.

"I'm coming. I want you inside first. I'll need to go in the back and I want you in the middle where you're protected. There'll be men on either side of you. Rio's team." He lowered his voice. "They won't hurt you."

She squeezed back. "I know. If you trust them, so do I. I'm just so . . ." Her voice trailed off.

"Yeah, me too, honey. Me too. But we're going to make it just fine. And then I'm going to fulfill a little promise I made."

Her brow wrinkled in question.

"You. Me. Naked. Me inside you. As many times as I can get there."

Color bloomed in her cheeks and she glanced hastily at Rio to make sure his murmured words weren't overheard. Rio's expression never changed. Sarah looked back, her cheeks still flushed, but there was heat in her eyes. He'd purposely reminded her of what they'd shared and what they would share to ease some of her shell shock.

A smile glimmered on her lips when she looked back at Garrett.

"Go with Rio. I'll feel better knowing you're safe."

She nodded and eased her hand from his. He didn't want to let her go even for a minute, but he wanted her in the truck, under guard while he got the report from his men and they got the hell out of this damn country. Nothing good ever came of him being in Mexico.

He watched as Rio ushered Sarah into the backseat of the SUV and Terrence stood guard outside the door. Then Rio walked back over to where Garrett stood.

"Okay, man, what's the plan? You need a hospital and Sarah isn't going to be happy if you don't go. She's all sorts of worried about you."

"Fuck the hospital."

"Don't make me whip your ass in front of your woman. It would be humiliating."

"We have more important issues to worry about than a hospital. Besides that, I don't want Sarah out in public."

"Who said anything about Sarah going to the hospital?"

Garrett tensed and fixed Rio with his stare. "She stays with me."

"I hate to bring this up but it needs to be said. You need to give this assignment up and let someone else in KGI take over. You're hurt and the entire mission is compromised because you've made this personal. You need to back off now."

It took all he had not to kick Rio's ass, even if it damn near killed him in the process. And Rio knew it pissed him off because he was watching Garrett with those dark eyes, studying every reaction and only convincing himself that he was all the more right. Well, maybe he was. He'd probably be preaching the same sermon to one of his team members if they were in the same position.

"I really don't give a shit about the mission right now," Garrett said in as controlled a voice as possible. "What I care about is keeping her safe, and don't feed me that bullshit about how any of you can keep her safe. Okay, I get that. I don't doubt your abilities. I trust you with my life. But I'm not trusting anyone but myself with hers. You said I've made it personal. You're damn right I have. She's mine."

"Well fuck, Garrett," Rio swore. "You've got yourself a hell of a problem then. Resnick's going to be breathing down our necks wanting to know where Sarah is—"

"Another reason for me not to show up in some damn hospital."

"There's also the fact that Lattimer will be looking for his sister and the fact that you're lying to her about who you are. You need to figure out what's more important to you, man. Nailing Lattimer or having Sarah. Because something tells me you won't get both."

"Look, I really don't want to get into this with you. Find me a damn clinic or fly me to Marin and let her check me over. Sarah goes where I go. End of story. This is my mission and I'll fucking figure out what the hell I'm going to do. But for God's sake, can we get the fuck out of Mexico?"

"You're the boss," Rio drawled. "I've got a chopper waiting about thirty miles south of here. We'll ditch the rides and hop the border into Corazol. I have a contact there who can help us get medical care for you. On the way I'll have to try to make contact with Van because they'll all be coming in hot."

"And I need to call home," Garrett said quietly. He could only imagine how his mom and sisters-in-law felt. Ethan and Sam both would have gone. He knew because in their shoes he'd do the same for his brothers. Rachel was probably taking it especially hard. They tried to arrange it so that both he and Ethan were never gone at the same time.

"Need help?" Rio asked. He signaled his remaining men. "Let's make tracks."

Garrett took an experimental step forward and then another. Rio kept pace beside him and opened the back to lay the third-row seat down. He tossed the equipment to one of his other men, who transferred it to the other vehicle. Soon, Rio had a large enough space for Garrett to crawl in and lie down.

Sarah turned in her seat and watched as Garrett inched his way forward. By the time he was in, sweat beaded his forehead and he felt like he was going to puke his guts up.

"Do you have water?" Sarah asked softly, looking at Rio who was still standing behind Garrett. "Neither of us has had anything to eat or drink."

"Of course," Rio said. "I'll have Terrence dig some out of his pack while I get us on the road. Okay, doll?"

She nodded. "Thank you."

"You all set, man?" Rio asked.

"Yeah," Garrett said. "Get us on the road and get me a damn sat phone."

CHAPTER 29

SARAH leaned her head back against the rest and closed her eyes. She was tired to her bones and worry for Garrett beat at her brain. Rio had pissed Garrett off by injecting him with a painkiller when he wasn't looking, but Sarah was glad he did it. The roads were terrible and lying in the back and being jarred by every bump and pothole would have been excruciating.

At least now he had fallen into a drug-induced sleep. She looked over her shoulder every few minutes, checking his expression for any sign of discomfort. There was no tension in his face and he looked at peace.

Beside her, Rio sat, his gaze constantly darting right and left and like her, over his shoulder to check on Garrett at intervals. Terrence drove, and another team member whom she'd heard referred to as Decker rode shotgun. Literally.

Alton and Browning followed in the other SUV.

"Where are we going?" she asked in a low voice.

Rio's gaze settled on her, and she regretted drawing his attention. She wanted to die over the fact that she'd darn near undressed in front of him. He'd certainly gotten an eyeful of her cleavage.

"Corozal."

"Belize?"

He nodded. "We're not too far from the border. Couple hours even on shitty roads. I want Garrett to see a doctor there."

"His family will be there."

It wasn't really a question since she'd heard Rio conversing with one of Garrett's brothers earlier. But it was a way to seek information because she was as nervous as hell at the idea of meeting his family.

"Oh, definitely," Rio said. "They'll probably be there before we will. They were en route to Mexico and rerouted to Corozal after I let them know we'd gotten Garrett out."

He continued to study her until embarrassment crowded in once more and she looked away.

"Sarah."

Her gaze flickered back to him.

"That was a damn brave thing you did back there. I don't think Garrett knows whether to turn you over his knee or kiss your feet. There should be no shame or embarrassment. You earned my respect today and my gratitude for taking such care of a man whose friendship I value and a man I'm extremely proud to work with."

Her throat grew tight and her eyes itched fiercely. She wanted to wipe them but the gesture would betray how shaky her emotions were.

"I feel like an idiot now," she muttered. "Garrett is probably furious. He made me promise several times not to draw attention to myself. He was so bent on protecting me. But I couldn't do it," she said painfully. "They'd already beaten him twice. I thought . . . when I heard you, I knew I couldn't allow them to hurt him again. If it meant sacrificing my . . . body . . . it was something I was willing to do."

"Most people would never make that kind of sacrifice."

"I showed you my breasts, for God's sake," she said in disgust.

He grinned, white teeth flashing. He was extraordinarily handsome and when he smiled, he transformed from dark warrior to someone with oodles of charm.

"And as a gentleman, I'll not comment on how spectacular they were."

She snorted and rolled her eyes, but she smiled, feeling a little lighter and less mortified than she had before.

"Thank you," she said. "For coming. Garrett said you would, but there were times I wondered. It felt like we were there for a week."

His expression grew serious. "We look after our own. No way we'd not come for him."

"Loyalty like that is priceless."

He nodded and then reached to the floorboard for one of the packs. "Are you still hungry? You didn't eat much before. And are you sure you're all right?"

She rubbed her forehead and then massaged the bridge of her nose between her fingers. "I'm okay. Just fried. I think if I ate anything else I'd be sick. My head is killing me."

He frowned. "You should have told me. I can give you an injection."

She shook her head. "No, I don't want to be out of it. The idea kind of freaks me out right now. Just some ibuprofen would be wonderful. I think it's just going to take a while for me to come down."

He dug into his pack and shook out several pills into his hand. Then he uncapped a bottle of water and extended it to her. After she took it, he handed over the pills and she threw them back and swallowed them with a gulp of water.

"Will you check in with Marcus? He'll be frantic that I haven't checked in. I assume you would have already told him that we're safe. I'd like to . . . talk to him if possible," she said.

Rio's face became expressionless. "Your brother knows you're safe. Garrett will handle reporting in. We work for Garrett but this is his mission. He took the assignment from Marcus."

She nodded. "It's enough that he knows. Garrett will handle it."

"Can you try to sleep?" Rio asked gently. "You can stretch out and put my pack against the door to lay your head on."

She sighed. "I don't know. I'm so exhausted and yet I feel like I'll never sleep again."

"Let me give you something," he said. "It'll relax you and allow you to rest. It'll alleviate some of the anxiety you're feeling."

She hesitated and he pressed. "You need the rest, Sarah. You're dead on your feet and when Garrett wakes up and sees you like this, he's going to wig out, and then we'll have no hope of getting him the care he needs. He'll be too worried about you."

"That was dirty," she said with a scowl.

"Thank you, ma'am. I do my best."

"Oh all right," she conceded.

"Pull your sleeve up," he directed as he dug back into the pack.

She complied and he uncapped a prefilled syringe. She looked doubtfully at it as he swabbed an area of her skin with alcohol. Then before she could question, he plunged the needle into her arm. She gasped and then rubbed when he withdrew.

"Sorry," he said.

"That seemed like an awful lot of medicine for something that's just supposed to bring me down and relax me a bit."

"Oh it'll knock you on your ass for several hours," he said cheerfully.

Already the world was going hazy around her and her eyelids grew heavy. "When I wake up, I'm going to kick your ass," she slurred.

Rio leaned her toward the window and tucked his pack underneath her head. He gave her a gentle smile. "Good night, Sarah."

SAM paced the tarmac with restless energy while Donovan and Ethan leaned against the door of the Kelly jet. Sam checked his watch for the third time in as many minutes and swore under his breath.

"Where are they?" he demanded. "What the hell's taking them so long? I hope they didn't run into trouble."

"We'd know if they did," Donovan said. "Rio can handle it. They'll be here."

Ethan remained silent, his expression tense. "Garrett called home. He knew the women would be upset. If he was thinking of Mom and Rachel and Sophie, he's fine."

The distant sound of a helicopter quieted the conversation. The hum grew louder until the chopper burst over the dense area of trees. A few minutes later, the chopper touched down several feet away from where the jet was parked and Rio hopped out of the cockpit.

Sam started over, his brothers on his heels. Sam waited for the engine noise to die before addressing his team leader.

"What the hell happened? Where's Garrett?"

"He needs medical," Rio said. "There's a clinic about thirty miles out. It's safe."

"That's stupid," Ethan cut in. "We can get him on the jet and take him home to a hospital there."

Rio shook his head. "Not going to happen."

"You want to explain why?" Donovan asked.

A dilapidated old van creaked onto the tarmac and drove noisily over to where the chopper had landed. Rio motioned to Terrence, who ducked into the helicopter and came out a moment later, a woman curled into his arms. He carried her toward the van while Sam and his brothers watched in confusion.

"Is that Sarah?" Donovan asked. "Was she hurt too?"

Rio shook his head. "Look it's a long story and one I'd love to tell you, but right now we need to get Garrett out of here."

Sam glanced at his brothers and then nodded. They hurried over to the helicopter to see Garrett lying on a makeshift stretcher.

"I can damn well walk," Garrett growled at Browning who had the misfortune of sitting next to Garrett's head.

"Yeah, well, it doesn't look like it to me," Sam drawled. Even though he purposely needled his brother, the relief at seeing him lying there bitching as usual nearly staggered him. He had to grip the doorway to steady himself.

"Goddamn it, Garrett, you scared the shit out of us," Donovan cursed.

Garrett picked his head up and saw his three brothers crowded into the doorway of the chopper. "Well, son of a bitch."

Ethan grinned back at him. "You look like a pussy."

Garrett rose up to flip Ethan the bird but groaned as the motion rippled pain across his midsection. Yet something else his brothers would give him hell over. He grinned as he stared at the roof of the chopper. Some things never changed, and he hoped to hell they never did.

"One of you assholes help me sit up. I can walk out of here, damn it. I don't need a goddamn stretcher."

Ethan chuckled but reached his hand out for Garrett to grasp. Donovan shouldered in and reached for Garrett's other. His muscles protested, but he was gratified to be able to get out of the helicopter without collapsing.

As soon as his feet hit the ground, he looked around, taking in the surroundings "Where is Sarah?"

"Relax. Terrence took her to the van. I gave her an injection to make her sleep. She was wound tighter than a spring," Rio said.

Garrett relaxed and then took a good look at the van in question. "Well, hell, Rio. Is this what you call a first-class ride?"

Rio chuckled. "It's all about blending in. Can't have a limo showing up at some out-of-the-way clinic."

"We have the jet here," Sam said with a frown. "You should damn well let us take you home. You can't continue this job in your condition."

Garrett ignored him and started toward the van. Ethan followed and grasped Garrett's arm to steady him. He was grateful for his brother's help, not that he'd admit it. The last thing he wanted was to face plant on the runway. He wouldn't live down that humiliation ever.

"Goddamn it, Garrett," Sam said in resignation. "I swear if you didn't already look like you've been rode hard and hung up wet, I'd kick your ass."

Garrett turned and shot a cocky grin over his shoulder. "You can try, big brother. You can try."

Donovan shook his head and followed the procession over to the van.

Garrett stuck his head inside to see Sarah curled onto the floor of the van. There were only two seats in front and the entire back was empty. She was out cold and her features were drawn into a tight grimace, but at least she was resting. The past few days had been hard on her, and she'd already been through enough.

He hesitated before entering the van and turned to face his brothers. "I'll make this quick. We need to get out of sight. I'm not going home with you." He held up his hand to stop the protest that Sam was already preparing to launch. "You three get your asses home. Make sure the women aren't worried. Tell them whatever you need in order to make them feel better. I don't want the family involved with this. Think about the danger we'd be bringing to our front door. Lattimer is a wild card. The whole point of this job was to flush him out. I'm not going to do that in any way that puts our family at risk, and you damn well know I'm right."

"My suggestion was to leave Rio with Sarah. Let his team take over the job. You need to get your ass home and be in a real hospital," Sam said.

"And I'm telling you right now, I'm not leaving Sarah."

He stared his brothers down. He saw Donovan shake his head and blow out his breath in resignation. Donovan knew. He already had a damn good idea that Garrett was in way over his head with the woman.

"There is still a threat to Sarah, one I haven't identified. And do you think for one minute that if we all go home, Resnick won't be all over us in a minute? Hell, he's probably on his way here right now. He's a complication I don't need."

"Are you forgetting that you're lying to her?" Sam asked in a low voice. "Whatever your feelings for her, she's not going to forgive being used as bait to lure her brother out of hiding. Get out now, Garrett. Let Rio do the job."

"Tell me something, Sam. Would you have left Sophie to Steele or Rio? Would you have backed off and let them protect her while you went home with your tail tucked between your legs?"

Understanding flashed in Sam's eyes.

Garrett turned to Ethan. "Would you have let us go in after Rachel while you stayed at home sitting on your hands because you were too emotionally involved?"

"Fuck no," Ethan bit out.

"Goddamn it," Sam bit out. "I hate when you have to make a goddamn point that I can't respond to."

Garrett grinned. "Go home, Sam. You have a wife and a new baby. Ethan has a wife to take care of. Sarah is mine to take care of. Rio and his team will stick with me. I trust them to do their job, but the only one I'm trusting with Sarah is me."

Sam rubbed a hand over his hair and made a sound of

disgust. "Okay, Garrett. Have it your way. Not that you ever do anything else. I hope to hell you know what you're doing."

"She's been hurt before, Sam," Garrett said quietly. "She trusts me. She's not going to trust another man."

"Yeah, and what are you going to do when the shit hits the fan?" Donovan asked. "She trusts you and you're going to betray that trust."

Pain that had nothing to do with his injuries washed through his chest. "I'm going to have to figure out a way to do my job—do what's right—and hope that she'll understand—and can forgive me—for doing what needed to be done."

CHAPTER 30

SARAH stirred and tried to blink away the groggy, hungover feeling that cloaked her like a thick fog. It took her a moment to even remember what had happened and that Rio had drugged her. She was also no longer in the SUV they'd traveled in, nor was she on a helicopter that she knew they'd intended to take into Belize.

She pushed herself upward, taking in her surroundings. Immediately her gaze locked with Garrett, who was sitting up, his back to the side of what looked to be an old utility van. Briefly she gazed around to see Rio also sitting in the back, as well as Terrence and another team member she hadn't caught the name of. Browning and Alton were in the front, Browning driving.

Then she glanced back at Garrett, who studied her with frank appraisal.

"How are you feeling?" he asked.

"That's a ridiculous question," she grumbled. "The real question is, how are you?"

He cracked a grin and then patted the small space beside him. She crawled over and nestled into his side.

"I prefer you close to me," he murmured. "And I'm okay. Just stove up. I'll be sore for a couple of days, but that's all."

She was skeptical of his self-diagnosis but she didn't argue. What she did do was glare over at Rio, whose lips twitched suspiciously.

"He's going to a clinic at least, right?"

Rio nodded. "Yes ma'am. Whether he wants to or not."

She nodded. "Good."

"Glad I have such a say here," Garrett said dryly.

She laid her head on Garrett's shoulder. "What do we do then? I mean, where do we go? I assume you'll need to check in with Marcus. I don't know what your arrangement is with him, but he's very used to being on top of things."

He tensed a moment before moving so he could put an arm around her. "You let me worry about Lattimer, okay? Rio and his team are going to stay with us so we don't get into any more situations like before."

She sighed and knew she needed to come clean with everything. Before . . . before there were several reasons she held back. She wasn't entirely certain she could trust Garrett—at first. That had faded away, and now he was the only person she did trust. And she was ashamed. Deeply humiliated by what had happened to her and her sense of betrayal had been so numbing that she hadn't been able to fathom telling anyone. Not Marcus—especially not Marcus.

Garrett needed to know exactly what he was dealing with, because from the moment he'd told her that Allen's brother had hired someone to find her, she knew. She was a threat to Stanley Cross. If she was ever hauled into court to testify against Marcus for killing Stanley's brother, the whole sordid tale would come out. Allen was dead, but Stanley wasn't, and he could still be held accountable for his role in her rape.

"Sarah?"

The question in Garrett's voice told her he knew something was bothering her. But she couldn't tell him now. Not in front of his men even though they'd have to know later.

So she shook her head to let Garrett know it was nothing. And later, after he'd been taken care of, she would divulge the last of her secrets.

CHAPTER 31

"OKAY, now that the doctor has assured you all that I'm not dying, can everyone stop with the babysitting?" Garrett grumbled as they exited the small, rural clinic where Rio had taken him to be examined.

Sarah rolled her eyes. "I wouldn't say all that bruising is nothing."

"No broken bones," Garrett reminded her. "Probably fractured a few ribs, but that's nothing I haven't done before."

They stood in the sunshine a step away from the van that had taken them thirty miles from Corozal. Rio and his men stood to the side, and Garrett leaned against the van as he looked to his team leader.

"Okay, what now? I assume you have a place off in the wilds somewhere where you can stash us. Donovan was going to send us to Alaska, but that's out now. Too risky. I don't want Sarah out in the open for that long."

It also needed to be a place where they could draw Lattimer. The sooner they ended this madness, the sooner Sarah would be safe again, and then he could address this thing between them.

"As a matter of fact I do," Rio said. "Always pays to have a few safe places that even the bosses don't know about."

Garrett shot him a look. Rio shrugged. "I'd be a dumbass if I didn't plan for every contingency."

Garrett couldn't argue with that logic.

"I have a place on the Belize River several miles from the nearest village. It's well stocked, isolated and it gives us several escape routes. I have a chopper there and a boat. We can bail at a moment's notice by air, water or roadway."

"And how big is this place?" Garrett asked. The last thing he wanted was to be tripping over five other men in close quarters.

Rio grinned. "Big enough. Besides, we'll be taking position in a perimeter around the house. No one will get within a mile unless we want them to."

Armed with painkillers, the trip over less-than-ideal roads wasn't as bad as it could have been. Still, by the time they turned onto the winding road that led to Rio's safe house, Garrett felt like he'd been beat all over again.

There was a large security gate that couldn't be seen from the road. Security cameras were mounted at each post on the left and right and Garrett raised his brow as Rio opened the gate by remote.

"Exactly how much are we paying you, man?" Garrett joked.

Rio snorted. "Not nearly enough."

The drive was a half mile long and looped around the incline to where the house rested atop a hill, completely surrounded and sheltered by dense trees.

Garrett whistled when he caught sight of the place. He'd been expecting a shack or maybe a stone building that more resembled a cave. Rio and his men had reputations for being staunch, cave-dwelling loners who kept to themselves when they weren't on assignment.

Rio liked his privacy—obviously—but he damn sure wasn't suffering in some hovel.

"Can't wait to see this," he muttered as they piled out of the van.

A high-security fence circled the house in addition to the barrier provided by the trees. The house was modern and sleek and spread out over at least three thousand square feet. When they entered, Garrett was struck by how clean and efficient the house looked, but what immediately took over his notice was the high-tech surveillance gear, the computer system and the weapons locker located just inside the door.

"Van would cream himself," Garrett said.

Rio laughed. "That he would. I'd have to kick his ass because he'd be touching my stuff."

He guided Sarah and Garrett into a kitchen that looked like something out of a catalog. All the modern appliances, granite countertops and a professional-grade stove with six gas burners.

"The kitchen is fully stocked. If it's edible I probably have it. Freezer and fridge have all the necessary foodstuffs. Staples in the pantry. Plenty of bottled water. Don't drink out of the tap. We don't have the best water."

They carried on into a sprawling living room, which Garrett immediately approved of. He cast a sideways glance at Sarah, wondering if she was noting the differences.

"This is the type of place you hole up in when you're hiding," he said. "There aren't any open areas for anyone to see into the living room or take a shot at you from a distance. All the windows are high to allow light to enter but this is a completely safe room."

"Oh yeah?" she muttered. "What if they have a grenade?"

Rio laughed. "Well then it's KYAG time."

At Sarah's raised eyebrow, Garrett supplied, "Kiss your ass goodbye time."

"Ah, very succinct."

"The bedrooms are through here," Rio said as he led them down a long hallway. "Each has its own bathroom and the master suite has a Jacuzzi tub and separate shower. Take your pick and make yourself at home."

"This is your home, isn't it?" Sarah asked softly. "Not just a safe house. I mean it's *your* safe place."

Rio was silent for a minute. "Yeah, it is. It's the place I go when I want to be alone, but hey, a guy likes his creature comforts too."

Sarah grimaced. "I'm sorry we're intruding then. But thank you for sharing your private getaway with us."

He smiled at her then and leaned over to ruffle her hair affectionately. "Well, if it was only Garrett I would have stashed him in some hovel somewhere. Much more in keeping with his winning personality. But I couldn't very well treat a lady like that."

"Oh, for God's sake. I'm going to puke over here," Garrett grumbled. "Don't you have something better to be doing?"

Rio grinned again and gave a snappy two-finger salute before he sauntered back down the hall to round up his men.

Garrett and Sarah were standing in the doorway to the master suite and Garrett waited for her to venture in. "It's beautiful," she said as she turned in a circle in the middle of the room.

Garrett dropped their bags on the floor, startling her. She looked at the bags, looked at Garrett and then color rose in her cheeks.

"I'll take one of the other bedrooms," she said as she started toward her bag. "You can have this one. I don't need much room."

He caught her wrist before she could bend to retrieve her bag and then he pulled her up close until they were flush against each other. "You're staying in here with me."

She trembled and her eyes took on a slightly glazed, hungry look that brought his body to immediate attention.

"In that bed. With me," he said as he nodded toward the big king-sized bed in the middle of the room. "Your legs wrapped around me, me inside you. I've thought of little else for the past few days. It's what got me through the two days in captivity."

She sucked in her breath and licked her lips nervously, leaving them plump and shiny and so damn irresistible. Then she put a hand on his chest and gave him a doubtful look.

"We can't make love, you idiot. What you need is a bath and food and rest. You should climb in the tub and soak while I go fix us something to eat. I thought I'd make your favorite. Meat, meat and more meat."

"Mmmm, that sounds good. But here's what I think. I think you should take that bath with me and then we'll both figure out something to fix."

She stared at him for a minute and then past him toward the bathroom. He could see she was tempted. He pulled her in closer and murmured in her ear. "You, me, lots of hot water. I'll wash your back. And your front. And all parts in between."

She shivered delicately just as he sank his teeth into her lobe, nipping with just enough force to excite her.

"And just so you know, Sarah, I'm going to make love to you. I don't give a damn if it kills me in the process. I'm going to have you. You're going to sleep in my bed, in my arms, your skin against mine. I want the last thing you feel before you go to sleep is me inside you, and the first thing you know when you wake up."

She made a soft, breathy, utterly feminine sound as she leaned into him, and he went painfully hard. God, but he wanted to touch her. He wanted to run his tongue from the tip of her nose to her toes and taste every delectable inch of her.

God, he had to quit or he was going to come in his pants.

"I'll go run the water," she said. "You sit down and rest while you wait."

He grinned at her bossiness. "Yes, ma'am."

Sarah pushed at him to get him to sit on the bed. When she was satisfied that he was comfortable and off his feet, she went into the bathroom. Her eyes widened when she took in the huge tub on an elevated platform. It was the centerpiece of the entire bathroom and would easily fit more than two people. Maybe Rio went in for more than one when it came to female companionship.

She laughed softly at the idea of the dark-eyed, quiet man being more frolicsome when it came to his private life.

On impulse, she searched the drawers for matches or a lighter and was delighted to find a long-stemmed candle lighter. She started the water running and then went around to light the candles placed at random spots around the bathroom. It seemed a girly thing to do but then a man owned this entire house, and the candles weren't girly smelling. The scent was more earthy and masculine. It reminded her of the outdoors.

She stood back to survey her handiwork and then let out a groan. It looked like she was bent on seduction. Then she chuckled. She could hardly be accused of seduction when Garrett had made it abundantly clear that he had every intention of making love to her.

She rubbed her hands up and down her arms as she watched the water grow deeper in the tub. She wasn't sure what had her on edge more. The idea of making love to Garrett or the fact that she wasn't more wary of giving herself completely and wholly to a man. Of trusting him.

She shrugged. The fact was, she wasn't afraid of Garrett. He'd been achingly tender and up front with her. He hadn't hidden from the mutual attraction that flared like a brush fire between them. She cherished the honesty between them, and she trusted him—in a way she'd never thought to trust another man.

After putting out towels and arranging the soaps and shampoo just so, she turned the water off and went back for Garrett.

She found him flat on his back, eyes closed, and for a moment she stood there, watching him. Absorbing everything about him. His broad chest rose up and down with his breaths and he looked oddly vulnerable, a fact she found extremely endearing.

She eased onto the bed and leaned over him, letting her hair fall to his shoulder. She rubbed one finger down his jawline, and his eyelids slitted open. He watched her with lazy regard as she ran her finger over his lips.

"Bath's ready," she murmured. "Need help up?"

"I could use help undressing," he said, an unholy gleam in his eyes.

"Of course you do," she muttered, but a smile hovered at the corners of her mouth.

She backed off the bed and watched as he rolled to the edge and put his feet down. Unsure of whether to help him or not, she waited and let him walk ahead of her.

"This is nice," he said as he looked around.

"Not too girly?"

He turned to look at her. "Nope, not too girly at all. As long as you like it, I like it."

He wasted no time stripping off his shirt. She winced when she saw the multitude of bruises that colored his abdomen. He looked like an Easter egg. When he started to shimmy out of his pants, she turned away and then shook her head at the absurdity of the action. She glanced back to see a prime view of his backside as he climbed over the edge into the water.

Damn but the man was built like a brick house. All hard lines, lean at the waist and hips, broad at the shoulders and a muscled back that made her mouth water. When he turned to lower himself in the water, she saw the rippled, discolored tight abdomen and the dark hair at his groin. And even at a state of semi erection, the man was impressive.

Even as large as the tub was, he seemed to fill every inch. He sank into water and stretched out with an appreciative groan. "Damn but this feels good."

Steam rose from the water—she'd been sure to make it hot—and he leaned his head back and closed his eyes. Unsure of what she was supposed to do—okay so she knew, but she felt damn awkward—she piddled with her shirt.

Finally she turned away and walked toward the far corner so she could undress. She hoped she didn't lose the nerve because she wanted that hot bath more than she wanted anything right now.

"Sarah."

She turned at the sound of his voice to see him watching her through half-lidded eyes.

"Come here."

Her head cocked to the side in question, she returned to the bathtub.

"Want to know what my fantasy is right now?" he asked.

Her eyebrow went up and she nodded.

"I want you to undress right there where I can watch."

She swallowed nervously. "You might not think it's such a fantasy when I get my clothes off."

His velvet gaze stroked over her body, touching fire to every nerve ending. "You have a beautiful body, honey. Perfect. I've had some pretty sweaty fantasies about it since meeting you. And that day on the beach when you wore that little suit. It was so modest but it made me even crazier because I kept imagining what was underneath."

Mesmerized by the low pitch of his voice and warmed to her toes by the stark truth in his eyes, she reached down to unbutton her shorts. His gaze followed her every movement as she unfastened and then slid the material down over her hips.

She gripped the hem of her T-shirt and pulled up and over her head, leaving her in just her bra and panties. She stood for a moment, gauging his reaction, but all she saw was pure, unadulterated male appreciation.

She wasn't sure which should go next, bra or panties, so she mentally flipped a coin and the bra won. She reached behind her to grapple with the clasp, because was there anything less sexy than taking the straps down and then twisting it around to undo from the front?

The band popped free and the cups loosened, but she held them over her breasts for the barest of moments before allowing the straps to tumble down over her shoulders. Then she let it fall to the floor as she lowered her arms.

She couldn't meet his stare now and instead looked down as she hooked her thumbs in the lacy band of her panties. With a little wiggle, she worked the underwear down her legs and let it fall.

"Come here," he said in a sexy, husky voice.

When she looked up there was a predatory gleam in Garrett's eyes. A look that told her she was his and he planned to lay claim. Oh but she loved that look. No one had ever looked at her with such intensity. Like he dared anyone to take what was his away. Like he wanted to devour her in a single bite and savor the taste.

He held up his hand to help her over the edge of the tub. She slid her fingers through his and stepped into the steaming water. As soon as it sluiced over her ankles, she moaned with the sheer pleasure of it.

He tugged her forward, closer to him and then downward until she knelt, facing him, in the water between his thighs. He reached around to cup her neck and then pulled her down into his kiss. His other found the swell of her breast, cupped one and ran his thumb over her nipple. It hardened instantly, becoming a rigid, sensitive point.

When he pulled away, they were both breathing hard. Arousal glazed his eyes, and the pupils were flared, making his eyes more black than blue.

"Turn around," he directed.

She complied and he pulled her into the V of his legs until her back was melded to his chest and she was surrounded by him, enveloped by his touch and smell.

"Relax," he murmured. "We can use this for a while."

She leaned farther into his embrace until they were both reclined, water lapping to their necks. His hands wandered lazily up and down her body, down her waist and then back up again, where he'd cup her breasts and bring her nipples to erect nubs.

Lulled by his light caresses, she closed her eyes and gave herself over to his touch and to the soothing hot water.

His touch grew bolder, lowering to the juncture of her thighs, teasing the curls at the apex. Her breath drew in painfully and she held it in anticipation as her body quivered—wanting and needing him to touch her more intimately.

He was patient, drawing lazy circles, dipping down to run his fingers over the closed seam between her legs. She sighed and parted her thighs, wanting him to have easier access. Slowly he worked one finger between her folds and rubbed lightly over her clit.

She gasped and tensed as pleasure shot through her body, tingling and burning its way through her veins and to all her pleasure points. Her breasts tightened and ached, wanting equal attention.

"Lay your head back on my shoulder," he whispered. "I want to see your face when I make you come."

Her head drooped back and she turned her face away as he nuzzled her neck. His fingers were magic, taking her up so close to her peak and then slowing and bringing her down until she was boneless in his arms.

His middle finger slipped lower, circling her entrance before entering the barest of inches, teasing and stroking. When her breaths were coming fast and shallow, he went back to her clit, exerting just the right amount of pressure as he found her sweet spot.

He licked her pulse point at her neck and then nipped lightly, his teeth grazing as goose bumps erupted over her flesh. "Come for me, Sarah. Right here. Right now in my arms. Let go for me, baby."

She twisted against him, arching into his hand as his fingers grew more insistent. He knew just how to touch her, just how hard to exert pressure and when to let off. As his mouth melted against her neck again, her orgasm flashed, quick and hard, exploding through her body. Wave after wave of intense, mind-bending pleasure curled through her pelvis and spread through her limbs until she was mindless and limp.

Slowly she came back to awareness as he rained a trail of kisses over the curve of her shoulder.

"That was amazing," she murmured. She yawned broadly and floated in the sweet aftermath as he stroked her body with gentle hands.

His erection was rigid against her back. Hot like a branding iron. Thick and large.

"*You're* amazing," he said sincerely. "What you did back there, Sarah. I'm humblèd. I'm furious with you for putting yourself between me and danger like that, and if you ever do it again, I'll spank your ass. But I'm so goddamn amazed at the courage it took for you to face him down like that."

"I was scared," she admitted. "But I figured whatever they did, it couldn't be as bad as what you'd suffered. I'd survive. I did it once. I can do it again."

He gathered her close and held on to her as he kissed the side of her face. "Thank you. I'm furious. I'm amazed. But thank you."

They soaked awhile longer, Sarah limp against his chest, content in the aftermath of his lovemaking. Finally, with the water cooling around them, she stirred and pushed herself upward. She turned to help Garrett, but he gripped the sides of the tub with bloodless fingers and strained to rise from the tub.

His face went pale and his lips formed a paper-thin line. His breaths spurted out raggedly as he stood a moment catching his breath. She hurried out of the tub and jerked a towel from the rack. She was there to help him as he stepped from the tub, not that she did him any good. But she was determined to take as good care of him as he had of her.

Gently she worked the towel over his body, wiping the wetness away. He was hugely aroused, and his cock strained upward toward his belly. Despite serious effort not to look, her gaze wandered to it more than once as she continued to towel him off.

Finally he seemed to be able to take no more. With a stifled groan, he gripped her wrist. "Finish drying yourself off. I'll be in the bedroom."

He walked stiffly from the bathroom, leaving her standing

naked and still dripping. She wrapped the towel around her and hugged the material close.

She wasn't afraid. She knew what was going to happen. More than that, she knew what she wanted to do. She didn't want to wait for Garrett to act. She didn't want to be a passive participant.

Hurriedly, she dried her hair and combed through it until the tangles were gone. There was a robe hanging from a hook on the back of the door, and as large as it was, it had to belong to Rio.

She pulled it on and tied the belt before walking out of the bathroom into the bedroom. Garrett was lying on the bed, a towel still wrapped around his hips. His eyes were closed and she frowned at the vivid bruising over his midsection.

Even battered and bruised, he was a beautiful man. Drawn to the vulnerable picture he posed, she crawled onto the bed beside him. His eyes opened and he focused on her as she knelt beside him.

He started to speak, but she lowered her mouth to his to hush him.

Just as she had while they were locked in the cell, she worked to soothe his hurts. Only this time there was no fear of discovery. No uncertainty of their fate. No reason for her to hold anything back.

Garrett watched the series of emotions that flickered across her face as she drew away. Her hand slipped up and down his chest, pausing low on his belly. Her fingers trembled against him, part nervousness and part excitement, if he had to guess.

A little shyly, she pulled at the towel until the ends fell away, baring him completely to her gaze. His cock shot upward as a surge of lust blew through his system. Every muscle in his body screamed its protest but at the moment he didn't give a damn.

There was a purposeful look in her eyes that had him hopeful and breathless all at the same time. Then she cocked her head and bit at her bottom lip as if she were unsure of what to do next. It was almost like she was looking to him for guidance. Or permission. Was she afraid of hurting him?

"Make love to me, Sarah," he whispered. "Touch me. You feel so damn good. Do what you want. You won't hurt me."

He could be lying or maybe he was hoping like hell he spoke the truth. All he knew was that he wanted her mouth on him like he wanted his next breath.

She kissed him again, this time in the center of his chest. As she kissed a delicate path down his midsection, her hand slid lower and her fingers circled his erection.

Ah shit.

He groaned and stirred restlessly, ignoring the pain he felt every time he so much as twitched.

Then she released him and slid her hand back up again as she kissed each area of his bruised ribs. Little butterfly kisses, each one bringing such pleasure that he was dizzy with it.

She loved every part of his ache, coaxed and caressed until the pain slid quietly away, replaced by warm euphoria. Her mouth crept lower until her tongue circled a wet path around his navel and to the sensitive skin underneath.

She hesitated when she licked down to his groin, and his breath caught in his chest and held until finally she grasped his erection. He exhaled in jerky puffs as her fingers circled him once again and she gently moved her hand up and down.

Again she lowered her mouth and brushed her lips just above the base of his cock. He was crazy with anticipation. Each breath was shallower than the last and every nerve ending in his body was screaming. He moved restlessly, ignoring the protest of his body. His skin was itchy and alive like he was about to turn inside out.

And finally she slipped her mouth over the crown of his erection and did a warm, wet slide down to her knuckles. He was already hard but the moment her tongue brushed over his length, he hardened to stone, his dick so rigid that it was as much pain as pleasure, and God, he wanted more.

She glided upward again, tasting every inch. Her mouth was the sweetest pleasure he'd ever known in his life. She took away the pain and replaced it with warmth he felt all the way to his soul.

He had to touch her. His hands curled and itched like crazy. He raised one to rest on her head and then delved into her hair, rubbing and moving down to her nape as he urged her on. He was careful not to push even though his mind and body were screaming to surge more fully into her.

She'd shared every part of herself. He knew how difficult it must have been for her to initiate this. He savored it, tasted it. His hand gentled, squeezing softly at her nape before sliding through her hair once more to the back of her head. He loved the feel of her hair around his fingers. He wanted her skin more.

As she sucked him deeper, he closed his eyes again and skimmed down to the side of her neck. She shivered when he caressed the skin just below her ear. He lingered there a moment and when she dipped again to take him deep, he traced a line around the hollow of her throat and then to her collarbone.

Her breasts swayed just underneath his reach. Her robe had come open and he could see the tempting swells. He wanted to cup the soft flesh and run his thumb over her nipple, feel it pucker and harden against the pad. But he didn't want to take more from her than she was willing to give, and so he contented himself with stroking the flesh of her neck and watching her throat work up and down as she swallowed against his erection.

His release was building and as much as he wanted satisfaction, he wanted to live in the moment. He didn't want it to end so soon.

He touched her jaw and she instantly went still. She turned, releasing him from her mouth and faced him, her eyes glowing softly.

"Should I stop?"

"Hell no." He couldn't contain the explosive denial and he worked to amend his statement. "Only for a moment. It's too soon. It's too good to end so quickly."

Her lips curved upward into a sensual smile of a female who knew she was pleasing her man. She stroked him with her hand, working up and down in slow, rhythmic motions as she continued to watch him.

"Lower," he said in a husky voice. "Touch me lower. Wrap your fingers around me, honey. I want you everywhere."

He moaned when she slid her hand all the way down to the base and then let go to cup his balls. She measured the weight in her hand squeezing gently and running her fingers over the sac.

"With your mouth," he whispered. "Do it while you use your mouth."

Her hair fell like a curtain as she lowered her head again. He pushed it aside, wanting to see her mouth as she closed it around his cock. As she massaged and rolled his balls in her hand, she sucked wetly down his length, exerting firm pressure with her mouth.

His breath escaped in a long hiss and every muscle in his body tightened. The pressure was painful as his bruised and aching muscles protested, but he urged her on, the pleasure of her mouth too much to deny.

"I'm close," he warned. "You can use your hand if you don't want me to come in your mouth."

She made a low purring sound in the back of her throat and then took him whole. He bumped against the back of her mouth and felt her swallow—an invitation—against the head. Oh God, he wasn't going to last.

Like silk, she glided sensuously over his cock, her tongue rubbing erotically along the underside. She increased the pace and tightened the pressure until he was nearly insane with the mounting frenzy.

"Sarah."

Her name tore from his lips just as his release boiled up and over. Fire shot through his groin and raced through his veins like quicksilver. He spurted against the back of her throat and then his release coated warm liquid in her mouth and over his cock. She swallowed and continued her downward motion, taking him and holding him like she savored every inch.

Nothing had ever been so good. He floated, free of pain, free of everything but her.

Gently, she coaxed the last of his release from him with soft sucking motions. Then she carefully pulled him from her mouth and then facing him, she laid her cheek on his thighs and slid her hand up his hip and to his belly.

She smiled up at him, her eyes soft and contented. He trailed fingers through her hair, stroking over and over.

"That was amazing," he murmured.

"I didn't hurt you?"

There was worry in her voice and even as she asked, she

slid her hand over the bruises as if she could wipe them away with her touch.

"I promise you I felt nothing but pleasure after I got inside your mouth."

She smiled again. "I'm glad. I wanted to take away the pain for a little while."

"You did more than that," he said softly. "You gave me something very special. Don't think I'll forget."

Her cheeks colored prettily and he brushed his fingers over her temple.

"Let's go eat," he suggested. "I imagine you're starving, and I promised you caramel num nums."

She laced her fingers with his and squeezed. "You've kept all your promises, Garrett."

CHAPTER 32

DINNER was fun. Sarah wasn't sure if it was due to her relief at being alive and safe or if she just enjoyed Garrett's company that much. He put her in charge of the three-meat dinner course while he worked on caramel num nums.

"I think you got the better work detail," she said as she sniffed at the caramel he was stirring.

"This is delicate work," he defended.

She snorted and cracked open the oven to peer at the chicken breasts and pork chops. "Almost done here. What about you?"

In response, he picked up the pot from the burner and carried it over to the pie dish, where he'd formed the graham cracker crust. He carefully spooned the mixture into the shell and then dropped the pot into the sink.

"It needs to cool before I pour on the chocolate, so we can eat first," he said.

They set the table and Garrett helped dish up the pieces of meat. By the time they sat down, Sarah's stomach was growling. She was starving!

As she ate, she was unable to keep her gaze from straying to Garrett. When they were in captivity together, she'd admitted to herself that she loved him. She'd wondered briefly if it was simply an emotional reaction to the possibility that they'd die in that shit hole. But now as she stared at him, she realized that her feelings for him couldn't be explained away that easily.

The words danced on her tongue, eager to be set free, but she was deeply conscious of the fact that to him she was a job. He worked for her brother. A brother who was extremely protective of her.

Yes, she'd tell him. Maybe not right this minute. She'd always chuckled at the idea of waiting until just the right time to tell someone you loved them. Wasn't any time good for such a thing? She realized now it wasn't as easy as that. There was marked difficulty in making yourself that vulnerable to someone else. Bearing your soul gave the other person power over you.

"What are you thinking?" Garrett asked.

She shook herself from her thoughts and then smiled. "I was thinking I'm ready for a caramel num num."

"I'll melt the chocolate right quick and then I'll pour it on. Thirty minutes in the fridge ought to set it right and then we can dive in."

She watched as he ambled back into the kitchen. Already his gait was smoother, though she could still sense tenderness in the way he walked. Garrett wasn't the type to dwell on pain, though. To him it was merely an inconvenience.

He looked up, caught her staring and his lips turned up into a smile. It took her breath away. Her pulse sped up and thumped against her skin until she was aware of every beat. His gaze smoldered with sensual promise.

She bit at her bottom lip and shivered. There was a lot she still had to tell him. Preferably before they became immersed in a sexual relationship.

A ridiculously giddy thrill rocketed up her spine, forcing a grin to her face. Sexual relationship. She was calmly contemplating a sexual relationship and furthermore, so far, she'd been the aggressor.

She had the absurd urge to stand up and do a double-fist pump with a *yeah* attached for emphasis.

What Allen and Stanley Cross had done hadn't been about sexual attraction or even sex. It was about power and the ability to inflict their will on someone weaker. Allen had raped her because he could, not because he was overwhelmed by desire.

Garrett wanted her. He desired her. But he held himself back because he was afraid of scaring her. She found that fact endearing, and it only made her want him all the more.

She watched as Garrett placed the dessert into the fridge and her breath caught in her throat as he returned to the table.

"So what do we do for the next thirty minutes or so?" she asked.

"Well, what I want to do is going to take a hell of a lot longer than thirty minutes."

Oh lordy. Her hormones just went haywire.

"Maybe we could just talk," she murmured. There was a lot she still had to tell him. Preferably before she got swept away and became so senseless she forgot her name.

He moved closer to her, put his hand on her face, stroking over her cheekbone and then into her hair.

"What would you like to talk about?"

She took a deep breath. "I have something I need to tell you."

His brow furrowed in concern and his fingers stilled on her face. "Okay. I'm listening."

Sarah glanced around. She hadn't seen Rio or his men since they'd arrived at the house, but she couldn't dispel the unease or the fear of being overheard. She peeked back at Garrett and chewed nervously at her bottom lip.

"Can we go into the bedroom? It's . . . private."

Garrett's look of concern deepened, but he turned without question, snagged her hand and pulled her gently toward the bedroom.

Once they were inside, he closed the door and faced her. "Whatever's most comfortable for you."

"You sit," she said. "On the bed. I'd prefer you not to loom over me. This is . . . hard . . . for me."

Garrett turned toward the bed, but he laced his fingers with hers and pulled her with him. He sat on the edge and then positioned her between his legs. He held both of her hands and looked up into her eyes. Then he squeezed. Just a simple gesture of support, but it meant the world to her.

"I've never told even Marcus this," she said frankly. "I

might have eventually but after what he did to Allen, I knew I couldn't. He would have gone crazy. Saying aloud that Allen raped me was bad enough. I couldn't bear the humiliation of telling the rest."

Garrett's face darkened. "The rest? You mean there's more?"

She nodded slowly and tears pricked the corners of her eyes. She sucked in steadying breaths and blinked to hold the burn at bay.

"Tell me," he said gently.

"You need to know. I should have told you the minute you told me that Stanley Cross had hired someone to find me. I was too ashamed."

Garrett's thumbs rubbed softly over her wrists and his gaze never left hers.

"He . . . he was there. The night Allen raped me. He . . . helped."

Garrett's lips curled into a snarl and his nostrils flared. She felt the quick huff of his breath and saw the tightening of his jaw. "The son of a bitch raped you too?"

Sarah closed her eyes and shook her head. "No. Well, yes, but not in the physical sense. He didn't penetrate me, but he may as well have. He watched Allen and laughed. Then he held my arms so Allen could finish the job. When Allen was finished, Stanley spit on me and told Allen to hire a new assistant because the one he had wasn't a challenge any longer."

Garrett swore long and hard under his breath and his fingers tightened around her hands.

"The night Marcus killed Allen, as I ran from the building, Stanley was there. He stopped me when I got off the elevator. He asked what the hell I was doing there. I knew he'd either think I killed Allen or that at the very least he'd know I saw who did. I also know he wouldn't want what he and Allen did to me to ever become public."

She shivered in Garrett's grip as the words fell baldly between them.

"I know I should have told you before," she said softly. "As soon as I knew Marcus had sent you to protect me. You needed this information. I was certain that the person who broke into my cottage on the island was someone Stanley sent to kill me. It's why I left and why I finally accepted help from Marcus."

"Come here," Garrett said softly as he pulled her into his arms.

He circled her body and hugged her close to him. It didn't seem to satisfy him. He pulled her down until she sat across his lap huddled to his chest. For a long moment he simply held her and pressed tender kisses to her hair.

Tension simmered through him. His muscles quivered beneath her skin and she could literally feel the battle he waged to get his anger under control.

"I'm going to do my absolute best to protect you, Sarah. I need for you to believe that." He pulled away and nudged her chin until she returned his gaze. "I also need for you to believe that you aren't just a job. This is personal for me. I care a lot about you. We have a connection. One I can't explain. I'm not really interested in why. I protect the people I care about with my life."

Tears shimmered making her vision grow blurry. He swam in her sight and her heart stuttered and jumped erratically. She raised shaking fingers to his face and traced the line of his cheekbone.

"I will kill any man who tries to hurt you. And you can believe, if you believe nothing else, I'm going to make Stanley Cross regret the day he ever took part in hurting you."

She shivered at the violence in his voice. She believed him. There was nothing but stark truth in his eyes.

She leaned her head forward until her forehead touched his. Their mouths were a mere breath apart. She closed her eyes as a tear slid down her cheek.

His warm lips kissed away the damp trail. He was so exquisitely gentle that her chest tightened unbearably with a swell of emotion.

"I'm sorry that happened to you, Sarah," he said in a voice tight with the same emotion knotting her throat. "I'm so damn sorry. If I could take it away I would."

She slid her mouth over until it aligned with his. "But you can replace it," she whispered.

"Are you sure?"

She nodded. "I need you, Garrett. Only you. I'm not afraid. With you I feel so strong."

He framed her face with both hands and kissed her long and leisurely, his tongue delving deep as he explored the inside of her mouth. She sighed and melted against him, his heat seeping into her bones.

When he pulled away, she saw something in his eyes that surprised her. He looked . . . uncertain. And now he hesitated as he stared softly back at her.

"What's wrong?" she asked.

"I'm afraid."

Her eyes widened. "Afraid? Of what?"

He touched her swollen mouth with one finger and ran it along the seam to the corner and back across. "I'm afraid of doing the wrong thing. I'm afraid of hurting you. Of frightening you. Sarah, honey, I'd die if I did anything to make you go back to that night. I'd do anything in the world to make this right for you."

She smiled then and for a moment she couldn't breathe around the sting in her nose and the hard knot in her throat. "You will. Oh, Garrett, you'll be just perfect."

She flung her arms around his shoulders and hugged him tightly. She buried her face against the side of his neck and inhaled his scent. Slowly he circled her body with his arms and hugged her back just as fiercely as she held him. Then he brushed his lips across the curve of her neck and spread a line of tiny kisses to her shoulder.

She felt free in a way she hadn't felt in a very long time. It was as if something inside her loosened and so much of what she'd kept suppressed came bubbling out.

Carefully she pushed away from Garrett and slid off his lap to stand in front of him once more. It was important to her to be an equal in their lovemaking. Oh, she had no doubt that Garrett would be exquisitely tender. But she wasn't going to be a wilting ninny who had to be coaxed at every turn.

She was a normal, healthy woman. She'd had lovers before. She wasn't a stranger to passion. She could *do* this.

Her gaze never leaving Garrett's intense blue eyes, she began to undress. Leisurely. Unhurried. She peeled off one item at a time, gauging his interest with every piece that fell to the floor.

His eyes smoldered. It was a wonder she hadn't gone up in flames. He watched her like a wolf watched his prey, his gaze stroking over her body like a paintbrush spreading liquid fire.

Finally she lowered her panties and let them pool at her feet. Then she pulled the straps of her bra down her shoulders until the cups fell away from her breasts. A mere second later, she tossed aside the bra and stood before him naked and trembling—not in fear—never in fear.

"Do you have any idea how beautiful you are?" he asked hoarsely.

"Right now I do," she whispered. "The way you're looking at me makes me feel like the most beautiful, desirable woman on earth."

"As you should."

Much as she'd done, he rose from the bed and stood just a foot apart from her as he began to slowly undress. His jeans dropped to the floor, leaving him in his boxer briefs. The material hugged his behind and his groin, outlining the sheer beauty of his physique. Her gaze was riveted to the bulge and to the thick erection being restrained by his underwear.

He pulled his shirt over his head. The muscles in his chest and shoulders rippled magnificently as he stretched. She simply couldn't help herself. She had to touch him.

She pressed her palms to his broad chest and smoothed them upward to his shoulders. He trembled and flinched, his breathing raw and harsh, pushed from his chest in torturous sounding spurts. His reaction surprised her but when she looked into his eyes, she saw the same desperate need that unfurled inside her.

She stepped even closer until his body heat wrapped around her. The first touch of his flesh against hers was an electric shock. He was lean and hard, rough and hairy. She wanted to rub herself all over him like a cat.

"You're killing me, honey," Garrett rasped out. "Lord have mercy, but you're killing me."

She smiled and reached for the waistband of his underwear. He sucked in his breath as she started working them down over his hips. His erection sprang free and bumped against the softness of her belly. She let go of the material, not caring where it went. She wanted to touch him. It was an urgent, restless need that took over. She ran her fingertips lightly up his sides, grinning when he shivered in response. They danced across his chest and then slid down to his belly and then lower still.

"Son of a bitch," Garrett muttered as he pried her hands away from his cock. "If you so much as breathe on me, I'm going to come and then I'll be so humiliated I'll never be able to get it up again."

She laughed and took a step back, more so she could look at him, all of him. Oh but he was beautiful. She thought that a lot about him, but it was so true. He was the perfect male specimen. Rough. Hard. Strong. A warrior in every sense of the word. There was nothing easy about him. She doubted there was a soft part on his body. And she wanted his hands on her more than she wanted to breathe.

"Touch me," she said in an aching voice. "I want to feel you."

He slid his hands over the sides of her neck and up to frame her face. His mouth came down on hers in a heated rush that stole her breath. His mouth was so gentle over hers, but insistent too.

The warmth of his tongue licking delicately at her lips sent a shiver down her spine. He tasted her like she was a delicious treat he was sampling. And as if he found it decadent, he pushed inward, wanting more. She met his advance, rubbing her tongue over the roughness of his. There was a hint of caramel, proof he'd snuck a taste while he'd been making dessert.

He sucked lightly at her bottom lip, pulling it then letting it go as he delved once more inside. Then he retreated and nibbled at her upper lip to the corner where he peppered her with tiny kisses. His mouth slid from her mouth to her jaw, tracing a line to her ear.

His breath blew over the delicate shell of her ear even as he sucked the lobe between his teeth.

"I want to savor you all night," he said in a rough, husky voice. "I'm going to take this slow. I want it to be perfect. So perfect. Now that you're finally mine, I'm going to kiss every inch of your body. I want to touch you and taste you and love you until you know in your heart that I'll never hurt you."

Her legs turned to jelly.

Which was okay because he bent and looped his arm underneath her quivering legs and hoisted her into his arms. He turned and walked the few steps to the bed and gently laid her down on the mattress.

He loomed over her, staring down at her like she was a feast he was about to devour. His gaze was fixed on her as if he was totally absorbed in her. Just her. It was a heady, giddy feeling that sent tingles of excitement through her blood.

The mattress dipped as he crawled onto the bed beside her. At first he contented himself with touching her. Just as she'd asked. And oh but his hands were wonderful. She was right. They weren't soft—she knew that already. But the way they glided up and down her body in a reverent manner made her feel as though she was a goddess being paid homage to.

He levered himself over her so that his body half covered hers and he stared down into her eyes, his expression serious. "If at any time I do something you're not okay with, tell me. I'll stop immediately."

She wanted to cry. Not because she was sad. Or afraid. But because he made her feel so protected and . . . cherished. It was a welcome change from fear and shame, from anxiety and fear.

"Promise me."

"I promise," she whispered. "Now kiss me."

His body pressed flush to hers as he lowered his mouth to capture her lips in yet another searing, soul wrenching kiss. Her breasts pressed into his chest, the light mat of hair teasing her nipples to hard points.

One hand wandered over her body, tracing a path over her curves, down her leg then back up again to her shoulder and then tangling in her hair. There was no sense of urgency about him. No rush—though she could tell by the betraying tremble of his body how hard he fought for control. She released a sigh of bliss that he swallowed up as his mouth possessed hers.

She wanted him. Not just wanted, but had to have. She wanted everything. His body. His touch. His tenderness. His love.

He shifted and his cock rested across her pelvis, hot and pulsing, so rigid and yet satiny smooth. But he made no move to end things that quickly. He pushed himself up and over her once more and dipped his head to nuzzle at her neck. He teased the sensitive flesh below her ear and nibbled a path to her shoulder, spreading a thousand chill bumps in his wake.

Soft, open-mouthed kisses caressed her flesh, ever closer to her breasts. She held her breath, waiting for his mouth to close around her nipple, but he continued to tease and lavish his attention on the plump swell.

She groaned in equal parts pleasure and frustration.

Then he dragged his tongue across the aureole and finally over her aching nipple. It puckered and thrust upward, so tight it was painful. He traced a damp circle around the bud before finally returning to it. His lips closed over the point and he sucked, keeping it between his teeth.

She arched off the bed, grasping wildly at his shoulders, something to hold on to, something for her fingers to dig into as she gasped her pleasure into the silence. He smiled against her breast and then carefully pulled away and fixed his gaze to hers.

"I'm not so good at pretty words," he admitted in a somewhat self-conscious voice. "I feel like I should be composing poetry or saying all the right things. You're so beautiful and the fact that you're giving yourself to me . . . I don't have the words."

She melted all the more under his steady gaze. She let all her love for him bleed into her smile as she raised her hand to stroke over his cheek. "The way you look at me, the way you touch me, tells me far more than words ever could."

He kissed her again, more fiercely than before. Breathless. Until she fidgeted with the restless, achy need that bloomed inside her. She wanted more. So much more.

He slid down her body, his mouth brushing over her breasts and then her belly. He paused at the juncture of her legs and gently kissed the area right above the patch of hair at her groin.

She shuddered, sighed and then arched upward, parting her legs in unconscious invitation. He repositioned himself so that he was between her sprawled legs, and again she held her breath as she watched his dark head lower until she could feel his soft exhale over her clit.

And then he touched her with his tongue. Just a simple flick over her clit and her hips bolted upward. Her knees shook uncontrollably and her fingers curled into tight fists at her sides.

With gentle fingers he parted her farther and swept his tongue over her quivering flesh to her opening. He circled it in a slow, teasing rhythm and then licked his way back up to her clit. He drew away for a moment and toyed with the swollen nub with his fingers, exerting just enough pressure to drive her insane. How could she withstand sweet and slow when he was killing her with just a touch?

He pressed his mouth where his fingers had just played and kissed her softly, sucking until she twisted and arched spasmodically.

"Garrett."

His name spilled from her lips, a soft plea, although she wasn't sure what she begged for.

"You okay?" he asked as he raised his head.

"Oh yes," she breathed.

He returned his attention to his gentle lovemaking, only this time he ran a finger through her folds. And when his mouth returned to her clit, he eased his finger inside her.

Lightning sizzled through her veins. Her orgasm welled up sharp and explosive. As he applied more pressure with his mouth, she went up in flames. Flood after flood of intense pleasure washed through her and over her.

It was several moments before she became aware of the fact that he was no longer between her legs. He lay beside her, gazing lazily down at her, smug satisfaction outlined on his face.

"Welcome back."

She stretched and turned into his arms, rubbing against his warm body. She sighed and laid her cheek on his shoulder.

"Feel good?"

"Mmm."

He chuckled lightly as he lifted a strand of her hair and let it fall from his fingers. "We're not done. Not even close to being done."

"You say the nicest things."

He cupped her cheek and kissed her lingeringly. When he shifted over, she could feel his hardness burning into her belly.

"I don't suppose you pack condoms in your soldier gear."

He reared back and then he laughed. "Soldier gear?"

She shrugged. "Whatever you call it. Aren't you Marines prepared for anything?"

"Oh yes, we routinely stop and fuck during a mission," he said dryly.

She giggled and punched him in the gut. "Smart-ass."

"I have two. We'll have to make the most of them."

"Somehow I don't think that'll be a problem."

"Me either," he murmured as he swept her underneath him.

He started all over again, coaxing a response and building and stoking the fire within her. He alternated kissing her senseless and licking over her body until she was panting and twitching from head to toe.

"Hold that thought," he rasped out as he rolled off her. She glanced sideways to see him dangle from the bed and fumble with his jeans. A moment later, her repositioned himself atop her and stroked his hand through her hair. "Now. Where were we?"

Feeling bold, she reached down and curled her hand around his latex-covered erection. She guided him toward her entrance and they both hissed out their breath when her heat surrounded him.

"Here."

"I like here," he said hoarsely.

"So do I."

Lowering to his elbows on either side of her, he eased forward, pushing into her with extreme patience and care.

"Stop me if I hurt you."

In response, she lifted her legs, curled them around his waist and arched her hips. Her movement caused him to sink farther into her body and she sighed. She stretched around him and the sensation was delicious.

"Almost there."

"Mmmm."

He surged forward the last few inches and her eyes flew open at the aching fullness. Tight, so very tight. She hugged his cock. Her body clenched with need and her pussy pulsed and rippled over his length.

"Tell me you're with me, Sarah. I can't hold back anymore."

The words came out in a pained-sounding rush. Sweat beaded his forehead and his jaw was clenched tight. Her fingers danced up his arms to his shoulders and she clasped her hands around his neck.

"I'm with you, Garrett. All the way. Let go. You won't hurt me. I want this. I want you."

With a groan he withdrew and thrust forward again. He only paused a second before he thrust again. And then again. He watched her the entire time and to ease his mind, she gave over to the all-consuming pleasure surrounding her like a cloud. She closed her eyes and threw back her head as the sound of his hips meeting the backs of her legs slid erotically over her ears.

"Tell me what you need," he strained out. "I want you to come again."

"Just don't stop," she said through clenched teeth. "Please don't stop."

No matter that he thought he was the one lacking control. She was already teetering on the edge of another orgasm, this one more intense, more explosive than the previous one. She bowed upward, her legs wrapped so tight around his waist that her body ached with the strain.

He thrust harder but he watched her the entire time and his fingers gently caressed her cheek. His body tightened and he closed his eyes, his gaze leaving her for the first time. She knew he was close and she wanted to go with him.

"Harder," she whispered.

A strangled sound escaped his throat and then he complied, rushing forward into her body. Once. Twice. She cried out his name, gripped his shoulders with bloodless fingers. Her name slipped from his lips in a husky, gravelly growl. Her orgasm burst over her like a balloon stretched too far.

She couldn't breathe. Couldn't think. Couldn't process anything but the mind-numbing ecstasy that fired through her brain. And through it all, Garrett gathered her close. Murmured her name. Whispered soothing words that were a balm to her ravaged senses.

She was breathing way too hard and too fast. Bright spots flashed in her vision and she closed her eyes, melting underneath him. Boneless. Mindless. She lay still as he came to rest atop her.

His chest heaved against hers and she felt the dampness as his forehead rested against hers.

"I've never seen a woman come like you do," Garrett said.

"If I wasn't so damn tired, I might take offense," she muttered.

He laughed. "It wasn't an insult. Right now I feel like Master of the Universe. It's a helluva ego trip for a man when his woman reacts that way to his lovemaking."

"Now you're going to get all smug on me."

He grinned and kissed her nose. "Oh, hell, yeah, I am." Then he sobered. "You okay?"

"Oh yeah. Never better."

He rolled to the side and then turned his back to her for a moment while he discarded the condom. A moment later he rolled back to her and wrapped his arms around her. She snuggled into his embrace and laid her head on his shoulder. After a moment he rolled to his back, taking her with him so that she was tucked firmly into his side. His arm curled possessively around her and he rubbed his fingers up and down her arm as their quiet breathing filled the room.

"I'm sorry I didn't tell you about Stanley before," she said quietly. "It's silly. Especially since I knew he was likely to come after me. I just didn't want anyone to know."

Garrett lifted his head and kissed her temple.

"I think I hate him more than I hate Allen. Isn't that stupid? Stanley didn't rape me. Allen did. But Stanley stood there with this smirk on his face the entire time. I begged him to help me and he just stood there looking at me like I was beneath his notice, like I deserved to be used. I'll always hate him for that. For being there. For allowing Allen to do what he did."

Garrett's arm tightened around her. "He won't get away with it, Sarah. I swear to you he won't."

His vow comforted her even though she doubted Garrett would ever have the occasion to come into contact with Stanley Cross. She stretched her legs, tangling them with his. She rubbed her foot up and down his hair-roughened leg as her hand glided over his chest.

"Thank you for making tonight so special."

Garrett kissed her again. "You're wrong, you know."

She rose up to look at him in puzzlement.

"It's you who made tonight special," he said in a low voice. "You're pretty special, Sarah."

She lowered her head until her lips touched his. "So are you, Garrett."

CHAPTER 33

THE next morning, Garrett waited until Sarah went into the bathroom to shower before he rolled out of bed and hurriedly dressed. He needed a moment to talk to Donovan because it was time to quit fucking around and end this.

He took the sat phone and stepped outside the reinforced, bulletproof glass doors to the enclosed patio off the master suite. The windows were tinted and was the only room in the house that allowed a sweeping view of the valley below.

Still, he remained in the shadows, in the corner and dialed up Donovan.

"Miss us already?" Donovan drawled a moment later.

"It's time," Garrett said quietly. "Send an email to Lattimer. Pretend you're Sarah and tip him off. I don't care what you tell him, just get him here. Let Resnick know so he can be in place. I need this over with as soon as possible. There are too many risks and Stanley Cross is the wild card here. He wants Sarah taken out."

"Allen Cross's brother?"

"Yeah, Allen Cross is the son of a bitch who raped Sarah, but his brother was there. He watched. He participated. His story about hiring a recovery firm to bring Sarah in because she can help bring his brother's killer to justice is bullshit. He wants her out of the picture so she can't hurt him."

"Damn," Donovan muttered. "What a fucking asshole. I vote that when this crap is over with Lattimer that you and I go on a little hunting trip."

Garrett grinned. One thing he loved about Donovan was that he had a very personal sense of justice when it came to certain crimes.

"What are you going to do about Sarah, Garrett? It's obvious she means a lot to you."

"Let me worry about Sarah," he said gruffly.

"I'll send the email. You need to alert Rio and be on guard. It's possible Lattimer won't even show. He might send his men in after her."

Garrett shook his head. "He'll come. Sarah is personal to him. He killed Allen Cross because he hurt Sarah. Personally. He didn't send someone else to do it though he could easily have done so. He risked a damn lot showing his face on U.S. soil again. Coming to Belize will be nothing to him."

"Be ready, Garrett. Lattimer's no amateur. He's a ruthless bastard with a very gray sense of justice."

Garrett thought back to when he faced Lattimer down all those years ago and felt the ripping sensation of the bullet Lattimer fired tearing into his leg. "You aren't telling me anything I don't already know. I've waited a damn long time for this, Donovan. I won't fuck it up. And tell Resnick he better damn well be careful. If he barges in here like a fucking idiot, Rio and his men are going to take exception. This is our show and Resnick better play by our rules."

"I'll let him know. I'm sure he'll be in touch."

Garrett hung up the phone and then called Rio to relay the news.

SARAH hummed contentedly as she set out the plates for breakfast. She dished up the eggs and bacon and then went to the oven to pull out the pan of biscuits that had turned golden brown. It was easy to forget that they were in some way out-of-the-way place in Central America, or that she and Garrett had endured a harrowing captivity just two days earlier.

Peace that she hadn't experienced in a long time settled over her like a warm and comforting blanket. She felt energized. She felt alive. And she felt hope for her future.

It was all silly. This giddy, feeling that gripped her. But it was fun and light and she wanted to laugh for the sheer joy of laughing. She smiled as she put the tray of biscuits on the counter and then she looked up and found Garrett across the room watching her with those intense blue eyes.

"Why are you smiling?" he asked as he ambled over.

A delicious thrill ran over her body all over again as she recalled the previous night. "I'm happy."

There was a brief glimmer of tension that rippled across his face before he walked over to where she stood and wrapped his arms around her, pulling her into his back. He kissed the side of her neck. "I'm glad you're happy."

She rotated in his arms and leaned up on tiptoe to kiss him. "Thank you for last night. For listening. For just letting me get it out without judging or reacting."

He squeezed her and kissed her long and lingering, his lips melting over hers. "He won't touch you, Sarah. Ever again."

"Have you let Marcus know what's going on? I don't want him to worry."

"He knows."

She stared up at him for a long moment as reality edged its way into her euphoria. Strange how it always worked that way. Thinking of Marcus had brought home the fact that her entire life had been upended. She was starting over with only Marcus to rely on for help.

She pulled away and placed the biscuits on a platter and then went to set them on the table. Garrett followed her and when she went to sit down, he put his hand over her wrist, holding her in place.

"Hey, what's wrong?"

She sighed and eased down into her chair. She picked up her fork and speared a piece of egg and then pushed it around her plate. "My life is a mess," she said honestly. "I don't know what I'm going to do. I've been in survival mode for so long, just taking it day by day, never thinking beyond the immediate. Marcus would like nothing more than to take care of me, for him to put me up somewhere where I never had to worry about money or work, but what kind of life is that? Existing, but not living. I can't return to Boston. I wouldn't, even if Stanley Cross got hit by a bus tomorrow."

"It's a pleasant enough thought," Garrett cut in.

She smiled. "Yes, I admit it is. But I wouldn't want him to die immediately. I'd want him to linger for several days and be in agonizing pain."

"I love it when you get all ruthless."

"You know what I love about you?" she said in an instant change of topic.

He blinked in surprise. "My amazing body? My ability to give you awesome orgasms?"

She laughed. "Aside from that."

"Do tell."

"It's really hard to throw a pity party because you know just what to say to make me laugh and smile."

His eyes grew serious. "I'm not making light of your situation, honey. If anyone has a reason to bitch, it's you."

She shook her head. "No, I mean it. Somehow it never seems quite so bad when I talk to you. I was sitting here thinking about what the hell I'm going to do after this is all over with. But then I think if it weren't for you, I wouldn't have those concerns because I'd probably be dead. And life . . . it's precious, you know? Even when it's bad, it's still good."

"Just when I think I've got you figured out, you do or say something that just makes me realize that I haven't even scratched the surface of the woman you are."

Her cheeks warmed under the blatant admiration in his voice.

"You're pretty damn special yourself, Garrett."

His lips tightened and he looked down at his food, forking up a bite of eggs and shoveling them into his mouth.

"Tell me about you and Marcus. You were raised in foster homes and yet he's your half brother. He seems pretty concerned about you now. Why weren't you raised together?"

The question caught her off guard and for a moment she sat there, fork frozen midway to her mouth. She lowered it to her plate and was silent a moment.

"Marcus and I shared a father. I never knew him, but from what I've heard he was a real bastard. Marcus hated him because he was unfaithful to Marcus's mom when he knocked my mom up. I would have thought that would give him reason enough to hate me. My mom wasn't self-sufficient. She was the type of woman who floated from man to man, looking for someone to take care of her because she had no desire to be responsible or hold a job. When she got pregnant with me, I think she thought I was her meal ticket. The problem was, my father wanted nothing to do with either of us. He sent her away without a dime and told her he'd kill her if she ever tried to make trouble for him. Granted, this was my mother's side and I was very young when she told me these stories, but Marcus did confirm that my mother did go to my father's house when she found out she was pregnant with me and that our father threw her out."

"Sounds like a real piece of work," Garrett muttered.

"She died when I was eight and I went into the foster care system. You already know all that. Marcus has always felt guilty because he knew he had a half brother or sister, and he also knew our father would never accept me. After our father died, he started searching for me. When he found me, he wanted to give me things. A home. Money. Cars. I don't know if he was trying to assuage his guilt or if just wanted the best for me. I was uncomfortable with it. I had a good job. I'd never get rich at it, but I was happy. And honestly just knowing he cared and that he'd been looking for me was enough. Suddenly I had someone when I hadn't since I was eight. Plus . . ."

"Plus what?" Garrett said as she drifted off.

She wrinkled her nose. "I don't say this to insult you because I know you work for my brother, but I know he's not perfect. I suspect . . . I suspect he's done a lot of things. Bad things. Our father wasn't a good man. Part of me doesn't want to know, because I love him and he's my only family. I feel guilty because I stick my head in the sand, but if I knew— if I really knew—that he'd done terrible things, it would crush me."

Garrett blew out his breath. Goddamn but this sucked. He didn't even want to respond anything because anything he said at this point would be a lie.

"I don't think badly of you," she said in a rush. "I mean, I know this is a job. You just work for him."

"You aren't just a job, Sarah. If you believe that, you're one hundred percent wrong. I don't give a damn about the job. What I care about is you and making damn sure Cross doesn't get close to you."

Pink dusted her cheeks and her eyes went soft. "Garrett, there's something else I wanted to tell you. Something I wanted to tell you when we were in that prison and I was so afraid. I didn't think that was the right time, and maybe it isn't now. I just—"

Garrett looked up in annoyance when Rio and Terrence let themselves in the back door. Sarah stood abruptly, her cheeks flushed and her fingers curled into nervous fists. What the hell had she been about to tell him?

"Do you guys want breakfast?" Sarah asked. "There's plenty, and I could put on some more eggs and bacon if the others would like to eat."

Rio glanced between Garrett's scowl and Sarah with a raised eyebrow. "Are we interrupting anything?"

"Yes."

"No," Sarah said. "Really. We were just eating and talking about nothing. Why don't you join us?"

Without giving Rio or Terrence a chance to answer, she hurried around to the fridge and took out more eggs and the rest of the bacon. She juggled another can of biscuits and plopped it all onto the counter.

"Your timing sucks," Garrett muttered as Rio and Terrence took their seats.

Rio glanced over at Sarah, who was busy beating the eggs in a bowl. "Van called. Resnick's sending one of his teams in. I don't like it, but we could probably use the backup. Lattimer has resources. I don't think it would be a bad idea to call up Steele for this. The last thing we want to do is underestimate Lattimer when all this goes down."

"Do what you feel is best," Garrett murmured. "My priority is Sarah. Your job is to make damn sure we're both safe. If you need to call Steele in, then do it."

Rio gave a short nod as Sarah walked over to put two plates in front of him and Terrence.

"What about the rest?" Sarah asked. "Aren't they hungry?"

"They can't leave their posts," Rio explained. "Terrence

and I won't be long. We just wanted to check in on you two and make sure everything was all right."

"Oh, we're fine," Sarah said breathlessly and gave Garrett a shy look that made him smile.

She sat back down, fiddled with her now-cold food some more and then looked up first at Garrett and then the others, and she frowned. "Do you really think they'll find me here?"

Rio shot Garrett a look that clearly told him he wasn't sure who the "they" were that she was referring to and furthermore, he wasn't going to venture onto shaky ground.

"Cross. Or the people he hired, I mean," she amended when no one immediately answered her.

Garrett reached over and squeezed her hand. "It's not impossible. But probable? It would take time to pick up our trail from Mexico and a lot of resources to track us here. I'm not saying it couldn't be done. We didn't have the cleanest exit in the world, and my brothers hauling ass to Corozal didn't help I'm sure. But regardless of whether they know where you are, what you need to realize is that we're not going to let those bastards take you."

Garrett glanced over at Rio. No, it wasn't Cross and company who concerned them. But make no mistake, once Lattimer was taken care of, Cross was definitely next on their list.

CHAPTER 34

THE slight bulge in Marcus Lattimer's jaw was the only indication of his mounting fury. He stared coolly at the email from Sarah he'd just opened and leaned back in his chair, eyes narrowed in concentration.

It shouldn't surprise him that someone had gotten to Sarah. She hadn't done the best job in disappearing. He'd tried to persuade her to come to him, but he'd understood her reasons why. Sarah had become a target from the moment Marcus had killed her rapist. It was one of the few times he'd lost control in his life. It was one of the few mistakes he'd made.

Not that he regretted killing Allen Cross even for a moment. But he'd handled it all wrong. He'd allowed his rage to rule his actions. Stupid. What he should have done was get Sarah away from Boston and settled. Somewhere she'd be happy and taken care of. Then he could have dealt with Cross. Sarah would be none the wiser and he could have returned to her. They could have been a family.

Damn Culpepper. Another of Marcus's recent mistakes. He was growing careless. Culpepper must have gotten information to the U.S. government before Marcus dispensed of him a few days earlier. He'd lasted longer than Marcus had thought he would. But no one could last forever under such horrific conditions.

Now Marcus wanted to kill him all over again for selling out Marcus's only family. Sarah, who'd never hurt anyone. Who'd already been dealt enough misfortune in her life. He'd been so determined to make it up to her, and in the end he'd only caused her more pain.

It was all too pat. Too easy. Marcus doubted that Sarah even composed the email staring him in the face. She was too careful. She'd never blab such explicit details through an email. The question was whether Sarah was even in Belize as the email stated. It was a trap. No doubt there. But were they using her for actual bait or were they just trying to get Marcus to walk blindly into capture?

They weren't the first to underestimate him. They wouldn't be the last.

He leaned forward and punched the button on the desk to summon his head of security. He needed as much information on Sarah's actual location as possible. If she wasn't in Belize, he could go in, destroy the sons of bitches who bent low enough to use a woman in their war. If she was in Belize . . . then he was going to have to be extremely careful. He wasn't going to give himself up, but neither would he allow Sarah to be sacrificed on his behalf.

It was time to call in a few favors.

CHAPTER 35

RIO wasn't happy when Garrett informed him Steele and his team were coming in hot. The team leader's lips thinned and his jaw went taut.

"Should have just hung up some balloons and announced a fucking party," Rio muttered.

Garrett gave him a look of sympathy. Rio was a loner and it had probably been hard enough to open up his private sanctuary to Garrett and Sarah but now he had to play host to Steele and his entire team and there wasn't much love lost between the two team leaders.

"Tell him this is my show. He's not barging onto my turf and taking over."

"He knows," Garrett said. "Van was clear. You're on point. You know this area. You have all the escape routes. Steele and his team are here to provide cover and support."

Rio nodded but he still looked pissed.

"Look on the bright side," Garrett said. "Van sent them to fucking Alaska first. Steele's probably not any happier that he's had to haul ass to Central America from Alaska."

Rio grinned. "Alaska, huh. Ouch."

Garrett rolled his eyes at how delighted Rio was over Steele's inconvenience.

"I'll stick Steele and his team on the perimeter. They can sleep in the trees. They'll have a bird's-eye view of the valley and the river. If someone comes after us, they'll come from the air or the river. Either way we'll nail them before they get here."

Garrett nodded. "I want Lattimer taken down the first time he shows his face. And Rio, tell your men to be careful. Lattimer is a ruthless bastard. He has no compunction about killing those he perceives as a threat. I don't want to lose a single man."

Rio's eyes went flat. "I already lost one man. I'm not losing another."

Months earlier, one of Rio's men had been killed when Garrett's mom had been abducted from the hospital where Garrett's dad had been taken after suffering a heart attack. It had been hard on the team leader. He'd felt enormous guilt over his man's death and Marlene Kelly's abduction.

Garrett put a hand on Rio's shoulder. "I know this sucks for you man, but I appreciate it."

"What's their ETA?"

"Two hours."

Rio nodded. "I'll meet them at the river and show them their posts."

Garrett stifled a smile. Anytime Rio rolled out the welcome mat, it was guaranteed to be interesting.

After leaving Rio, Garrett went in search of Sarah only to find her curled on a couch in Rio's library with a book in hand. It still amazed him that Rio had such refined tastes. In addition to the well-stocked library, the man had a wine cellar that would make royalty green with envy. It was obvious that Rio had spent a lifetime stocking his house in all the things he loved the most. Sarah had called it right when she'd suggested that this was Rio's refuge. His home. Something he kept away from the rest of his life. It made Garrett look at his team leader in a whole new light. It also made him realize how little he knew about the men—and the woman—that KGI employed.

"Hey," he said from the doorway.

She looked up, setting her book down on her lap. "Hi."

A broad smile spread across her face, and her cheeks bloomed with color. It gave him a kick in the gut that she was obviously glad to see him.

"Enjoying yourself?"

She patted the spot on the couch beside her in invitation and he ambled over to settle beside her.

"It's weird in a way. I feel almost guilty to be eating good food and enjoying good books. I keep thinking I should be looking over my shoulder and worrying."

"That's my job," he pointed out. "Yours is to relax and *not* worry."

She snuggled into his arms and lay her head on his shoulder. "You're spoiling me, Garrett."

He stroked a hand down her hair and kissed the top of her head. "Being spoiled isn't a bad thing, surely."

She sighed and rubbed her cheek over his chest. "No, it isn't." Then she raised her head up so sharply she almost butted him in the chin. "Hey, I never got a caramel num num."

He chuckled. "They haven't gone anywhere. Well, not unless Rio and his men found them."

She scrambled out of his arms and hurried toward the door. "I'll fight Rio for them."

Garrett pushed up to follow her, grinning the whole way. In the kitchen, Sarah jerked open the fridge and stared inside, her brow furrowed in concentration. Then her eyes lit up and she reached in and pulled out the pie dish.

Garrett took it from her, turned the dish upside down onto a glass platter and tapped until the whole thing came out. Then he tossed the dish into the sink and began cutting the dessert into little pieces. Sarah hung impatiently at his side until he offered her a bite.

She pounced on it and nibbled at the treat. She closed her eyes and groaned. "Oh my God. This is wonderful, Garrett. Give me more."

She shoved him aside and picked out several of the larger pieces. He chuckled as she viewed him suspiciously, like she was an animal guarding her food.

"They're all yours," he said, putting his hands up in defense.

He watched as she put another bite into her mouth and closed her eyes with a soft groan.

"Rio has an enclosed pool off the left wing of this house. Wanna go for a swim?" he asked.

She lowered the candy and scrunched up her brow. "Is it safe?"

"I wouldn't have suggested it if it wasn't. Rio is a paranoid bastard. He's made this place virtually impenetrable."

"I'd like that."

Garrett pushed in closer to her, swaggering as he said the next. "Skinny-dipping?"

Color rose in her cheeks. "Garrett! I don't want anyone seeing me."

"Did I mention this pool is completely enclosed? No one will see you but me, honey, and I'm going to end up seeing you whether you wear a suit or not. I just figure it'll make my job easier if you forego a suit from the start."

She laughed. "Incorrigible!"

"Yes ma'am, I am," he said. "My mama has said so many a time."

She shook her head. "Okay. Skinny-dipping it is. But if anyone else sees me, I'll kill you."

He lowered his mouth to hers with a growl. "If anyone else sees you, I'll kill *them*."

"YOU ever think we spend most of our time in transit?" P.J. asked as she hopped into the boat beside Cole. Behind her, Dolphin, Renshaw and Baker piled into the next boat while Steele stood on the dock coolly surveying the river.

"I'd say we spend most of our time getting jerked around," Cole muttered. "First it's fucking Alaska. Now it's the damn jungle. I hate the fucking jungle."

"You only say that because you got shot the last time we ventured into the jungle."

"It was a ricochet," Cole pointed out.

P.J. shrugged. "You still took a bullet and had to be carried out."

Cole scowled as he stared at the smaller woman who serenely stared over the water. Steele climbed aboard and gave the motion to shove off. Damn woman was yanking his chain again and, as always, he rose to the bait beautifully.

"I wonder what we'll have here," she said as she turned. "In Alaska, it was BAFB. I guess here it's BAFS."

"BAFS?" Cole asked cautiously. He wasn't even sure he wanted to know.

"Big-ass fucking snakes," she said cheerfully. "They have anacondas here. They can swallow a man whole."

"Great. Just fucking great."

"You're way too easy Coletraine," Steele said, a hint of amusement in his voice.

"I hate snakes. They freak me the fuck out."

P.J. patted him on the arm. "I'll protect you, Cole. I won't let the big bad snakes get you."

"I'm tempted to feed you to them."

Steele chuckled and turned his attention back to the river as the boats glided soundlessly through the water.

"I hope wherever we're going, we get some sleep," P.J. said with a yawn.

"The accommodations will be up to Rio," Steele said through his teeth.

"Great," Cole said glumly. "I think the man's idea of first-class accommodations is having a rock for a pillow."

"Rio has a nice place here," P.J. piped up.

Steele raised an eyebrow while Cole turned sharply. "How the hell do you know what Rio has?"

P.J. shrugged. "He told me about it. Sounds like a nice place. He worked on it for years. Pretty high-tech too."

"You had an actual conversation with Rio?" Cole asked in disbelief.

"Yeah, he's cool."

Cole's gaze narrowed. "Just how well do you know him?"

"We talk."

"When the hell do you have time to talk? When we're all together for a mission, there sure as hell isn't time for chit-chat."

"Duh, I have a life outside our missions, you know."

Cole's mouth popped open. Granted he didn't know jack about what his team members did outside the job. If he was honest, most of the time they lived, ate and breathed the job. Sometimes they spent weeks together, day in, day out. It was hard to imagine anyone's life outside the team.

"I saw him when he was in Colorado a few months back," she said with a huff of impatience. "He knew I lived in the area so he looked me up. We had a few drinks. Talked shop."

Cole scowled again and glanced over at Steele to see how

he took the news. He appeared as unruffled as ever, but then that was Steele. He never interfered in their private lives. When they were on a mission, their asses belonged to Steele. No questions asked. They followed his command without question. But when they finished, they each went their own way, and until now, Cole never gave a thought to how his teammates lived when they weren't together.

P.J. was a good looking, very in-shape woman. She was smart. Sharp as a tack. And she could damn well look after herself. Any red-blooded male would be tripping over his tongue to hook up with her.

Now it was going to bug him to wonder what had happened between P.J. and Rio. Not that it was any of his business. P.J. was just a teammate. Nothing more.

But as they slipped farther down the river, Cole couldn't help but imagine P.J. with Rio.

He scowled harder.

Thirty minutes later, they docked at a bend in the river. It was a moonless night and they were far enough from any town that the entire area was shrouded in a cloak of darkness. Cole's eyes rapidly adjusted and he caught movement at the other end of the dock.

He pushed P.J. back and stepped in front of her, then barked a low warning to Steele and pulled up his rifle.

Rio rippled out of the shadows and murmured a greeting to Steele and his team. P.J. shoved by Cole and then got into his face, her eyes spitting fury.

"What the fuck was that, Coletraine? You ever pull a stunt like that again and I'll cut your balls off."

"Yeah, we're clear."

Hell, he didn't know what had possessed him to do that. She had a right to be mad. He'd treated her like she was someone in need of protecting. Not like an equal.

"Let's go," Steele said shortly. "We've got until dawn to scout and get into position."

CHAPTER 36

SARAH yawned and gave a gigantic stretch as she pried open her eyes. According to the clock at her bedside, it was already past noon. Noon? Holy cow.

She bolted upward and started to leap out of bed but then she flopped back onto her pillow and stared up at the ceiling. Why did she have to hurry? There was absolutely no place she had to be. Nothing to do other than whatever she wanted.

It was a nice feeling to know that she was safe and that she could slow down and stop the incessant worrying that had plagued her for so long that she'd forgotten what it felt like to just be.

She had Garrett to thank for that. Well, and Marcus, but mostly Garrett. The man had made her feel like living again. She smiled and yawned lazily. After a moment, the sounds coming from the bathroom pricked her ears and she realized Garrett was showering.

Feeling devilish, she scooted from the bed and hurried into the bathroom. Sure enough, he was in the shower and steam rose, fogging the shower doors and the bathroom windows. With a grin, she shed her nightshirt and opened the shower door to see Garrett standing with his eyes closed, face turned up into the spray as water cascaded over his muscular, lean body.

All the breath left her as she simply stared. He was so gorgeous. Sweet merciful lord. but the man was simply lethal.

Water slid over his belly, down through the dark hair of his groin and then down thickly corded legs. She frowned when she spotted a large, ugly scar on his upper leg that she hadn't noticed before. It was old but large. It didn't look like it had been stitched well. There was a mass of scar tissue, still angry looking, white at the edges and dull pink in the center.

When she glanced back up, she saw that his eyes were open and he was staring at her. His cock twitched under the onslaught of water and stiffened until it rose toward his navel.

She smiled.

He scowled.

"It's disgusting how little control I have around you," he muttered.

She stepped into the shower and shut the door behind him. Water bounced off him and pelted her as she sidled up to him and pressed her body to his. They both moaned when their flesh met. His erection was pressed between them but she was aware of his length, pulsing against her belly, growing more turgid by the moment.

"I thought I'd give you a little help," she said as she reached for the washcloth and the liquid soap.

"Oh, I can always use your kind of help."

He stretched his arms up to rest on the walls of the shower so she had full access to his body. She lathered soap onto the cloth and began at his shoulders. Gently, she lavished attention over his entire body, taking special care around the still-vivid bruises at his midsection.

She might have washed his behind more than necessary, but she was mesmerized by the full cheeks and the contrast between them and his lean hips and muscular legs. The pale globes were a stark contrast to his tanned arms and legs. It was all she could do not to lean over and take a bite out of his ass.

She knelt and rubbed up one leg and then the other. Each time her gaze was drawn to his thick cock thrusting upward from his groin. Deciding it needed extra special attention, she tossed aside the cloth and curled her hands around the base, guiding it down toward her mouth.

"Oh hell," Garrett groaned.

He dropped one hand and thrust it in her wet hair just as she sucked him deep into her mouth. He trembled from head to toe and thrust impatiently over her lips.

Before she could really get into it, Garrett reached down and hauled her up into his arms. He slammed her against the wall of the shower and devoured her mouth like he was starving.

"No condoms in here, damn it," he said in frustration.

He spun around, threw open the shower door and stepped out. She shivered as cooler air hit her wet body. Garrett stalked through the bathroom and into the bedroom. He tumbled her onto the bed and before she could take a breath, he flipped her onto her belly. She heard the nightstand drawer open and then slam. Felt his hands gripping her hips and pulling her to the edge of the bed.

"That's the last condom," she teased. "Better make it good."

His fingers slipped between her legs and pushed inward as if testing her readiness. She was wet. She was definitely ready. She squirmed impatiently as his hand left her.

Firm hands gripped her legs, spread her and then he thrust into her from behind.

She cried out at the instant fullness. The indescribable pleasure at having him buried to the balls inside her body. The tightness, the sensitivity. Her heart raced. Her blood pounded through her veins. Her pussy pulsed and clenched around him. Every nerve ending was on fire, sizzling like the shortest of fuses.

"Are you okay?" he murmured close to her ear. He'd gone completely still as he awaited her response. Her chest lurched and she closed her eyes, smiling at the depth of his concern and caring.

"I'm fine," she groaned. "Please don't stop. You feel wonderful."

He chuckled then and pulled out slowly, his length rippling over her swollen tissues until she squirmed underneath him. He pushed forward again, gaining depth at his hips pressed into her buttocks.

His hands smoothed over her back and he leaned down to kiss between her shoulder blades. He slid his tongue over her shoulder to her neck and then he nipped, eliciting shiver after shiver to quake down her spine.

He began pumping against her, the noisy smacks echoing erotically through the room. He maintained a steady rhythm, one destined to drive her insane. He drove her to the very brink of orgasm and then he'd pause and change his speed and strength, forcing her to start all over again.

She panted frantically through her mouth until it was dry and all she could do was croak out her protests. Halfhearted protests. She even managed to confuse herself. Stop. Don't stop. You're killing me. That feels wonderful.

He was patient and he had the staying power of a damn machine. How could he hold out that long? She was exhausted and he still fucked her like he'd just begun.

His body blanketed hers, pressing her into the mattress. There wasn't a part of her body that wasn't enveloped by him and his heat. His hips moved rhythmically against her behind, pushing her harder and further. She closed her eyes, curled her fingers into the sheets and arched up as high as she could with his weight pressing down on her.

By the time she realized that this time he wasn't going to stop, she was exhausted and so dizzy with pleasure that she was senseless. She moaned as the pressure increased. Burned. Sharp. A razor's edge. Higher and higher. Harder and harder. She didn't have the strength. This orgasm was going to kill her.

A high keening wail split the air and she realized it was her. Garrett pushed himself up off her by pressing his hands into the mattress on either side of her head and he began working into her hard. Much harder than before. He was as close as she was.

Her legs spread wider and the force of his thrusts pushed her up the bed until her head crept over the opposite side. She stared down at the floor, her vision going blurry and fuzzy as she arched painfully.

Then the pressure suddenly blew like a tire under pressure. She gave a gasp of relief and then moaned as the aftershocks splintered through her, painful, edgy, so good. So very good.

His teeth sank into his shoulder like he was a beast marking his mate and his hips pressed firmly against her, holding himself deep as if to tell her there was no escape. She was his. He was a part of her.

She melted into the covers and turned her face so that her

cheek was pressed flat against the mattress. She closed her eyes and panted softly as he sprawled over her body, his cock still buried deep inside her.

She was pinned, filled, covered, and she loved it.

Garrett kissed her shoulder but continued to lay on her as his chest heaved. When he finally pushed himself up, she felt bereft of his touch. Felt naked and cold. She shivered and turned, seeking his warmth.

He stood by the bed, quickly rolling the condom off to toss in the trash. She stared up at him as he turned back to her and she sighed in utter contentment at the look in his eyes. No, words simply couldn't replace the way he looked at her, the way he touched her, the way he loved her like there was no one else in the world for him.

The words bubbled up again, and this time she knew she was ready to tell him.

She reached for his hand and he slid his fingers over her palm as he crawled back into bed beside her. She crawled into his arms, cuddling against his side. She threw one leg over his body, holding him as possessively as he often held her.

"I love you," she said softly.

He tensed beneath her and she smiled. Before he could respond, she put a finger to his lips.

"Shhh. Don't say anything. Please. I've wanted to tell you, but the time just wasn't right. Maybe it's not now, but I can't hold back any longer. But the thing is, I don't want you to respond. I don't want you to say anything at all. I just need you to know how much I love you. How grateful I am for you. How utterly amazed I am that a man like you exists."

She levered up and over him and stared down into his eyes as earnestly as she knew how.

"No matter what happens, I wanted you to know that you are the most special man I've ever met. I'll never forget you. I'll never forget our time together. I never considered that I'd be able to trust someone again. Somehow you made it easy. You made it second nature. I didn't even have to think about it long. You just snuck past my defenses and you made yourself at home."

She kissed him warmly, pressing her mouth softly to his. "I love you," she whispered again. "So much I ache. Thank you for helping me take back everything Allen and Stanley Cross took from me."

Garrett gathered her in his arms and squeezed her so tightly she couldn't breathe. "Sarah, I—"

The door burst open and Garrett rolled Sarah underneath him to shield her from view.

"What the fuck?" Garrett roared.

Rio stood in the doorway, his expression grim.

"We have to move. The whole damn jungle is on fire and we're in its path."

CHAPTER 37

GARRETT pushed himself from the bed and yanked up the sheets to cover Sarah. He strode naked to the door where Rio stood. "Tell me."

"Big fire. It's moving rapidly in our direction. The smoke's made using the helicopter impossible. We'll have to go by boat. Meet at the trucks in five. We're moving out."

Garrett cursed and turned in the direction of the bed, where Sarah sat up, the covers pulled to her chin. Her eyes were wide and concerned and her fingers were white against the sheets.

"Get up and get dressed, honey. We've got to move fast."

She scrambled out of bed and ran to the drawers to yank out her clothing.

"Get what you can stuff into your bag. Leave everything else. We don't have time," he said as he pulled on his jeans.

While she thrust items into her bag, Garrett retrieved his holster and shoved his Glock into it. He threw the strap of his rifle over his shoulder and patted his pockets for his knife.

"I'm ready," Sarah said in a remarkably steady voice.

He kissed her forehead and then thrust her into the hall ahead of him. They hurried down the hall, through the living room and to the garage where Rio and the others waited.

"Steele and his team are covering our exit. Then they'll

rendezvous with us at the river," Rio said as they piled into the two trucks.

As soon as they burst from the dark garage, Garrett saw the hazy film of smoke in the air and the smell of scorched earth assaulted his nostrils. In the distance, the sky was blocked by a film of dark smoke and as they rounded the corner of Rio's drive, they got a glimpse of orange flames shooting skyward.

Rio accelerated as they lurched from his smoother drive onto the rough, narrow roadway that would take them to the river. They roared over bumps and holes and Garrett's grip tightened around Sarah so she wouldn't hurt herself or land on the floor.

The river was visible ahead when suddenly two dark SUVs pulled directly in front of their vehicle and blocked the road. Rio slammed on the brakes, fishtailed sideways and in the same instant, jammed it into reverse and gunned the motor. Rio turned to look over his shoulder as he steered with his left hand and roared backward down the path they'd come.

Garrett shoved Sarah to the floor and drew his weapon as Terrance did the same. The other SUV that occupied the rest of Rio's men was racing backward just behind Rio. The two vehicles were nearly back to the main road when yet more SUVs pulled onto the path to block them.

"Son of a bitch," Rio swore. "I knew this was a setup!"

He braked, jammed the gearshift into drive and started forward again. They were nearly to the first vehicles that had blocked them when an explosion sounded and the vehicle careened wildly to the right. Rio fought for control and managed to reign the vehicle in but too late, they rolled to a stop against a tree.

The vehicle lurched on impact, throwing Garrett against the passenger seat.

"Sarah!" he barked. "Are you okay? Stay down."

"I'm fine," she returned.

"Fuckers shot out our tire," Rio bit out.

"Fuck," Terrance muttered.

Garrett looked up to see what Terrance was swearing over only to find five heavily armed men just outside the vehicle, their rifles all pointed directly at them. One motioned with his rifle for them to get out.

"Fuck," Garrett echoed.

Rio raised his hands from the steering wheel. "I hope to fuck Steele and company make it here fast. As much as it pains me to say, they're going to have to get our asses out of this one."

"Garrett?"

Sarah's fear-filled voice rose from her position on the floor-board.

"Come up, Sarah," Garrett said. "Slowly. Don't make any sudden movements. When we get out I want you to stay behind me and Rio at all times. Understand?"

She nodded as she slowly climbed onto the seat.

Terrance opened his door and slowly got out. Rio followed suit and then Garrett carefully got out on his side and then motioned for Sarah. He gripped her wrist and pulled her out but was careful to tuck her behind his back as he turned to face their threat.

Behind them, the rest of Rio's team got out of their trucks and closed ranks around Sarah from behind. Garrett could feel Sarah shaking against him and he squeezed her reassuringly.

Several feet ahead of the men holding them at gunpoint, another person got out of one of the vehicles. When he turned in Garrett's direction, instant recognition flashed through Garrett's mind.

Marcus Lattimer slid the shades from his eyes and stared coldly in Garrett's direction as he slowly walked toward him.

Garrett's grip tightened around Sarah.

"Sarah, come out here," Marcus called softly as if he had no desire to frighten her either.

Sarah stiffened against Garrett's back and then cautiously she stuck her head around Garrett. "Marcus?" she whispered.

"Are you all right?" Marcus demanded.

"Of course. Garrett has taken good care of me."

"Come away from *Garrett*," Marcus ordered. "He's no friend, Sarah. He's using you to get to me."

Sarah took a step forward, but her face wrinkled in confusion. "I don't understand. You hired him, Marcus. He's only done the job you hired him to do. He's protected me."

Marcus held out his hand and as soon as Sarah took it, he yanked her to his side.

"He lied," Marcus said shortly. "I didn't hire him. He quite likely works for the U.S. government. He would have done whatever was necessary to draw me out, including hacking into your email and sending me messages to draw me out."

Garrett's stomach churned as Sarah only looked more confused.

"No, Marcus, you're wrong. Garrett didn't use me. He protected me. He . . ." She trailed off when she turned haunted eyes on Garrett. He stared stoically at her and something died in Sarah's expression. "It's true?" she whispered as she stared dully at Garrett.

"No, it's damn well not true," Garrett growled.

"Then why did you tell me Marcus hired you? Marcus says he didn't."

Garrett wasn't going to explain the whole goddamn thing here. He hoped to fuck that Steele and his team were moving in fast. It would be nice if for once Resnick was on tap at the right time.

"Your brother is a traitor," Garrett spat.

Marcus lifted one brow even as he pulled Sarah closer to him. His hand slipped comfortingly over Sarah's shoulder and squeezed reassuringly. At least the bastard seemed to genuinely care for Sarah. He wouldn't hurt her.

"I remember you now," Marcus said casually. "You were the Marine I shot in Libya."

Garrett's nostrils flared and he snarled in Marcus's direction, "A lot of American soldiers lost their lives trying to save your ass."

"I don't recall asking your government to do anything," Marcus said calmly.

Sarah looked between Garrett and Marcus, her confusion and hurt mounting by the minute. "What's going on?" she croaked out.

Marcus turned gentle eyes on her. "I'm sorry, Sarah. I have many enemies. Men who would think nothing of stooping to using women in their war against me. I'm so sorry he got to you before I did. I wouldn't have had you hurt for the world."

She turned to Garrett for confirmation but his cold stare said it all. He hated Marcus. She glanced at Rio and to his men, all men who'd sworn to protect her. All the time they were using her to draw her brother out. The very thing she'd feared the most had come to pass. She had been used against Marcus. Only it wasn't the judicial system as she'd feared. These were men who'd think nothing of killing her brother in cold blood. She'd led them directly to him.

Nausea welled in her stomach. She'd trusted Garrett as she'd never thought to trust another person. She'd made love to him. She'd given him everything and all along he was involved in some sick vendetta against her brother.

She'd told him she *loved* him.

"How could I have been so stupid?"

The whispered words came out in a painful rush. Garrett flinched and raised his glittering gaze to her. "Sarah—"

The ground exploded beside Sarah as dirt flew in all directions. The distant retort of a rifle shot echoed and she stood there, stunned as she stared down at the dirt all over her feet.

Garrett and Marcus both lunged for her at the same time, but Marcus was there first, leaping in front of her and turning her so she was trapped between him and the vehicle.

Marcus's body lurched against her as another shot sounded and Marcus grunted in pain. She shoved at Marcus, wanting to see. The next thing she knew, Garrett had pulled her away from Marcus and flung her to the ground, his big body covering her as the world went crazy around her.

"Sniper at three o'clock!" Garrett roared. "Take cover!"

Pandemonium ensued. Sarah shoved at Garrett but she couldn't see or hear what was going on. Gunfire sounded loud in her ears, deafening her to all else. Her chest squeezed painfully as she glanced to the side to see Marcus lying on the ground a mere foot away, blood trickling from his mouth.

P.J. heard the shot and jerked her gaze in the direction of the gunfire. The shooter was close—at most, twenty yards. She drew her pistol and stalked stealthily through the heavy cover, her nose quivering as her gaze took in every inch of thick foliage. She didn't dare radio. The sniper would hear.

She smelled him before she spotted him. Stupid asshole. His stench wafted through the leaves. Sweat. He reeked of it. He wasn't a professional, which took the challenge right out of it for her. This would be like taking down an infant.

She crept up behind him, disgusted that he hadn't even heard her. She pressed the barrel of her pistol to his head. "Down, asshole!"

The man whirled around and tried to charge her. She rolled her eyes, stuck out her foot and in a lightning move, yanked his arm back as he went down. She fell on top of him, his arm twisted painfully behind his back. His face was in the mud and her barrel was dug into his back.

She shoved him over and kicked away his rifle. The man ought to be shot for not taking better care of his equipment. It was a sin to abuse such a fine piece of weaponry. She dug her pistol into the side of his neck as she sat astride him.

"Talk motherfucker. Who do you work for?"

The man spit at her and she punched him. "You're pissing me off. Don't make me cut off your nuts."

She reached her knife and flipped it open until the blade gleamed wickedly in the light.

"I'd listen to her. She's pretty mean when she's pissed off," Cole drawled.

P.J. looked up to see her teammate leaning against a tree several feet away, amusement glittering in his eyes.

She returned her gaze to her prisoner to see disbelief in his eyes.

She cut the button off his fly and used the knife blade to pry open his pants. He sucked in his breath when she got to his underwear, and she made quick work of the material covering his dick.

She shot him a pitying glance. "Not that there's a whole lot to be prideful over, but still, most men would rather not do without. Though in your case, I can't imagine it makes much difference."

The man's face flushed with anger and he tried to roll her off him. She rammed her fist into his nuts and brought the pistol stock down over his jaw.

"Now, let's try this again. You tell me who you are and who you work for or I cut off your dick and make you eat it."

"Now, P.J.," Cole chided, "you don't want to add it to your collection?" He shook his head at the man underneath her. "I used to think she had dick envy or something. Now I just know she's one mean bitch. She collects dicks, you know, like trophies. Dries them out, tans them like an animal hide and then hangs them on her wall. Kind of sick, if you ask me, but everyone has their hobbies."

"You're lying," the man gasped out. But sweat rolled down his face and his eyes bulged out of his head as he stared at the knife in horror.

"Well, granted yours isn't anything to brag about, but I'm sure I have a place on my wall for it," she said with a shrug. She made another cut to his pants and the acrid smell of piss assaulted her nose.

"Well hell, he pissed himself, Cole. That's going to make this a little more difficult."

"Okay, okay!" the man shouted. "Stanley Cross hired me. Wants me to take out the Daniels bitch. Doesn't care how. He wanted me to bring back photographic evidence of her death. If I do, he pays me a mil."

P.J. sat back and faked a look of disappointment. "Well, damn."

"Get her off me!"

Cole chuckled. "I don't usually mess with P.J. I'm kind of fond of my dick."

P.J. rolled off but was careful to keep her pistol aimed at the man's head. "Get up, asshole."

As P.J. walked over to where Cole stood, he murmured low enough for only her to hear. "Dick collection, Rutherford? You didn't have to have quite so much enthusiasm."

She chuckled. "As fond as you men are of them, I figured he'd squeal sooner if I threatened his dick."

SARAH scrambled over to Marcus as soon as Garrett moved off her. Marcus lay partially on his side and she rolled him to his back, terrified at the copious amount of blood staining his chest.

"Marcus," she pleaded. "Talk to me please. I'll get you help."

Marcus's eyelids flickered and he trained his unfocused stare on her. "You're safe. That's all that matters."

Tears slid soundlessly down her cheeks. She shut out the goings-on around them. There were men everywhere. Garrett directed most of the action while Marcus's men were taken into custody. There were too many for it to just be Garrett's team. Marcus was right. Garrett had used her to get to him.

"Please be all right, Marcus. You're all I have. I love you. This is all my fault. I shouldn't have told you. I should have fought my own battles."

Marcus raised a hand to wipe at her tears. "No, Sarah. You had to fight them for far too long. You should have had a home. Me. A father who loved you. Neither of us had that, I'm afraid. But I could have done more for you. I'm sorry. I love you, you know. You're the only person I've ever loved and who loved me back."

"We have the sniper who shot at Sarah in custody," Garrett said.

Marcus slid his gaze sideways to Garrett. "You tried to be the one who took the bullet."

"Yeah," Garrett acknowledged.

"My sins are my own. Sarah shouldn't be punished for them."

"Yeah, I know that too."

Marcus's face spasmed in pain and he coughed, blood pouring from his mouth. "Take her away. She doesn't need to see this."

Sarah hunched over Marcus, pulling him into her arms. "No!" she said fiercely. "I won't leave you." She whirled, her angry gaze going to Garrett. "Are you going to let him die?"

"I've called in a helicopter," Garrett said softly. "It's hard because of the smoke. We're going to have to meet them downriver."

"You hear that, Marcus? You hold on. We're going to get you help."

Marcus shook his head. "It's too late, Sarah."

Hot tears poured over her cheeks. "No. No, I won't let it be too late." She leaned down and pressed her lips to his cheek. "I love you, Marcus. I don't care what you've done. I love you. Do you hear me?"

He smiled faintly and his face whitened with the effort. "You're the best thing my father ever did. Everything . . . else . . . wrong. Don't . . . know . . . how . . . you . . . turned . . . out. The way you did."

He raised a violently shaking hand to touch her cheek and then he closed his eyes, going still beneath her.

"Marcus?"

His name came out brokenly, a sound she didn't even recognize.

"Marcus? Oh God . . ."

"Sarah, honey."

Garrett put his hands on her shoulders but she shrugged him away, unable to bear his touch. She buried her face in her hands and wept, rocking back and forth on her knees.

When men she didn't recognize came to cover Marcus with a blanket, she went crazy. "You don't touch him! Get away from him."

She yanked the blanket down and then arranged it herself, pulling it to his chin so that the blood was covered but he appeared at rest, his expression surprisingly peaceful.

"Sarah," Garrett said quietly. "Come away, honey. We need to get out of here."

Where did she have to go? The thought was bleak. Her mind was numb, but one thought was clear. Garrett wasn't who he said he was. He'd lied to her. She'd trusted him and he'd violated that trust.

A moan throbbed in her throat and welled out painfully. He tried to help her up, but she wrenched away from his grasp. "Don't touch me. Just stay away from me."

Ignoring her protests, he picked her up and carried her to one of the trucks. "Stay here," he said grimly and shut the door, leaving her alone, numb, so devastated that she couldn't imagine anything ever being right again.

CHAPTER 38

GARRETT swore long and hard as he approached Adam Resnick. Resnick flicked his cigarette butt a short distance away and promptly lit another one, taking a deep drag as he surveyed the scene around him.

"Goddamn it, Garrett. I wanted Lattimer alive. This is fucked up. His men can't do shit for me."

"I didn't kill the bastard."

Steele and his team stalked out of the dense line of trees all but dragging a dirty, bedraggled man with them. P.J. smirked as they drew closer, and she shoved the man forward.

"Here's your sniper, Garrett. Dumb asshole was easy to peg. He says Stanley Cross hired him to kill Sarah. He wanted proof of her death."

"Christ," Resnick swore as he tossed yet another cigarette. "My entire mission was ruined by a fucking amateur."

"Shut the fuck up, Resnick. I'm not any happier about how all this went down," Garrett snapped.

"If you hadn't ditched me, this might not have happened," Resnick snapped back. "What the fuck was with your going rogue on me? This was a highly planned mission. You were supposed to follow my instructions to a T."

Garrett held up his middle finger and walked away. He

stopped a few feet from the truck where Sarah sat, her features pale and drawn, pain swamping her eyes until he couldn't bear to look at her. What a clusterfuck. Her selfish bastard of a brother had finally found a conscience and took the bullet meant for Sarah. Unfuckingbelievable. Yet one more thing Garrett was going to have to be grateful to the son of a bitch for.

Sarah turned then and found his gaze. Her eyes turned to ice and her lip curled before she looked away, refusing to stare at him any longer. Christ, she hated him. She had every reason.

"Garrett, I'm going to have to take her in," Resnick said behind him.

Garrett whirled around. "What the fuck? You know damn well she has nothing to do with her brother's business."

"Yeah, I know. But I'm more interested in what she can tell me. I'll need to access the emails they exchanged. I need to question her. Don't make this harder for me than it needs to be. You know this is how it has to go down."

"That's just fucking great," Garrett hissed. "She already hates me for betraying her. Now her brother's dead and it's my fault and you're going to haul her away for questioning."

"I'll explain my role in this," Resnick said quietly. "I doubt it'll make a difference. And I swear to you I'll keep you in the loop, every step of the way. Give her some space, Garrett. She's pissed right now. She's not going to listen to anything you have to say. I'll keep her safe. I'll go easy on her. And when it's over, I'll let you know."

Garrett glanced again at Sarah and knew Resnick was right. If he pushed now, he'd only lose her. Forever. He'd give her a few days to cool off while he attended to other matters. Mainly one Stanley Cross.

"You tell her I'm coming for her, Resnick. You tell her there's no way in hell I'm letting her go. Don't you dare let her think I deserted her."

"Yeah, yeah," Resnick grumbled. "I'll tell her all that mushy shit. Jesus, man. You and your brothers are driving me insane with the women."

Garrett wanted to tell Resnick to tell her he loved her, but he figured he'd save that one for the next time he saw her. Hopefully by then some of the shock of today would have worn off and she could view the events more objectively. If not, he was going to have a long, hard fight ahead of him. Giving her up wasn't an option. She belonged with him, in his arms, in his bed. He wouldn't settle for anything less.

"We need to get the fuck out of here," Resnick said. "You and your men should clear out too. The government here is only going to be so understanding. Lattimer and his men have already done millions of dollars' worth of damage by setting the damn world on fire. It'll take them days to get this under control."

"I need to stay and help Rio. He could lose everything."

Resnick nodded and started toward the truck where Sarah sat, two of his men on his heels. Garrett watched, his fists clenched tight at his sides while Resnick spoke in soft tones to Sarah. A moment later, he guided Sarah from the truck and down to one of the waiting boats.

Sarah walked stiffly, like an old woman without any fight left. Her gaze was fixed on the ground and never once did she look back at Garrett.

More of Resnick's men led the sniper away, hands cuffed behind his back. The rest of Resnick's team quickly and efficiently cleaned up the scene, carried Marcus's body away. Five minutes later, only Garrett and his men remained.

Rio turned in toward the smoke and then back in the direction of his house.

"Think it'll take your house?" Garrett asked quietly.

Rio shrugged. "If it does, it does. Not much I can do. I can always rebuild."

"We need to move out," Steele said crisply. "I don't want to be here when the locals show up."

"You go," Rio said. "My men and I will stay and take any heat. I have contacts here. We'll be fine." He looked up at Garrett. "You go with Steele and his team. Get the fuck out of the country. The boat will take you downriver to a waiting chopper."

"You sure?"

"Yeah, I'm sure," Rio said.

Garrett gestured for Steele and his team to follow him to the dock. They hurried down and got into the last remaining boat. Rio rattled off a terse stream of Kriole to the young man operating the boat and then waved to Garrett as the boat pushed away from the dock.

"You just going to let her go like that?" P.J. demanded.

Startled, Garrett turned on P.J., his lips curled into a snarl. "What the fuck do you mean?"

"I saw the way you looked at her, and yet you let that asshole Resnick walk away with her."

"Back off, Rutherford. You don't know what the fuck you're talking about."

"Men are such dickheads," she muttered. "She just watched her brother die. Of course she's upset. But she needs you with her, not hundreds of miles away while Resnick drills on her."

"I have a few things I need to do before I go after Sarah," Garrett said tersely.

P.J. snorted and turned her back. To Garrett's surprise, Steele eyed him with a grimace as well.

"Not you too," Garrett muttered. "You're supposed to be a fucking machine. The last thing I need is you nagging my ass too."

A glimmer of amusement flickered across Steele's face, but he remained silent and turned his attention to the shoreline as he watched for any threat.

They traveled a mile upriver and veered off into one of the fingers that drifted farther inland. The water shallowed to a couple of feet as they slogged closer to a sharp bend in the offshoot. A helicopter came into view as they hung a sharp left and drifted into the cove.

Garrett scrambled off the boat with Steele and his team and they piled into the helicopter. As it rose and hovered close to the ground, Garrett stared out the window and wondered how Sarah was doing. Resnick had sworn he'd take good care of her, and Garrett knew he would. He wasn't quite the asshole he and his brothers liked to label him.

He may have taken the coward's way out but there was a lot he had to sort out before he could face Sarah again. He couldn't afford to fuck things up with her. First he had to remove any and all threats to her. Only then could he go to her and plead his case.

Maybe by then her grief wouldn't be so raw, her pain not so sharp. Maybe by then she'd have a better perspective.

One thing he knew for sure, and he'd known it the moment that Sarah had looked at him with such pain and betrayal in her eyes. He loved her and he'd settle for nothing less than having her in his life. Until the day he died. He simply wouldn't consider any alternative. If it took him the rest of his life to convince her, then that's what he'd do.

CHAPTER 39

RUSTY trudged from the school building toward the student parking lot. Today was just another shitty day in what was shaping up to be a shitty year. Her senior year. So much was made of a person's senior year. Magical. Time-of-your-life sort of thing. She barely held back a snort. The only good thing was that so far, Matt Winfree hadn't opened his mouth. Whatever Sean had said to him seemed to have worked. At least for now.

Instead he and his group avoided her like the plague.

At least she'd gotten her car back. Almost like new. She'd been afraid that Marlene and Frank wouldn't let her have it back after what had happened. But they hadn't said a word. Just handed her the keys and said that no one was allowed to drive it but her. Fine by her. She wouldn't make such a stupid mistake again.

She was so focused on her thoughts that she didn't see the men standing at the front edge of the parking lot until she heard the murmur of voices around her. When she did look up, her mouth fell open and her first thought was oh shit. What had she done now?

The Kelly brothers—well, almost all of them—stood in a formidable line. Even Garrett was there, and he was supposedly off on some supersecret mission after everyone had worried he was up shit creek.

Sam stood the far left. Ethan was next to him and Donovan and Garrett stood together. They were wearing army-looking fatigues with boots and shit. Damn, they looked like they were ready to kick some serious ass. She sighed. Probably hers.

"Winfree, just the guy we're looking for," Garrett called.

Oh shit. This was even worse. Rusty squeezed her eyes shut as the brothers looked beyond her. Then she slowly peeked around to see Matt standing several yards away, looking for the world like he was about to wet his pants. Maybe this wouldn't be so bad after all.

"Come over here, boy," Sam said in a terse voice that you simply didn't ignore.

"Yes, sir?" Matt asked as he approached warily.

"Heard you've been messing with our sister," Ethan said with a growl.

Unexpected tears burned Rusty's eyes as she stared agape at the scowling brothers.

Donovan curled his lip back and took a step forward. Matt shrunk about three inches and went even paler. "Do you know what we do with punks like you?" Donovan asked.

"N-no sir."

"I have no respect for little pricks who beat up on women," Garrett snarled. "Especially a woman who happens to be a part of my family. Let me give you a little advice, Winfree. Stay away from Rusty. Far, far away. If I ever catch you near her, if you ever even say her name to anyone, I'll find a dark hole for your body and trust me, no one will ever find you. You got me?"

Matt's head bobbed up and down, his eyes so wide that he looked like a deer in the headlights. Rusty wiped at her eyes, determined she wouldn't cry. But damn if her chest wasn't about to burst open. Their sister. They'd called her their *sister*. A part of their family. They were sticking up for her. Hell, they'd just threatened to kill a guy if he ever messed with her again.

She stared at them in wonder as Matt all but ran to his car. A moment later, in a squall of tires, he roared out of the parking lot.

"I can't believe you did that," she whispered. "For me."

Sam grimaced and his expression softened as he took a step toward her. "We meant every word. You're our sister. Mom's taken you under her wing, and her chick you're going to stay. No one fucks with the Kellys, and I mean no one. You've been around us long enough to know that by heart. Well, you're a Kelly now and no one's going to mess with you."

Without pondering the rightness or whether he'd be appalled, Rusty launched herself into Sam's arms, nearly toppling them both over. She squeezed him so tight that it was a wonder he could breathe, and she'd never felt anything better in her life.

Brothers. Protective older brothers. The mind boggled. That they gave a shit about her stunned her. And it felt better than she could have ever imagined.

"Thank you," she said as she gripped him harder. "No one's ever done anything like that for me."

When she finally drew away, she was embarrassed by the tears streaking down both cheeks. Her nose was all snotty and she probably looked ridiculous.

"Got a hug for your other brothers?" Garrett drawled.

She eyed him suspiciously for a moment. He was nice enough to Rachel, and Rusty saw him be affectionate and lovey with both Rachel and Sophie, but the truth was, he scared the shit out of her. But when he opened his arms, she forgot all about her fear and launched herself into his embrace.

One by one they all hugged her until she was a weepy, snotty mess. She cried all over them and they sighed indulgently, just like big brothers should. It was the best day of her entire life.

CHAPTER 40

"SO what are you going to do now?" Donovan asked quietly when he and Garrett were finally alone.

Garrett dropped onto the couch in the war room and stared tiredly at his younger brother. "I'm going to Boston to kick the shit out of Stanley Cross and make sure the little bastard never tries anything with Sarah again."

"I'm going," Donovan said tightly.

Garrett nodded. "Rio called a while ago. He wants in too. I'm going to make that little son of a bitch pay."

"We could always make him disappear," Donovan said with a shrug. "There are places where his body would never be found."

"Don't tempt me. I've never contemplated cold-blooded murder in my life, but I'd do it now and suffer no regrets."

"And afterward? What then?"

Garrett knew what Donovan was asking. "Then I'm going after Sarah. I'm bringing her home with me. I'm not coming back without her."

"I figured."

"Yeah, I know you did," Garrett muttered. "I'm head over ass for her. I can't imagine my life without her. She may not forgive me. I don't know what the hell I'll do then."

"You've never been the type to give up," Donovan said dryly. "You're a stubborn bastard."

The security doors opened, admitting Sam.

"Thought you were on kid duty," Garrett said.

Sam wore a frown and Donovan and Garrett exchanged uneasy glances.

"Joe's been hurt. Busted his leg. He's being flown to Fort Campbell."

"Shit," Donovan swore. "What about Nathan?"

"No word on Nathan. Ma got the call a while ago. All they told her was that Joe was hurt in combat. They patched him up and were flying him to the base. He'll be there tomorrow."

"That's it, though? How did he break it? Bullet or what?"

"They didn't tell her shit," Sam said in frustration. "She's pissed and ready to go kick some army ass. I'm going over with her tomorrow to keep her in line or she'll end up behind bars."

Donovan chuckled despite the seriousness of the situation. Then he glanced at Garrett. "Should we wait to see Joe before we head to Boston, or you want to go now?"

"What the fuck are you going to Boston for?" Sam demanded.

"A little unfinished business," Garrett said quietly.

"Shit. Don't call me to bail your asses out of jail."

"I won't let him kill him," Donovan promised. "Rio and I will be there to witness what goes down. I guarantee you that Cross will fall down a few flights of stairs. Maybe more than once."

Sam chuckled and shook his head. "I can't even bring myself to call you down. I'd like a piece of the bastard myself for what he did."

"We'll wait for Joe to get in. I want to make sure he's all right," Garrett said. "Van, get the Kelly jet fueled and ready to go. I'll let Rio know what's going on so he can meet us there."

THE whole Kelly family descended on the base the next day. Even Rusty came along and Marlene evidently had been made aware of the fact that her boys had showed up at Rusty's school because she beamed at them nonstop the entire afternoon.

At least she hadn't kissed them and pinched their cheeks in front of the military personnel on the base.

Sophie had little Charlotte bundled up, and Garrett had to admit the kid looked cute as a button in all that pink. She was a beautiful girl, just like her mama. Garrett gave Sam shit about how glad he was she hadn't taken after her daddy. Sam just grinned and agreed wholeheartedly.

Rachel had hugged Garrett so tight that he'd felt immediate guilt for not going over to see her the minute he got back. He'd been too preoccupied with thoughts of Sarah and calling Resnick every five minutes to get a status report.

"Hey, sweet pea," he murmured into Rachel's ear as she hugged him. "You doing okay?"

"I'm fine. It's you I've been worried about."

She drew away and he could see the concern darken her already dark brown eyes. It gratified him to see that she'd filled out more and the shadows she wore under her eyes like permanent bruises had lightened. She looked . . . happy. Content.

"You look terrific," he said. "Ethan's been taking good care of you, I see."

She smiled, her entire face lighting up. Rachel was a beautiful woman, but when she smiled, it seemed the sun shone just a little brighter. Ethan and Sam had chosen well with Rachel and Sophie. Now Garrett couldn't wait to bring Sarah home to meet his family. They'd love her. He just knew it. And she'd love them too.

"She'll forgive you, Garrett," Rachel said softly so only he would hear. "Donovan told me some of what happened. Don't be angry at him. I did puppy dog eyes at him."

Garrett laughed, making the rest of his family look over at him to see what was going on. He lowered his voice and turned Rachel to the side. "You're evil, Rachel. You know Van can't resist you when you do that."

"That's the point," she said with a mischievous grin. Then she sobered slightly. "You love her a lot."

Garrett sighed and glanced sideways again. It wasn't as if he was ashamed of his feelings. He just wasn't ready to share them with the world yet. "Yeah, I do. I fucked up though."

Rachel touched his arm and then wrapped her arms around him in a tight hug. "I know a lot about pain. And forgiveness."

Garrett squeezed her back. "I know you do, sweet pea. Ethan's so lucky to have you."

"She'll forgive you if she loves you. She's hurting right now, but she'll realize that being without you hurts more."

"I hope you're right. I'm a stubborn son of a bitch. I don't plan to come home without her."

"I can't wait to meet her. I can only think she must be an amazing woman if you love her."

"Well, I love you and you're amazing," Garrett said.

She smiled. They were interrupted when the doctor came into the waiting area where the Kellys had been stashed. Marlene pounced immediately, though Frank wasn't far behind.

"How's my son?" she demanded.

"He's doing quite well," the doctor said as he surveyed the gathered family members. "A bullet shattered the fibula and we're taking him into surgery shortly to reconstruct the bone."

"Can we see him before you take him to surgery?" Marlene asked anxiously. "I want him to know we're here."

The doctor chuckled. "Oh, he knows you're here. I think the entire base knows you're here. I'll let you in to see him for five minutes. You'll be able to see him again when he comes out of recovery."

The entire family crowded into the small holding room where Joe was propped against several pillows, his leg swathed in tight gauze to anchor the break.

"Ma, Dad!" His entire face lit up when his parents entered the room, his brothers right behind them. "Hell, you all didn't have to come."

Sam snorted. "As if we wouldn't come, little brother. What the hell have you done to yourself this time?"

Garrett watched as Marlene fussed and clucked, kissed and petted. He grinned as Joe ate it all up just like he was a young boy with a boo-boo again.

"It's damn good to see you again, son," Frank boomed out. "I'd rather not have had to see you in the hospital, though."

"Joe, do you know anything about Nathan?" Marlene asked anxiously.

Joe grimaced and shook his head. "Sorry, Ma. He wasn't with me. Things were pretty tense. We were separated into two teams. Our team came under attack. I took a bullet. Two of our guys died. I don't know about Nathan's team. No one has told me jackshit."

"I'm sorry," Marlene said softly. "I'm sorry about your team members."

Joe leaned back, his face white with pain and fatigue. "Yeah, it sucks. We were coming home after this mission. Most of us were getting out. We talked about nothing else for the last weeks. We all had plans. Now two of them aren't coming home and three of us are in the hospital. I'm lucky to be alive, I guess."

"Guess you'll be home faster than you thought," Ethan piped in. "Might take them a little while to get you discharged, but you sure as hell won't be going anywhere after this."

"Nathan and I were supposed to get out together," Joe said through a clenched jaw. "This sucks. It wasn't supposed to happen like this."

"I'm just glad you're alive," Marlene said as she kissed his cheek again. "My prayers are so close to being answered. My babies back home, where they belong."

The nurse stuck her head in the door and looked pointedly at the gathered Kellys.

"Time for us to go, Joe," Frank said as he rose. "We'll be here, though. We aren't going anywhere. We'll see you when you get out of surgery."

Garrett stepped forward and took Joe's hand. "Hey man, I'm shoving off for a few days. I have some loose ends to tie up. I'll be back soon. I'll be checking on you through Ma."

Joe gripped his hand in return. "Let me know if Nathan gets in touch with any of you. Promise me."

"Yeah, sure, no problem. Take care of yourself, baby brother."

Joe glared at him and flipped him the bird. "I'll show you baby when I get out of the damn hospital."

The nurse herded the Kellys out the door and back toward the waiting area. Marlene plopped down in a chair and let out a huge sigh. Rusty, looking worried, sat beside Marlene and put an arm around her shoulders. "He'll be all right, Marlene."

Marlene smiled at Rusty. "I know he will, baby. I'll always worry about my children, though. I'm afraid it's a mother's curse."

"I'll stay with you and Frank," Rachel said as she sat on Marlene's other side. She glanced up Ethan and he nodded. "Of course we will."

Marlene frowned up at Sophie and Sam. "Let me kiss my granddaughter and then you get her home where she belongs. Last place she needs to be is a place full of sickness and germs. I'll call you as soon as I know anything."

Garrett leaned down and kissed his mother's cheek. "Van and I are shoving off. I'll call you."

Marlene patted his cheek and then studied him as she rubbed her hand over his face. "You look tired, son. You need some rest. You're working way too hard."

"I'm bringing someone special home to meet you. I love her, and you'll love her too."

His mom's mouth gaped open as he stepped back. "Why am I always the last one to know these things?"

Garrett smiled. Just saying it aloud had infused him with even more determination. Sarah belonged here with him. With his family. Surrounded by love and acceptance. He just had to make her see it.

CHAPTER 41

SARAH sat on the porch of the beach house where it all had begun. She was tired. Numb. Beyond exhausted. Her mind was in chaos. And she missed Garrett with every breath.

For several days, Adam Resnick had questioned her, albeit very politely. He'd made sure her every need was met. She was catered to, waited on, treated like an important guest instead of the sister of the CIA's most wanted man.

It had hurt to hear the truth about her brother. She knew he'd been involved in some questionable activities, but she'd been shocked to know the extent. It horrified her to know of the things he'd done. The people he'd killed. The lives he was responsible for wrecking. She'd finally covered her ears and demanded that Resnick stop his recitation of Marcus's many crimes.

She hadn't been able to help them. She would have, if she had any way to. But Marcus had never given any information to her. He'd kept his dealings completely separate from her. He'd been careful not to ever let that aspect of his life touch her in any way.

She'd even given Resnick the number of her offshore account since Marcus had funded it. Now that she knew precisely how he'd gotten it, she had no desire to ever use it again.

As a result, she was broke with less than a thousand dollars left in her personal account. If Resnick hadn't offered to set her up any place she wanted to go, she wouldn't have been able to afford to come back here.

It was here that she wanted to sort out her life and pick up the pieces. Here is where her life had irrevocably changed. Yes, it had changed the moment Allen Cross raped her, but the island was where she'd been given a new lease on life. Garrett had done that for her. And then he'd crushed her in a way Allen Cross hadn't been able to. That was the height of irony.

For three days she'd done nothing but sit on her deck and stare sightlessly over the water. She had no idea what she'd do next. At some point she'd have to make a decision. She couldn't spend her life hiding.

It shouldn't have surprised her to look up and see Garrett walking down the sand toward her cottage. But it did. It took all her willpower not to turn and flee into the cottage and lock the door behind her.

Instead she sat as calmly as she was able and watched him approach.

He wore jeans and a T-shirt. Judging by the irritation of his face and the way he shook his feet at intervals, he'd gotten a buttload of sand in his tennis shoes during the walk from town. Clearly he hadn't learned anything from his time here.

When he got closer, she saw that he held something in his hand. She forced herself to look away, out over the water as he approached.

He hesitated for a moment and then settled on the step beside her. Just as he'd done weeks before. He piddled with the object in his hand and then extended it until she looked down to see what he held.

A smile quivered on her lips. How could she want to smile when she hurt so damn much on the inside?

"I brought the big guns this time," he said as he held up the caramel chocolate bar. "No holding out this time."

He set it on her lap and turned to stare at the water as she'd done.

"I love you, Sarah."

She sucked in her breath and felt herself come apart all over again. Pain ripped through her heart and left a bloody cut as deep as a wound could go. She went so rigid that she shook. She started to bolt to her feet but his fingers circled her wrist and he tugged until she was forced to remain seated.

"Please," he begged softly. "Hear me out."

She couldn't look at him. Not and maintain her composure. She closed her eyes to keep the tears at bay. She'd shed enough over the last week. Her head still hurt and her sinuses had gone to shit. She wouldn't cry anymore.

"I know you feel hurt and betrayed."

"You have no idea how I feel," she said bitterly.

"I have an idea. If it's anything close to what I've felt since Resnick took you away, I know it's pretty damn awful."

She ignored his statement. She fixed her eyes back over the water, determined to get through this even if it killed her.

He sighed. "Let me start from the beginning. I was asked to take this job because Resnick knew I had a personal score to settle with . . . your brother. Six years ago, I led a mission to rescue your brother, when he made a deal with the wrong people. In return, he was going to work with the CIA to take down several terrorist networks that he'd supplied arms to.

"We went in and Lattimer double-crossed us. He murdered two of my men and shot me in the leg. Resnick knew I hated him, and so when he got the information that Lattimer had killed Cross and that you had taken off, he asked me to tail you, stay close to you until your brother showed up."

"You used me," she said painfully. "And now he's dead."

Garrett blew out his breath again. "I know you're hurt, honey. I'd do anything in the world to change what happened, but I'm not sorry he's dead. I won't lie to you just to get you to forgive me. He was a bastard of the first order. However, I'll always be grateful that he saved your life. Given a choice between his death and yours? I'll take his hands down."

Her gaze flickered as a fresh wash of tears flooded her eyes.

"The thing is, the first time I laid eyes on you, things changed for me. I felt this connection between us and I was determined to keep you safe. Somehow you became mine from the first time I met you. After you left the island, I gave Resnick the slip. Told him to hell with the job. I just wanted you safe, and I wanted to remove any threat to you.

"I fell in love with you, Sarah. I fell in love with you but

I still had a job to do. Lattimer was responsible for the deaths of many innocent people. I was sworn to take him down. I loved you, but I couldn't look the other way. Not for you. Not for anyone. I know he was your brother and that in his own way he loved you and protected you. You loved and protected him. I understand that, but I couldn't let him walk away after everything he'd done."

Sarah closed her eyes against the tears. Against the pain of his words. She clenched her fingers into tight fists as Garrett's impassioned words hit the very soul of her.

"I know he wasn't a good man," she whispered.

Garrett reached for one of her fists and gently pried her hand open before lacing his fingers through hers. "I know you don't trust me after what happened, Sarah. I know trust is a big thing to you after what Cross did. I just want the chance to make it right. I want to show you that you *can* trust me. I love you. I want you with me. And I'll do whatever it takes to have you in my life. Always."

She raised her gaze to meet his and saw soul-deep pain reflected in his eyes. He was suffering too. He hurt like she hurt.

"What are you asking, Garrett? What do you see for us? I have to tell you. I'm a mess. I don't have a job. I have less than a thousand dollars to my name. I'm still coming to grips with the fact that I was raped. I buried it deep and just existed from day to day."

His eyes softened as he stared back at her. "What I see is a strong, resilient woman who knocks me on my ass every time she looks at me. I see someone who's been hurt so badly she's afraid to trust again. I see someone who has such a loving spirit, who strives to see the best in people despite being shown the worst. What do I see for us? I see you with me, making me happy until I draw my last breath. I see us living and laughing together, having children eventually. Enjoying sunsets and growing old together."

His voice grew hoarse and shaky with emotion. "Honey, I don't care if you don't have a penny to your name. I don't care if you have a job. Those things will come. What I want is for you to be with me so we can work this out together. Together we can do anything. You don't have to go through this alone. I'll be with you every step of the way. That's what love is about."

She glanced down at their entwined fingers, watched as his thumb caressed the top of her hand.

"I'm scared, Garrett. I feel . . . alone. I mean, before I was alone, but I had Marcus, and I always knew that if I really needed someone, he'd be there, no questions asked. This past week I've had to come to grips with the fact that I have no one. I have no idea what I want to do. I just feel numb and terrified all at the same time."

He pulled her into his arms and held her tightly against him.

"I'm terrified too," he admitted. "I'm scared shitless you won't forgive me and I'll have to go back home without you after I promised my mother I was bringing you back with me. She can't wait to meet you, you know. I'm pretty sure she's already planning our wedding."

Sarah smiled against him and shook her head.

He tucked a finger beneath her chin and prodded her upward so he could stare into her eyes. "I love you, Sarah. I think I fell in love with you when I looked into those eyes and saw your determination not to be scared. I know I hurt you, honey. I can only promise I won't hurt you again. Not like that. But I have to be honest with you. I don't regret what happened, only that you had to be involved. It's who I am. I have a very strong sense of justice."

"Who are you really, Garrett? You didn't work for my brother obviously. Do you work for the CIA? Will I even ever see you?"

He palmed her cheek and stroked gently over her face. "We do contract work for the government. We also work in the private sector too. I work for myself. Me and my brothers. We do things like hostage and fugitive recovery. As for whether you'll ever see me? You're going to be seeing a damn lot of me. So much of me you're going to want me to take a mission just so I'll leave you alone. My work is important to me, Sarah. It's part of who I am. But you're the *most* important thing to me."

He poked his finger at her for emphasis and she felt some of the ice around her heart crack and start to melt.

"You'll always come first. You and our children. Is there risk involved in my work? Hell, yes, and I know it's a lot to ask you to take on. But for every mission I take, the goal is going to be the same. Coming home to you. Always."

She leaned forward, resting her forehead against his chin. "You make it sound so . . . easy."

He tugged her back into his arms and hugged her so tight she could barely breathe. "I love you. I think you love me. What could be simpler? Everything else we'll work out. Together."

She raised her head back up and took a deep breath as she drowned in those intense blue eyes. "I do love you, Garrett. Even when I hated you for lying to me, I loved you. I want to be with you. I just feel so overwhelmed. Like I'll never get my life together. I feel like it's spiraled out of control."

He touched her cheek, and she was shocked to see a wash of emotion in his eyes. They glistened with unshed tears and when he spoke, his voice broke.

"Right now, the first step is saying you'll try," he said. "Come home with me. Let's work on our relationship together. You can decide what you want to do there. If you want to talk to someone about the rape, we'll find you a damn good counselor. If you want to go back to work in your current field, you can do that. Or you can study to become a teacher. We have a great university just thirty minutes away. The thing is, you have choices, Sarah. You have all the choices in the world. All I ask is that you let me be part of them. Let's tackle the problems together."

She curled her arms around his neck and hugged him. Not content with any part of her not touching him, she crawled into his lap and burrowed into his chest until they were smashed together like two lovebugs.

"There's still Stanley," she sighed.

He tensed and pulled slightly away. He tipped up her chin until their gazes met again. "Stanley won't ever be a problem for you again."

She frowned at the conviction in his voice. Then her eyes narrowed in suspicion. "What did you do?"

"Let's just say that me, Rio and my brother Donovan took care of the little asshole. He might have fallen down a flight of stairs. Twice. Or at least that's the story, and I'm sticking to it."

She laughed helplessly, appalled that she found such satisfaction in the image but at the same time desperately wishing
she could have witnessed it all. Then she squeezed him tight
again.

"I love you, Garrett. I do. I want us to be together. You
make me not so . . . afraid. You make me think that things
really will work out."

"They will, honey. They will. I want to take you home.
You're going to love my family and they're going to love you. I
have some things to work out too. For instance, right now, I live
with my two brothers and my oldest brother's wife. It's kind of
crowded," he said ruefully. "Sam—that's my oldest brother—
has started construction on a complex for the entire family. It's
impressive, really. We'll have all the facilities we need. A private airstrip, a helicopter pad, training facilities, a gun range
and most important, we'll all have our own house. That's where
you come in. I have the decorating sense of a mule."

Sarah smiled and felt her heart lighten with every beat. "I
should warn you I have girly tastes. I won't allow my living
room to be decorated in camo. Oh, and Patches." She glanced
anxiously up at him. "She's back with me. Can we bring her
home too?"

He smiled. "Yeah, you and Patches are a package deal. For
you I can put up with a cat."

"And girly? You don't mind your house being girly?" she
asked with a grin.

He pretended disappointment. "I suppose I can live with
girly."

"You need to get used to it for all the daughters you'll have."

His eyes lit up with such joy that it took her breath away.
"Did I tell you I have a new niece? She's beautiful. Not as
beautiful as our daughters will be, but she's cute as a button."

She squeezed him again, unable to contain her excitement.
"All week long I've thought of the future with such dread.
You've made me think it will be filled with wonderful things."

He slid his hand into her hair and gently ran his fingers
through the strands. "I'm making you a solemn promise. For
as long as we both live, I'm going to spend every day giving
you wonderful things. You will never doubt for one moment
that you are as loved as a woman will ever be."

She smiled and wiped at her damp cheeks in irritation. "I love you."

"And I love you. Think we can go home now?"

She kissed him, warm and sweet, letting her lips melt over his. She breathed a sigh into his mouth and let herself go limp against him. "I can't wait."

He tucked her firmly against him, and they sat there on the steps until the sky shimmered in gold and pink and the sun was a fiery half orb on the horizon. It was the first of many more to come. In the years ahead, they often returned to Isle de Bijoux. Though they enjoyed sunsets in a multitude of places, none was ever quite so beautiful as the ones here, where it all began.

ZAC took his arm from around Natalie's shoulders, unlocked the door to their hotel room, and drew out his Glock, motioning for her to stand just inside the door. He quickly cleared the room, checking beneath the bed and behind the shower curtain, then nodded to her that all was well.

She set down his gear bag, shut the door, locked it, and slipped the door guard into place. Then she took a few steps backward and sat on the bed, once again motionless, her gaze fixed on the door as if she expected all the demons in hell to charge through it any minute now. There were dark circles beneath her eyes, her face was pale, a haunted look in her eyes.

Something inside him hurt to see her like this, the girl whose smiles had made his teenage heart pound harder, now battered and terrified. Again, he found himself wanting to comfort her but not knowing what to say or do. His years in WitSec had been spent shielding criminals, people who'd turned state's witness to save their own hides—drug dealers, thugs, counterfeiters. After a meth dealer he'd protected had taken advantage of a new identity to start a life of crime with a clean slate, Zac had left WitSec and gone to work apprehending fugitives, a job that had suited him better. He had no experience protecting the innocent or comforting the victims of crimes.

God only knew what they'd done to her. In the five days it had taken him to reach her, they could have . . .

Don't go there, McBride.

Zac reined in his imagination, sickened by the images it conjured. He holstered the Glock and knelt down in front of her. "Hey, there's a shower in the next room with your name on it—hot water, towels, soap."

She shifted her gaze from the door to him, then nodded. "You won't go anywhere will you? I . . . I don't want to be left alone."

He'd planned on slipping down to the little shop he'd seen in the lobby to buy them both some personal supplies and get her something decent to wear. But he would have room service bring what they needed instead. He took her hand, squeezed it. "I'll be right here."

Natalie willed herself to stand; even the appeal of a shower was not enough to break through the strange numbness that had taken hold of her. For the past twenty-four hours all she'd done is run. Now she could barely move.

She walked into the bathroom, flicked on the light, then shut the door behind her and began to undress, letting her clothes fall to the floor. She heard Zac's voice on the other side of the door, the deep sound of it reassuring. He was probably calling to let his commanding officer know where they were so that someone could come pick them up and drive them back across the border.

Deliberately avoiding the mirror—she was afraid of what she might find there—she turned on the shower, stepped beneath the spray, and let it carry away a week's worth of sweat, dirt, and fear. She shampooed her hair twice, massaged in conditioner, then scrubbed with a soapy washcloth till her skin was pink—wanting to be clean again, needing to feel clean. Then she rinsed her hair and her body, watching the bubbles swirl down the drain.

It's over. I'm alive. I'm going home.

The thought hit her, putting a lump in her throat—but close on its heels came another. So many people *weren't* going home. Tears spilled down her face. How many had died on that bus? Twenty-five? Thirty? All of them journalists, all of them there because they wanted to make the world a better and safer place. Killed without mercy. Shot down.

Screams. Flying glass. Blood.

Oh, God, no! No! I've got a wife and—

Bam! Bam! Bam!

The bathroom seemed to dissolve, and she was on the bus again. She didn't hear Zac's knock at the door, didn't hear him call her name, didn't know he was there until he turned off the water and wrapped a towel around her, murmuring reassurances, lifting her into his arms, carrying her to the bed.

He sat down beside her, held her, kissed her hair, his words reaching her, bringing her back to the present. "It's okay, sweetheart. Let it out."

She couldn't have stopped crying if she'd tried, her body shaking as she sobbed out the past week's horror, her face pressed against Zac's chest, the strength of his embrace a sanctuary. How much time passed she couldn't say. Slowly, her tears subsided, leaving her feeling drained—and ashamed.

She sniffed. "I'm sorry."

"You have no reason to be sorry." He handed her a tissue, his gaze soft. "If you want to talk about it, I'm here."

Natalie shook her head. The last thing in the world she wanted to do was to talk about it. But then the words came on their own, slowly at first, then tumbling out of her, bringing a fresh wave of tears. "Why didn't they kill me? Why didn't they kill me, Zac?"

The question haunted her. She needed an answer.

He drew her into his arms, stroked her hair. "I don't know, sweetheart."

"All those people . . ." Grief tightened its grip on her heart— and some other emotion, as well. *Guilt.*

"It's not your fault that they died and you lived." Had he read her mind?

She drew back, saw a wet stain on his shirt. "I got your T-shirt wet."

"Tears are probably the best thing this shirt has ever known." He stood and drew the shirt over his head, the bandage she'd made for his shoulder still in place. "You should try to get some sleep while you can."

"When are they coming to get us?"

He frowned. "When is *who* coming to get us?"

"The other Marshals or the State Department or whoever you're working for. The good guys."

He ran a hand over his unshaven jaw, looked down at the floor. "No one is coming to get us."

She felt a little spike of adrenaline. "What do you mean?"

"I'm not working for anyone." He met her gaze. "I didn't come here for the U.S. Marshal Service, and I didn't come here for the State Department. I came for you, Natalie."

FROM *NEW YORK TIMES* BESTSELLING AUTHOR

MAYA BANKS

THE KGI SERIES

THE KELLY GROUP INTERNATIONAL (KGI): A super-elite, top secret, family-run business.

QUALIFICATIONS: High intelligence, rock-hard body, military background.

MISSION: Hostage/kidnap victim recovery. Intelligence gathering. Handling jobs the U.S. government can't . . .

THE DARKEST HOUR
NO PLACE TO RUN
HIDDEN AWAY
WHISPERS IN THE DARK
ECHOES AT DAWN
SHADES OF GRAY
FORGED IN STEELE
AFTER THE STORM

mayabanks.com
facebook.com/AuthorMayaBanks
facebook.com/LoveAlwaysBooks
penguin.com

M1054AS0813

Meet Gabe, Jace, and Ash: three of the wealthiest, most powerful men in the country. They're accustomed to getting anything they want.

Anything at all.

FROM *NEW YORK TIMES* BESTSELLING AUTHOR
MAYA BANKS

THE BREATHLESS TRILOGY
RUSH
FEVER
BURN

PRAISE FOR THE NOVELS OF MAYA BANKS:

"Hot enough to make even the coolest reader sweat!"
—*Fresh Fiction*

"Superb...[an] exciting erotic romance."
—*Midwest Book Review*

"You'll be on the edge of your seat with this one."
—*Night Owl Reviews*

mayabanks.com
facebook.com/AuthorMayaBanks
facebook.com/LoveAlwaysBooks
penguin.com

M1266AS0213